KNOT YOUR PROBLEM, COWBOY

WILD HEARTS RANCH

COZY COWBOY OMEGAVERSE

HARLEY KNIGHT

CONTENTS

KNOT YOUR PROBLEM, COWBOY
WILD HEARTS RANCH

I'm not staying.

But these three Montana cowboys might just change my mind.

I was matched once. An Alpha who promised me forever, who made me believe in all those things they say about true mates. And then I lost him.

After that, I stopped dreaming. Stopped hoping. I told myself some bonds only come once in a lifetime... and mine was already gone.

So when a surprise inheritance drags me from city life to a dusty ranch in the middle of nowhere, I plan to keep things simple. Sign the papers. Sell the land. Drive away and forget this place ever existed.

Then I meet them.

Cash. Walker. Ridge.

Three Alphas with stubborn streaks, patient smiles, and that maddening cowboy charm that makes me question every rule I made for myself. They've spent years building Wild Hearts Ranch into something solid, and the moment they catch my scent, they know exactly what's been missing.

Me.

But I didn't come here to stay.

And with my heat cycle closing in fast and no heat clinics in town, everything I've buried starts to unravel. I'm tangled in legal delays, family secrets, and a book club that gossips more than it reads. And those three cowboys? They keep showing up. In my space. In my thoughts. In my heart.

I promised myself I'd never need anyone again.

They're not asking me to need them.

They're asking me to belong.

Honeysp

Wild Hearts Ranch
Brutus the Bull
River
Fire Station
Medical Centre
The Rusty Spur
Bakery
Hardware Store
BBQ Joint
Moonlight & Magnolias Dance Barn
Craft / Quilt Shop
Toy Store
Gas Station
Music Store
Copper Canyon Guest Ranch
Honey

Meadow

Maggie's Diner
Antique Store
Flower Shop
Convenience Store
General Store
Produce Store
Thrift Store
Drug Store
The Dust Jacket Bookshop
Post Office
POST
ater Creek Reality
Wildflower Bakehouse & Cafe
Hartwell & Associates
Santos Rodriguez's Feed Store
Market
Honey Spur Rodeo Arena
Police Station
POLICE
Town Hall
Hensley's Ranch (Longhorns)
al Grounds
TICKET

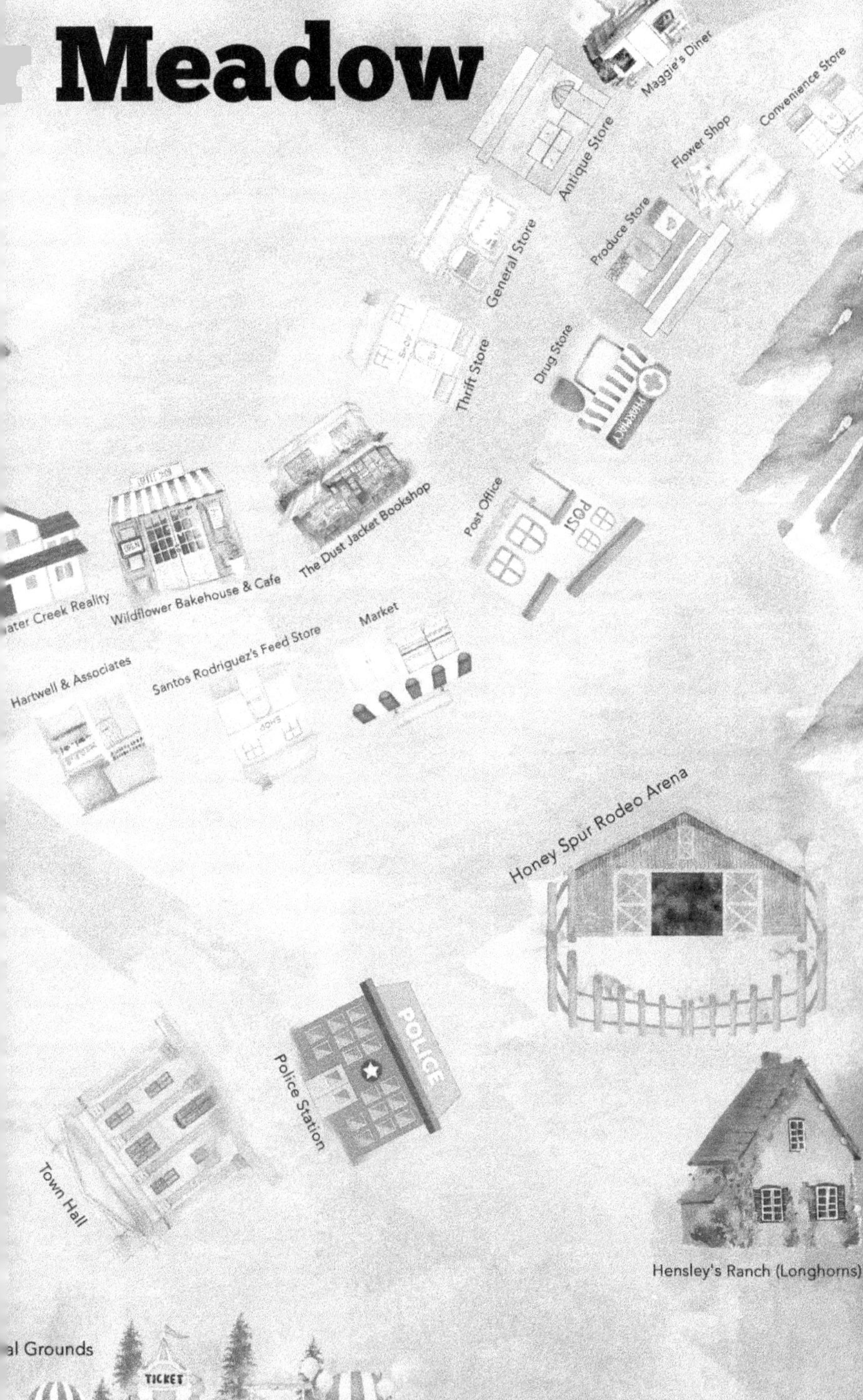

1

SOPHIA

I should assume the GPS is lying when it tells me to turn down a dirt road that looks like it hasn't seen maintenance since the last ice age. But after six hours of driving in the Montana heat wave with a broken air conditioner and a car that makes more noise than a dying whale, I'm desperate enough to follow Siri into the gates of hell if it means finding civilization.

What I find instead is a massive bull standing in the middle of this narrow dirt road, staring at my rental car as if I've personally offended him.

The beast is enormous, all rippling muscle under a hide so black it seems to absorb sunlight. His horns curve wickedly, and his tail swishes from side to side.

"Okay, big guy," I say through the windshield, as if reasonable conversation will work on a two-thousand-pound animal with an attitude. "I just need to get past you. Can you move?"

I squint into the distance and spot a weathered wooden sign that reads *Wild Hearts Ranch*. Just beyond it stands a sprawling house—the kind you'd see in a Western soap opera, complete with a wide porch. Well, credit where it's due, the GPS got something right. At least I've made it to the right place. That's... something.

The bull snorts, drawing my attention back to him as he paws the ground, sending up little clouds of dust.

That's when I honk the horn, and I regret it instantly.

The bull's head shoots up. Eyes locked on me.

For one terrifying moment, we stare at each other through the windshield. His nostrils flare as he lowers his huge head.

"Oh, fuck!"

Then he charges.

I floor the gas pedal, hoping to swerve and speed past him, but the rental car's tires hit the loose dirt and immediately lose traction. The wheel spins in my hands as the car fishtails wildly across the road.

I'm going too fast on ground that's basically powdered dust, and my heart is in my throat. The car skids sideways, completely out of control, and I have just enough time to think that this is how I die, taken out by a furious bull in Montana.

The passenger side slams into a large oak tree by the side of the road.

I scream.

The impact throws me against the driver's-side door, luckily not hitting my head, and the engine dies with a pathetic wheeze. My hands shake as I grip the steering wheel, trying to catch my breath. *Holy shit.* I almost died. Like, actually died.

I turn the key frantically, but all I get is a horrible clicking sound. "No, no, no!" Through the rear window, I see that the bull has found my car's new location and is expressing his displeasure by charging back.

BANG!

He rams his horns into my trunk, sending the entire car into a shake with each impact. *BANG.* The rear window spider-webs. *BANG.* Something that sounds expensive falls off the undercarriage.

I scream again, gripping the door handle as I'm rattled around.

"Thank God I got the full insurance package with the rental company," I mutter hysterically. "Shit!"

I have two choices: stay and become the filling in a car-bull sandwich, or make a run for it to the house about sixty feet away. Especially as there's no one coming out to help with this psycho bull.

I glance at the house again, which is grand. Two full stories, wraparound porch, windows everywhere. It looks exactly like the photos the lawyer sent, only bigger. Older. Real. The kind of place that's seen generations come and go, probably along with a few ghosts and a scandal or two.

Right now, it's also my salvation.

So I grab my red handbag, say a quick prayer to whatever deity protects idiotic city girls from rural disasters, and bolt from the car.

Several fast steps toward the house and I glance back.

Big mistake. The bull's head swivels toward me, those dark eyes locking on to mine like a heat-seeking missile. His muscles bunch.

"Shit, shit, shit!" I sprint across the yard, my flats slipping on loose gravel. Behind me, hoofbeats are thundering closer. My heart hammers so hard I think it might explode.

I hit the wooden steps at full speed, taking them two at a time. My hand fumbles for the door handle. *Please be unlocked, please be unlocked.* I throw myself against the front door, and it swings open. A blast of loud country music finds me right as I tumble inside. Something about whiskey, heartbreak, and boots stomping on gravel.

I spin and slam the door shut just as the bull crashes into the porch from outside.

Breathless, I stand there trembling. Shit, that was too close. And seriously, what the hell is wrong with that bull?

The loud music cuts out mid-lyric.

"Um, excuse me?" a woman's voice asks behind me.

I snap around, still breathing hard. What I see makes me question whether I've hit my head in the crash.

Three men are positioned around a rustic living room, each one holding a tiny, fluffy kitten and wearing no shirt. Not just holding—posing.

Sweet baby Jesus.

One man sits in a leather armchair with an orange tabby kitten perched on his broad shoulder. He has dirty-blond hair that's short on the sides but longer on top, falling across his forehead in that perfectly messy way that probably takes effort. His blue eyes study me with an intensity that makes my knees weak. When he tilts his head, I notice the slight crook in his nose.

Another leans against the grand staircase rail, cradling a black-and-white kitten like it's made of spun glass. This one is built like a mountain, with auburn hair that drapes to his shoulders and a black cowboy hat perched on his head. Lord, those shoulders could probably bench-press my rental car.

The third kneels on the floor with a gray kitten tucked against his chest, his expression as serious as death. Dark brown hair trimmed short except for the front, which falls over one eye in a way that should look ridiculous but instead looks unfairly attractive. He has the longest eyelashes I've ever seen on a man. Add to that the most beautiful mocha-colored eyes.

Plus, so many muscles that I'm unsure of where to look. Who are these gorgeous men?

The loud grunt outside me echoes in my ears, and that's when the guy with the black-and-white kitten moves fast. He tucks the cat gently under an arm and strides to the door, then opens it just a crack, peers outside, and closes it again.

"It's Jack's bull," he states, giving a small nod to the others. "He's not hurt."

Not hurt?

"I almost died," I blurt out, still breathless. "That thing chased me across the yard like I owed him money."

"Who *are* you, and why are you interrupting my shoot?" A woman with purple hair buzzed short on one side stands in the center of it all, surrounded by enough camera equipment to shoot a movie. She has one hand on her hip, cinching in her blue floral dress.

The porch shudders again behind me, reminding me why I'm here. "As you now know, there's a crazy bull outside trying to murder me, and your muscular models are holding kittens. I think we're past normal social conventions here."

She tilts her head to the side, deadpanning me. "Honey, these are real cowboys, not models. Plus, this is a calendar shoot for the local animal shelter," the woman says with exaggerated patience. "*Cowboys and Kittens—Adopt Love.* We're already three hours behind schedule."

The man with the orange kitten shifts in his chair, a smile curling on his lips. Is it suddenly burning hot in this room?

"Ma'am? Are you injured?" The one with the gray kitten stands slowly, and sweet mother of pearl, he's even taller than I thought.

"Only my dignity," I manage, trying not to stare at the way his abs move when he breathes. "And possibly my rental car. That bull, Brutus or whatever he's called, wasn't interested in negotiations."

The mountain who checked outside is patting his kitten,

remaining by the door. "The owner just calls him 'Bull,' but 'Brutus' seems more fitting. And he normally doesn't come out of his pasture."

"Well, he made an exception for me. I'm honored. Really. It's not every day you get personally victimized by livestock."

They all laugh—well, except the photographer, who is still eyeing me like she wants to kill me.

The third cowboy, still seated with his orange kitten, has eyes that seem to see right through me. "You lost? It's not often we have gorgeous women burst into the house."

Wait, did he just call me *gorgeous*?

"I was looking for Wild Hearts Ranch. And I guess I found it." I glance around the open hall, taking in the polished wood floors and exposed beams, but this isn't some rustic shack. It's expensive, and it shows.

The room is massive, with a high ceiling and a sweeping staircase that curves up one side like something out of an old Western mansion. The hallway branches off in both directions, leading to other rooms.

Sunlight filters through big windows in the nearby room I can see into, framed by heavy navy curtains. A bronze chandelier hangs above us. There's a coatrack by the door with actual cowboy hats hanging from it and, yes, a pair of spurs.

It's not flashy; it's intentional.

"You're at the right place," the man with the orange kitten says, his deep voice raising the hairs on my arms in a way that has nothing to do with fear. But has everything to do with attraction. I normally don't react to Alphas this way, this quickly. Yet, these men are pure Alphas. That much is clear in their appearance, their voices, even the way they stand and stare at me. "Question is, what are you doing here?" he continues.

Before I can answer, the porch gives another ominous thud, and I step farther away from it.

"I think Brutus might have other plans for me," I say weakly.

The three men exchange looks. Then the tall one with the gray kitten steps forward.

"Here," he explains, gently transferring the tiny ball of fluff to my arms. Before I can process what's happening, I'm suddenly juggling three adorably soft kittens as the other two cowboys deposit their furry charges on me as well.

"Wait, what—"

But they're already grabbing lassos from hooks by the door. Then they rush outside, leaving the door slightly ajar behind them.

"This is exactly why I don't normally work with animals or children!" the photographer mutters, throwing up her hands.

I stand there, trying not to drop any kittens while simultaneously trying not to openly drool over three shirtless cowboys preparing to wrangle a bull. The orange kitten is attempting to climb me, the gray one purrs against my chest like a tiny motor, and the black-and-white one seems content to bat at my hair.

"So, does this happen often?" I ask, because apparently my mouth works independently of my brain.

"Which part? The bull attacks, the ruined photo shoots, or random women falling through the door?"

The orange kitten makes it to my shoulder and promptly gets tangled in my hair. "All of the above?"

"Welcome to Wild Hearts Ranch," she says dryly. "Where chaos is just another word for Tuesday."

Through the gap in the door, I study the three men approaching the bull, who's back on the dirt road. I can't hear what they're saying from this distance, but the one with dark hair is making slow gestures with his hands while apparently having a full conversation with Brutus.

The one with auburn hair takes the lead, twirling his rope before sending it flying. It lands around Brutus's thick neck, and the bull loses it, bucking and twisting like a demon possessed.

I gasp, clutching the kittens tighter against me, one of them meowing loudly.

The other two cowboys come in from the sides, ropes snapping through the air. Within seconds, they've got the bull triangulated, muscles straining as they hold him steady.

I can't stop staring.

They're all shirtless, just jeans, boots, sun-drenched skin, and pure focus. Dirt kicks up around them, sweat gleaming on their backs as they wrestle with an actual monster like it's just another day.

How are they not terrified? That thing nearly killed me.

The bull releases a furious grunt, hooves tearing into the dirt, but they hold their ground, tension in every muscle I can see. And somehow, unbelievably, they win. Brutus finally calms, sides heaving, as they guide him down the road like it's no big deal.

I blink. Did that actually just happen?

"Impressive," I admit.

"They're good at what they do," the photographer mutters while she packs up some of her camera equipment. "Been running this place for years now. I'm Belle, by the way. And you are?"

"Sophia Hollis. Believe it or not, I'm actually supposed to be here. I inherited this place from Rose Martinez's grandson."

Belle's eyebrows shoot up so high they nearly hit her purple hairline. "Oh, this is going to be interesting."

My shoulders pull back at her loaded tone. "Why do you say it like that?"

"Because those three out there? They think this ranch is theirs. They had some agreement with Rose about buying it after working here for five years. And, well, she passed before the five years were up."

My stomach drops. "But... it was left to me. I have the paperwork."

"Well then, honey, you're about to have one hell of an awkward conversation."

I'm staring at Belle packing up her photography equipment while I still hold on to the gorgeous kittens. After a long moment, the front door opens wider, and the three cowboys file back in. My knees actually wobble in response. Traitor knees.

These men are tall, still shirtless, and I'm suddenly breathless.

They stop short when they see me standing there with their kittens, and something shifts in the air. It makes breathing difficult.

"Well," Blue Eyes almost grunts, his voice rougher than before. "Brutus is back where he belongs. Though your car has seen better days."

I try not to stare at their bare chests, all those muscles, the way they shift when they move. I really do. But my body isn't listening to my brain right now, and every inch of exposed skin seems to radiate heat. They're all just standing there like a calendar come to life, towering over me, jeans slung low, dust on their arms, muscles still tense from the whole bull-wrangling thing. How many men in Chicago can say they've taken on a charging bull with nothing but a rope and raw nerve? Yeah... not exactly a common skill set back home.

My fingers tighten around the kittens. Distraction. That's what I need. I spot a single-seater sofa nearby and shuffle over, gently placing the fluffballs down. They immediately pounce on each other like tiny gremlins, batting tails and chewing ears.

The room goes quiet.

Then the Alpha with blue eyes and dirty-blond hair says, "Guess introductions are in order. I'm Cash Winslow."

The one with dark brown hair and bewitching mocha-colored eyes gives a short nod, sending my stomach into a ridiculous flutter of butterflies. "Walker Stone, and we live here on the ranch."

Of course his voice is low and smooth. His jaw is dusted with stubble, and there's this quiet steadiness in his eyes that makes it really hard to look away.

And the third, with a cowboy hat and auburn hair, doesn't say anything right away. Just watches me with those green eyes in that judging way.

"Ridge Colter," he finally says in a deep voice that shouldn't captivate me, but damn him, it does.

I nod, trying not to let it show how off-balance I feel. Cash, Walker, Ridge. The names click into place. Blue eyes. Mocha eyes. Green eyes and a hat. Now with identities.

Then Walker tilts his head slightly. "So now that Brutus isn't trying to murder you... you want to tell us what you're doing here?"

Right. That.

I straighten up, clearing my throat. "Sophia Hollis. That's my name." Sweat rolls down my spine. Why do they make me nervous?

More silence. They're waiting.

"Well," I start, shifting under their combined stares. "I, uh... recently inherited Wild Hearts Ranch."

That lands heavily. Their eyes wide, breaths fast. Belle is just watching us with a smirk. She is enjoying this way too much.

I push forward, words rushing out. "Technically, not from Rose. It was her grandson Nolan Martinez. He left it to me."

Their expressions don't change right away, but the shift is immediate. Like I just dropped a match into something I didn't realize was flammable.

I almost wish I'd kept a kitten in my arms. At least then I'd have something warm and nonthreatening to hold when the fallout starts.

"Oh," Walker murmurs.

"That's impossible," Ridge states flatly. "Rose promised us—"

"We had an agreement," Cash finishes, all traces of amusement gone from his face. "Five years of running the place, and then we could purchase it at fair market value."

"I'm sorry," I say, and I mean it. The looks on their faces make my chest tight. "I had no idea. But I have the will, and the lawyer confirmed everything."

"Are you a Martinez?" Ridge asks, suspicion clear in his voice.

"It's... complicated." Understatement of the century. "But, legally, the ranch is mine. Look, if you want to buy it, that makes things easier for everyone. I need to get back to Chicago, and you want the farm. We can work this out." My heart is thumping loudly in my chest as the words rush past my lips.

"You would sell it to us?" Walker asks, tilting his head like he's trying to read between my words, like he's just waiting for the story to fall apart.

I open my mouth, then close it again.

Everything is happening so fast. I nearly died earlier. I've been charged by a bull, hit a tree with a rental car I can barely afford to fix, and now I'm standing in a room with three shirtless Alphas watching me like I might be their next problem. I can't tell if they're being polite, suspicious, or silently plotting to throw me off the porch.

All I know is I didn't come here to fight. I came to get my inheritance, sell it, and finally have enough cash to breathe. Because Omegas like me? When we lose our mates, we don't get safety nets. We get silence. Unless I want to sign up for one of those Omega auctions and let some Alpha buy and claim me like I'm a prize pig at the county fair.

Hard pass.

I've already done the whole owned thing. Look where it landed me—broke, alone, and clawing my way out of the wreckage with nothing but sarcasm and caffeine.

This inheritance? It's my one shot to stand on my own feet. No Alpha. No collar. Just me, finally choosing my own damn future. And if Lady Luck is feeling generous, maybe she'll throw in the kind of Alpha I've only dreamed of... one who doesn't want to own me but actually stands beside me. Supports me, no matter what I choose.

And I'll be damned if anyone gets in the way of that.

"I wasn't planning to keep the ranch," I say finally, quieter than I expected. "This place... it wasn't meant for me."

And it wasn't. The place was left to Nolan—my Alpha. Or, my deceased Alpha, who passed eleven months ago. A man I didn't love, not really. Definitely not in the way everyone assumed. He hurt me more than he ever helped me, but... this? Leaving me something in his will? Even if it was just the thing his grandmother left him? That was the one decent thing he ever did.

Nolan never updated his will after Rose passed, just a month before him. With both of them gone, the lawyers spent nearly a year working through challenges from the family before they finally contacted me. Apparently, someone tried to contest it, but that was eventually sorted. So, legally, here I am.

An Omega who doesn't belong here, outnumbered and completely out of her depth. My friend, Meredith, and her brother were supposed to come with me as my backup, my buffer, but they bailed at the last minute because of a family emergency. So now it's just me, standing on shaky legs in the middle of unfamiliar territory, trying to pretend I have a clue what I'm doing.

I don't.

There's nothing for me here. Just the overwhelming scent of three Alphas, which scares me because of how attracted I am to it, whose home I've just dropped into like a grenade.

For a second, none of them speak.

Then Ridge runs a hand along his jaw, exchanging a look with the others. "We'd be open to discussing price," he says slowly, like he's still trying to wrap his head around the fact that this is even happening. "But maybe you should talk to your lawyer first. Get the full picture before anyone signs anything."

"Yeah," Walker adds, his voice calm but guarded.

Cash just watches me, jaw tight.

I nod quickly, grateful for the pause in pressure. "I actually have his info." I dig in my shoulder bag with shaky hands until I find the printed email, crumpled but legible. "Ben Hartwell. He's based in town. Says his office is on Front Street?"

Belle perks up. "Hartwell? I saw him this morning when I grabbed coffee." She eyes me, already shifting into motion. "How about I take you into town? We'll swing by his office, and you can figure things out from there."

"Are you sure?" I ask.

"Yeah." She nods toward the door. "Grab your stuff, and we'll go."

Then she turns to the guys. "I think I got all the shots I need anyway. Thanks for the last-minute heroics. You three just sold every calendar in a five-state radius."

Walker gives a small smile. "Glad we could help."

"Anytime," Ridge adds, tipping his hat slightly.

Cash just nods, his expression unreadable. "We'll be here when you return, Sophia."

His voice hits with just enough weight to make my stomach flip. I really can't pin down their reactions. Are they happy, pissed? What is their deal?

I glance back once as I follow Belle out. The three of them are still standing there, shirtless, gorgeous, and silent. And I can't help but feel like I've dropped a huge bomb on them. I'm just as rattled. Walker goes to collect the kittens in his arms as we walk away, my pulse racing, my stomach knotted. I'm so far out of my comfort zone right now.

"Thanks for the help," I say awkwardly. "Even if we are on opposite sides of this situation."

They just smile, and it leaves me more uneasy. Tough crowd, but I can't blame them. Yet, how was I supposed to know they'd made a deal with Rose?

Belle's truck is a cheerful yellow monstrosity that looks like it could survive the apocalypse. As I climb in, I sense three sets of eyes burning into my back.

"So," she says conversationally as we bounce down the dirt road once we take off in her truck. "On a scale of one to ten, how screwed do you think you are?"

"What do you mean?" I glance at her, tugging on my seat belt.

"Oh, honey." Belle laughs, one hand on the wheel like this is her favorite soap opera. "The way those boys were checking you out? Scenting you? And then you hit them with the little detail that you're inheriting their home out from under them?"

I scoff. "They weren't checking me out. They were shocked. Just like me."

Belle arches a brow without looking away from the road. "Uh-huh."

"They were probably just processing. You know, the whole surprise-stranger-just-claimed-their-ranch thing. Not everything is about pheromones and... and shirtless dominance vibes."

I groan and slump in my seat, staring down at my black leggings, flip-flops, and my favorite cropped tee with tiny rhinestone stars on the collar, the one I wore because it's cute and comfortable. There's a smudge of dirt near the hem and a streak of kitten fur clinging to the front. I try to brush it off like that's somehow going to make me look more put together.

I sigh dramatically and mutter, "All I'm missing is a tiara and a nervous breakdown, and I could headline my own rodeo."

Belle just grins. "You're gonna fit in just fine around here."

We drive through the countryside that belongs on a postcard—rolling hills, wildflower meadows, mountains in the distance. Belle chats about the town, pointing out landmarks and sharing gossip.

Grabbing my phone, I decide to email the lawyer and tell him I'm popping over to see him soon if he's free. Hoping he can slot me in.

"That's where Cash got into a bar fight with three truckers last year," Belle continues. "Won, too, though don't ask me how. Ridge used to be a huge rodeo star before his accident. And Walker, he's got some kind of weird Dr. Dolittle thing going on. I swear animals understand him better than people do."

"Good to know," I say, turning to stare out at the ridiculously beautiful green landscape. I'll be out of the cowboys' hair soon enough anyway. And as gorgeous as they are, drop-dead, drive-into-a-tree gorgeous, they didn't exactly seem thrilled to see me.

"Word of advice? Those cowboys might seem like trouble, and they are, don't get me wrong. Cash especially has a reputation for being a bit intense when something catches his interest. But they're good men. Whatever happens with the ranch, don't write them off too quickly."

I snort. "Great. Intense Alphas with broody streaks. Just what every emotionally *stable* Omega dreams of."

Belle smirks. "Yeah, well, stable is overrated."

I shake my head. "I'm not here to catch feelings or collect cowboys. I came to sign paperwork and head back home to Chicago, where I have semi-control over my life."

"Whatever you say," Belle murmurs.

"This is going to be fine," I say, more to myself than to her. "I'll talk to the lawyer, we'll sort out the sale, and I'll be back home eating overpriced sushi and ignoring emotionally unavailable men in no time."

And maybe, if I keep repeating it, I'll actually believe it.

We drive in silence for a few minutes, the truck bouncing gently along the road. Then Belle glances over at me.

"Can I ask you something?"

"Sure."

"How'd you end up coming out here on your own? No pack escort or anything?" Her tone isn't judgy, just curious. Maybe a little surprised.

I huff a small laugh. "You mean, how did an unclaimed Omega dare to breathe country air without a personal bodyguard?"

She holds up a hand, amused. "I'm a Beta. My stepsister is an Omega, though, so... I get it. She's not even allowed to go to the corner store without someone shadowing her. Last year she snuck off with some friends to a night market two towns over, and the next morning, Dad signed her up for the mate-dating institute. Said she couldn't be trusted to make her own decisions."

"Yikes." I wince. "That's... harsh." I've heard plenty of stories. Some Alpha parents treat their Omega daughters like delicate glassware, terrified they'll get scratched if they so much as look at the wrong male. There's this disgusting belief floating around in some circles that a *tainted* Omega, one who's been out in the world, has opinions, has spent time around Alphas, somehow loses her value. That she won't be as desirable.

Because God forbid an Omega have a life before getting claimed.

Some Alphas want them pure. Untouched. So innocent they've barely exchanged two words with anyone outside their family. Like that's supposed to be a virtue.

It's bullshit, if you ask me.

I grew up that way, sheltered, careful, constantly reminded of how a good Omega behaved. And it still landed me in a cold, loveless relationship I hated. But I stayed, because that's what was expected. That's what Omegas do, right? Obey. Settle. Serve.

Never again.

I refuse to live like that. And hearing about Belle's sister, about anyone else being shoved into that mold, makes my skin crawl.

Belle shrugs. "Yeah. She's still pissed about it. But, you know, Alpha dads and control issues."

I nod, jawline tight. "My best friend, Meredith, was supposed to come with me on this trip. She's a Beta too, and she was going to drag her brother along. But they had a family emergency, and I had to come settle the property stuff alone."

I don't add *Because I need the money. Because one of my freelance social media clients just ghosted me, and another pushed their campaign back a month.* But I grit my teeth and keep going. "Didn't really have the luxury of waiting around."

Belle is quiet for a second, then offers a half smile. "Well, look at it this way: If you're staying anywhere near those three cowboys, no one's going to question whether you've got protection."

"I'm not staying," I say quickly, too quickly.

She raises an eyebrow but doesn't push it. "Right. Of course not."

We drive the rest of the way with light chatter about the town, where to get the best coffee, the fact that everyone knows everyone's business, and how the mayor's cat has more Instagram followers than the actual town account.

Eventually, Belle pulls to a stop in front of a brick building with Hartwell & Associates etched on a brass plaque.

"Good luck," she calls out, putting the truck in park.

"Thanks." I open the door, then glance back with a smirk. "And best of luck with your cowboy calendar."

Belle grins. "I don't need luck. I've got abs."

I laugh, shutting the door and making my way toward the lawyer's building.

I step into the reception area, greeted by the scent of old leather and lemon polish. A woman behind the desk looks up from her computer with a polite smile.

"Hi," I say, brushing kitten fur off my shirt.

At that exact moment, a side door opens and an older man steps into view—late sixties, gray hair neatly combed, wire-framed glasses, crisp shirt tucked into perfectly pressed slacks. He moves to a side cabinet, searching for a file.

I glance back down at the receptionist, saying, "I'm Sophia Hollis. I emailed earlier about meeting with Mr. Hartwell to discuss an urgent matter."

She stares around to the older man, who is now turning his attention to me.

Recognition flashes across his face. "Ah, Ms. Hollis, yes, I was just reviewing that file. You're right on time."

He gestures toward the side door in reception. "Come on back. I've got a few minutes to spare."

I follow him into a warm, wood-paneled office lined with legal books and framed photos.

"Please, have a seat," he says, settling behind his desk. "Can I offer you some water? Coffee?"

"I'm good, thank you." I sink into a chair. "Mr. Hartwell, I'm hoping we can make this quick. I've already met the current tenants of the ranch from my inheritance, and they're interested in buying. I am happy to sell the ranch to them immediately. So if we could just—"

"Ah." The corners of his mouth curve down, and my stomach sinks. "I'm afraid it's not quite that simple."

He pulls out a thick folder and adjusts his glasses. "Mrs. Martinez was very specific in her will. The inheritance comes with conditions."

"It does?" My voice comes out higher than intended.

"The person who inherits the place must live on the ranch premises for three months before he or she can claim full ownership or authorize any sale."

The world tilts. "I'm sorry, what?"

"Three months' residency, Ms. Hollis. The will was originally written for her grandson, but upon his passing and your designation as his beneficiary, the terms transfer to you."

"Three months?" I stand up so fast the chair rolls backward. "I have to live there? With cowboys who are already unsure about me?"

He leans back in his chair. "I'm afraid so. If you choose not to fulfill the residency requirement, the ranch defaults to the next of kin, a Mr. Ronan Blackwood, as per Rose's will conditions."

"This has to be a joke." I sit on the edge of the seat because I need the money from this ranch to survive.

Not want... *need.*

I have less than five hundred dollars to my name. My job as a social media freelancer sounds great on paper, but after rent, utilities, groceries, and the endless stream of bills I keep shoving to the bottom of a drawer, I'm barely staying afloat. One emergency, like, say, a bull wrecking my rental car and me needing to pay the excess, and everything starts to unravel.

This ranch... it's the first good thing to land in my lap in a while. A chance to breathe. Maybe even get ahead for once instead of clawing just to stay even. I didn't plan for it, and I sure as hell didn't expect it, but when I saw that will, I thought, *Finally, something breaks in my favor.*

And now this?

Three months, stuck in a place I don't belong, surrounded by strangers who look at me like I just stole their future.

I press my palms to my thighs, trying to ground myself, but all I feel is that tight coil of panic under my ribs. I can't afford to lose this chance. I won't.

"I understand this is unexpected—"

"Is there any way around it?" I ask weakly.

"I'm afraid not. Mrs. Martinez was quite clear. She believed the ranch needed someone who would truly understand it before making any decisions about its future."

Three months in Montana with three Alphas, a bull named Brutus who has it out for me, and I have no idea if this small town even has a heat clinic.

What could possibly go wrong?

3

I stumble out of the lawyer's office like someone just told me Santa isn't real and I owe them months of back rent.

Three months.

Three fucking months in Montana with cowboys who probably want to lasso me off their property.

The afternoon sun hits Front Street beautifully. Everything glows golden, the vintage lampposts with their hanging flower baskets overflowing with petunias, the brick storefronts with hand-painted signs, the mountains in the distance looking like God's own screen saver.

"Get it together, Sophia," I mutter. I survived Chicago rush hour for years. I can handle a few cowboys and a ranch. Then I sigh, feeling slightly lost on *how* to handle this.

That's when the sweet, buttery scent of cinnamon finds me. My stomach growls in betrayal, reminding me I've skipped both breakfast and lunch in my rush to get to the town of Honeyspur Meadow. I turn around, and across the main street, nestled between The Dust Jacket Bookshop and Sweetwater Creek Realty, sits the Wildflower Bakehouse & Café.

I wait for a pickup truck to rumble past, then cross the quiet road like I'm on a mission from the carb gods.

The window display is pornographic. I'm talking full-on, should-be-illegal levels of baked seduction. Croissants so flaky you can see the layers from outside. Cupcakes topped with buttercream roses. A chocolate cake coated in shiny ganache. And there, front and center, a tray of Portuguese custard tarts with their signature burnt edges, calling my name like sirens.

A little bell chimes as I push open the door and step into what can only be described as carbohydrate heaven. The interior is all warm wood and mismatched vintage tables, with mason jar lights hanging from exposed beams. A chalkboard menu stretches across one wall in looping script, and the display case, sweet mother of pastry, is even more glorious up close.

"First time?" comes a soft female voice from behind the counter.

The woman speaking has flour in her straight, dark hair and a dusting of powdered sugar on her cheek. Her apron is a rainbow of patches, cats, and one suspiciously bedazzled donut. She wears a cherry-print blouse buttoned all the way up. She looks my age, in all honesty, around twenty-four years old.

Her name tag reads "Kitty," and somehow that tracks more than it should.

"You've been staring at my tarts like they hold the secrets of the universe," she says, tilting her head.

"Is it *that* obvious I'm drooling over them?"

She nods sagely. "We've had priests, brides, and a biker gang cry over that tart tray. You're in good company."

"They might hold the secrets," I say seriously. "Can I get two of those and a latte, half vanilla, half hazelnut? I'll have them here."

"A woman who knows what she wants. I *like* it." Kitty

snatches a pair of tongs. "You're the city girl, aren't you? Here about the Martinez ranch?"

I blink. "How did you—"

"Small town, sweetie. Plus, Belle swung past here earlier to pick up some pastries. If this town loves anything more than rodeos, it's gossip." She giggles as she plops the tarts onto a delicate china plate with painted violets.

The espresso machine hisses as Kitty works her magic. In moments, she slides over a latte with a flawless rosetta in the foam, like she just casually moonlights as a latte art champion.

I carry my goodies to a small table by the front window, the view overlooking the old town road where the occasional car rolls by and locals wander past in no particular hurry. My table has a single bud vase holding a daisy and a tiny crocheted doily that someone's grandmother probably made. The chair creaks as I sit, but it's the kind of creak that says *Welcome*, not *You're about to die*.

The first bite of tart is a religious experience. I moan, sinking into my seat.

The custard is silky and just sweet enough, with a surprising hint of lemon that tastes perfect with the caramelized edges. It's not what I expected, but it's a twist I didn't know I needed. The pastry shatters at the slightest pressure from my fingers, flaky, buttery deliciousness that makes my eyes flutter closed.

"Oh my God," I groan, not caring who hears me. "I might survive three months here after all."

Kitty beams from behind the counter. "My grandmother's recipe. She always said good pastry could solve half the world's problems."

"And the other half?"

"Good tequila." She grins widely.

She wipes her hands on a flour-dusted apron, then leans

an elbow on the counter, eyeing me with open curiosity. "So, you're staying in town for three months? That's exciting."

I raise an eyebrow. "You fishing for info for the rumor mill?" I tease.

Kitty laughs, utterly unbothered. "You walked into Honeyspur. We trade stories faster than we trade pies."

"Well, if I get these tarts every day, it's probably worth it."

Kitty chuckles. "Careful. They've been known to cause addiction."

I laugh and lean back in my chair, already reaching for the second tart. "I can tell."

Her gaze flicks toward the window, and she lowers her voice just a bit. "You know, most of the women in this town have been trying to catch the eyes of those Wild Hearts boys for years."

I blink. "Really?"

She gives me a slow, meaningful nod. "Mm-hmm. But none of them ever stuck. Those guys are the kind who know what they want, and I guess no one's been good enough yet."

Something in the way she says it makes goose bumps rise on my arms. Not a warning exactly, just a quiet truth.

"Lucky me," I murmur, half to myself, half to the custard tart, which is suddenly the safest thing to look at.

I'm halfway through the tart, sipping my latte and watching the town move like a live-action snow globe, minus the snow, when a familiar figure across the street catches my eye.

Cash.

My stomach does a wild somersault. He's standing there with that same quiet confidence, one hand on his hip, casually scrolling through his phone, completely unaware that he and his pack brothers broke my brain this morning just by existing shirtless. That image is burned into my memory in high definition, and no amount of caffeine is going to blur it out.

I straighten in my seat, realizing that I'll be living at the same ranch as these men. For three months. With nowhere to hide.

My brain tells me to look away. My body pretends it doesn't speak the language.

Of course he's here. Of course I'm suddenly hyperaware of the fact that I'll be staring at that jawline for the next three months. Someone really should've put a warning label on this whole situation.

He's now leaning against the entrance to Santos Rodriguez's Feed Store, and even from here I can tell his jeans should be classified as a public safety hazard. Then he turns the phone screen toward an older man working there. They both glance at it... then look straight at the café.

Straight at me.

"Shit," I mutter, ducking behind my latte like a coward and praying Kitty's foam art is thick enough to block their line of sight.

Nope.

Cash says something to the man, pockets his phone, and starts crossing the street with that infuriatingly confident cowboy walk that makes my ovaries threaten to unionize.

The bell over the bakery door chimes, and suddenly the air feels ten degrees hotter.

"City girl," he drawls, touching the brim of an imaginary hat like he's in a spaghetti Western. "Fancy meeting you at this café."

"It's a small town," I reply, trying not to gape at how stupid good he looks in that fitted Henley. "Fancy meeting anyone anywhere."

His grin spreads, lazy and lethal. "Fair point. Mind if I join you?"

Yes. No. Maybe. My brain stutters like a dial-up connection.

"Free country," I manage.

Built like a linebacker, he slides into the chair across from me. The guy is huge. And his eyes aren't just blue but the color of morning glories after a storm, his jawline sharp. Someone can fall so easily staring at that face.

Cash leans back in his seat, his chair creaking slightly beneath his weight. "So... how'd it go with Ben?"

I swirl my latte, lowering my attention to the foam losing its pattern. I should ease into telling him, give him the news gently.

Instead, the words come rushing out. "I can't sell the ranch right away."

He lifts one brow. "Come again?"

"The lawyer said... to inherit it, I have to live on the property. For three months." I take a gulp of my coffee like it might drown the nerves clawing up my throat. "If I don't, it goes to some cousin of Nolan's I've never even met."

Cash frowns. "Ronan Blackwood," he hisses.

I blink. "You know him?"

"A little. That man's about as welcome in these parts as a rattlesnake at a square dance." He scratches his jaw. "So you're staying, then?"

"I guess I'm going to be a nuisance." I laugh, but it comes out a little tight. "Definitely not the plan. I work online, so I can do my job from anywhere, but I didn't exactly pack for ranch life. And now I'm crashing at your home for three months." My breaths are rushing.

He just watches me for a beat, then says, "We've got plenty of space at the ranch. No one's asking you to sleep in the hayloft, unless you're partial to mice and itchy blankets." He grins, and my chest tightens at the sight, that small dimple in his chin, the slight peek of teeth. God, who is this man?

I huff a laugh.

"As long as you're fine living with the three of us," he adds, "you're welcome to stay. It's been our home for over four years now, but it's still Rose's house at heart. And if she wanted you there, that's good enough for me."

Something hot and awkward crawls into my chest. "I mean, I would never ask you to move out. I—" I fumble with my tart plate, nearly sending flaky crumbs everywhere. "But also, it wasn't Rose who left it to me, but her grandson. I guess he never updated his will after she passed."

"Then maybe it's a blessing in disguise," he says, lifting one shoulder. "One of my foster dads used to say, 'If the gate swings shut, check your boots and climb the fence.'"

I blink. "That... actually makes sense. Anyway, my plan is to sell the ranch to you three, but I guess we need to wait three months."

He smiles again, nothing judgy behind his expression, and heat skitters across my skin. "So, you from Chicago, then, Sophia?"

"Born and raised," I say with a wry smile. "Shocking, I know. Guess I'll be getting very familiar with Montana real soon."

"It ain't the worst kind of strange."

"I'll let you know."

He chuckles, then glances toward Kitty, who's pretending not to eavesdrop while wiping the counter in tight little circles.

"My usual, Kitty?" he calls.

She perks up, her grin downright devilish. "Already got it started, sweetheart."

He looks back at me, and I try not to gape. Okay. So he has a usual here. He has a smile that could melt steel. And Kitty said all the women in town would kill for a chance with him and his friends. Why haven't they picked someone? Are they impossible to please? Or is there something deeper, something none of the town gossips know?

Someone walks into the café, sending a flurry of air inside and, with it, smothers me in Cash's scent. Fresh sage, strong coffee, old leather. It's not overwhelming, but it settles low in my belly, and something deep inside stirs and stretches like it's been asleep for years. I shift in my seat, heat flushing my neck.

He grabs his coffee from Kitty, who winks at me as he turns. "Come on," he says. "I'll give you a lift back. Sun dips behind those mountains, the temperature'll drop faster than gossip at a funeral."

I finish my tart in two bites, draining the last of my latte as Kitty gives me an exaggerated eyebrow waggle. I try not to laugh but end up giggling like a fool anyway. "Thanks again," I say, following him out.

"Hey!" Kitty calls, hurrying over with a white paper bag printed with her logo, the sides puffed out like it's about to burst. "Packed you a few pastries for later just in case you need a little sugar to survive ranch life." She flashes a smile so warm it softens something in my chest. I already like her.

Outside, the breeze is cooler, brushing my cheeks and setting the bakery sign to swaying. We walk down the sidewalk toward where his truck is parked, our footsteps falling into an easy rhythm.

As we pass the post office, something catches my eye. A hand-painted billboard near the window, bright and cheerful with a slice of apple pie nearly the size of my head.

Honeyspur Meadow's Annual Pie Festival. Enter. Eat. Judge. Repeat.

I grin to myself. I've officially stepped into a cowboy movie, and now there's pie.

Cash's truck is big and black, with chrome accents that catch the fading sunlight and a dusting of country roads clinging to the wheels. He opens the passenger door for me like it's second nature, and I hate how much I like that.

"Thanks," I mumble, climbing in.

When he gets in beside me, the cab fills with his scent all over again, stronger now, warmer. My breath hitches while I watch his nostrils flare, as I assume he is now catching mine. Something about the look in his eyes makes my pulse skitter... but then he reaches over and rolls his window halfway down without a word.

Oh.

Right.

Subtle.

Clear.

Not interested.

Got it.

I fold my hands in my lap and try not to die inside.

We drive in silence for a stretch, the mountains casting long shadows across the valley as the sun starts to dip. The road is mostly empty, just us and the hum of the tires.

"So," he says finally, eyes still on the road. "You said earlier that Rose's grandson left you the ranch?"

I hesitate. "Yeah. Nolan."

He glances at me briefly. "Your Alpha?"

"He was," I admit.

A long pause.

"I'm real sorry," he says softly. "Losing your Alpha... that kind of pain sticks."

I stare out the side window, watching the trees blur past. "It wasn't like that. Nolan and I weren't true scent matches. We tried. It just... never clicked."

I remember one night, one last try. The way he pulled away like I'd burned him, frustration and apology all tangled on his face. I swallowed the lump in my throat then, like I do now.

"It was more about expectations," I murmur. "His family

wanted it. Mine encouraged it. And I stayed, thinking I should. But I don't want to be someone's obligation. I want to live by my own rules. Even if it means figuring everything out from scratch."

He hums, thoughtful. "Well, sometimes the map's wrong, but the trail's still worth walkin'."

I smile despite myself. "That one's actually pretty good."

We turn off the main road onto a wide gravel lane framed by two open iron gates, the words *Wild Hearts Ranch* welded across the top in curved lettering that's seen a few Montana winters. As the truck rumbles forward, I catch glimpses of the land stretching out ahead, rolling pastures dotted with wildflowers, white-fenced paddocks, and clusters of trees that sway lazily in the breeze. Horses graze in the distance, their tails flicking, their coats glossy in the afternoon sun.

Cash slows to a stop just past the gates, shifts into park, and hops out.

I watch through the windshield as he walks back to swing the gates shut. It shouldn't be a thing, just a man closing gates, but somehow the way he moves is... confident. Comfortable. Cowboy. He climbs back into the truck, then flicks the blinker, and we take off again, gravel crunching beneath us.

"Back entrance," he says with a little grin, like he's letting me in on a secret. "Main road's prettier, but this way keeps the horses from getting too interested in traffic."

We drive deeper onto the property, and the ranch starts to take shape. Wide barns painted a deep red with white trim, a sprawling training arena, fenced pastures in every direction, and the main house perched up on a gentle rise. It's big, old, and even more gorgeous from this angle.

"Wow," I murmur. "This place is... bigger than I expected."

"Six hundred acres," Cash says, his voice low and proud.

"We do horse sales and breeding, some boarding and training too. Couple of the guys compete in local events when we've got time, and we lease out parts of the land now and then. We've got a team who lives in the bunkers and helps us run the place."

"That sounds like a full plate."

He tosses me one of his captivating winks. "Walker handles most of the training. Ridge is the numbers guy. I keep things movin' and deal with folks who need talkin' to."

I raise an eyebrow. "Is that cowboy code for intimidation?"

He grins. "Depends who I'm talkin' to."

We roll up the driveway, his thick, muscular forearms catching the gold wash of late sunlight. One hand grips the wheel, the other rests against the open window, wind teasing his dirty-blond hair like we're in some kind of rugged romance novel I did not sign up for.

I have no idea what I've gotten myself into.

Three cowboys. One ranch. Zero backup plan.

But until I figure out how to make this work, or how to get paid for the ranch, I'm stuck here.

With him. With all three of them.

And I really need to stop staring at his arms.

4

CASH

I practically leap out of my truck the second we roll to a stop behind the main house, sucking in lungfuls of fresh Montana air like a drowning man. That twenty-minute drive from town nearly killed me.

Her scent. God Almighty, her scent is everywhere, clinging to my clothes, burrowing under my skin, wrapping around my cock like a silk fist. Jasmine tea and vanilla bean with rain on summer grass. It's strangling me in the best and worst way possible.

I watch her climb out of the passenger side, those impossibly toned legs unfolding from my truck. This morning my biggest worry was dealing with that ornery stallion who keeps breaking through the north paddock fence. Now? Now I'm trying to wrangle the goddamn beast in my jeans that's been rock hard since she slid into my truck.

She catches me staring, and I snap my gaze away, moving to the driver's seat to grab my hat. Perfect. I'll just hold it casually in front of me, totally natural. Nothing to see here, folks. Just a grown man hiding behind his Stetson like a teenager at his first dance.

"Everything okay?" Her voice has this little lilt to it, like she knows exactly what she's doing to me.

"Peachy keen," I manage, gesturing toward the back door. "After you."

Fuck me sideways, those leggings should be illegal. Black fabric hugging every curve, following the gentle swell of her hips, the perfect roundness of her ass. My fingers itch to trace those same lines, to peel that material down and discover if she tastes as good as she smells.

I guide her through the mudroom, past the kitchen, and into the front parlor. It's the nicest room in the house with a massive stone fireplace, leather couches that have seen better days but are comfortable as hell, and that big round table in the back where we play poker every Thursday with whoever wants to join us.

"Ridge! Walker!" I holler toward the stairs and outside the front door. "Get your asses in here!"

Sophia settles onto the single armchair, crossing those legs that are going to haunt my dreams. She's spectacular. Not in that obvious, trying-too-hard way I've seen in town. She's got this natural elegance that tightens my balls.

Her reddish hair catches the afternoon light streaming through the windows, all those shades of copper and gold twisted together like expensive whiskey. She pushes it off her face and over her shoulders, leaving her neck exposed, and sweet merciful hell, I want to press my mouth right there where her pulse flutters. Her skin looks as soft as cream, scattered with tiny freckles across her nose.

But it's her eyes that really get me. Deep green like summer pine needles. She's got this way of looking at you dead-on, no bullshit, but then her gaze will skip away like she's remembered she's been caught staring. Makes me want to dig into every single thing about her. What happened to her and Rose's grandson? What's her life like in

Chicago, and is she happy there? What would it take to make her look at me without that careful distance?

Ridge appears from upstairs, Walker from the direction of the rear rooms, and they both stop dead in their tracks just outside the parlor room when they see her properly. Walker's breaths speed up. While Ridge, who *claims* his busted scent senses make him immune to Omega appeal, shifts his weight like he's been sucker punched.

"So," I drawl, settling onto the couch across from her. "Sophia's got some news from the lawyer."

She uncrosses and recrosses her legs, and I have to bite back a groan. "Well, this is awkward." She laughs, but it's nervous as the guys enter the room and take seats on either side of me. "Turns out I'm not just inheriting a ranch. I'm inheriting... roommates?"

"I need a bit more information." Ridge's voice is flat, careful.

"According to the will, I have to live here. On the ranch. For three months." She rushes through it like ripping off a Band-Aid. "Starting immediately. Or I forfeit everything. So... surprise? You've got a house guest who has no idea what she's doing but evidently needs to figure out the whole rent situation back home and probably buy some actual boots because these"—she gestures at her flats—"are going to get ruined."

The silence stretches out like taffy.

"So what do you think?" She's twisting her fingers together. "I really didn't plan this, but I guess when life hands you lemons, you... move to Montana and pretend you know anything about horses?"

"Yep. When life bucks you off, from the saddle," I say automatically, "you dust off your ass and climb back on."

Walker snorts. Ridge rolls his eyes so hard I'm surprised they don't fall out.

"Really?" Walker grins. "That's what you're going with?"

"It's wisdom," I defend.

"It's a bumper sticker," Ridge counters.

Sophia's fighting a smile; I can tell. "So... three months of bumper sticker wisdom? This should be interesting."

"Anyway," Ridge says, settling back in his chair. "We're happy to have you here. Ranch could use a fresh perspective."

"Plus, Cookie will be thrilled," Walker adds. "He's been complaining that we don't appreciate his cooking enough. Says we eat like bears."

"We do!" I point out.

"Exactly. You'll class up the place."

"Oh!" Walker suddenly jumps up, heading to the corner of the room. "Almost forgot. We had your car towed to Murphy's Garage in town earlier. Grabbed your duffel bag from the back." He holds up the bag.

"You did? Oh my God, thank you! I didn't even think... Crap, I still need to call the rental company." She's already pulling out her phone. "Let me just... I'll step outside for a minute. Excuse me."

The second the patio door closes behind her, we all exhale like we've been holding our breath underwater.

"Well?" I look between them. "What do you think?"

"I think," Walker says slowly, "that we're in trouble."

"Big fucking trouble," Ridge agrees, but he's almost smiling. "Did you see how she didn't even flinch at your philosophy? Most people run."

"She gave it right back," I say, probably sounding too pleased about it. "She's an Omega, and I swear to God she's doing something to me that no female ever has." I adjust my thick cock through my jeans, not even trying to be subtle about it.

Walker grins like a beast. "Her scent is fucking hypnotic. Like sinking into warm honey. Makes me want to roll around in it until it's all over me."

"Makes me want to bend her over that chair and find out what other sweet sounds she makes," I admit.

"Fuck," Ridge mutters, but he's shifting in his seat. "You two need a cold shower."

"You're telling me you don't feel anything?" Walker challenges. "Not even a little?"

"I'm broken, remember?" Ridge cuts him off, but there's something in his eyes that says different.

"Bullshit," I call. "I saw you lean in when she walked past."

"I was being polite."

"You were sniffing her like a bloodhound," Walker accuses, grinning.

"Like a dog who found bacon," I add.

"You know my sense of smell doesn't work, assholes," Ridge mutters, but his lips are twitching.

The patio door opens and Sophia returns. We all pull back into our seats. I catch the worry on her face before she even speaks, the way she's nibbling on her bottom lip between her teeth.

"All okay?" I ask.

She drops into the chair, looking deflated. "Well, that was fun. Apparently, I need to send them the mechanic's details and pay a hefty deductible that I definitely don't have right now. Not until..." She waves vaguely. "You know, three months, when I can actually access any of this inheritance money from selling the ranch."

"How much?" Walker asks.

"Two thousand." She waves her hand like it's nothing, but I see the tension in her shoulders. "Plus whatever the mechanic charges for the repairs."

"That's fucked," Ridge says bluntly.

"Yeah, well." She shrugs. "Story of my life lately."

There's something raw in her voice that makes me want to dig deeper. What else has gone wrong for her?

"We could lend you the money," Walker offers.

"No." The word comes out sharp, almost angry. She takes a breath. "Sorry. I mean, thank you, but no. I don't take charity."

"It's not charity," I say carefully. "It's—"

"It's three strangers offering to pay my bills on day one." Her green eyes flash. "I know what that looks like. What it leads to. Thanks, but I'll figure it out myself."

The temperature in the room drops about ten degrees. She thinks we want something from her. Payment in another form. Lone Omega, three Alphas, middle of nowhere. She'd be stupid not to be suspicious.

"Fair enough," Ridge says, breaking the tension. "Your ranch, your rules."

"Right. *My* ranch, sort of." She says it like she's trying to convince herself. "For three months, anyway."

She suddenly straightens in her seat. "I want to help out around the ranch. Earn my keep, learn the operation. I may be selling, but I'm not going to be a freeloader."

"You own the place," Ridge reminds her. "You don't need to earn anything."

"Maybe not." That stubborn chin lifts. "But I'm going to anyway."

"That's fair and I admire that," I add.

"Well, the only thing is," she adds, staring down at her hands, "I'm not sure I feel comfortable living in the house with you all. You're still strangers. And it's just... I'm an Omega and... But I'm not kicking you out. I see there are other places on the property. Maybe I can stay in one of those instead?"

She gestures vaguely at us, cheeks turning pink.

Fuck me, but that blush makes me want to find out how far down it goes. I notice Walker's hands clench on his thighs, see Ridge's jaw tick. The biological imperative is already working on all of us, that primal need to claim, to protect, to possess.

I've met plenty of women, both Betas and Omegas, over the years. None of them made me want to throw them over my shoulder and lock them in my bedroom until they smelled like me inside and out.

That's exactly why unmated Omegas shouldn't live with Alphas. Hunger can drive you mad, make you do things you'd never consider with a clear head. It's why they usually travel with protection, why they stay indoors, and why many end up in cities with the Omega institutes, dating match organizations, and heat clinics.

Walker is staring at her with an intensity that borders on predatory. Even Ridge is barely blinking.

"The guesthouse," I blurt out before anyone says something stupid. "You can have the whole thing to yourself. It's private, no Alpha scents. Far enough from the bunkhouses and anyone else, but close enough if you need anything."

Relief washes over her face as her shoulders drop. "That would be perfect. And I promise to stay out of your way unless I'm helping on the ranch. I work from home anyway. Social media management. As long as there's Wi-Fi, I can work from anywhere."

"You're covered, then," Ridge adds.

"Amazing." She almost smiles.

"Come on, then." I push to my feet, needing to move before the tension in this room suffocates us all. "I'll show you the guesthouse. I'm sure you're exhausted."

I grab her bag from where Walker left it. She says goodbye to the guys and follows me out, and the late afternoon air is a relief after the charged atmosphere inside. I catch myself slowing down just to keep her in my peripheral vision.

"So this path continues on to the main barn," I point at the stone passage as we walk, my voice remaining neutral. "That's where we keep the horses for training. Over there is the cattle barn, and past that is the equipment shed. You'll want to stick to the marked paths until you learn your way around."

"The ranch is huge." She sounds genuinely shocked.

"Easy to get lost if you don't know where you're going."

We keep walking, then she says, "So your friends seem nice."

I almost laugh at the careful way she says it. "They're good men and my pack. Little rough around the edges, but solid. Rose gave us a chance by hiring us when no one else would."

That's when we approach the guesthouse. It's smaller than the main house but newer, built maybe ten years ago when Rose was thinking about taking in paying guests. Never happened, but we've kept it maintained.

"It's perfect," she says, smiling at the sight.

"Two bedrooms, full bath, kitchen's stocked with basics." I pause in front of the porch steps. "Now, the big building on the other side of the main house is where Cookie holds court," I continue. "We've got a full kitchen and dining hall there. Breakfast at five, lunch at noon, dinner at six. You're welcome anytime. Cookie makes enough to feed an army, and he'll be thrilled to have someone new to fuss over. Anyway, your guesthouse keys are on the kitchen table inside."

"I don't have to cook? Sounds amazing," she muses.

"Not unless you get a hankering for it." I grin. "Most doors are also almost never locked anyway, ranch tradition, but feel free to keep yours locked if you feel safer."

We stand there, awkward. Then she's got her hand out for her bag, but I don't want to give it up yet. Don't want this to end.

"Well," she says finally. "Thanks for... everything. Really."

"Our door's always open," I manage. "If you need anything. We're just..." I gesture vaguely toward the main house. "You know. There."

Smooth, Winslow. Real smooth.

She wrestles her bag from my grip and heads toward the door. I force myself to walk away, not sprinting like my body wants. About halfway back, I risk a glance over my shoulder.

She's on the porch, watching me. Our eyes meet and she flushes, disappearing quickly inside.

I grin all the way back to the house.

Ridge and Walker are still in the parlor, now with beers in hand. Ridge tosses me one without asking.

"So." I collapse onto the couch. "We've got ourselves a house guest for three months. Should work out fine."

"Yeah, if you can keep it in your pants," Ridge states. "Saw the way you were drooling over that poor Omega."

"Fuck you very much. She's just... different."

"Think it might be a scent match?" Walker asks, way too casual. "She smelled like temptation, but I'd need to get closer to be sure."

"Sure you would." I take a long pull of beer. "For science."

"We should give her space," Ridge suggests, ever the practical one. "Girl looks ready to bolt if we breathe wrong. What she needs is protection, not desperate Alphas sniffing around her door."

"I can protect her just fine up close," I argue.

"With what? Your animal magnetism?" Walker snorts. "Face it. You're already half gone on her."

"When the horse fits," I start, but Ridge throws a cushion pillow at my head. I dodge it.

"No. No more wisdom. Go make a fucking advice column for the local paper already."

"Y'all are just jealous of my philosophical nature."

"Sure!" Walker grins. "Thought it was just another symptom of being dropped on your head as a baby."

"Fuck you both sideways." But I'm grinning too. This is what I love about my pack. We can go from intense to stupid in seconds flat.

"Seriously, though," Ridge leans forward. "We need to be careful. She's our boss now, technically. And she's alone, unmated, probably scared under all that sass. If we spook her, she could make our lives hell."

"Or kick us out," Walker adds quietly.

The reminder sobers us all. This ranch is everything to us. The only real home we've ever built together.

"We'll be smart about it," I promise. "Keep things professional."

They both stare at me.

"What? I can do that."

"You were just hiding a hard-on with your hat earlier in your seat," Ridge points out.

"That's... Shut up."

"Anyway, I got a few more things to finish," Ridge adds, so he and Walker head outside. I end up in my bedroom, needing space to think. To breathe air that doesn't carry her scent.

Except my room faces the guesthouse. And there she is, moving inside, past the window.

This is bad. This is very, very bad.

I've gone too long without sinking into a woman. Plenty of Betas in town are happy to scratch that itch, but I haven't had any desires. And I've never been with an Omega. Never wanted to deal with the complications.

But this one... Christ, this one is calling to something primal in me.

I unbuckle my belt, pop the button on my jeans. My cock springs free, already leaking. What the hell? I haven't been this worked up in a long time.

She appears on the porch for a moment, staring out at the fields. The setting sun turns her hair to flame, and I'm already fisting my cock, rough and desperate.

One hand braced on the wall, the other working my length like a man possessed. I picture her in my truck again, that scent wrapping around me. Imagine peeling those leggings down her thighs, spreading her out on my bench seat.

In my mind, she's bare and perfect, crawling over my lap. She's dripping wet, her breasts in my face as she straddles me. I take one pink nipple into my mouth, and she moans my name...

"Fuck, fuck, fuck," I hiss, pumping faster. My knot is already swelling at the base, something that usually takes a lot more work.

She shifts on the porch, hips cocking as she leans against the railing, and I'm done for. I come with a growl, barely managing to grab tissues in time. Still make a mess on the curtain like some kind of animal.

I'm panting, watching her disappear back inside.

Three months of this sweet torture.

She's going to destroy me. Turn me inside out and leave me howling at her door like a beast stripped of its mate.

And the worst part? I'm already looking forward to it.

Damn it all to hell.

5

SOPHIA

I stand in my fairy-tale cottage, trying to process the last twelve hours. This morning I was in Chicago, thinking I'd sign some papers and be home by the weekend. Now I'm living in Montana with three cowboys who make my body burn like it hasn't gotten the memo that I'm doing just fine on my own.

My phone buzzes. A text from my bestie, Meredith.

Signs of life? Do I need to send a search party?

I text her back.

Survived. Long story. Can I call you?

Her response comes in seconds.

About to jump on a Zoom call for work. Will call you once done.

So I unpack quickly, needing something normal and routine to ground me. Laptop, chargers, the silk pajamas that are wildly inappropriate for ranch life but that I packed anyway. Once everything is in its place, I feel marginally more human. Though I'll seriously need more clothes and toiletries if I'm actually going to live here for three months.

Maybe I can make a quick trip home? If someone's

willing to lend me a car. That wouldn't break the contract... right?

I start wandering around the guesthouse, and it's not what I expected.

From the outside, it's a charming little wooden cabin with whitewashed panels and flowers along the front yard, like it belongs on a greeting card. Inside, it's cozy in that lived-in, well-loved way. Not overly modern, but not a time capsule either. The kind of place where someone once cared about the details.

The entry opens into a small lounge with a plaid couch, a rug with horses galloping across it, and a little brick fireplace. To the left is a kitchenette with cheerful yellow cabinets and an honest-to-God mint-green fridge that hums like it's survived five generations and a few heat waves. Down the short hallway, I find a snug bedroom with soft linens and a quilt folded neatly at the end of the bed. The bathroom is clean and bright, smelling faintly of lavender soap.

I pause at the back door and peer through the window. A tiny brown bunny is hopping lazily through a vegetable patch just beyond the porch, pausing to sniff the air. Its nose twitches like it's caught me watching, and in a blink, it darts away under the fence, white tail flashing like a retreating puffball. I press a smile to my lips. Cute. Unexpected. And maybe a small sign that this place isn't out to chew me up and spit me out after all.

Then I find the last room and... it steals my breath.

A miniature library.

The walls are lined with shelves, some crammed full, others half stacked with books lying sideways or tucked in at odd angles. Light filters in through a wide window, and nestled in the corner is the coziest reading nook I've ever seen. A hanging bamboo chair curled like a crescent moon, with a plush mauve cushion practically purring my name.

Okay, universe. I get it.

I backtrack to the kitchen, find a cold lemonade soda waiting in the fridge like some small miracle, and then hurry to grab my laptop, phone, and charger from the bedroom. My arms are full, wires tangled, soda tucked awkwardly under my chin as I half stumble, half slide into the library nook. There's a power outlet behind the seat, and I quickly plug in my laptop. The suspended chair wobbles dramatically, swinging just enough to make me yelp, but somehow I manage to settle in cross-legged, tech gear piled around me like I'm preparing for battle.

The chair sways slightly, but it's comfortable. Absurdly so. The cushion cocoons me in just the right way, and for the first time since I landed in this dusty town, something inside me eases.

I pull out my laptop, open it with a soft chime, and fire up my blog. The familiar interface blooms to life in the way only something truly mine can. My little corner of the internet. This, at least, hasn't changed.

I lean back into the cushion, legs tucked beneath me. Then my fingers find the keys as I read and reply to a few people from my last post.

I started this blog two years ago as a total shot in the dark, keeping it a secret from Nolan, my then Alpha. Just me, no name shared, and a whole lot of frustration. I was tired of being told what I could and couldn't do. Where I should go. Who I should be. What I should feel. And the worst part? Most of those opinions didn't even come from other Omegas. Just people telling us how we ought to behave for our own good.

So I did something a little rebellious that no one knew about, except my bestie.

I made a space for Omegas. For anyone who needed it, really. I wanted to share my life as it happened—the awkward parts, the messy bits, the painful ones too. And in return, others started sharing their stories. Omegas from all over. Some scared. Some furious. Some who just wanted to feel like they weren't the only ones questioning the old rules. We're not a huge demographic, but we've got experiences worth telling. And apparently, a lot of people want to listen.

The blog has just under fifty thousand followers now, which still blows my mind. Most are Omegas, sure, but some have outed themselves in the comments as Betas. Even a few brave Alphas. Surprisingly respectful too. No unsolicited scent matches or mating proposals. Yet.

There's something kind of magical about that. This odd little patch of internet land where everyone is just... decent. Curious. Supportive. Sometimes snarky. Sometimes sad. Always real.

Leaning back, I breathe easy and start typing, unsure of exactly what I want to say.

Confessions of a City Omega
In Which Our Heroine Discovers Cowboys Are Real and Very Distracting

Dearest Diary,

Remember how I always said I'd never leave Chicago? Well, surprise! Your girl is currently sitting in what can only be described as a Pinterest board come to life, in the middle of Absolutely Nowhere, Montana.

Why, you ask? Inheritance drama. Long story. The short version is I now own a ranch. Yes, you read that correctly. Me. Owner of actual land with actual animals.

But let's talk about the REAL issue here. Cowboys. Not the Halloween costume kind. Real ones. With the hats and the boots and the way they say "ma'am" like it's stitched into their DNA—it's honestly unfair to the rest of us.

Current survival status:

- Found good coffee (critical)
- Located bakery with life-changing Portuguese tarts (extra critical)
- Survived an attempted murder on me by livestock (barely)
- May have accidentally inherited three Alpha cowboys along with the ranch (help)

The guesthouse they've put me up in looks like something out of a fairy tale. I'm literally sitting in a hanging chair in a reading nook, surrounded by books and definitely not thinking about the cowboys. Nope. Not thinking about them at all.

Send wine. Send chocolate. Send a guide on *How to Not Develop Feelings for Cowboys Who Technically Work for You but Also Kind of Don't.*

Will report back tomorrow if I survive.

City Omega out. (From the country. The irony isn't lost on me.)

I post it, and within minutes, it gets likes and comments from my regular readers. The familiar ritual of engagement soothes something in me. At least this part of my life hasn't changed.

My phone suddenly rings. Meredith.

I answer immediately.

"Hey, I'm back," she says. "Zoom call from hell is over, I've got wine in hand, and I just reread your blog post. So I'm double caffeinated, slightly tipsy, and triple needy for details. Spill. How's the trip?"

I let out a long breath. "Well, remember how this was supposed to be a quick one? Sign some papers, come home?"

"Yeah?"

"Plot twist. I have to live here for three months, or I lose the inheritance."

Dead silence. Then: "WHAT?"

"Right? And there are three Alpha cowboys who basically already live here and thought they were buying the place. So now I'm the evil city witch squatting in their home."

"Okay, okay, slow down. Three Alpha cowboys? Sophia Marie Hollis, why would you bury the lead like this?"

"It's not like that."

"Tell me what they're like. Scale of gas-station calendar to Marvel movie."

I groan into my hand. "Marvel movie. Possibly the director's cut with bonus footage. Very high-definition."

"SOPHIA."

"I know. And one of them I'm certain already dislikes me. Another one may dislike my scent. I'm living in a fairy-tale cottage, and I found the world's best Portuguese tarts, so maybe I'll just stress-eat myself into a coma and hope the problem solves itself."

"Breathe. This is spiral thinking. What did your therapist say?"

I inhale through my nose and count to four. "You're right. I'm okay. This is manageable. Completely fine."

"Important question. Are any of them single?"

"Mer!"

"What? It's a practical question. You're stuck there for three months with three hot cowboys. The universe is writing you a romance novel, and you're ignoring the plot."

"The universe needs an editor. These guys think I'm stealing their legacy. Romance isn't even in the prologue."

"Mm-hmm. What do they smell like?"

"I'm hanging up now."

"You can't smell them through the phone. That's the one upside to long distance. Just tell Auntie Mer."

I sigh. "Sage and coffee. Cedar and cinnamon. Honey and fresh bread."

"O. M. G. You're living in a damn bakery. And they're all single?"

"I don't know! I've only known them for less than twelve hours!"

"Enough hours of smelling like a Williams Sonoma catalog. Girl, your ovaries must be writing poetry."

"My ovaries are drafting their resignation letter. One more whiff and they'll unionize."

I shift in the hanging chair, trying not to smile, but it's impossible with Meredith. "How's your mom?"

"Doing better. Hip surgery went great. She's already bossing around the nurses, so clearly she's on the mend."

"Good. Tell her I said hi."

Another pause. Then her voice softens. "You sure you're okay? This is a lot. Way more than the plan."

"I don't really have a choice. I need the money, Mer. Nolan's accounts are basically dry, and it's not like he let me have a job. I only started my freelancing gig after he passed. I'm surprised he even left me the ranch inheritance. So I've got to make this work."

"You could ask your parents for help."

"Right. Let me just call them up and say, 'Hey, remember how I didn't try hard enough to make Nolan happy? And then after he died, you sent me all those guilt texts? Well, now I need a loan.'"

"They don't really believe you didn't try." Her voice dips low.

"They never said it, not directly. But they didn't have to. Dad barely looks at me when I go over, and Mom only calls when he's out of the house. She checks in, but she's too scared to cross him. And honestly? I think they were just relieved when Nolan died. Now they don't have to pretend anymore."

Meredith sighs. "They're wrong. And you're doing your best."

"Yeah, well, my best is currently avoiding eye contact with guys who could break the internet with one smolder."

"Again, you say this like it's a bad thing."

I glance out the window where the last of the sunlight casts long shadows across the ranch. The guesthouse feels quieter now, the kind of quiet that dares you to unpack your thoughts.

"I should probably go," I say, my voice softer now. "Spotted some yogurt and fruit in the fridge and I'm planning to raid the pantry like a raccoon in silk pajamas."

Mer snorts. "Sexy."

"You know it."

"Well, I'll let you hide for the rest of the night, then. But if you need help clearing out your place back home or packing more of your things, just say the word. I've got a duffel bag, two working arms, and an unhealthy love for bubble wrap."

"Thanks." My throat tightens, but I smile. "You're the best."

"Damn right I am. Now go eat your raccoon dinner, and try not to fall in love with any more emotionally unavailable cowboys."

"No promises."

"Love you, Soph."

"Love you more."

I hang up and let the silence settle. For a moment, it's just me, the soft hum of the fridge, and the slow sway of the hanging chair.

And maybe, just maybe, things will start to make sense tomorrow.

6

Something pulls me from sleep, and for a moment, I'm floating in that hazy space between dreams and waking. My neck aches from an odd angle. The bed beneath me sways gently, and I reach for my nightstand that isn't there.

Chicago. I'm in my Chicago home with the broken radiator that clangs at 3:00 a.m. and the neighbor's Yorkshire terrier yapping outside.

Except there's no dog. No radiator. Just... silence so complete it feels like pressure against my eardrums.

My eyes adjust slowly to the darkness. Moonlight filters through lace curtains I don't own, illuminating a room full of built-in bookshelves. The suspended chair I've somehow pretzeled myself into creaks as I shift. I must have fallen asleep in it from exhaustion. My laptop slides off my legs with a soft thud onto the thick rug below. My phone follows, screen briefly lighting up to show that it's 2:47 a.m.

Right. I'm in Montana at a ranch I inherited from my Alpha's grandmother, surrounded by three cowboys who... no. Not thinking about them right now. Not thinking about how Cash's eyes follow me everywhere, or Walker's gentle smile, or Ridge's brooding silence that intrigues me more than scares me off.

The scratching comes again; that's what woke me. Long, deliberate drags against glass that make my skin prickle. The library window is maybe ten feet away, curtains drawn tight except where moonlight sneaks through gaps.

I untangle myself from the chair, still wearing yesterday's leggings and shirt. My bare feet hit cold hardwood, and I suppress a squeak. These floors are freezing.

The scratching continues, patient and rhythmic.

What lives in Montana that scratches at windows? Bears (do bears have claws that scratch, or do they just maul?), mountain lions (definitely have claws), wolves (more likely to huff and puff and blow the house down), serial killers who've watched too many horror movies (statistically unlikely but not impossible).

Then Brutus flashes through my mind. That massive black bull appearing from nowhere on the road yesterday. The sickening crunch of metal as I'd swerved into that oak tree. Then he chased me. My skin crawls.

Another scratch. Then another. More insistent now.

I creep toward the window, wishing I'd thought to locate a weapon. Or a light switch. Or my common sense, which apparently stayed in Chicago.

The floorboards creak under my weight, and the scratching stops. Great. Now whatever is out there knows I'm awake. I hold my breath, waiting.

A sound comes through the glass, high-pitched, almost like a rusty hinge that needs WD-40.

I reach for the curtain edge with shaking fingers and peek through the tiniest gap possible.

An enormous orange tabby cat sits in the flower bed below, one paw raised to scratch again. When it spots movement, it opens its mouth and produces the squeakiest meow I've ever heard from something that size.

Like someone stepped on a particularly melodramatic dog toy.

Relief makes my knees weak. Then annoyance kicks in.

"Seriously?" I whisper to the glass. "All that drama for a cat?"

The furball meows again, more insistent, pressing its whiskered face against the window. In the moonlight, its eyes reflect green, pupils wide. It glances over its shoulder, then back at me, pawing more frantically. Its tail is puffed up, not quite Halloween-cat level.

Was something chasing it?

I struggle with the window latch while the cat continues its squeaky serenade, throwing in some deeper yowls now. Finally, the latch gives with a screech that probably carried to the next county and woke up every cow in a five-mile radius.

The cat shoots inside like its tail is literally on fire and only indoor safety will do. An orange blur streaks past my legs, nearly taking me out at the knees before disappearing into the darkness of the house.

"What's chasing you?" I mutter, quickly closing the window and making sure the latch catches this time. "Please don't be fleeing from a mountain lion that's now going to eat me instead."

Then I follow my uninvited guest to the kitchen, where the light switch is mercifully easy to find. Harsh fluorescents flicker to life.

"Oh, you know exactly where you are, don't you?" I study the feline more closely. Definitely well-fed—actually, that might be understating it. This cat has achieved a level of round that speaks to regular meals and probably some stolen extras. Coat glossy and thick, white bib pristine despite its outdoor adventure.

The cat butts its broad head against my hand, purring

intensifying to jet-engine levels. I swear the vibrations are making the windows rattle.

"Fine, but no counter surfing." I scoop up what has to be at least twenty pounds of cat. Good Lord, what are they feeding the barn cats here, entire cows? I set it on the floor with effort. "House rules. Well, temporary house rules that I'm making up as I go because apparently I live here now and make rules about cats."

The fridge is mostly empty. But there's a can of something in the back, behind a jar of pickles and what might be homemade jam. Tuna pâté, according to the label. The expiration date is still two months away.

"Fancy food it is." I peel open the can, nose wrinkling at the smell.

The cat winds between my legs, nearly tripping me as I search for a plate. I dump the pâté and set it down, watching the cat attack it with enthusiasm that suggests it hasn't eaten in days. Which, given its substantial girth, seems unlikely.

"Easy there, chunk. Leave some for—"

A different scratching interrupts me. This one is at the door, more aggressive, accompanied by what sounds like battle cries.

The cat doesn't even pause in its eating. Clearly, whatever is outside isn't its problem anymore.

I creep to the front door, acutely aware that I have no idea what's on the other side. The door is solid wood, no peephole, no side windows. I reach for the door, my trusting nature way too comfortable right now when there could be anything from a rabid raccoon to a bear on my porch.

The scratching intensifies, followed by a sound that's definitely not threatening, more like an indignant squeak.

I crack the door open an inch, ready to slam it shut if something with more teeth than I'm comfortable with appears.

Two balls of orange fluff stare up at me, kittens, maybe twelve weeks old, carbon copies of the cat that I assume is their mother, down to the white bibs. One takes the open door as an invitation and darts between my legs with the speed of a tiny rocket. The other locks eyes with me, and I swear I see its little face scrunch up in disgust before it hisses with all the ferocity its tiny body can muster, arches its back, and bolts into the bushes.

"Oh, no. No, no, no." I shove my feet into flip-flops abandoned by the door. "Come back! You're all alone. Do you have any idea what's out there?"

I step outside and immediately realize how very alone I am out here. The main house is dark, maybe two hundred yards away, but it might as well be a hundred miles. The barn structures loom like sleeping giants against the star-filled sky. And beyond that? Miles and miles of wilderness where things eat other things and nobody would hear me scream. Well, maybe the coyotes would hear, but they'd probably just consider it a dinner bell.

The thought makes my skin prick with goose bumps, but the cat...

"Here, kitty kitty," I whisper-call, following the direction it fled, which is down the path away from both houses. My flip-flops slap against the dusty ground with each step, completely inadequate for the terrain.

Every shadow could hide something with teeth. Every rustle of wind through grass sounds like approaching danger. The rational part of my brain that navigated Chicago's streets at night without issue is screaming at me to go back inside, lock the door, and let nature take its course. But I keep seeing that tiny orange face, and I can't.

"I'm going to die out here," I mutter under my breath. "They're going to find my body clutched around a kitten, and my obituary will read *City Girl Dies Trying to Save Cat, Surprising No One Who Knew Her.*"

A flash of orange disappears into a patch of wildflowers to my right. In the moonlight, they're silver, as though they've come right out of a fairy tale. The good kind, not the Brothers Grimm kind where everyone dies horribly. The flowers release a sweet honey scent as I push through them.

Then I spot the kitten, paused.

It watches me with eyes that glow green in the darkness. "You know if you come to me, you can live in the house," I call, stumbling into the darkness. "Big house, no forced snuggles unless you want them. Your mom's inside with food!"

A sound carries through the night—yipping calls answered by others at a distance. Coyotes, my brain supplies helpfully.

"Hear that?" I tell the kitten. "That's why indoor cats have longer life expectancies. And more toys. And those fancy water fountains. You could have a water fountain!"

It just stares at me like it might bolt.

I lunge. My hands close around warm fur and fragile bones.

"Gotcha!" I smirk. "And joke's on you. I lied about the 'no snuggles' thing. I give them in abundance."

The kitten immediately transforms into a spitting, clawing ball of fury, needle claws finding every gap in my defense and some I didn't know existed.

"Okay, okay, you're very fierce," I gasp, trying to contain the tiny tornado without actually hurting it. "But you're also literally two pounds, so maybe save the murder mittens for something your own size? Like a grasshopper?"

I tuck the kitten to my chest, using my shirt as a shield against its claws. Gradually, miraculously, it settles. A tiny motor starts up.

"See? This is much better than being a midnight snack for—"

A sound cuts through the night air from behind me.

Low, rumbling, emanating from the direction of the trees. Not quite a growl but something that makes every primitive instinct in my body scream *Danger!* The hair on my arms stands up, and my throat goes dry.

This is it. This is how they'll find me tomorrow, city girl turned cat lady, killed by local wildlife. My father will be mortified. *She died doing what?* I can hear him now. *Chasing cats? In flip-flops?*

I turn slowly, each degree of rotation feeling like an eternity. My eyes strain to make sense of shapes in the darkness. There, by a cluster of trees, is something large. Bulky. It's hunched oddly, as if leaning against a tree stump, and it's holding a small shape that I can't make out...

A bear, my brain supplies. Has to be a bear. Bears can use tools now, right? I saw a documentary once. Or was that about crows? Either way, this bear has clearly figured out tools and is about to use them on me.

"You should be careful offering snuggles so freely here."

A male voice rolls through the darkness. Deep, masculine, with an edge that makes my stomach do complicated things that have nothing to do with fear and everything to do with other four-letter words.

"Never know what might turn up on your doorstep."

My brain finally processes what I'm seeing. Not a bear. A man. Sitting on a huge tree stump, glass catching moonlight in his hand.

Ridge.

"Holy sh—" I catch myself, heart hammering against my ribs like it's trying to escape. "You scared me! I thought you were a bear!"

His laugh is low, rough, like he doesn't do it often and his throat needs practice. "If you see a bear drinking whiskey from crystal, we've got bigger problems than a midnight kitten rescue."

He stands in one fluid motion, sets his glass down on the

stump, and strolls toward me. I notice the slight favor to his right leg. "You okay?"

The moonlight finds him as he steps from the shadows, and my mouth dries. Black jeans fit him like they were tailored by someone who understood that cowboys are basically walking advertisements for Wrangler. His leather belt sports a buckle that, now that I can see it clearly, depicts a bronco rider frozen in silver, hat flying, one arm up for balance, the other gripping for dear life. It's intricately detailed, the kind of thing you win, not buy.

Blue button-up shirt open at the throat—three buttons, not that I'm counting—revealing a triangle of tanned skin and the hint of a chain disappearing beneath the fabric. The sleeves are rolled to his elbows, exposing strong, powerful forearms. No wonder romance-novel readers are obsessed with cowboys.

His auburn hair, earlier hidden under that black hat, falls loose to his shoulders. The breeze plays with it, sending strands across his face that he doesn't bother to push away. Without the hat shadowing his features, I see him more clearly, the sharp angle of his jaw with light stubble, the way his mouth naturally turns down at the corners, giving him a perpetual serious expression even when he's almost smiling.

"Barn cats get out sometimes," he states when he's close enough that the night breeze carries his scent to me. Cedar, cinnamon, and whiskey. "Orange mama and her babies. They're escape artists with a capital *E*. Been sneaking out for weeks now."

"Maybe they prefer actual houses?" I aim for light, teasing, trying to ignore how my body wants to sway toward him like he's magnetic north and I'm a very confused compass. "You know, with walls and heating and a distinct lack of things with sharp teeth and appetites?" I scratch the kitten's ears in my arm, and she just purrs back.

Ridge doesn't respond immediately, simply watches me with green eyes like mine but darker, like forest shadows. There's a weariness there, carefully hidden but visible if you know where to look. He's studying me too.

"Careful out here," he drawls finally. "Wild country. Wild animals."

"Is that why you're out here?" I adjust the kitten against my chest, needing something to do with my hands that isn't reaching out to touch him. "Playing security guard for wayward city girls and escaped cats?"

"I can't sleep sometimes." The words come out clipped, final, like a door closing on further questions. But there's something underneath, pain maybe, or memories that have teeth.

"So you drink whiskey on tree stumps in the middle of the night?"

"Better than staring at the ceiling, counting cracks in the plaster." He pauses. "Or watching shadows that aren't there."

There's definitely a story there. Several, probably. But I don't push. We all have our 3:00 a.m. demons.

A sound carries through the night, long, mournful, answered by another at a distance.

"Wolves?" I can't help the way my body tenses.

"Coyotes." He tilts his head, listening with the ease of someone who knows this land's language. "Wolves sound different. Deeper. More..." He searches for words. "Primal. Coyotes are gossipers, calling to each other about their night. Wolves mean business."

"Comforting." The kitten shifts against me, tiny claws pricking through fabric. "Really making me feel better about my midnight adventure."

He tips his head back, looking at the sky, and I follow his gaze. The sky here is nothing like Chicago's orange-tinted dome. Stars crowd together in impossible numbers, so bright and close that I understand why ancient peoples thought they could read destinies in them.

"Ever *really* looked at the stars?" he asks, voice different now, softer.

"From my home roof once. Mostly I saw airplanes and what might have been Venus. Or a satellite."

That almost smile quirks his mouth. "That pattern there..." He points with one hand, and I notice scars across his knuckles. "Seven stars that look like a ladle. That's the Big Dipper."

"Oh, I know the Big Dipper," I say, only slightly too excited.

"Did you know it's part of Ursa Major? The Great Bear?"

"I... no."

"The handle is the bear's tail. The cup is its flank." His voice takes on a different tone, like he's sharing secrets. "Ancient Greeks saw a bear where we see a kitchen utensil. Says something about perspective. What we see depends on what we're looking for."

"How do you know all this?" I'm genuinely curious now. This is not what I expected from a taciturn cowboy who seems to brood more than he speaks.

"Books. Long winter nights." He shifts slightly, that subtle favor to his right leg more noticeable. "Started reading about them after..." He stops, jaw tightening. "Just started reading. Got a telescope in my room now. One of those fancy computerized ones that find things for you. Cost more than my truck, but worth it."

"A cowboy with a telescope." I can't hide my surprise or the warmth it brings. "That's..."

"Not what you expected from a dumb ranch hand?" There's challenge in his voice now, defensive, like he's been judged before.

"Impressive," I finish firmly. "Really, really impressive.

And kind of romantic. Cowboy by day, astronomer by night."

He looks at me sharply, searching for mockery, but I mean it. There's something deeply attractive about hidden depths, about tough men who study stars between dawn cattle drives and have expensive telescopes in their bedrooms.

"That cluster there," he continues, apparently satisfied that I'm not mocking him, pointing to a different section of the sky. "Looks like a tiny ladle, or maybe a question mark. That's the Pleiades. Seven Sisters."

"I can only count six stars."

"Most people can. Need perfect conditions and exceptional eyesight to see the seventh. The lost sister, Merope, who hid her light in shame for falling in love with a mortal."

"There's a story?"

"Always is. Greek myth says they were seven daughters of Atlas, pursued by Orion until Zeus took pity on them and turned them into stars for their own protection."

"And Orion?"

He points to another section of the sky. "There. See the three stars in a perfect line? That's his belt. He's still chasing them across the sky, night after night. Doomed to always follow, never catch. Forever wanting what he can't have."

"That's heartbreaking."

"Most myths are. Gods were cruel in their mercy. Better to suffer for eternity than not suffer at all, apparently."

We stand in comfortable silence, him teaching me constellations while I cuddle a purring kitten and try not to notice how the moonlight catches in his hair, turning auburn to copper and flame. The night breeze picks up, carrying his scent stronger now, wrapping around me like invisible silk until I feel drunk on it.

"So," I say when the silence stretches too long, when my awareness of him becomes too acute, when the space between us feels both too vast and not nearly vast enough. "Belle mentioned that you three aren't really the settling-down kind."

His shoulders tense, the relaxed atmosphere evaporating like morning dew under sudden sun.

"Not that I'm interested," I add quickly, feeling heat flood my cheeks that has nothing to do with the cool night air. "God, I'm not. That came out wrong. I just meant... you have such a perfect setup here. Ranch, brotherhood, stability. Seems like the kind of place you'd want to put down roots. Maybe find someone to share it with. If you were into that. Which you're not. According to Belle. Who could be wrong. Is she wrong?"

Stop talking, Sophia. Stop talking right now.

He's quiet long enough that I wonder if I've stepped on some invisible land mine, triggered some cowboy code violation about asking personal questions under starlight.

"Walker wants to settle down. Eventually. Cash is still having fun dating and stuff. But when the right person comes along, they'll both know it." He pauses, jaw working like he's chewing on words that taste bitter. "Deep down, they both believe in that kind of thing. Forever. Mates. Family."

"But not you?"

He turns to look at me fully, and even in the moonlight, the intensity of his gaze has me catching my breath. There's something raw there, quickly shuttered but not fast enough. Pain, maybe a badly healed break.

"We don't need an Omega here." The words come out flat, decisive, like a judge passing a sentence. "Well, at least I don't."

The words land like ice water on overheated skin, dousing the warm feeling that had been building with each constellation, each shared moment of quiet understanding. Of course. I'm the interloper, the complication in their perfect bachelor paradise. The temporary inconvenience who'll be gone in three months.

"That makes two of us." I force my chin up, summoning every ounce of city-girl brass to cover the unexpected sting of rejection. Pride is the only thing keeping me steady when my body wants to sway toward him like he's gravity and I'm a poorly anchored satellite. "I don't want any Alphas. I'm not here for that. Three months to satisfy the will, then I'm gone, back to civilization where the only predators wear suits and the stars hide behind smog. You don't have to worry about me getting ideas."

Something flashes across his face. Regret? Relief? Pain? It's gone too quickly to identify.

The kitten chooses that moment to squirm with sudden determination, slipping from my grip like it's made of liquid rather than fur and tiny bones. Probably bored with all the human drama and wanting to get back to important kitten business.

It lands softly in the grass, immediately crouching for a spring toward the shadows where things with appetites lurk.

Ridge moves surprisingly fast. He scoops the kitten up before it can take two steps, large hands impossibly tender around the tiny body. The kitten, probably shocked by the sudden altitude change, goes limp like a little orange noodle.

"Here," he says, stepping closer to hand it back.

Our fingers brush in the transfer, and the contact sparks through me like touching a live wire. Every nerve ending lights up, sending urgent messages to parts of my body that really need to calm down. This close, I can see details, the darkness and distance hidden, the faint lines around his eyes that speak of squinting into too many suns, the way his pupils dilate as he breathes in, nostrils flaring slightly like he's scenting me.

He doesn't retreat.

I can't move, can't think beyond the warmth radiating from his body, the way his scent smothers me, and I'm left breathless. We're suspended in moonlight and possibility, the space between us charged with everything we're not saying, everything we're not supposed to feel.

His free hand lifts, moving with dreamlike slowness. A strand of my hair has escaped, hanging across my cheek like it has any business being anywhere but firmly behind my ear. He reaches for it, and I stop breathing entirely, every cell in my body focused on the approach of his fingers.

He tucks the strand behind my ear with incredible gentleness, fingertips barely grazing skin. The touch is lighter than butterfly wings, softer than whispers, but it burns through me like wildfire. The point of contact leaves a trail of heat that spreads outward until I'm burning from the inside out.

The world narrows to this moment—his fingers lingering near my ear, the kitten purring between us like a tiny furry chaperone, the sound of synchronized breathing in the vast Montana night. Time stretches like taffy, seconds becoming hours becoming lifetimes.

My thighs clench involuntarily, heat pooling low and insistent in places that have no business responding to an almost touch. Every Omega instinct I've spent years learning to control roars to life, desiring things I can't name, shouldn't want, definitely can't have with a man who just made his disinterest crystal clear.

His hand drops, but he's still too close, close enough that I notice his pulse jumping in his throat, quick and hard as if he's been running. His gaze lowers to my mouth, holds there with a purpose that makes my lips part without my permission, like they're offering an invitation I didn't authorize.

"You should go back," he says, but his voice has gone

rough, dropped an octave to a sound that vibrates through my bones like bass through speakers.

"Should I?" The question comes out breathier than intended, like I've been running too. Which I haven't. Unless you count running from good sense.

"Yes." The word is gravel and smoke and warning, but he still doesn't move, doesn't step back, doesn't do any of the sensible things that would break this spell.

"Why?" I'm playing with fire now and I know it, but I can't seem to stop.

"Because if you don't..." He doesn't finish, but the promise and threat in those unfinished words melt my knees, making me want to know exactly what happens if I don't.

"Ridge—"

"Go." This time it's almost a growl, Alpha command bleeding through his voice. Not quite an order but close enough that my Omega instincts whimper. "I'll watch. Make sure you get there safely."

I clutch the kitten tighter, using it as armor against the insanity building between us. The poor thing mews in protest at being squeezed. My legs feel unsteady as I turn away, each step an effort when every cell in my body screams to turn back, to find out what he's hiding.

The walk back to the guesthouse feels endless. I'm hyperaware of the inadequate slap of my flip-flops against the ground, the whisper of grass against my leggings, the way the kitten's purr synchronizes with my too-fast heart-beat. But mostly I'm aware of his eyes on me, the weight of his gaze across my body, making me want to put extra sway in my walk just to see if he'd react.

At the porch, I can't resist looking back. He's still standing where I left him, a shadow cut from darkness and moonlight and barely leashed want. He touches two fingers to his forehead in a gesture that might be mockery or promise or both, then fades back into the shadows like he was never there at all.

Inside, I set the kitten down with its family. The mother cat barely pauses in grooming the adventurous sibling to sniff at the returned prodigal. Crisis averted, maternal duties resumed, no thanks necessary.

I move to the window, pressing close to the glass, but the angle is wrong and blocks my view. Is he back on his stump with his whiskey? Walking the property like some kind of midnight guardian?

My body thrums with unused energy, skin too sensitive, every nerve ending alive and wanting. I press my forehead to the cool glass and try to make sense of what just happened.

Ridge doesn't want an Omega here. His words were clear, unambiguous, as final as a slamming door.

So why did he look at me like I was salvation and damnation wrapped in one impossible package?

Why did one barely there touch feel more intimate than any kiss I've ever shared?

And why, despite his rejection, despite my own plans to leave, despite every logical reason to keep my distance, do I suddenly need to know everything about him? What broke him? What makes him study stars like they hold answers? What would it take to see him smile, really smile, not just that bitter quirk of lips?

What made him so certain he doesn't need an Omega? Or is it just this Omega he doesn't need?

The kitten mews at my feet, probably wondering why its rescue has turned into standing at windows like a Gothic heroine waiting for her brooding hero to return.

"This is your fault," I tell it. "If you hadn't needed rescuing, I wouldn't have just had my world tilted off its axis by a cowboy who smells delicious and looks at stars."

The mother cat gives me a look that suggests she's not buying my deflection.

"Fine," I concede to my feline audience. "Maybe it's not entirely the kitten's fault. Maybe I was always going to end up in the darkness with Ridge."

I think about Orion and his eternal pursuit, about gods who were cruel in their mercy, about cowboys who study stars and push away with both hands what they might want.

Three months suddenly feels like both forever and no time at all.

The really terrifying part? I'm starting to think Ridge might be worth the heartbreak I can already see coming like storm clouds on the horizon.

But maybe, just maybe, some things are worth chasing across the sky.

Even if you never catch them.

7

RIDGE

I'm in the chute at Cheyenne Frontier Days, the metal rails cold under my gloved hands despite the July heat. Diesel Rage shifts beneath me, two thousand pounds of pure meanness compressed into black hide and muscle. The bull's breathing matches mine, heavy, controlled, waiting. We both know what's coming.

"Ridge Colter on Diesel Rage!" The announcer's voice booms over the packed arena. "This cowboy's sitting second in the world standings, folks, and a good ride here could move him up to first going into Vegas!"

My hands are steady as I work the bull rope, wrapping it around my right hand. Suicide wrap—that's what we call it when you wrap it tightly enough that only God or gravity can get it loose. The rosin makes the rope sticky against my glove, insurance against the violence about to come.

I can see Cash and Walker pressed against the arena fence from here, close enough that I can make out Cash's worried frown and Walker's encouraging nod. They've been at every major ride for the past three years, my unlikely pack brothers who understand that rodeo isn't just what I do; it's who I am.

Three rows behind them, Abby waves when she catches my

eye. Beta female, sweet as honey, with a laugh that made me stop mid-sentence when I first heard it at that bar in Sheridan. We'd been talking about books. One conversation led to another, which led to her driving four hours to watch me ride today.

"Looking good, Colter," Jake Chase calls out from the bucking chute over, waiting for his turn. "Heard you drew a spinner."

"Diesel always goes left," I confirm, settling deeper into position. "Hard and fast."

"Just how your girl likes it?" another rider jokes, and laughter ripples through the cowboys hanging on the rails.

"Shut your mouth, Thompson, before I shut it for you," I shoot back, but I'm grinning. This is how it is—crude jokes and bravado masking the very real possibility that any of us could leave here in an ambulance. Or worse.

The arena director leans over the chute. "You ready, Ridge?"

With my free hand, I pull my hat down, a black Stetson that's seen a hundred rides and never let me down. My other hand grips the rope so tightly my knuckles ache inside the glove. Diesel's muscles bunch beneath me, coiled energy waiting to explode.

"Ready," I call out, though ready is relative when you're about to try to stay on a tornado for eight seconds.

I nod sharply.

"Let's see if Ridge Colter can tame this storm!"

The gate swings open and the world explodes.

Diesel launches out of the chute like he's been shot from a cannon, immediately spinning hard to the left like I knew he would. My arm jerks up high, maintaining the perfect form the judges want to see, free hand never touching the bull, never touching myself, never touching anything but air.

The first jump jars every bone in my body, spine compressing and releasing like a violent accordion. The arena blurs past— faces, lights, signs, all of it smearing into a kaleidoscope of color and sound. The crowd roars in approval as Diesel really gets into it, bucking and spinning with a fury that makes him one of the best bulls on the circuit.

Time stretches and compresses simultaneously. Eight seconds feels like eight hours and eight milliseconds all at once. My thighs burn from gripping, shoulder screaming at the repeated jerking, but I'm centered, balanced, in that perfect sweet spot where bull and rider become one violent dance.

I catch glimpses as we spin. Cash on his feet now, fist pumping. Walker's hands cupped around his mouth, probably whooping, though I can't hear individual sounds over the crowd's thunder.

Five seconds. Maybe six. I'm counting in my head, feeling the rhythm of Diesel's bucks, anticipating each twist. I'm going to make it. I'm going to—

On the next spin, I see Abby. But she's not watching me anymore. She's turned to the man beside her... When did he sit down? She's laughing at something he's said. Her hand touches his arm, casual, friendly.

My concentration shatters.

For one crucial instant, my balance shifts. My free arm drops just a fraction, and my grip loosens just enough. Diesel feels it immediately because bulls always know the second you're vulnerable.

He changes direction mid-spin, a move I'm not ready for. My weight goes wrong, sliding sideways. I try to recover, muscles screaming as I fight to regain position, but physics has already chosen sides.

Fuck!

The world tilts.

My heart is thundering in my ears.

I have a perfect moment of clarity as I leave Diesel's back, seeing everything in crystalline detail. The bull's head whipping around, the arena dirt rushing up, the horror dawning on Cash's face. I'm airborne, hat flying one direction, body another, completely at gravity's mercy.

Then I hit.

Not the dirt like I'm supposed to. The side of my head

scratches against the top rail of the arena fence, a glancing blow that sends lightning through my skull. The crack is audible even over the crowd's sudden gasps. I slide down and hit the dirt hard, right shoulder taking the impact before I roll.

There's a moment of absolute silence in my head despite the chaos erupting around me. Then sound rushes back, distorted, wrong, like I'm underwater. Ringing fills my right ear, high and sharp and endless.

"Ridge! RIDGE!" Walker's voice, closer than it should be. When did he jump the fence?

I try to push up, but the world spins violently. Something warm runs down the side of my face. Blood. I can taste copper, smell iron mixing with arena dirt.

"Don't move!" Cash now, hands on my shoulders. "Medical's coming. Just don't move."

Through the haze, I hear the announcer: "...looks like Colter got hung up there, folks. Let's hope he's all right..."

Six point nine seconds. That's all I lasted. Not even close to eight. But that's not what terrifies me as I lie in the dirt with my Alpha pack and medical personnel rushing over.

It's the ringing that won't stop. The way sound warbles in and out of my right ear like a badly tuned radio. The certainty, bone-deep and immediate, that something fundamental just broke. Not just my body, but my whole life.

"Can you hear me?" The paramedic shines a light in my eyes.

"Yeah," I manage, though my own voice sounds strange, distant on one side.

"Don't try to sit up. We need to—"

Yet I'm already trying to see past him, to find Abby in the stands, but someone is holding my head down. However, I caught a quick enough glance at where she was standing now, hand over her mouth, that man's arm around her shoulders. Comforting her. Like he has the right.

"Who's that?" I say, my words slurring slightly.

Walker follows my earlier gaze. "Ridge, buddy, we need to focus on—"

"WHO?"

"Another rider," Cash answers quietly.

All I see is her hand on his arm, resting there like it belongs, and it guts me worse than the fall. She was here for me. And still, she found someone else to hold her. Like I'm already gone. Like I never mattered.

They get me on a backboard, then a stretcher. The crowd applauds, that polite acknowledgment that I'm moving, not dead or paralyzed. As they wheel me toward the ambulance, I catch sight of the replay on the arena's big screen.

There I am, perfect form until the instant I'm not. The fall plays in slow motion, my head grazing against the rail with a violence that makes me nauseous to watch.

Three years of dominating the circuit. Three years of almost reaching the top, unstoppable. All of it ending in six point nine seconds because I let a Beta's disinterest in me break my concentration.

"You're going to be okay," Walker says, jogging beside the stretcher. "You hear me? You're going to be fine."

But the ringing in my ear says different. The way medical is moving, fast but careful, says different. The look in Cash's eyes says different.

I'm a rodeo cowboy. Was. We know injuries, live with them, collect them like badges of honor. And this is the one that ends me.

Three years later, and I still wake up tasting arena dirt and lost dreams.

I shoot right out of bed, sheets soaked with sweat, phantom pain screaming through my skull. My ear rings with the memory of it. Sharp, high, endless. The pain radiates from my temple down my neck, across my back, following pathways that exist only in my dreams.

"Fuck." The word comes out rough, angry. Three years, and the damn dream won't leave me alone. Of waking up tasting failure.

I grunt. My room is exactly how I need it, with white walls, bare of decoration, spacious enough for the king bed, walk-in closet, and the leather couch where I sometimes sit when staring at the sky doesn't cut it. My guitar waits on its stand in the corner, a Martin D-28 that's seen me through too many sleepless nights.

The dream clings like cobwebs. Abby's laugh. Her hand on the rider. That split second of distraction that cost me everything.

Anger floods through me, hot and familiar. Not at her, as I got over blaming her years ago. The fury is all for myself. If I'd been good enough, strong enough, focused enough, I would never have fallen. Would never have let something as simple as a woman's attention shatter my concentration.

I shake off sensations that aren't real anymore and stumble into the adjoining bathroom. The shower runs hot, almost scalding, but it helps wash away the phantom aches. By the time I'm out, I can almost pretend I'm whole again.

I pull on blue jeans, worn soft from years of ranch work. My belt slides through the loops, the buckle catching the early morning light. It's a bronze piece depicting a rider on a cutting horse, working cattle. Cash bought it for me two Christmases ago, said I needed something that showed who I was now, not who I used to be.

A gray button-up comes next, pearl snaps instead of buttons because some habits die hard. I run my hand through wet hair that's getting too long again, auburn strands falling past my collar. My stomach growls, reminding me I skipped dinner last night in favor of whiskey and stars.

The sun is just cresting the horizon as I head out, painting the Montana sky in shades of pink and gold. Walker is already out there somewhere, probably in the round pen with that new colt that's been giving everyone hell. Cash will surface eventually, the lazy bastard.

We've been a pack for eight years now, bonded by choice. After my family couldn't handle having a damaged Alpha in their ranks, couldn't stomach that my scent glands got fucked in the fall along with my hearing, these two became everything. Walker and Cash.

They pulled me through those first months when I couldn't see past the wreckage of my career. When I'd stare at the prescription bottles and wonder if it wouldn't be easier to just... not. They gave me purpose again, showed me I could be more than Ridge Colter, fallen rodeo star.

This ranch became our salvation. Just over four years, we've poured everything into it, every sunrise, every blister, every sleepless night when the horses were sick or the fences were down. It's in my bones now, this land. These mountains. This life we've built from nothing.

Which is why Sophia scares the shit out of me.

She could destroy it all with a signature. Sell to some developer who'd turn our home into vacation condos for rich assholes who think Montana is quaint. The thought makes my jaw clench hard enough to ache.

Last night replays through my mind—her in the moonlight, clutching that kitten, looking at me like I was someone worth knowing. She almost made me forget why I don't need complications shaped like beautiful Omegas with curious eyes.

Christ, she's gorgeous. I'm damaged, not dead, and my cock certainly isn't broken. The way those leggings hugged her curves, how her eyes caught the starlight, those lips that made me think about all the filthy things I wanted them to do...

No. Focus on the job. The ranch. The life we've built. Last time I let my mind wander to what I wanted instead of what I needed, I lost everything that mattered. Besides, she's... addictive. Beautiful in a way that gets under your skin if you let it. *But she's just another Omega to me. A pretty face. That's all*, I remind myself.

The dining hall sits between the main house and the bunkhouses, a long building that's the real heart of the operation.

As I walk the gravel path, something feels... off. Or maybe right. My hip isn't aching. The usual pull in my leg is just... gone today. I must have slept better than I thought, even with that damn dream.

Then the smell finds me of bacon, eggs, biscuits, and Cookie's famous gravy that could make a grown man weep. I follow it toward the door, trying not to read into anything.

Laughter finds me as soon as I enter, more than usual for this early hour. I stop in the doorway, taking in the scene.

The dining hall is simple with long wooden tables scarred from years of use, benches on either side, a buffet-style serving area where Cookie sets up. The old Army cook runs this kitchen like his personal kingdom, feeding fifteen-plus ranch hands, including us, three meals a day without complaint.

But this morning is different. There's energy in the air, sparked by a certain redhead holding attention at the center table.

Sophia has half the ranch hands hanging on her every word, gesturing with a fork as she tells some story. "...and then the system completely crashed! Three million people watching my client teaching yoga when the screen freezes mid-downward dog—right as Bob the goat strolls into frame with her sports bra dangling from his mouth like it's lunch."

The men roar with laughter. Even Cookie is grinning as he flips pancakes, and that man hasn't smiled since... ever.

"So what'd you do?" asks Dennis, one of our younger hands.

"Only thing I could do. I turned it into content!" Sophia grins. "Posted about *Technical Difficulties and Goat Overlords*. Got more engagement than the original video would have."

She fits here like she was born into it.

Cash appears at my elbow, nudging me. "Look who's making friends."

"She's certainly... adaptable." I head for the serving line, trying not to notice how her laugh scrapes something raw in my chest, reckless and too damn bright.

"Adaptable," Cash repeats, loading his plate with enough food for three men. "That your explanation? From my point of view, she's got half the ranch wrapped around her little finger, and she hasn't even been here forty-eight hours."

"She owns the place," I remind him, adding bacon to my pile. "Makes sense to play nice."

"Uh-huh." Cash grabs the syrup. "That's why you were having a private conversation with her at three in the morning?"

I shoot him a look. "You were watching?"

"A new Omega shows up smelling like heaven? Of course I'm watching." He lowers his voice further. "Saw you two in the moonlight. Very romantic."

"It wasn't—" I stop myself. No point in arguing with Cash when he's in this mood. "We agreed to keep our distance, remember? Too much riding on this."

"Right," Cash drawls, clearly not buying it. "Because you looked real distant when you were tucking her hair behind her ear."

"How the fuck could you see that detail from the house?"

"I've got skills." He grins. "Also binoculars."

"You're a sick bastard."

"And you're so wound up I could play you like a fiddle." He nods toward Sophia. "When was the last time you reacted to an Omega like this?"

"Never." The answer is immediate and unwanted. I've been with women since the accident. But none of them made me feel like I was burning from the inside out. Except, the reality is that we can't ever have a true bond, a scent match, not what an Omega and an Alpha should, what she deserves.

"Doesn't matter," I say finally. "Three months and she's gone."

"That what you're telling yourself?" Cash loads his plate higher. "Because from where I'm standing—"

"With your binoculars like some creep?"

"—she doesn't look like someone who's planning to leave."

I follow his gaze. Sophia is still chatting with the ranch hands, but there's something in how she leans in, how she listens, how she engages. Like she's putting down roots already, even if she doesn't know it.

"Incoming," Cash mutters.

Walker pushes through the door, all six feet, three inches of him commanding instant attention. The chatter dims slightly. Walker has that effect. Not through meanness but through sheer presence. The man radiates an underlying strength that makes even hardened cowboys step carefully.

But today he's in a good mood. I can tell by the set of his shoulders, the almost smile playing at his mouth. He heads straight for Sophia's table.

"Oh, this should be good," Cash murmurs.

Walker settles next to Sophia like it's the most natural thing in the world. She beams up at him.

"Morning, sunshine," Walker says in that deep rumble of his. "Sleep well on your first night at the ranch?"

"Like a baby," she says.

"You finished eating? Want to show you something."

I tilt my head to the side, watching how damn easily he talks to her, how she looks at him like the sun cracked through the clouds just for him.

It shouldn't bother me. Not the way she laughs, not the way she leans in. We're a pack and we share everything. That's how it works.

But it does bother me.

Because it feels like hell just to look her in the eye, let alone talk like nothing is broken. And deep down, some dark, festering part of me wonders... if the others want her, and she doesn't want me—the busted one—what the hell happens then?

Do I just sit on the sidelines? Watch them build something I'm not welcome in? Be the one left behind while they find a future without me?

"Show me something?" Sophia's eyebrows rise. "You've got me intrigued."

"There's a spot near your guesthouse. Think you'd like it." Walker's voice stays casual, but I know him too well. He's fucking interested.

"Oh, he'll show you his special spot all right," Tom drawls from the table, earning a few muffled chuckles.

"Just don't follow him too deep into the woods," another hand mutters. "Ain't no one ever come back the same."

Sophia lifts her coffee with a sly grin. "I figured he was just being polite."

Cookie barks a chuckle from behind the griddle. "If that boy's being polite, I'm a damn ballerina."

"I'm just showing her around and being helpful," Walker states, palms up like he's the picture of innocence, but the corner of his mouth twitches.

"Helpful is what you do with a fence that's fallin' down. You? You're one sweet talk away from handing her the deed to your truck and a key to the bunkhouse."

The room cracks up, boots tapping and forks clinking on plates.

Sophia just raises an eyebrow like she's not buying any of it. "Should I be worried?"

Walker smirks. "Only if you're scared of good manners."

"That's bait," Cookie mutters.

And Sophia laughs, big and unbothered, right in step with the rest of us. Like she's been here all along.

"You ready?" Walker asks when the noise dies down.

"Lead the way, cowboy." Sophia stands, clearing her plate. "But if this *special place* turns out to be a muddy pond or a pile of rocks, I'm going to be very disappointed."

"Have a little faith."

They head out together, Sophia barely reaching Walker's shoulder but matching him stride for stride. Everyone in the dining hall watches them go.

"You keep staring like that," Cash observes, "and people might think you're obsessed with our new Omega."

"Fuck you," I tease, stabbing at my eggs while still standing by the buffet.

"Just saying. Your eyes didn't leave her until she walked out."

I have to agree, damn him. I force myself to focus on my plate, but my mind is already wandering.

I risk one last glance toward the door they disappeared through. Three months and she'll sell the ranch and go back to Chicago, where she belongs.

Except Cash is right about one thing: She doesn't look like someone who's planning to leave.

And that terrifies me more than any bull ever could.

8

Walker leads me out of the dining hall, his boots beating a steady rhythm against the packed-dirt path, the sun rising, already promising a hot day. I have to do a little skip-step occasionally to keep up with his longer stride, but I don't mind. The morning air is fresh, carrying scents of hay and horses. There's something calming about being on a ranch.

"So," I start, then stop, suddenly feeling awkward. How do you ask virtual strangers about borrowing their stuff? "I was wondering... is there maybe a vehicle I could use sometime? To get back to Chicago for clothes and things?" I gesture at my limited outfit of jeans and a shirt that I'm wearing today. "I only packed clothes for a few days."

Walker glances down at me, and a piece of dark hair falls over his eye. He's wearing a faded denim shirt today, sleeves rolled to reveal forearms I can't stop staring at. His muscles bulge against the fabric. His jeans are worn, and those boots... why are cowboy boots so attractive?

"Got a spare truck you can use anytime," he says easily, like lending vehicles to almost strangers is perfectly normal. "Old Ford, nothing fancy but she runs well. Keys are on the hook by the kitchen door. Just let me know when you want to head out, and I'll show you her quirks."

"Really? Just like that?"

"We've got more vehicles than sense around here," he says with a slight smile that speeds my pulse. "Happy to have someone actually use her. She gets cranky sitting too long."

"The truck gets cranky?"

"Definitely. Stubborn in second gear, likes to stall if you don't sweet-talk her." He says it completely seriously, but there's warmth in those brown eyes that suggests he's teasing.

I smile. "Thanks for letting me borrow her, but I should warn you, I can't drive stick."

"Well then," he drawls. "I might have to teach you."

The grin of mine widens at the thought and no judgment.

"Anyway, how'd it go with the rental company? They giving you grief about the car?"

I groan. "They're being a nightmare. Apparently, *attacked by bull* isn't covered under standard insurance. Who knew? But I managed to work out a payment plan for the deductible, six months instead of all up front. Small miracles."

"That's good. Brutus has damaged more vehicles than I can count. We keep offering to pen him up better, but old Mr. Crawford insists he's a free-range bull in his yard, yet he keeps escaping." Walker shakes his head. "Free-range pain in the ass is more like it."

"Walker Stone!" a woman's voice calls out.

We both turn to see a woman practically bouncing toward us. She's about my height but seems taller because of her energy alone, curly brown hair escaping from what might have been a bun at some point. Her sundress is covered in sunflowers and looks genuinely vintage, not the fake kind from boutiques. Freckles dust her nose and cheeks, and her hazel eyes spark. She is beautiful and maybe younger than me by a couple of years.

"Morning, June," Walker answers, and there's definite fondness mixed with resignation in his tone. They know each other. "You're out early."

"Early? It's practically noon!" She smirks at her joke, then stops in front of us, slightly out of breath but still vibrating with enthusiasm. "Well, okay, it's nine thirty, but that's basically midday for ranch folk, right?" She glances at me with a small smile.

"June, this is Sophia Hollis," Walker says, gesturing to me. "She's inheriting Rose's place. Sophia, June Calloway. Local real estate agent and—"

"Information specialist," June interrupts, sticking out her hand to me with a grin that could power a small city. "Oh my gosh, you're exactly who I came to see!"

"Oh?" I shake her hand, already charmed by her enthusiasm.

"Yes! Okay, so Mrs. Henderson was at the café and told me she heard that someone new was at the ranch and might be the heir Rose mentioned and—" She pauses for breath. "Is it true? Are you really going to sell?"

"June," Walker says, a warning in his tone.

"What? I'm being professional! This is my professional face." She schools her features into what I assume is meant to be serious but mostly looks like she's trying not to sneeze. "See? Very professional."

I can't help but laugh. "Most likely, yes. The will says I have to live here for three months before I can make any decisions."

"That's perfect! Anyway, as Walker hinted, I run Sweetwater Creek Realty. Well, technically, it's my parents' agency, but Dad discovered bass fishing three years ago and hasn't come back to reality since, and Mom decided she'd rather grow prize-winning tomatoes than deal with people. So it's basically mine now, which is great because I have all these ideas about sustainable development and preserving the town's character while still allowing for growth and—"

"June, will this take much longer?" Walker interrupts gently.

"Right. Rambling." June presses a hand to her chest like she's reeling herself in. "What I meant to say is, when you're ready to talk options, I'm here. No pressure. But also... you should totally come to town today. Meet some locals. Maggie's Diner has chicken and dumplings on special, plus tonight is meatloaf night, and I swear they sell out of both faster than secrets at church."

"That does sound really good," I admit. My stomach growls, traitorously, even after Cookie's breakfast.

Walker shifts beside me, arms loosely folded. "Guess that means we're skipping lunch."

June perks up. "Perfect! I'm heading over around five. You could ride with me, Sophia. Give us girls a chance to gossip without your long shadow looming."

I open my mouth to answer, but Walker cuts in, easy as ever. "Or Sophia and I could both meet you there. I was already planning to head into town."

I blink. Was he? Since when?

June's smile stretches. "Oh, how convenient. But surely you've got something ranch-y to do, Walker. Fix a fence? Mourn a tractor? Stare meaningfully at the horizon?"

"I could pencil that in for tomorrow," he says with a smirk, not taking his eyes off me. "Unless you've got other plans?"

His voice is low, but it hits something sharp and sweet in my chest. Damn him.

"I mean, I'd love to," I say, lifting my chin. "But I can handle myself. No need to chaperone."

"Didn't say you needed one," he murmurs. "Just offering the ride."

June fans herself dramatically with her clipboard. "Mercy. I should've brought popcorn." She turns to me, voice dropping like she's sharing a secret. "Or you can come with me and ditch this one. I'm going to a book club after dinner. We're reading that one with the demon prince who bites ankles and redeems himself with smut."

That earns a quiet laugh from Walker. "Is that what counts as literature these days?"

June winks. "Don't knock it 'til you've read chapter eight."

I bite back a grin. "Honestly? That sounds like the perfect girls' night." I shift my weight, caught somewhere between flattered and flustered. "Thanks for the offer, Cowboy Uber," I say to Walker, trying for light. "But... I might actually do the girls' night thing tonight."

"I can handle it," Walker says, tossing the words out casually, but then he presses a palm to his chest like I've wounded him. "Picked over an ankle-biting demon. That stings."

June snorts. "You'll live, cowboy."

He casts me a look, all mock betrayal and slow smirk. "Barely."

"Oh, I'm sure you will," June cuts in with a wink. "But don't worry. I'll return her in one piece."

Walker tilts his head, gaze flicking to me. "You sure?"

There it is, that undercurrent again. Not pushy. Just... something steady and unspoken. And it does ridiculous things to my pulse.

"I'm sure," I say, then immediately feel the need to backpedal. "I mean, you can take me to dinner another night."

June gasps so dramatically that you'd think I'd just proposed marriage. "Wait. Was that a date offer? Did I just witness an actual date invitation from the elusive Miss Big City to one of our very own ranch cowboys?"

My eyes go wide. "What? No! I meant like... you know, showing me around town, checking out the sights... not a date."

Walker raises a brow, clearly enjoying this way too much.

June fans herself with mock flair. "Oh, girl, it's about damn time someone realized what a catch he is. He can cook, fix engines, ride like a dream, and once I caught him bottle-feeding a litter of abandoned piglets while humming a lullaby. A lullaby, Sophia."

Walker groans. "You promised you'd never bring that up."

"And you promised you wouldn't ghost me at karaoke night, but here we are."

"I had the flu, and you won with Cash stepping in for me!"

"I'll give you that." June winks. "Sure did. And for the record, I fully endorse that dinner idea. I mean, if you don't snatch him up, someone else will."

"I didn't mean it like that," I say, heat blooming in my cheeks. "I meant dinner in a... town orientation sense. Oh God, I'm making it worse."

June links her arm through mine like she's won a trophy. "Too late, sweetheart. You flirted. It's canon now."

I shoot a helpless glance at Walker, who's clearly trying not to smirk. Traitor.

But my brain short-circuits somewhere between "dinner idea" and "snatch him up." And the karaoke thing. And the piglets. And—wait. I untangle myself from June.

"Were you two... like, together or...?" The words tumble out before I can stop them, mortifying and loud.

Walker chokes on a laugh.

June blinks at me, then throws her head back with a

cackle. "Oh, hell no. Don't get me wrong, he's easy on the eyes, but Walker's like a brother to me. Always has been. I've known him since the three of them moved into Rose's place."

She nudges me with a sly grin. "And trust me, I've got no room for men in my life right now. Things are... a little complicated."

The look she gives me is dry, a touch wry, and it's clear there's a story behind it.

June leans in conspiratorially. "Anyway, I'd better go hunt down the rest of your trouble trio."

"They should still be in the dining hall," Walker states.

She sighs. "Perfect. Wish me luck. If Ridge is in a mood, I'm bribing him with pie."

June starts to leave, then spins back with a grin. "Oh, Sophia? Just a heads-up, I've heard the book club can get a little... enthusiastic. It's my first night joining, but I've almost finished the book for discussion. I'll give you the full report over dinner. I've heard about Loretta, who runs the events, though. She once read a steamy scene out loud with full sound effects. Be prepared."

She's gone before I can fully process that image, practically bouncing away with the same whirlwind energy she arrived with.

"Is she always like that?" I ask, watching her disappear around the corner toward the barn.

Walker chuckles. "Pretty much. I've only known her a little over four years, but she came in hot and never slowed down. One of the most genuine people I've met. Always has a dozen ideas and twice as many opinions." He pauses for a beat. "But... things with her family are a little rough. Not many people know. And I won't speak for her."

I nod. "Of course. If she ever wants to talk, I'll be around. But I'm not one to pry."

Even if I'm absolutely dying to know.

"Come on," Walker says, tipping his head toward the barn. "Got that something to show you if you're still interested?"

"You bet!"

We walk in comfortable silence for a few minutes, leaving the main cluster of buildings behind. The path winds through a grove of cottonwoods, their leaves whispering in the morning breeze. Walker guides me with the lightest touch on my lower back when the trail narrows, barely there, but somehow I feel it everywhere. Heat flares from that single point of contact, blooming outward like a spark in dry grass.

Then there's his scent.

Masculine. Warm. Delicious. Honey and freshly baked bread. And it hits me harder than it should. Like it's wrapping around my ribs and tugging me closer, threading into my veins and anchoring itself in my chest. I suck in a breath, like that might help, but it only makes it worse. Stronger. More real.

Why is it doing that?

This isn't normal.

I've never reacted to anyone like this. Not even Nolan. Not once did his scent make my knees weak or my thoughts skip like a broken record. I didn't crave his nearness or feel like something essential in me tilted toward him without permission.

But now it's like my body is attuned to Walker in ways I don't understand. Like there's a string connecting us, pulled taut.

Please don't let this be a scent match. Please not that. Surely not.

I would've known, right? There would've been signs. Something. Anything. And yet—

"Close your eyes," Walker says suddenly, his voice low

and rough, pulling me out of my spiraling thoughts before they can fully swallow me.

"Excuse me?" I blink at him, but he just gives me a look, the annoyingly confident one with the soft eyes and the tilted smirk that has me forgetting how to put together a sentence.

"Trust me," he says, quieter now. Rougher. And somehow that makes it worse. "Promise it's worth it."

Those brown eyes are warm and sincere, maybe even a little shy, and against every last shred of logic I own, I close my eyes.

I feel his hand slide into mine, calloused, hot, steady. I try not to react, but my skin betrays me, goose bumps racing up my arms.

"Careful now," he murmurs. "There's a root... that's it. Few more steps."

Without sight, every other sense sharpens. I pick up on the birdsong above, the rustle of our shoes in the grass, the way sunlight brushes my cheeks. But mostly, I'm aware of him. The way his scent wraps around me, pulling something loose and vulnerable inside me. Every inch of me is eager, ready to curl up at his feet like a damn stray.

I shouldn't feel like this. Not over a man I barely know. Especially not one who probably thinks I asked him on a date earlier like a blushing idiot. I mean, maybe I did kind of imply that... but not on purpose. And now I'm walking through a forest while holding his hand like some sort of woodland courtship ritual, and I'm spiraling.

"Almost there," he says. "Okay. Open your eyes."

I do, and my breath stutters to a halt.

We're standing at the edge of what can only be described as animal paradise. The enclosure stretches wide and deep, two acres at least. The fencing is tall and curved inward at the top like a serious fortress, and I can see where it burrows into the ground. Heavy-duty netting creates a canopy overhead.

But what's inside makes my heart squeeze.

It's not just a shelter; it's magic.

Cat trees built like real ones stretch toward the netting above. Houses dot the space like a miniature village, some bright and painted with cheerful murals, others like rustic cabins or tiny castles. Bridges and tunnels connect them all, like a skyway system for the four-legged. Water trickles from a central fountain, shaded hammocks sway between posts, and one corner even has a fake beach, complete with warm lamps and a sandpit.

And there are cats everywhere. I might have squealed.

"Walker," I breathe. "This is... I don't have words."

He rubs the back of his neck, suddenly a little bashful. "Took me and the boys a year to build. I just wanted a place where they could be safe. Run. Climb. Do what they need to do without worryin' about traps or coyotes or—"

He breaks off, jaw flexing. I glance at him, and my chest aches at how much this clearly means to him.

"It's incredible," I say softly. "They're lucky. You made them a whole kingdom."

He shrugs, but his ears turn a little pink. "Just figured if we were takin' them in, we should do it right. When we first moved into town, there was a huge feral cat problem, so I fixed it."

I stare at him then, really look, and he's watching me. Not the enclosure. Me.

My stomach dips. There's something in his gaze that hits deeper than it should. Heat prickles up my neck, across my cheeks, and curls low in my belly, warm and unsettling. He's watching me like he sees something no one else has, and I can't seem to look away.

Then he says, "It's my animal sanctuary." And just like that, everything in him shifts.

His whole face lights up, easy and unguarded, like I've been handed a glimpse of the man beneath the hat and the slow drawl. Not just the cowboy. Not the mystery. But the kind of man who builds something like this with his own hands. Who cares so deeply it shows in every detail.

"We take in the ones nobody else wants, kill-shelter overflows, abandoned pets, ferals that need care. Animals with nowhere else to go. We have more farther ahead for dogs and other animals, and I have a team who helps with them—feeding, medical care, watching and engaging with them."

And somehow, I can't breathe right. Because I didn't expect this. Him. And it comes at me with sharp clarity that he's not just handsome or broody or unfairly charming; he's good. The kind of good that sinks under your skin before you can stop it.

"How big is this sanctuary?" I ask, hoping my voice doesn't betray how shaken I feel.

"Pretty large and I'm in the process of expanding it." He nods toward the far fence. "Got a barn for the bigger animals too—couple horses that were bound for slaughter, a donkey named Fernando who thinks he's a lapdog, some goats that just wandered in and never left."

A laugh escapes me, too real to hold back. "You run an animal commune."

"Something like that," he states with a grin. "They're misfits. But they've got a home here."

His gaze catches mine again, and something shifts between us. Less playful now. Quieter. Steady.

And it scares the hell out of me how much I don't want to leave this moment.

"I can't believe you built all this." I turn in a slow circle, trying to take it all in.

"Well, Ridge designed most of it. Man's got an engineer's brain hiding under all that brooding. Cash handled the legal side, permits and regulations and all that paper-work that makes my eyes cross." He rubs the back of his neck, and something about the motion, broad shoulders shifting, his head ducking slightly, makes my breath catch.

"Gathering the animals and the team to help me was mostly me. Needed something to focus on after—"

He stops. Silence stretches for a beat, but his expression doesn't go blank like those of most people when they shut down. No, this is something else. He's letting me see it. The weight.

"What happened?" I ask.

"I grew up in Oklahoma," he says, gaze tracking something in the distance. "Out there, tornadoes are just part of life. You learn the signs, the sky going that strange green, the way the air goes still, too quiet. We had drills in school, a shelter dug behind the barn, even a go-bag by the back door."

He pauses, jaw working like he's chewing over something too bitter to swallow. I can't help but reach out and rub his arm.

"I used to think we were ready. That we'd be fine, no matter what hit." His voice dips. "But one night..."

A breath hitches in his chest, so faint I almost miss it.

"It hit us hard. Real hard." He avoids my gaze. "The house didn't stand a chance. Neither did the barn. Animals were gone in an instant."

Another beat of silence. Then, quieter, he says, "So were my folks."

The words land heavily between us. Not dramatic. Just true. Raw. My chest squeezes, my throat tight.

He exhales slowly, like letting it out is both relief and punishment. "We had this old mutt, Misty. Slept at the foot of my bed since I was five. She didn't make it either. But even now... sometimes I swear I hear her claws on the floor. Like she's still checking in on me."

My throat chokes up. I squeeze his forearm gently, unsure if it's for him or me. His muscle tenses under my fingers, but he doesn't pull away. Doesn't flinch.

"Sorry," he says, clearing his throat roughly. Then he runs a hand through his hair, a little tousled from the wind. It's a distracted motion, like he doesn't even notice how much space he takes up or the way the morning sun catches on the dust clinging to his shirt. "Didn't mean to unload."

"You didn't." My voice is soft. "I'm glad you told me. And I'm so sorry for your loss."

Walker glances down at me, something unreadable in his expression, but it's not cold. It's not guarded. It's something deeper, heavier, and... searching. Like he's trying to figure out what it means that I'm standing here, looking at him like this, listening.

The air shifts. I feel it before I understand it. That thick, magnetic stillness that coils between us. Our bodies haven't moved, but everything inside me is suddenly too much—heart pounding, breath hitching, blood roaring in my ears like a summer storm.

His gaze drops to my mouth.

And stays there.

My lips part, instinctively. I don't even realize I'm leaning in until I feel the heat of him brush against my skin, until I swear the earth tilts beneath my shoes. Time slows. My heartbeat pulses somewhere low and deep, like every cell in my body is reaching for his.

He leans down, just a little, close enough that I feel the ghost of his breath against my cheek. His scent swims around me, sinking under my skin, and I swear I want to drown in it.

Just a few more inches...

A shrill yowl pierces the air.

We both jerk back as if awakened.

Walker barks out a laugh, wrecking me in a different

way. I laugh as well, a little too loud, a little too breathless, trying to smother the way my whole body feels like it's been short-circuited.

"Guess they're not fans of public displays," he says.

"I—uh—I should…" I swipe my hands down my jeans, needing something to do with them. "Wow, okay. That happened. And it didn't. But almost. And… yeah."

"Yeah," he echoes, but there's a smile tugging at his lips that says he's not nearly as flustered.

I take a careful step back, trying not to combust. What am I doing?

This was not the plan. No matter how warm his eyes are. No matter how safe I feel near him.

Get a grip, girl. Control. You're here for the ranch. Not the cowboy.

Still, as he swings open the gate and ushers me in, my pulse hasn't settled. And I'm starting to wonder if it ever will again.

He approaches the entrance, a double-gated system with metal fencing and a keypad, and punches in a code. "Security system," he explains. "Had some incidents with people dumping animals after hours. This way we know who comes and goes."

We step through the first gate and wait for it to shut behind us before moving through the second. And then—

They descend.

A group of cats explodes out of the enclosure. They emerge from cat houses, drop from high walkways, appear like living shadows from under benches and platforms.

"Oh my God." I laugh, dropping to my knees as cats swarm me with headbutts and purrs. "How many are there?"

Walker smiles. "About thirty-two. Unless someone gave birth overnight. Which is possible. And we have fifteen dogs too."

"The cats are so friendly."

"We work on socialization every day. Local school brings kids out twice a week. Gives the animals attention and teaches the kids responsibility. Plus, we have volunteers who just come to cuddle cats. Turns out it's therapeutic for everyone involved."

A gray kitten with impossibly blue eyes climbs into my lap, purring loudly enough to rival a motorcycle. I look around, taking in more details. Each of the houses has a name painted on it in different handwriting, clearly a community effort.

"Fluffy's Palace?" I read. "Chairman Meow's Estate? The Purrfect Hideaway?"

Walker actually blushes slightly. "The kids from the local school get creative with naming. And once something's named, can't really change it. Chairman Meow would be offended."

"Obviously. Can't offend the chairman." I'm charmed beyond words by this gentle giant who builds cat palaces and worries about feline feelings. "Oh! Speaking of names, I've been calling the orange escape artist who broke into my house Chonkarella. She and her two kittens have claimed my guesthouse."

Walker's smile is immediate and delighted. "She got in? That sounds like her. She's one of our part-timers, prefers the barn life but visits houses when she feels like it. Rose used to leave windows open specifically for her visits."

"Said she had visiting rights," I tease.

He nods, grinning. "Want to see inside the main shelter?"

"You bet."

Walker offers his hand as I stand—not that I need help, but I don't exactly mind the excuse to touch him again. His fingers curl around mine, warm and sure, and his other hand briefly steadies me at the waist. It's a blink of contact, but my body registers it like a live wire.

We make our way through the cat village. Inside, the main building is surprisingly modern. Rows of sleek cubbies line the walls, each one a tiny sanctuary with a plush bed, toys, and a nameplate.

"This is their home base," Walker explains. "Heated floors for the cold months. Medical and intake rooms through there. Those back sections are for the older ones if they seek quiet time."

I glance at him out of the corner of my eye, and my stomach does a slow flip. He almost kissed me earlier. Or I almost kissed him. *God.* What would've happened if that cat hadn't interrupted?

He points to a sleek, high-tech-looking machine in the corner. "Timed feeders. Some of the shy ones eat better when it's quiet. They all get late-night snacks."

"This is incredible," I say, and mean it. "Most shelters are barely surviving. This feels like... luxury."

"Every animal deserves more than just surviving," he says simply. "Doesn't matter if they're missing an eye, or bite when they're scared. They still need love."

I blink hard, trying to hide how much that affects me. I'm not even sure we're talking about cats anymore.

"Seriously, Walker. This place, it's amazing. You built all this for animals no one else wanted."

He shrugs, rubbing the back of his neck, and I catch myself staring again. Not just at the breadth of his shoulders or the way his shirt pulls across his chest—though, yes, that too—but at the man himself. Quiet. Kind. Devastating.

Butterflies riot in my stomach.

"I could help," I blurt, desperate to redirect my thoughts. "With the website. Marketing. Social media campaigns. That's my world."

He turns to me, surprised. "You'd do that?"

"I want to," I say, more breathless than I intended. "This place deserves attention. You do."

His gaze lingers on me a second too long. "You're kind of a force, you know that?"

Not usually, I want to say. *Not before here. Not before you.* But I just smile, trying to ignore the way my knees feel like they're moments from buckling.

We start walking back toward the guesthouse, a companionable silence between us, until my foot catches on a slick patch of mud and my balance vanishes.

I yelp, slipping straight onto my ass with a wet splat.

"Oh my God," I groan, sitting in the mess, utterly mortified. "Of course. Of course this would happen."

Walker's laughter rumbles low before he's suddenly crouched beside me, strong arms sweeping me up as if I weigh nothing. "Gotcha."

"I'm fine! I can walk," I protest, squirming in his arms.

"Mm." He gives me a long, amused look. "Not sure you're exactly trustworthy on two feet right now."

He starts walking again, carrying me like it's nothing, one arm behind my back, the other under my thighs. I'm all muddy jeans, flailing limbs, and utter humiliation, but the only thing I can focus on is him. The heat of his chest pressed against mine. His scent. That deep, rich honey and fresh-baked bread that feels like coming home.

I try to breathe through it, but my body is betraying me —nipples tightening, pulse fluttering, skin buzzing like live wire. I can't not feel him.

"Go get cleaned up," he murmurs eventually. "After lunch, I'm taking you into town for some new clothes."

"I don't need—" My voice croaks in protest. "I can just wash what I have—"

"My treat. Least I can do after throwing you to the wolves this morning. Or cats, technically."

"I don't want to spend your—"

He cuts in smoothly. "I'd be honored to help you out until you can retrieve your stuff from Chicago. Deal?"

It's impossible to argue when you're cradled against a man built like a carved statue, your brain swimming in his scent and your heart trying to claw its way out of your chest. "Fine. Deal."

He carries me right to the porch of the guesthouse before gently lowering me to my feet, those warm, calloused hands lingering just a second longer than they should. My body misses him immediately.

"I'll let June know I'm driving you in tonight," he states, stepping back like it's the easiest thing in the world, like he didn't just unravel me completely.

I nod, heart thudding. "Okay."

His gaze lingers on mine, unreadable. "Don't be late." He winks, and I almost fall over from swooning.

Then he walks off, and I'm left standing on the porch, soaked in mud and confusion, attraction and dread swirling in equal measure.

Because I'm not just flustered or overwhelmed.

It scares me how fast I'm falling for them.

And I don't know what the hell I'm supposed to do about it.

9
WALKER

As I head back toward the barns, I adjust my jeans with a frustrated grunt, trying to will away the hard-on that's been throbbing since I left Sophia on the porch. Hell. She has no idea what she's already doing to me, and I mean that in every damn sense. One soft look, one teasing smile, and I'm walking around half wrecked. I'd prayed for this moment more times than I'll admit—finding her, my Omega. The one the world promised would fit beside me like fate knew what it was doing. But no one tells you what it feels like when she's actually here. Real. Complicated. Beautiful. And already starting to unravel the neat little order I'd forced into my life.

She's going to destroy us. I can feel it in my bones.

But fuck, I've never wanted anything more.

I never told the others how much I wanted this. I kept that shit locked up tight, played it cool. But I've been waiting. And now she's here. Of course it'd happen now, with the inheritance mess, with emotions already raw. Is there ever a good time for your entire world to tilt on its axis?

And this is exactly why I didn't say anything yet. I need her to trust me, not question whether I'm using her for the ranch. These are two different things, no matter how tangled up they might feel. That's why I watched instead. I paid attention. To her gasps. Her shallow breaths. The way those big eyes locked on mine like I was the only thing anchoring her. The way she clung to me without even thinking, her fingers fisting in my shirt like letting go wasn't an option.

And beneath it all—fuck me—that delicious, slick-sweet undercurrent of her scent, thick and needy and buried under her nerves. It damn near brought me to my knees. I wanted to pin her to a tree right then and claim her as mine, every raw inch of her.

But I'm getting ahead of myself.

She doesn't look ready to give in.

And I sure as hell won't be the reason she runs.

So I lock it down. Push the heat back under my ribs and put one boot in front of the other. The ranch doesn't stop spinning just because I'm losing my damn mind.

Cash leans against the rail like he owns it, toothpick between his teeth, that calculating look in his eyes that means he's trying to run numbers, which is what Ridge normally takes care of. Probably figuring transport costs for the three horses we sold to that Texas breeder. High-dollar deal, clean money, no complications.

Well. We're about to get messy.

"Need to talk," I say, pushing through the gate hard enough that it slams against the post with a metallic clang.

The round pen is about sixty feet across, dust-packed earth underfoot, the fence solid pipe panels that circle like a corral cage. Ridge has the lead rope in one hand, gloved fingers loose but firm, body still and measured. He doesn't look up at the sound, but the horse does, ears twitching back, nostrils flaring.

Animals always know when the energy shifts.

"Thought we settled on sending the buckskin with the

others," Ridge states without breaking rhythm. He gives a quiet click of his tongue, and the sorrel gelding moves at a lazy walk around the inner edge of the pen.

Cash has one boot hooked up on the lowest rung as though he's settled in for the show. Hat low, sunglasses on. Classic. He squints toward me now, head tilting just a fraction.

"Not about the horses," I mutter.

That gets Cash's full attention. He straightens, flicking the toothpick away, brow cocked like he's just been handed something interesting. "What crawled up your ass?"

I step into the center of the pen, dust kicking up around my boots, the kind that clings to your jeans and settles in your lungs. My body is still thrumming from having Sophia in my arms when I carried her back, her laugh and her scent short-circuiting my brain.

"Sophia."

The name drops between us like a live grenade.

Ridge pulls the horse to a stop, finally looking at me. Cash goes still in that dangerous way of his.

"What about her?" Ridge's voice is carefully neutral, but I see his knuckles white on the lead rope.

"She's my scent match."

The words hang in the air like a challenge. Like a confession.

"Fuck yeah," Cash mutters.

Ridge hands off the horse to Miguel, who'd been hanging back near the fence. He's smart enough not to ask questions, just leads the gelding out of the round pen with a glance over his shoulder.

"You sure?" Ridge snaps.

"Sure as a man can be when his insides are trying to claw out of his skin." I rub the back of my neck, jaw clenched. I haven't been right since leaving her side. Since I held her. Since I caught her scent and everything in me lit up like someone dropped a match in a dry field. I still feel it tight in my chest, low in my gut, wrapped around my damn cock like a vise.

Sophia.

"Hit me like a freight train," I say. "Couldn't breathe. Couldn't think. Just needed…"

"To claim," Cash mutters, voice rough though he's smiling like a damn fool. "I fucking knew it!"

There's silence. A heavy one.

Then I add, "She's our scent match."

"Ours?" Ridge scoffs. "Pretty sure scent matches don't come in group packages."

I step toward him, pointing a finger. "Don't play dumb. You've been acting off since the second you met her. Don't need working scent glands to know your instincts are screaming."

Ridge's mouth tightens. "I told you, mine got damaged in that rodeo accident. Nothing has screamed at me in years. And without that connection, what Omega wants a nonexistent binding?"

"But your body knows," I say. "You shift closer when she talks. You track her movements even when you think no one's watching. Don't act like that means nothing."

He stays silent, but that flicker in his eyes is answer enough.

I swing toward Cash. "And you—you practically orbit her."

He shrugs, trying to play it off. "What can I say? Girl's got great tits."

I give him a look that could cut steel.

He rolls his eyes. "Fine, fuck. You want the truth?"

"That'd be a first," Ridge mutters.

Cash glares, then sighs and pulls a folded sheet from his back pocket—half wrinkled and smudged. "I did some digging. After she mentioned Nolan. Didn't sit right."

"She told us he was dead," I remind them, trying not to growl the words.

"Yeah, but dead is just the final chapter. You want the rest?" He holds up the paper. "Arranged mating. Old-school-Alpha bonding contract. Her father handed her over like she was nothing but leverage in a business deal. Nolan Martinez, CEO, power-hungry bastard, real poster boy for toxic dominance."

My hands curl into fists.

Cash goes on. "She was twenty. He was thirty-five when they mated. Known for being ruthless. Controlling. Hated by damn near everyone who ever worked with him. There are court records, sealed, mostly, but what's public paints a dark picture. Rumors of aggression. Emotional abuse. Bond manipulation."

"And no one helped her?" Ridge asks, voice low, jaw tight.

Cash shrugs. "Hard to know. No social media. No public appearances. Then he dies, and she resurfaces. Quiet, alone, out from under his thumb."

"Jesus," I mutter, scrubbing my face. "No wonder she's so adamant about not reconnecting with Alphas."

"Yeah," Cash says, gaze dark. "That kind of shit leaves marks. Doesn't matter how strong she is now—he did damage."

"And now she's here," I say quietly, more to myself than to them. "Right in front of us."

Cash sighs and runs a hand through his hair. Then, after a beat, his voice drops to something different. Quieter. "You wanna know the real truth? I think she might be mine too."

Ridge turns his head sharply.

Cash shrugs like it costs him. "I've been trying to ignore it. Figured it was just proximity. Interest. Lust. But it's not. No one's scent has ever crashed into me like that. Not even close. It's like she cracked something open in me, and now I can't shut it."

He swallows hard, gaze flicking toward the fence line. "She's in my head, man. Every fucking second. I want to protect her. Tear down anyone who hurts her. It's not just want. It's need."

The silence that follows feels like a damn earthquake.

Then Ridge crosses his arms, stiff. "And I'm just the third wheel?"

"You feel something," I say. "Don't lie."

"I don't need to lie," Ridge snaps. "I can't scent her like you two can. Doesn't mean shit."

None of us speak for a beat. The wind whistles through the fence slats. The buckskin kicks at a patch of dirt.

"Point is," Cash continues, "our girl's been through hell. She's not gonna trust easily."

"Which is why we're not pushing." I glance between them. "We show her. Slow. Careful. Make her feel safe. Let her see that she belongs here."

"With us," Ridge says flatly, arms crossed, that storm brewing behind his eyes.

"Yeah," I say. "With us."

Ridge snorts, jaw tight. "And how exactly do you see that working? We line up and tell her we're all nuts about her? *Hey, Sophia, wanna be our shared mate and adopt thirty stray animals while you're at it?*"

Cash barks a laugh. "Hell, I'd pay to see that."

"We court her," I say, simple and solid.

There's silence.

Cash raises a brow. "Court her? What is this, the goddamn 1800s?"

"You got a better plan?" I shoot back. "You wanna walk up and say, 'Hi, Sophia, we caught your scent, and now we're ready to knot you into next week'? Think she's gonna stick around for that?"

Cash holds up his hands. "All right, all right. No knot jokes."

"Too late," Ridge mutters, running a hand down his face. He starts pacing, and I notice his slight limp isn't there today. "Why complicate things? Why not just take her on normal dates? You know, movies, coffee, shit real people do instead of... whatever *courting* means."

Cash smirks. "Well, I'm not gonna show up in a suit with a guitar, but maybe we *could* take her out. Individually. Not as dates. Not labeled like that. Just... spend time. Ease her into it. She has to feel the same toward us, so let her open up to us first."

"Yeah," I add. "Take her to the market in town, see if she wants to check out the bookstore, maybe show her the ridge trail."

Ridge shrugs. "Not terrible."

"Coming from you, I'll take that as glowing praise," Cash mutters.

"You're both missing the point." I push off the fence, pacing now too. "This isn't just about doing things with her. It's how we make her feel. Protected. Wanted. Free. We can't risk her thinking we're doing this to manipulate her over the ranch or the inheritance. This—us—has to be separate. Has to be real."

They go quiet.

"You think I haven't imagined this? Fuck, I've dreamed about finding my match since I was old enough to understand what it meant. But never once did I think she'd fall into my lap like this. But here she is. And she's real. She's unsure and confused."

My voice drops. "But I saw it. The gasps. Her breathing all hitched up. The way her eyes went wide like a deer, but she didn't run. And that sweet Omega slick just starting to bloom. How long before her heat comes?" We all know the truth: Alphas bring out heat in Omegas a lot quicker, another reason they tend to be kept away from us.

Ridge exhales, low and hard, his voice quieter when he speaks. "So, what... we each take a shot? One at a time?"

"It's not a fucking competition," I growl. "We're not here to fight over her. This isn't about ego. If this bond is real, then we give her reasons to believe it."

"Without pushing," Cash echoes.

"Exactly."

Ridge leans his arms on the top rail, staring out past the paddock. "And what if she doesn't want it? What if she doesn't want any of us?"

I don't say anything for a moment. That thought has been lodged in my chest since the second I caught her scent.

"Then we let her go," I say eventually. "Even if it kills us."

Cash mutters, "You always gotta be so dramatic? I ain't letting her go."

I shoot him a look.

He smirks, then kicks a boot at the dirt. "All right. This is happening, then."

"Yep," I say, dead serious. "You want her? You act like it. Earn her."

Cash nods.

"Looks like it," Ridge says quietly.

"God help us," Cash mutters.

"No," I say, voice flat. "God help *anyone* who tries to get between us and her."

They're on board, even if Ridge is still fighting it. All three of us, pursuing one Omega. It should feel wrong. Complicated. Instead, it feels like pieces clicking into place.

"Oh, and tonight," I start.

Ridge frowns. "What's tonight?"

"Five fifteen. Be at Maggie's Diner," I repeat, voice firm. "Don't be late."

Cash arches a brow. "You setting curfews now, Daddy?"

"Fuck you. She's having dinner with June," I say. "Thought it'd be a good time to see how she is without us breathing down her neck. Just... watch her. Get a read."

"Jesus," Ridge mutters. "You *are* stalking her."

"I'm observing," I snap. "There's a difference."

"Yeah. One's got a restraining order," Cash says under his breath, grinning.

I roll my shoulders, jaw ticking. "You two wanna sit around here and pretend we aren't already circling her like wolves, be my guest. But I'm going. Not saying we sit with her. She has her dinner. We have ours. But I want to see how she holds herself when she's relaxed. If she laughs. What she looks like when she's not worrying about the ranch or her damn inheritance."

Ridge eyes me. "You planning to take notes? Build a fucking psychological profile?"

I smirk. "Nope. Just watching my scent match in the wild."

"Creepy," Cash deadpans.

"Practical," I correct.

Cash and Ridge exchange a look.

"I'll go," Ridge says eventually. "But I'm not making small talk with June. It's terrifying how that woman doesn't stop talking."

"You'll survive," I grunt, turning toward the barn. "Come hungry. It's meatloaf night."

"You just said the magic words," Cash says.

"Good choice," I mutter, already walking off.

Behind me, their voices drift into banter, footsteps following. They're in. We're doing this.

And as the sun starts to rise over the hills and the scent of hay, horse sweat, and pine fills my lungs, one thing settles deep in my chest like a promise...

We may not be playing fair.

But we're playing to win.

10

At exactly two o'clock, Walker knocks on my door. I've spent the past few hours doing everything I can not to think about him.

Not about the almost kiss. Not about the way his voice curled around me like smoke. And definitely not about the fire smoldering between my thighs that refuses to go out, no matter how many icy showers I take. My body feels like it's betraying me, aching for him in ways that terrify me. Because what if this isn't just lust? What if this is a scent match and my heat responding?

God, no. Though, that would explain the way I nearly came apart just from him carrying me in his arms. How my chest tightened when I caught his scent. And now how I feel like I might actually *die* if I don't see him again soon.

So I distracted myself.

I dragged every clean item of clothing I have out of my bag, hardly anything, and tried them all on like I was auditioning for a runway show in the middle of nowhere. The kittens didn't care. Chonkarella lounged at the foot of the bed, one paw slung over her twin furballs like she was judging my wardrobe with regal disdain.

I finally settled on a sundress I'd thrown in as an afterthought, a pale yellow number embroidered with tiny wildflowers along the hem. It cinches at the waist and floats to mid-thigh, soft cotton against sun-warmed skin. Not exactly ranch wear, but it's clean and doesn't smell like barn animals.

And maybe I want him to look at me the way he did earlier.

Even if I know I'm not ready to admit it.

I open the door and immediately forget how to breathe.

Walker has changed too, and the sight of him makes my mouth go dry. He's wearing dark jeans that fit him perfectly, showcasing long, strong legs that seem to go on forever. A blue-and-white-checked shirt stretches across his broad shoulders, pearl snaps catching the afternoon light like tiny stars. His belt buckle is different from the one he wore this morning and depicts a big silver star. The tan-colored Stetson sits at just the right angle, shadowing his warm brown eyes in a way that makes them look darker, more dangerous, more... everything.

He's so tall that I have to tilt my head back to meet his gaze, and when I do, the look in his eyes makes my stomach flip. He's staring at me like I'm something precious and edible all at once, his stare tracking slowly from my face down to where the dress hugs my curves, lingering on the way the fabric clings to my chest before forcing his eyes back up.

"You look..." He clears his throat, Adam's apple bobbing in a way that shouldn't be attractive but absolutely is. "That's a pretty dress."

"Thanks. You clean up pretty well yourself, cowboy." I aim for light and teasing, but my voice comes out breathier than intended, like I've been running.

"Ready to go?"

"Lead the way."

His truck is exactly what I expected, a well-maintained Ford, vibrant blue paint and a bench seat covered in a wool blanket. He opens my door without fanfare, but his hand on my elbow as I navigate the high step sends sparks through me. The dress rides up slightly as I climb in, and I catch his sharp intake of breath.

"First stop," he states as we pull onto the main road, his voice rougher than usual. "Western wear store. Can't have you chasing animals in those city shoes. Then there's a dress store nearby you might like."

I want to argue, not about the practicality but about the spending. I hate the idea of racking up any kind of debt here, even temporarily. My current wardrobe consists of too few clothes. I need to work out when I'm going to drive to Chicago to grab some more and deal with my rental. Thinking about it makes me breathe too quickly.

"Okay," I agree softly. "But I'm paying you back. Every penny."

"Wouldn't expect anything less," he says, glancing at me with a faint grin.

The rest of the drive slips into silence. Not an awkward one, but a charged one. The kind that crackles beneath your skin and hums low in your stomach. I keep sneaking glances at him, at the way his forearms flex as his hands grip the steering wheel, the concentration in his jaw, the way the sun filters through the windshield and catches the dust in his hair like flecks of gold.

His scent is strong in the cab, honey and man, but thank God the window is cracked, letting in fresh air. It helps. Barely. I grip the seat belt as if it'll save me from drowning in pheromones and don't dare bring up the scent match thing. If I pretend it's not there, maybe it'll stop pulsing through my bloodstream like some kind of Omega fever.

The scenery outside helps ground me. Wide-open green fields stretch on either side of the road, dotted with cows and rust-colored barns. A red-tailed hawk cuts through the sky, and somewhere far off, a tractor hums. Then, just like that, the countryside gives way to the town of Honeyspur Meadow. It might as well have been plucked straight from a Hallmark movie set. Quaint. Charming. A little too perfect with its tiny whitewashed fences outside some of the buildings, flower boxes, and cheerful storefronts with hand-painted signs.

Walker pulls into a spot right out front of the Western wear store, a prime location that feels suspiciously lucky. He throws the truck in park and hops out before I can unbuckle my seat belt.

I've barely opened the door before he's there, pulling it the rest of the way and offering a hand to help me down.

"I can get out of a truck by myself," I tease, slipping my hand into his anyway. The contact is brief, but the warmth lingers.

"Sure you can," he says, lips twitching. "But you don't have to."

As I step onto the sidewalk, an older couple, maybe in their sixties, walks by, hand in hand. They smile warmly at Walker, but their eyes shift to me... and linger. Their smiles widen, a little too knowing, and then they move on, whispering to each other as they go.

I clear my throat. "Friendly town."

"Everyone knows everyone," he replies easily, but his voice has an edge of amusement. "And they've got theories about everything."

Of course they do.

Then I finally take in the store itself, larger than I expected, stretching half the block. The windows are filled with mannequins decked out in rhinestone-studded shirts, pearl-snap dresses, worn leather jackets, and enough cowboy boots to start a stampede. A pair of fringed chaps hangs dramatically near the entrance, daring someone to try them on.

The Western wear store feels like another world. Rows of boots in every color and style imaginable line one wall—snakeskin, distressed leather, embroidered roses, even a pair that glitters with gold sequins. To my left, there's a whole section dedicated to denim, and to the right, enough hats to outfit a country music video.

Walker tips his head toward the back. "Boots first. You'll want something sturdy for the mud. And maybe something else for when we go into town that won't get you strange looks."

He's close to me again. Too close. And his scent is thicker inside, no breeze to save me this time. I try not to visibly lean toward him. Try even harder not to imagine what his mouth felt like almost pressed to mine.

He gestures for me to go ahead but stays near enough that I feel him at my back. It's stupid how aware I am of him. I've known him, what? A few days? And yet he's already embedded himself under my skin like he belongs there.

I stop at a display table of short ankle boots with low heels and nudge one with my toe. "These could work."

"They'll break your ankles before the week's out."

"Okay," I sigh. "Function over fashion. Got it."

We wander into the work boot section, and I can't help but be drawn to a pair of chestnut leather boots with subtle floral embossing and a reinforced sole. Sturdy. Practical. But still... me.

"These," I say, picking one up and turning it over.

Walker crouches down beside me and takes the boot from my hands to check the size. "These'll do. Try them on."

It's ridiculous how flustered I get at something so basic. I lower onto the bench, then pull off my flip-flops, and he kneels in front of me like he's about to propose. He doesn't say a word, just reaches for the thin try-on socks from the box. The disposable kind every shoe shop has, the ones that feel like half a whisper against your skin.

My heart damn near stops when he reaches for my foot and slips on a sock, then the boot like it's the most natural thing in the world. Same on the other foot.

"This isn't a Cinderella moment," I mumble, staring anywhere but at his face.

"No," he agrees. "You're more real than any fairy tale."

The words crash into me somewhere near my pelvis. My breath stutters. I glance down, and his gaze is already on me, intense and unreadable. My cheeks flush, heat creeping up my neck.

"Fits?" he asks, voice lower than before.

I nod. "Perfectly."

By the time I'm standing again, I feel steadier on my feet, but not in my head. Not in my heart. Everything in me is on fire, and he hasn't even touched me more than necessary.

I take a few strides and know these boots are perfect.

We browse a bit more. He's picky and has opinions on materials, cut, and durability, but it's weirdly comforting to watch him be so serious about it. I end up with a few shirts, a durable denim jacket, and four pairs of jeans that don't hug my hips like a vise. It's practical, but... kind of sweet, the way he guides me without taking over. I also make sure to grab half a dozen pairs of thongs, as I'm in desperate need of new underwear.

Walker pays with an Amex black card as I gather the bags and walk toward the door.

Outside, the breeze has picked up, and the late-afternoon sun paints everything gold. It's too pretty, too picturesque, and I'm too caught up in the way Walker lingers near me even now, close enough that his arm brushes mine as we walk. He collects my bags and puts them into his truck, then we are strolling toward a shop with pastel-painted trim and a big glass window lined with mannequins in sundresses, cowgirl boots, and sparkly fringe. The hand-painted sign overhead reads *The Gilded Cactus* in gold script, with a tiny cartoon cactus wearing a tiara next to it.

It's adorable.

Inside, the place smells like vanilla candles and clean linen. It's huge too. Racks of flowy skirts, denim, and floral prints line the space, with a few cowhide chairs scattered in corners beside full-length mirrors. Then I spot more racks of clothes way in the back. Soft acoustic music plays from an old stereo behind the counter, where two girls glance up the second we step inside.

"Walker," one of them says with a grin, dragging out the syllables like they taste sweet. She's all legs and lip gloss, blonde braid swinging as she leans on the counter. "Don't tell me you're finally here for a makeover."

The brunette beside her perks up too, bright-eyed and clearly just as delighted. "Or maybe you're here to finally buy that flannel we tried to talk you into last winter?"

Walker lifts a hand in greeting but doesn't stray far from me. "Actually, she's the one doing the shopping today."

Both girls turn their eyes to me then, and I swear their smiles twitch—not mean, exactly, but assessing.

"Ohhh," the blonde drawls. "We're gonna have fun."

The brunette nudges a rack closer. "Shout if you need a dressing room. We've got three in the back. The middle one has the best mirror."

Walker shoots me a reassuring smile, as if to say he'll be close, then peels off to browse a table of belts and boots, giving me space.

I let out a breath and drift toward the dresses.

That's when I see a deep blue one with silver threading along the hem, fitted through the bodice, then flaring at the skirt in soft, swooping waves that might graze my calves. The kind of thing you wear to a barn dance, or maybe a date you don't want to end. I grab it and keep on shopping. Before I know it, I have a massive pile in my arms, and the shop assistants are nowhere to help. So I head into the middle dressing room and pull on the blue number first. Then I turn in front of the mirror, startled by my reflection.

It hugs me in all the right ways, makes me look... different. Softer. Brighter. Like someone who hasn't been battling for an easier life for as long as she can remember.

Which is why I'm trying really hard not to think about Walker.

Not his stupid crooked smile. Not the way he looked at me when I tried on boots, like he was seconds from devouring me whole.

I step out of the dressing room.

Walker is lounging in one of the cowhide chairs outside my dressing room, one ankle crossed over the opposite knee, his sinful smile aimed straight at me like it has its own gravitational pull.

His posture straightens. Eyes darken. Mouth parts. And for a few loaded heartbeats, he just stares.

"You're fucking stunning."

Not the dress. He's staring at my face. *Me.*

Heat rushes up my neck. "You don't think it's too much?"

"No," he says, low and growly. "It's spectacular."

It's impossible to ignore the way his gaze drags up and down my body. Or how he shifts in that ridiculous cow-print chair, legs spread like he owns the whole damn store.

I duck my head and mutter something about trying on more outfits. He doesn't push. Just nods, silent as I disappear behind the curtain.

The next outfit is a white linen skirt and a soft green crop top. A little too revealing for my usual taste, but something about today feels different. I tug at the hem, hesitate, then square my shoulders and step out.

Walker doesn't whistle, thank God, but the look he gives me? It burns.

His mouth curves, slow and wicked. "That one's dangerous."

My brow lifts. "Why? Because it's not flannel?"

"Because if you wear that around the ranch, I'll get nothing done."

Heat flushes through me. I spin for effect, flipping the skirt like I'm in a commercial. "Maybe that's the goal."

He chuckles, low and gravelly. "You keep talking like that, and I'm gonna start thinkin' you want trouble."

I hold his stare. "Look at you being Mr. Flirt," I tease, though my face feels as if it's on fire.

Silence hums between us like electricity in the air before a storm. Then I break eye contact and dart behind the curtain again, pulse hammering.

What the hell am I doing?

I change quickly into a soft pink dress. Not the fanciest, but the one I liked most, as it looked comfortable and sweet, with a square neckline and capped sleeves.

I'm about to call out when I hear the curtain shift.

Walker slips into the changing room, one hand curling the fabric shut behind him.

My heart lodges somewhere in my throat.

"Walker—"

"I know. I'm crossing a line," he says, voice pitched low and rough. "But I couldn't help myself. You look like a fucking dream in those outfits."

My spine presses against the wall, the cool plaster grounding me while he steps closer.

"I didn't ask you to come in here," I whisper, my words shaky. Weak. Wanting.

"No," he murmurs. "But you didn't tell me to leave yet either."

He's so close I can feel the heat of him. One hand lifts,

slow and careful, fingers brushing my jaw. My whole body tightens in response. His thumb strokes my cheek. I lean into it before I realize I'm doing it.

"You smell like jasmine and vanilla," he says. "And rain. And fuck, Sophia... your scent's been driving me insane since the second I met you back at the ranch."

I grab his wrist. "Maybe we shouldn't."

"No?" His voice is all husky temptation. "Don't act out what we're both desiring? That you've been looking at me like you want to tear me apart just as bad?"

My mouth parts, but no words fall out.

"Tell me to go, Sophia. Tell me to fuck off, and I will do anything you ask."

I try to speak.

Nothing happens.

His other hand slips to my waist, fingers curling just above my hip. I let out a soft breath that's almost a whimper.

"You're not ready," he says quietly. "I get it. But I'm not gonna pretend I don't want you. That I don't feel this... connection. You walk into a room, and my whole body reacts."

"I thought I was imagining it," I whisper.

He grins wickedly.

I tilt my head up. Our faces are inches apart.

Too close.

The air between us feels charged. His scent wraps around me with something darker now, spiced heat and want. It pulses in time with my heart, which is currently thundering in my ears like it's trying to rip free from my chest.

He leans in just enough that I feel his breath fan across my mouth. Not touching. Not quite. Just there, hovering like temptation incarnate.

My knees nearly buckle.

His lips are a hairsbreadth from mine. Not even a full breath separates us. Just heat. Just hunger. My body aches, slick pooling between my thighs like a betrayal. This is why Omegas aren't supposed to be alone with Alphas. Because when this need ignites, there's no logic. No safety. Just instinct and devastation.

A single touch would ruin me. A kiss might kill me.

I can't breathe. Can't think.

Why the hell did I think shopping with Walker was a good idea? He's not just dangerous; he's lethal. And not because he's trying to be. But because he isn't. That's what makes it worse.

He doesn't move. Doesn't speak. He just looks at me with those searing eyes like he's stripping me bare. And I can't look away. Can't run. I'm locked here, heart in my throat, chest rising and falling too fast.

My fingers curl into the fabric of my dress like it might anchor me. Like I might survive this.

And then his gaze drops to my lips. "I won't do anything unless you want me to. Do you want me to?"

I swear I feel the moment it happens, as though gravity itself shifts toward him. My lungs squeeze. My body screams out for him, thrashing like it's being denied oxygen.

His lips twitch, almost a smirk. A dare.

And I snap.

I rise onto my toes and crash my mouth to his like I've waited lifetimes to do it. Because if I didn't, I would've exploded from the ache. From the pressure of wanting something so badly it hurts to breathe.

And God help me—

I don't regret it for a second.

Just the shock of him groaning into my mouth and the strength of his arms banding around my waist, hauling me against his chest, are enough to destroy me. His kiss isn't polite. It's possessive, deep, full of the kind of hunger that makes me ache.

His tongue sweeps into my mouth, tangling with mine, slow and thorough. My hands fist in the front of his shirt. I gasp when he turns me, pressing me to the wall with his body. I can feel every hard line of muscle, the tension thrumming under his skin.

He kisses my neck like he wants to ruin me.

"Tell me to stop," he whispers.

But I can't. And when I twist my head to look him in the eye, my answer burns hot on my face. I'm on fire for him.

One of his hands slides under my dress, fingers brushing the back of my thigh, drawing a trembling moan from me. My back arches. I just crave more.

We're both panting.

"You're the sweetest thing I've ever kissed," he rasps. "And, darlin', if you keep lookin' at me like that, I'm gonna lose what little control I've got left."

"Walker—"

"We're scent-matched, Sophia."

I flinch and turn around to face him. "Don't say that."

His eyes narrow. "Why? Because you already know it's true?"

I shake my head and go to step away, but he grabs my hips and pulls me back, pinning me to the mirror with his body.

"You didn't kiss me because you're scared," he murmurs. "You kissed me because your body's screaming for mine."

"I didn't mean to—"

"You did," he growls. "And I fucking loved it. So did you."

I hate that he's right.

His mouth crashes into mine again, harder this time. "Be quiet for me, baby," he whispers against my collarbone. "Just feel."

His breath is hot against my throat. Then lower. Lower

still. And he's sinking to his knees before me, his hands already sliding up my thighs. And in moments, he's dragging my panties down slowly as he looks up at me like I'm the only thing that's ever mattered. I step out of them.

"I need to taste you properly. Is that okay?" he asks gently.

I swallow hard and nod, having forgotten how to speak.

He fists the hem of my dress and pushes it up, baring me inch by inch until the cool air hits the inferno between my legs. I'm trembling already. No underwear. Nothing to hide me. And God, I want to hide, but I don't. I widen my stance instead, shaky but willing, because if he doesn't touch me soon, I might fall apart on my own.

He exhales. "Fuck me. Look at you."

His thumbs stroke over the crease where my thighs meet my lips, spreading me open just enough to expose the mess he's made of me. I can't even look down; I'm too close to combusting.

"You're so damn pretty," he murmurs, more to himself than to me. "All pink and glistening like you were made for me. You want my mouth here, darlin'?"

"You have no idea," I manage.

He chuckles, dark and satisfied. "Good girl."

And then his tongue is on me, slow and deliberate, licking through my folds like he's savoring every inch. My hips jerk, a whimper slipping past my lips as he drags the flat of his tongue over my clit, then back down, teasing, tasting, claiming.

"Mmm," he groans against me. "Fuckin' soaked. Sweetest damn thing I've ever had on my tongue."

His grip tightens as he spreads me further, tongue circling, flicking, then diving deep. I bite down on my lower lip again, knees going soft, body lighting up in waves that crest too fast to process.

Suddenly, two thick fingers push into me, fast and sure,

filling me to the hilt. I nearly cry out, back arching against the wall as he curls them just right, dragging across that spot that has my vision going white.

"That's it," he murmurs. "Take it. Let me feel how bad you need it."

The stretch, the fullness—it's too much and not enough all at once.

He keeps working me with his mouth, tongue flicking my clit while his fingers pump slow and deep. I try to hold still, but I'm trembling, grinding into every stroke like I've lost control of my own body. Because I have.

I'm gone.

Just a slick, gasping girl pinned against the wall with a man between her legs who knows exactly how to bring her to her knees.

A moan escapes me even though I've been trying to be quiet and not draw attention to us in the dressing room.

Too loud.

He pulls his mouth away, just barely, and looks up through heavy lashes, fingers still buried deep inside me.

"You're bein' too noisy," he murmurs. "Don't want those salesgirls hearing how wet you get for me, do you?"

I shake my head, hardly able to breathe.

He withdraws his fingers slowly, soaked and glistening, and brings them to my lips. "Bite down on these."

My breath catches, but I part my lips without question. His fingers press past, sliding over my tongue, and I moan before I even realize I've made a sound.

The taste is heady. Sharp with arousal, rich and earthy beneath it. My scent is strong, impossible to ignore, but there's something unexpectedly sweet layered in, like dark vanilla left too long in the sun. It coats my tongue, addictive, like something forbidden I shouldn't crave.

But I do.

My cheeks flush hot as I suck around his fingers, my own

flavor mingling with the salt of his skin. I shouldn't find this hot. I shouldn't be so turned on by tasting myself from his hand.

But I'm drenched. Burning. Hungry for more.

And the low, filthy groan he makes when he sees me suck harder?

That sound alone nearly tips me over the edge again.

And then he's back on me, tongue rough and relentless as he sucks my clit into his mouth, hard. I gently bite down, just like he told me to, barely muffling the scream that rips from my throat as my orgasm detonates like a firestorm.

I convulse.

Every muscle locks and then breaks loose. I shake violently, legs threatening to give, and he doesn't stop. Doesn't even pause. He licks me through it, holding me up with his hand on my thigh, his tongue claiming every last pulse and tremor until I'm wrecked.

Completely destroyed.

My head falls back against the mirror with a soft thud, breath coming in broken gasps, and I swear my soul might've left my body.

But he's still there, between my thighs, licking over the seam of my pussy lips, eyes wild with something raw and possessive.

"Sweetest damn thing I've ever devoured," he whispers.

Then he slowly rises from where he's kneeling, a man in no rush to let go of what just passed between us. He merely stares at me. Then his hands cradle my jaw, tilting my face up as his mouth descends.

His kiss is deep. Devouring. His lips seal over mine with a hunger that melts every bone in my body. There's no softness now, no hesitance, just possession and the kind of need that makes you forget your own name.

When he finally pulls back, breath ragged, I'm trembling again for an entirely different reason.

"That was..." I swallow, voice catching. "That was incredible."

A slow smile curls his lips. "I don't do halfway, darlin'."

But the high starts to slip. Doubt creeps in at the edges of my mind, fast and sharp and unwelcome.

"It might've been a mistake," I whisper. The words feel like sandpaper in my throat.

Walker doesn't flinch. Doesn't look away. "I don't think so," he states. "When you find your scent match, you claim her. And if she's not ready to be claimed..." His thumb brushes my bottom lip. "Then I wait. For as long as you need."

"God," I breathe, stepping back, heart jackhammering. "Why do you have to be so... you? So perfect. So damn sexy. So everything."

A flicker of darkness passes through his gaze.

"We have time to deal with this stuff later, right?" I joke, but it comes out thin.

Walker doesn't laugh. He sees too much. Feels too much.

I look away. "Well, I'd better get changed."

My hands fumble to pull my dress back down, heat flushing my face. I grab my underwear off the floor and fist it in my palm. "I just need to go to the bathroom real quick," I mumble, already turning.

"I'll pay for the clothes," he says. "All of 'em. You just breathe." His voice follows me as I slip past the curtain.

In the bathroom, I lock the door and sag against it, pulse still racing, body still slick and aching. But now the rush is giving way to something cold.

What if I've opened Pandora's box?

I should've kept pretending. Pretending that I felt nothing. That the chemistry was one-sided. That I could control this.

Because what if it all falls apart?

What if I don't belong here, on the ranch, in this town, with them?

What if I want to leave?

What if the other two don't want me? What if I'm the Omega that breaks their pack instead of binding it?

Nolan was caring at first too. Attentive. Kind. Until I bonded with him... and eventually he stopped touching me. Stopped even looking at me. Wouldn't help me through my heat. Not even once.

I had to pay strangers at a clinic to get me through it. Had to sign a waiver. Had to lie and say I was fine.

My stomach twists, the weight of everything crashing down.

I need tonight. I need June. I need alcohol, loud music, and food.

I need a night where I don't feel like I'm standing on the edge of a cliff, begging not to fall.

And maybe... I need to fall anyway. Just not tonight.

11

CASH

Ridge and I climb out of my truck in the parking area behind Maggie's Diner, our boots crunching on the gravel scattered between the painted lines. The lot is about half full with a mix of dusty pickups, a few sedans that probably belong to the townspeople, and one shiny red Mustang that's got to be some tourist's ride. A handful of motorcycles are lined up near the back fence, chrome gleaming under the security lights that are just starting to flicker on.

The sun hangs low, painting everything in shades of amber and crimson. September is settling in with that crisp bite to the air that promises winter is not far behind. A couple of ravens are pecking at something near the dumpster, and the smell of fried food and barbecue smoke drifts out from the kitchen vents.

Walker is leaning against his truck, arms crossed over his chest. "About damn time," he growls as we approach. "I was starting to think you two got lost between here and the ranch."

"Had to make a pit stop," I reply, adjusting my button-down. It's one of my nicer ones, a deep blue that brings out my eyes, and I'd be lying if I said I didn't pick it hoping Sophia might notice. "Ridge here insisted on buying half the gas station's inventory of jerky."

"Man's got to fill up his supply back home," Ridge states with a smirk, settling his hat more firmly on his head. He's wearing his good jeans tonight, the ones without holes in the knees, and a burgundy flannel that makes his auburn hair look like fire in the dying light.

But Walker isn't laughing. There's something wound tight about him, like a spring ready to snap. And now that I'm close enough, I can smell why.

That scent clinging to him makes every Alpha instinct I've got sit up and roar. It's sweet and spicy and feminine, and it's definitely not his usual masculine one. Without thinking, I step right into his personal space, close enough that our chests are almost touching, and take a deep breath, filling my lungs.

Walker shoves me back, but there's more surprise than real aggression in it. "What the fuck, Cash?"

"Don't play dumb with me," I rebut, grinning because now I know exactly what happened this afternoon. "You smell like Omega pussy. You've been rolling around with our pretty little Omega, haven't you?"

"Goddamn it, so fucking what?" Walker mutters, but his cheeks are flushing.

Ridge's head whips toward us so fast I'm surprised he doesn't get whiplash. "This is so fucked up," he groans. "If I miss one thing about losing my sense of smell, it's that sweet scent of pussy."

Walker and I both stare at him. It's the first time he's actually admitted what losing his scent abilities has cost him beyond the day-to-day stuff. But I'm too wound up to process that right now.

"Well, our boy Walker here," I say, still grinning, "has been sampling the merchandise."

"It wasn't like that," he protests, but he's not denying it either.

"You pushed us to keep it in our pants and go slow with her, and now, I can smell her on you. Faint, but hell, man, I can only imagine how good she would have been."

Walker chuckles, running a hand through his dark hair. "Funny story..."

"Real funny," I state flatly.

Ridge crosses his arms, waiting.

Walker gives us the quick rundown about helping Sophia buy clothes and then somehow ending up in the changing room with her, on his knees, between her legs. The bastard is trying to play it casual, but I can see the satisfied gleam in his eyes.

"Oh, you just fell into that position, right?" I ask, my voice dripping with sarcasm. "What, did you trip over your own feet and accidentally land face-first in paradise?"

Even Ridge cracks up at that. "Yeah, Walker, that's some real graceful navigation there. Next you'll tell us you were just helping her tie her shoes."

Walker's cheeks actually flush a little. "Look, she's my scent match. Ours, most likely." He glances at Ridge meaningfully. "I think yours too, but that's a different battle. When you get near her... fuck me, but I couldn't resist. I've never experienced anything like this."

I cross my arms and lean back against his truck. "Spill it. And I want details. Because I've been wondering if she's a natural redhead since the day she walked onto the ranch."

Walker's face goes even redder. "Jesus, Cash."

"What? It's a legitimate question." I drum my fingers against my crossed arms. "Come on, don't leave us hanging. What's she taste like? Sweet as she smells?"

"You're both sick," Ridge says, but he's listening intently.

Walker runs a hand through his hair, making it even messier. "Look, it just happened, okay? And yeah, Cash, she's a natural redhead. The softest damn hair I've ever felt against my face."

The mental image that creates makes my jeans uncomfortably tight. "Fuck me sideways."

He shakes his head. "I've never lost control like that. Never wanted anything as much as I wanted to make her come apart under my tongue."

Ridge has gone very still. "Both of you are certain about this scent match thing?"

"As sure as I can be," Walker says gently. He understands this is hard for Ridge to hear, knowing he might never be able to confirm it himself. "But I think you'll realize when you're close to her. There are other signs."

Ridge just shrugs.

"Listen, man," Walker continues. "Like the way every instinct you've got screams at you to protect her. Like how you can't think about anything else when she's around. Like how you want to claim her so badly it makes even your teeth ache."

"And here I thought I was just developing an unhealthy obsession," I say.

"Oh, you are," Walker says with a grin. "We all are."

"So what happened after?" I ask. "Did you... finish the job?"

"Afterward, she panicked," Walker explains, his expression sobering. "Ran out of there so fast she practically left skid marks. I think it scared her, how good it was between us."

"Can't blame her for that," I say. "Probably didn't expect to get her world rocked in a clothing store's changing room."

"No, probably not." Walker pushes off his truck. "But she's ours, whether she wants to admit it or not. And I'm not letting her run back to Chicago. Can't leave the animals at the shelter, and I sure as hell can't leave my Omega. Simple solution to me—she has to stay."

Ridge adjusts his hat, a sure sign he's thinking hard about something. "And if she fights us on it?"

"Then we convince her to stay," I say simply. "However long it takes."

We start walking toward the back entrance of the diner, our boots echoing off the brick wall. The music and voices from inside grow louder.

"All right, enough talking," Ridge says as we reach the rear door to Maggie's Diner. "Let's go see what our girl is up to."

We all remove our hats, and the moment we step inside, I'm transported back to the Old West. Maggie's hasn't changed since we moved into town and started coming here. The walls are covered in dark wood paneling, and every inch is decorated with vintage Western gear, old spurs, faded photographs of cattle drives, branding irons, and even a couple of antique rifles mounted above the bar. The floors are original hardwood, scarred and worn smooth by decades of cowboy boots. Red checkered tablecloths cover round wooden tables, and mason jar lights hang from the ceiling, casting everything in a warm, amber glow.

A massive stone fireplace dominates one wall, unlit now but surrounded by leather chairs that have seen better days. The bar runs along the back wall, manned by Maggie herself, a woman in her sixties with steel-gray hair and arms like tree trunks from lifting beer kegs. She's got a no-nonsense attitude that keeps even the rowdiest cowboys in line.

The jukebox in the corner is playing something by Garth Brooks, and the whole place hums with conversation and laughter. It's Friday night, so the place is packed. Families occupy the larger tables, couples share intimate corners, and a group of ranch hands from the Morrison ranch has claimed several stools at the bar.

But none of that matters, because I've spotted my target.

Sophia and June are tucked into a corner booth near the front windows. The warm light from a vintage lamp has Sophia's red hair resembling liquid fire, and she's wearing a yellow dress and has her back to us. She leans forward to say something to June, and I get a glimpse of the pale skin of her arm that makes me want to mark her up with my teeth.

I guide my packmates to a table in the back corner, positioning myself so I have a perfect view of her profile. She's animated tonight, talking with her hands, throwing her head back when she laughs at something June says. Every gesture makes that dress shift and cling in new ways.

"Well, this is pathetic," Ridge mutters as we settle into our chairs. "Three grown men stalking a woman during her girls' night out."

"We ain't stalking," Walker protests. "We're... observing."

"That's the definition of stalking," Ridge points out.

"Ain't always clean work wranglin' what you care about," I say, which makes both of them look at me sideways. "What? It's good advice. Sometimes you've got to embrace the uncomfortable position to get what you want."

A waitress appears at our table, a young blonde with pigtails and a smile that says she's probably working her way through college. "Evening, gentlemen! What can I get started for y'all?"

"Three beers," I say immediately. "Coldest you've got."

"And food, please," Ridge adds. "I'll take the sixteen-ounce rib eye, rare, with loaded mashed potatoes."

"Make that two steaks," Walker says. "But I want the porterhouse, same temperature, with the works."

"Meatloaf special for me," I finish. "With butter biscuits and extra gravy on the side. And keep those beers coming."

The waitress scribbles down our order. "Y'all must work up quite an appetite."

"You could say that," I reply with a grin that makes her blush, then she heads off.

"So, about those new horses coming in next week," Walker starts.

"Nope," I interrupt. "We're not done talking about your afternoon adventure. I want to know everything about you breaking your word. What was she wearing under that little sundress? How loud did she get? I need to be able to picture it in my head like a movie."

Ridge leans forward, interested despite himself. "Go on, I'm invested now. Don't leave us hanging."

Walker glances around to make sure no one's listening, then leans in closer. "She was wearing this little white lace thing that barely covered anything. And when I got my mouth on her..." He closes his eyes for a second. "Sweetest thing I've ever tasted. Like vanilla and rain and something that was just purely her."

"Fuck," I breathe.

Just then, our beers arrive, and we all fall silent while the waitress is there. "Food'll be out real soon," she says cheerfully. "Y'all need anything else right now?"

"We're good," I tell her, already reaching for my beer as she leaves. The cold liquid hits my throat like salvation, helping to cool some of the heat that Walker's story has stirred up.

Then he leans in again. "And she got so loud I had to press two fingers into her mouth. Same ones I'd just been using inside her."

He lets that sink in, his grin slow and wicked. "Swear to God, it was the hottest damn thing I've ever experienced. The way she moaned around them? Like she couldn't decide if she wanted to scream or keep suckin'—"

I choke on my beer.

My hand jerks under the table, adjusting myself before I

embarrass us all. Because that image? It detonates in my head like a wildfire.

Sophia, mouth open and gasping, her legs trembling, dress hiked to her waist while I drop to my knees between them. Her taste on my tongue. Her fists in my hair. Her slick heat coating my fingers while she makes those sounds for me. Just for me.

Fuck!

I press my palm hard against my thigh like it'll ground me. It doesn't. The overhead fan is rattling too loudly, and the damn lights feel like spotlights aimed right at my guilty conscience.

This is a public diner. There are grandmas eating cobbler a couple of tables over. And here I am, two seconds from unzipping and making a damn fool of myself because I pushed Walker to share.

I blow out a breath and force my focus back to my beer, swallowing a curse. If he keeps talking like that, I'm gonna lose it.

Or worse—

I'm gonna stand up and walk across this diner, pull Sophia into the goddamn bathroom, and make her scream loud enough that everyone in this place will know exactly who she belongs to.

Small blessings as our food arrives faster than usual, probably because they know we tip well. The waitress sets down three plates that would make a lumberjack weep with joy. Ridge's steak hangs off both sides of his plate. Walker's porterhouse is even bigger, accompanied by a baked potato the size of a softball. My meatloaf is smothered in brown gravy, with a side of mashed potatoes that could feed a small army and biscuits so buttery they're practically glowing.

"Half the cow's on my plate," Ridge declares with a grin, already cutting into his steak.

"Look at that beautiful piece of beef," Walker adds, admiring his porterhouse. "Almost too pretty to eat."

"Almost," I agree, digging into my meatloaf. "But not quite."

We eat in silence for a few minutes, but I keep glancing over at Sophia's table. She hasn't looked our way once. For the best, perhaps.

That's when I spot the waitress heading to their table with a tray of drinks. She points across the room toward the bar, and I follow her gesture to see two men raising their glasses in the girls' direction.

"Son of a bitch," I mutter, my grip tightening on my fork.

Walker follows my gaze, and his whole body goes rigid. "Fucking hell."

Ridge squints across the room, then his face darkens. "Is that Ronan?"

I focus on the tallest of a small group of men, and recognition comes at me like a sucker punch. "Yeah, it's that piece of shit."

Ronan Blackwood. Rose's worthless grandson who showed up at the ranch every few months with his hand out, looking for money he hadn't earned. The bastard who once told Rose to her face that he was just waiting for her to die so he could claim what was *rightfully his*. The ass who dressed like a cowboy but had never done an honest day's work in his life.

"What's he doing here?" Walker sneers, his voice tight with anger.

"Nothing damn good," I reply, watching as Ronan stands up from his barstool.

He's dressed to impress tonight, designer jeans that probably cost more than most people's monthly rent, a shirt that's been pressed within an inch of its life, and boots so shiny they could blind a pilot. His black hair is slicked back with enough product to waterproof a roof, and there's something sickening in the way he's staring at Sophia.

"This isn't going to end well," Ridge hisses, his whole body tensing.

I'm on the edge of my seat as Ronan strolls toward the girls' table with the kind of swagger that comes from too much money and not enough sense. But before he can reach them, Walker is on his feet, moving through the crowd with deadly purpose.

I've seen Walker handle spooked horses and aggressive dogs, but I've never seen him look as dangerous as he does right now. Bunched-up shoulders, chin high, hands in fists, and people instinctively move out of his way, all six feet, three inches of intimidating Alpha muscle.

He reaches Ronan just before the bastard gets to Sophia, who has no clue, as she and June are deep in conversation, laughing.

Giving Ronan no chance to react, Walker grabs him by the collar and hauls him toward the back exit like he's wrangling uncooperative livestock—forceful, fast, and with zero patience. Chairs scrape back as he shoves past tables, the air thick with tension. Conversations stutter to a stop. A fork clatters onto a plate.

Most of the locals know Walker. They don't interfere. Hell, a few even tip their hats or mutter things like "'Bout time" under their breath. No one tries to stop him. No one asks questions.

Ridge and I are right behind them, leaving our half-finished meals without a second thought.

The parking lot feels different now, darker, more isolated. The security lights cast harsh shadows between the parked cars, and the temperature has dropped enough to make our breath visible.

Walker releases Ronan with a shove that sends him stumbling forward. "What the fuck do you think you're doing? You have nothing to do with those girls in there, understand?"

Ronan stumbles and whips back around, that oily smirk never leaving his face. "That's where you're wrong. Sophia has something that belongs to me," he snaps. "And no little bitch in a sundress is going to keep what's mine. Especially not with you three assholes playing gatekeeper like this town is your personal fucking kingdom."

Walker's entire body coils, muscles straining like a live wire about to snap. Ridge's jaw flexes, fists at his sides. I feel the burn of rage crawl up my spine, and I take one deliberate step forward.

"Say that again," I growl. "And I'll knock the teeth outta that smug face of yours."

Ronan scoffs, but his hand twitches. He's nervous. Good. He should be.

He straightens his expensive shirt again. "Wild Hearts Ranch is mine. Always was. Rose had no damn right handing it off to someone else, let alone a stray Omega just 'cause her dead grandson dipped his dick in there. And you three? You're nothing. Just overgrown mutts sniffing around."

Walker shifts forward, slow and deliberate, like a wolf closing in. "Say her name again," he murmurs, voice flat and as sharp as a knife. "I fucking dare you."

Ronan snorts, but the sound is thin. He opens his mouth—

The rear door of the diner bangs open behind us.

Boots hit gravel.

I glance back just as the five men he was at the bar with pour out. Must be Ronan's crew. One adjusts a ring on his swollen knuckle. Another grins, tongue running along his teeth like he's already tasting blood.

But I shift my weight, jaw tightening. Five on three. We've had worse. I lean just a little closer to Walker and

Ridge, sizing up the other men. "We can take those fuckers," I mutter. "I'll swing first."

"No doubt," Ridge says grimly, cracking his neck. "But we take them here, and it's gonna bleed inside. Sophia's in there."

That's all it takes.

I turn back to Ronan. "You're done here. You hear me? Don't show your face again, or we'll bury your sorry ass so deep in this town's dirt, even the worms'll be scared to touch you."

Ronan's jaw ticks, but he doesn't move.

The diner door creaks open behind us. An older couple steps out. The man squints into the dusk, taking in the squared shoulders and the twitchy fingers.

"This ain't the place for whatever this is," he commands. "Y'all wanna throw down, take it to the canyon. Not where folks are eatin' their supper."

No one moves. Walker is still locked on to Ronan like a loaded gun with no safety.

Ronan lifts his hands in mock surrender. "Wouldn't dream of causing trouble," he says, all syrup and smirk. "Just sayin' hi to some old friends."

"Then you said it," I growl. "Now get the fuck outta here."

The older couple moves on toward their car.

Ronan eyes me, then Ridge, then Walker. Doesn't say another word. Just turns and heads for his truck, his little pack of bootlickers trailing after him.

Walker takes a step forward, fury in every inch of him as he clenches his hands into fists.

Ridge grabs his arm. "Not now."

Ronan chuckles low. "See you boys real soon."

The engine roars to life, and their truck peels out in a spray of gravel and dust, leaving the air thick with exhaust and threat.

We watch them go.

Silence settles.

I spit to the side, glaring after them. "Next time, we don't let them leave on their feet."

Walker nods once. Ridge doesn't say anything but just stares into the dark, jaw clenched.

We need to tell Sophia.

But not tonight.

Tonight, we let her believe the world is still safe.

For now.

As we head back inside, I catch sight of Sophia. She's laughing at something June said, completely oblivious to the storm gathering around her. But that's okay.

We'll handle the storm. That's what Alphas do for their Omegas.

Even if this one doesn't know she's ours yet.

The evening air is cooling as June and I step out of Maggie's Diner, stomachs full of the best chicken and dumplings I've ever tasted. The main street of Honeyspur Meadow stretches before us, busier than I expected for a weekday night. Shop windows glow yellow, the hardware store is still open, and a few people are browsing inside. Kids race past on bikes.

"So, about chapter eight," June says, linking her arm through mine like we've been friends for years instead of hours. The casual intimacy of it makes my chest warm. "When the demon prince does that thing with his tail while she's trying to read her grandmother's spell book?"

I nearly stumble on the sidewalk. "Okay, I may need to read just that chapter before we arrive at the book club."

"Well, he wraps it around her thigh and slowly slides it up while whispering in a demonic tongue about how her soul tastes like cinnamon and secretly bonding her to him?" June finishes, completely shameless. Her hazel eyes sparkle in the streetlight. "Apparently, it's Loretta's favorite scene. She's the one who owns The Dust Jacket Bookshop, where the club is held. You'll love her. Or be terrified. Possibly both."

"Tell me more about this Loretta," I ask, stepping around a couple strolling with their ancient beagle who seems determined to sniff every single lamppost. "I need to know what I'm walking into."

June's soft curls bounce as she glances at me. "Loretta Honeycutt. Forty-six, divorced twice, currently dating a mechanic but also flirting outrageously with the new veterinarian who's, like, twelve years younger. She inherited the bookstore from her aunt and turned it into this whole community hub thing. Also runs the food bank, organizes the harvest festival, and somehow finds time to read approximately ten books a week."

"Ten?"

"I'm barely exaggerating. The woman consumes books like I inhale coffee." June leans in closer. "Also, rumor has it she's writing her own romance novel, titled *Roped and Ruined*."

"Stop." I laugh, the sound echoing off the storefronts. It feels good to laugh like this, freely and without weight. June reminds me so much of my best friend, Meredith, back in Chicago, with the same rapid-fire speech and the same ability to make even mundane things feel like adventures.

"Oh, and she has this theory that everyone in town is secretly harboring passionate desires for inappropriate people," June continues, her free hand waving dramatically. "Last month she tried to convince us that Earl from the hardware store and Gladys from the post office have been carrying on a torrid affair for thirty years."

"And have they?"

"God, no. Earl's been happily married to the same woman since high school, and Gladys thinks romance is what happens to other people while she's sorting mail."

We pass the darkened windows of an antique shop,

ghostly furniture shapes visible inside. A tabby cat watches us from the windowsill, eyes reflecting green. June slows our pace, and I can see her working up to something by the way she's biting her lower lip.

"Okay, but speaking of people harboring passionate desires..." She pauses dramatically, watching my face.

My stomach does a little flip. "What?"

"Did you notice that your cowboys were at the diner earlier?"

I stop so abruptly that June stumbles, her grip on my arm the only thing keeping her upright. My heart kicks into overdrive. "They were what? Where? How did I not see them?"

June's grin spreads slowly, like she's savoring this moment. "You had your back to them. They were in the corner by the kitchen. All three of them, trying very hard to look like they weren't watching you."

"All three were there?" My voice comes out higher than intended. Heat crawls up my neck. Why were they there? They knew I'd be there. Were they... following me? "But I didn't... they didn't say anything to us."

"Well, they're not exactly the pushy type," June says, tugging me back into motion. We pass the barber shop, closed now but the traditional pole still spinning lazily. "Though God knows they could be. Half the single women in town, and a few of the married ones, would tackle them given half a chance. But your boys tend to keep to themselves."

"They're not *my* boys," I protest, but the words feel hollow. Walker's kiss is still burned into my memory, the desperation in it, the way he held me like I was precious.

"Sure they're not. That's why they just happened to show up at the exact same diner at the exact same time you were there." June's voice drips with sarcasm. "Total coincidence."

My mind races. Are they... what, checking up on me? The thought should annoy me, but instead there's a flutter in my stomach.

"Maybe they just wanted dinner?" I try, but even I don't believe it.

"Right. Because three grown men who have a personal chef at the ranch suddenly needed to eat at Maggie's." June shakes her head, soft curls bouncing.

"So, what, they were... watching me... us?"

"Watching over you, more like," June says thoughtfully. "Which, okay, sounds a little intense when I say it out loud, but it's actually kind of sweet. Like in the book I read for the book club, when the demon prince follows Serena to her job at the occult bookshop because he can sense that other demons might attempt to claim her? How he lurked in the shadows, ready to intervene if needed but also respecting her independence. Except there were actual demons in that book trying to steal her soul."

"I don't think Maggie's Diner posed any danger to me."

"You never know," June explains with mock seriousness. "That new cook she hired? Definitely suspicious. No one makes pie that good without supernatural assistance."

I laugh despite myself.

We walk in silence for a moment.

June squeezes my arm. "Get used to it. Small-town life means everyone's in your business whether you want them to be or not. At least your gossip involves three extremely attractive cowboys. Some of us just have nosy neighbors who report on our recycling habits."

"Oh! There it is!" I exclaim maybe a bit too enthusiastically.

The Dust Jacket Bookshop sits next to the Wildflower Bakehouse & Café, where I ate the most divine Portuguese tarts.

The bookshop itself is housed in an old brick building

painted a cheerful yellow. Flower boxes overflow with petunias and what might be lavender. A hand-painted sign swings gently in the evening breeze, creaking slightly. The window display features an alarming number of shirtless male torsos on book covers, arranged around a central pyramid of copies of *Infernal Temptation*.

"Subtle," I observe.

"Loretta wants to give the people what they crave," June says, pulling open the door. A bell chimes somewhere deep in the shop, a tinkling sound that seems to echo longer than it should.

The smell comes first, of old paper and fresh coffee mixed with something that might be sage or incense. Books are everywhere, not just on shelves but stacked on every available surface. The organizational system seems to be based more on feeling than on any logical method. A velvet fainting couch sits beneath a window, currently occupied by a huge, fluffy white cat. Two wingback chairs face each other near the register, mid-conversation frozen in furniture form. And is that an actual church pew against the far wall?

"Oh my God," I breathe, turning in a slow circle. "It's like someone's eccentric grandmother's library exploded."

"Wait until you see the romance section," June says, steering me left. "Loretta believes this genre deserves its own room. Behold!"

The side room is painted a deep rose color that should be overwhelming but somehow works. Twinkling lights crisscross the ceiling like stars. The shelves are labeled with increasingly specific subgenres from Historical, Paranormal, Cowboys, Alien Cowboys, and I swear to God, Time-Traveling Alien Cowboys Who Are Also Dukes.

"That last one can't be real," I protest, moving closer to read the spines.

June pulls a book from the shelf. The cover features a man wearing both chaps and a cravat, holding what appears to be a laser lasso. "*Lady Pemberton's Galactic Rancher.* It's actually pretty good once you accept the premise."

"Which is?"

"That love transcends time, space, and species. Also that aliens apparently look exactly like hot humans but with better abs."

"June! There you are!" a female voice booms from behind us. "And you must be the friend she said she was bringing. Sophia?"

I turn to find a woman who can only be Loretta. She's wearing a flowing caftan covered in what appear to be quotes from famous novels, the text spiraling across the fabric in different fonts. Her silver-streaked hair is piled in an elaborate updo held in place by what I realize are chopsticks with tiny books glued to the tops.

The woman is practically a walking library display with her necklaces clinking with every movement, one boasting a pendant shaped like an open book and another that might be a tiny typewriter. Plus she's wearing a charm bracelet covered in miniature book covers. It's... a lot.

"Yep, this is Sophia," June says, completing the introduction. "Sophia, Loretta is the owner, operator, and high priestess of all things romance in town."

"Oh, aren't you just adorable!" Loretta grabs my hands. "You are most welcome here."

"Thanks, I'm excited. It's my first book club."

She glances at her watch, a vintage piece with books on the face instead of numbers. "You two are the last ones. Let me just lock up, and we'll head upstairs. The ladies are probably already deep into the wine."

She bustles to the front door, flipping the sign to CLOSED and turning multiple locks. "Can't be too careful," she says. "Last month someone broke in and rearranged my entire mystery section alphabetically. It took me weeks to get the ambience right again."

June and I exchange glances, both fighting smiles.

"Now then," Loretta continues, leading us toward a narrow staircase hidden behind a bookshelf that swings open like something from a mystery novel. "Fair warning, we really embraced the theme this month."

The door at the top opens into what can only be described as hell having a midlife crisis. Red string lights cast everything in a demonic glow that has everyone looking vaguely sunburned. Fake flames made from red and orange cellophane flutter in front of a fan that's seen better days. Plastic pitchforks stand in vases like the world's most concerning flower arrangements, and are those plastic skulls from the dollar store?

But the *pièce de résistance* is definitely the cardboard cutout of a shirtless man propped in a chair. Someone has enhanced his abs with black Sharpie and made him a tail made from Christmas tinsel. A speech bubble has been added to his mouth, reading "Welcome to my lair, ladies."

"Join us," Loretta announces grandly, "in hell! Population: us!"

Three women are already present, each sporting their own interpretation of the theme. The woman closest to us, probably mid-forties with purple-tinted hair, wears full bat wings that definitely came from a Halloween costume. She's paired them with a T-shirt reading *Sinner* in glittery letters.

"Everyone, this is June and Sophia," Loretta announces. "Sophia's new in town and living at Wild Hearts Ranch!"

The room erupts in excited chatter, all three women talking at once.

"Oh my God, is it true?" Bat Wings leans forward eagerly, wineglass already half empty. "We heard you were a mail-order bride for those three cowboys!"

I nearly choke on air. "A what?"

June starts giggling beside me, pressing a hand to her mouth. "I hadn't heard that one. That's amazing."

"Well, what else would a young woman from the city be doing out here?" This from a woman wearing a surprisingly normal outfit except for light-up devil horns.

My face burns. "I'm in the midst of inheriting the ranch. Rose was—"

"Oh, we know who she was," the third woman interrupts. She's wearing a shirt that reads *I'd Sell My Soul for Chapter 8* and has added a red feather boa for flair. "Lovely woman. But you, a pretty Omega living with three handsome cowboys? The math writes itself."

"Any girl who lands that pack is going to be lucky," Light-up Horns adds with a knowing look. "And exhausted. Lord have mercy, can you imagine? All that stamina."

They all laugh, and I try to join in, but my face is burning for entirely different reasons now. If only they knew I'd had Walker pressed between my legs just earlier today, his hands everywhere, his mouth doing things that definitely belonged in chapter eight of the demon book.

"Let's get you girls some wine and get started!" Loretta claps her hands. "Dolly, Rita, Karen, make room on the couch."

June and I sink onto a love seat facing the fireplace, which has been decorated with paper flames. We exchange looks, both trying desperately not to laugh. This is unlike any book club I've ever heard of.

"First things first," Loretta announces, producing two jars that might have once held pasta sauce. "Everyone needs their demon name for the evening. Take one slip from each jar."

I reach in and pull out two pieces of paper. "Writhing Muffin," I announce, and June completely loses it, nearly sliding off the couch in her laughter.

"Mine's Throbbing Crumpet," she gasps between giggles. "Why are half of these baked goods?"

"I ran out of sexy nouns," Loretta admits cheerfully. "But

baked goods can be very sensual! Have you ever watched someone eat a chocolate croissant? Pure seduction."

"Now, let's start with a quick recap for our new members," she continues, settling into what's clearly her designated chair, a throne-like thing that might have come from a community theater production. "Who wants to summarize *Infernal Temptation*?"

Rita, the one with light-up horns, raises her hand enthusiastically. "Ordinary girl Serena accidentally summons hot demon prince Malphas while trying to make a soufflé—"

"It was a summoning circle, not a soufflé," Dolly corrects, her bat wings rustling.

"The flour made a circle! Same difference. Anyway, demon prince appears, there's a binding contract involving his ability to claim her soul through orgasms—"

"Seven orgasms specifically," Karen adds helpfully, adjusting her feather boa. "Very important plot point."

"Right, seven orgasms, and she has to resist while he tries increasingly creative methods to seduce her." Rita fans herself with her hand. "Chapter eight being the most creative."

"The tail thing," everyone says in unison, then dissolves into hollering laughter. It's contagious, and I find myself joining in.

June leans over to whisper in my ear, "I have so many questions about the mechanics of that scene."

"I may need to borrow your book after this and read this scene."

"Now," Loretta states, pulling out what appears to be an actual cauldron—plastic, but still impressively theatrical. "Before we discuss the literary merits of tail-related seduction, we need to vote on which local man would make the best demon prince."

"Oh, this should be good," June murmurs.

"I want everyone to write down one name," Loretta

announces, shaking the cauldron with glee. "One man in this town you'd bind yourself to for seven lifetimes. No judgment. No explanations. Just go with your gut or whatever body part is talking the loudest tonight."

A chorus of cackles ripples through the room.

She starts passing out little slips of red paper and glitter pens. Some of the women immediately lean over their wineglasses with wicked grins, scribbling fast like they've been waiting their whole lives for this moment.

I glance at June. She bites her lip to keep from laughing, then scrawls something on her paper before dropping it into the cauldron.

"I don't really know enough people," I whisper, hesitating with the pen.

Then I picture Ridge in the moonlight, whiskey in hand, jaw tight, eyes shadowed. That stubborn set to his shoulders like he's holding up the whole world and refuses to let it fall. Before I can stop myself, I write his name.

I fold the paper quickly and toss it in.

Once everyone has contributed, Loretta gives the cauldron a theatrical shake and begins pulling names one by one, reading them aloud like the results of a very inappropriate county fair raffle.

"First up… Earl from the hardware store." She cackles. "That man alphabetizes his nails and screws. Nobody organizes screws that meticulously without dark secrets."

The women giggle in agreement.

"Next—ooh, Sheriff Cade." Loretta raises her brows. "You just know he's got a tragic backstory and a single tear he lets fall exactly once a year. Classic book-boyfriend material."

Someone fans themselves dramatically.

"Dr. Hendricks," Loretta reads next, her voice going dreamy. "That vet has forearms built by God and hands that cradle baby goats. You know he'd make a woman feel seen… and stretched."

June chokes on her wine. I have no idea what kind of book club we've just entered, but I'm rolling with it.

Loretta plucks out a slip and squints. "No great Betas in town."

A few of the ladies make sympathetic noises, then all turn to give June a pointed look.

"You know," Dolly says, shaking her head. "Alphas accept Betas too. It's not all Omegas and heat drama."

June snorts, swirling her drink. "Sure they do. Right after they win the lottery and grow wings."

The room erupts with knowing laughter.

Loretta pulls the final slip and pauses. Her gaze lifts, locking on me with a twinkle. "Ridge Colter."

The room falls quiet just long enough for every head to turn and glance my way.

I sit frozen, cheeks warming. June doesn't help, as she's already grinning at me.

Loretta fans herself with the paper. "Silent type. Brooding. The man reeks of demonic potential. I respect it."

"Maybe too much potential," someone mutters.

"Oh, no," Loretta says with a wink, "that's half the fun."

"All that auburn hair and those shoulders." Rita sighs, horns blinking in what might be Morse code.

"Plus he's got that whole damaged hero thing," Dolly adds, wings drooping sympathetically. "Nothing sexier than a man with scars and secrets."

My face is on fire. The whole town seems to know about his accident, though no one has told me specifics. What happened to him?

"I just… he seemed… I mean, I barely know him," I stammer.

June nudges me with her elbow, her expression gleeful.

"Sure you don't. That's why you picked him out of all the men in town."

"He'd make an excellent demon prince," Loretta declares with authority.

"Can we please talk about the actual book?" I beg, desperately needing to change the subject before I spontaneously combust.

"Of course!" Loretta settles deeper into her throne. "Let's discuss the themes. Who wants to start?"

Dolly raises her hand, wings catching on the lamp beside her. "The power dynamics are fascinating. Here's a demon who could destroy her with a thought, but he's bound by ancient laws to only take what's freely given—"

"Speaking of power dynamics," Karen interrupts, leaning forward conspiratorially, "did anyone else see Mayor Buchanan coming out of the high school at ten p.m. last Thursday?"

Rita gasps, hands flying to her chest. "The drama teacher's car was still there!"

"That man needs to be more careful," Loretta says, shaking her head. "His wife has a cousin who's a private investigator in Billings."

"Wait, are we talking about the book or—" I try.

"I'm not sure," June adds, then looks surprised at herself.

Loretta waves a ring-laden hand. "Literature is life, life is literature. We discuss both. Very philosophical. But while on the topic, June, when are you going to let me set you up with Marcus from the feed store? He's a Beta, you're a Beta, it's perfect!"

June's cheeks pink prettily, and she fidgets with her bag strap. "I'm focused on my career right now."

"Career schmeer." Dolly waves dismissively, nearly knocking over her wine with a wing. "That boy has been making moon eyes at you for months. I saw him nearly walk into a door while watching you at the farmers' market."

June laughs, but I catch something flickering in her expression. "Shouldn't we actually discuss chapter eight? That's why we're here, right?"

"Chapter eight!" Loretta claps. "Yes! The tail scene. Now, who wants to share their interpretation of the deeper meaning behind the demon's use of his tail as a method of seduction and penetration?"

The conversation miraculously goes longer than fifteen minutes about the book.

"Wine break!" Loretta announces loudly. "Let's refill before we dive deeper into demon anatomy."

During the break for snacks—devil's food cake and hell cookies that are just regular snickerdoodles with red food coloring—I notice June pulling out a serious-looking camera from her bag. She's snapping close-ups of the food, of the decorated room.

"That's quite the equipment," I say, admiring the professional-grade camera. "You into photography?"

"Hobby of mine," she says, checking the battery. "I'm trying to put together a book about the town. Show people we're more than just some rural backward place. We have culture! Drama! Romance!"

She glances around to make sure the others are distracted and not near us, then clicks through photos on the camera's display.

"Look at this," she whispers, angling the screen toward me.

I'm expecting something funny, maybe Earl organizing his screws or the mayor sneaking around, as they all seem obsessed with this. Instead, I'm staring at a beautifully composed photo of a couple beneath a tree. They're wrapped in each other's arms, faces close, the golden-hour lighting making everything look like a movie still. The inti-macy of it makes my chest tight.

"Gorgeous and perfect lighting," I say carefully, not sure why she's showing me this.

June snorts. "Forget the lighting. See him? That's Bryce Waverly. His family owns the second-biggest ranch in the valley. And her? That's Iris, adopted daughter of the Castillo ranch foreman."

"And this is significant because...?"

"Because Bryce has been promised to Anastasia Hensley since they were in diapers. Their marriage is supposed to unite the two most powerful Alpha-led ranch families in town. The Hensleys basically founded this place, and the Waverlys own half the valley. Meanwhile, Iris is... well, nobody expected her. She came to town as someone's girl-friend, got a job at the Castillo ranch, and stayed."

"Do they know you took this?"

June shakes her head, looking troubled. "I was trying to get a shot of the old oak tree for my book, and they just... appeared. Started kissing like the world was ending. What do I do with it?"

"What do you mean?"

"Do I tell them I have it? Warn them they're not being as discreet as they think? Or do I delete it and pretend I never saw anything?"

I study the photo again. The way they're holding each other speaks of desperation, of stolen moments. "Delete it," I say finally.

"You think?"

"You want to start a war between the families? This is their secret. Their choice."

June sighs. "Yeah, but wouldn't you want to know if someone had evidence of your secret relationship? So you could be more careful?"

Now it's my turn to sigh. "I guess."

"Ladies!" Loretta's voice cuts through our whispered conversation. "We're starting again! So glad to have fresh blood here. New perspectives are always welcome!"

June quickly shuts off the camera and tucks it away, and we settle back in for round two of the most chaotic book club I've ever experienced.

The rest of the evening passes in a blur of increasingly wild discussions, more wine than is probably wise, and laughter that makes my sides ache. These women have thoughts about demon anatomy, the implications of soul-claiming through orgasm, and whether the heroine should have just given in by chapter three to save everyone time.

"I mean, seven orgasms to claim her soul?" Karen says, adjusting her boa for the hundredth time. "That seems like a pretty good deal. My first husband couldn't even manage one most nights."

"That's why he's your ex," Dolly points out.

I nearly spit out my wine from laughing.

By the time we finally leave, it's nearly eleven and Front Street is quiet except for the occasional passing truck. June and I stand outside the bookshop, me slightly giggly from wine and the absurdity of the evening. She stuck to water most of the night, clearly the smarter one.

"That was..." I search for words.

"Insane? Ridiculous? The best night ever!" June supplies, linking our arms again.

"All of the above." I lean into her slightly, feeling wonderfully loose and happy. "Thank you for bringing me. I needed this."

"Hey, what are new friends for if not to drag you into demon-themed book discussions with the town's most colorful ladies?"

We stroll slowly toward where June parked. The stars are bright overhead, and I think about Ridge teaching me constellations, about Walker's kiss, about Cash's devious grin. About three cowboys sitting in a diner, watching over me from afar.

"You know," June says thoughtfully. "Those boys of yours might be onto something with the whole protective thing. Not that you need protecting, but... it's nice. Having people who care."

"Yeah," I agree softly. "It is."

By the time we reach her car, I'm still smiling. My cheeks hurt in the best way. I've laughed a lot with Meredith back in Chicago, and tonight reminded me of that easy kind of joy. But this feels different, too. Like something inside me unclenched. I wasn't overthinking or pretending or trying to hold it all together.

And here, in this small Montana town, I feel more like myself than I have in years.

"Same time next month?" June asks as she unlocks her car and we get in.

"Wouldn't miss it," I say and mean it. "What's the next book?"

"Something about a vampire motorcycle club. Loretta's already planning a leather theme."

"Of course she is."

We're both laughing as June drives me back to the ranch, windows down to let in the cool night air.

Tonight, I'm just a girl who made a friend, joined a ridiculous book club, and laughed until her face hurt.

For now, that's enough.

13

SOPHIA

June's taillights disappear down the ranch road, leaving me in the kind of darkness Chicago never achieves. I fumble with my keys, slightly unsteady on my feet. June had one glass of wine, responsible designated driver that she is. I, on the other hand, discovered that Loretta's book club pour is apparently measured in *yeses*.

"Mrow?" a familiar squeaky voice greets me from the shadows.

"Chonkarella!" I squint at the porch where three orange shapes wait like fuzzy sentinels. "And babies! Were you waiting long? I'm so sorry. Mommy was out discussing demon anatomy with the town ladies. Very educational."

The mama cat winds around my legs as I finally get the door open, nearly sending me sprawling. Her two kittens dart inside like they're being chased. Or maybe they just know dinner time when they see it.

"Yes, yes, I hear you," I tell them, flipping on lights and making my way to the kitchen. "Demanding little fluffballs, aren't you?"

I find two cans of tuna in the cupboard, the good stuff, apparently, not the bargain brand I usually buy. "Look at me, feeding you fancy tuna. You're already living better than I did in Chicago."

They attack the food. I make a mental note to ask Cookie about cat food tomorrow. Although, watching them eat with such enthusiasm is oddly satisfying.

I grab a bottle of water from the fridge, chugging half of it in an attempt to preempt tomorrow's wine headache. Before I shower off the evening's... everything... I need to update my blog. My followers have been begging for news, and boy, do I have news.

Laptop open, sitting cross-legged on my bed with three cats already claiming territory on my comforter, I start typing.

Confessions of a City Omega

Book Clubs, Barn Cats, and Bad Decisions

Dearest Diary,

Second night in Montana and your girl has already:

- Joined a book club
- Adopted three cats (or they adopted me—jury is still out)
- Discovered the ranch has a cat sanctuary (I'm in heaven)
- Made questionable life choices involving cowboys (I'm fanning myself)

But let's start with the important stuff: BOOK RECOM-MENDATION ALERT!

Infernal Temptation — a literary masterpiece about a woman who accidentally summons a demon prince while trying to bake. I haven't technically finished it yet (I'm savoring chapter eight like fine wine).

The ladies of the book club take their demon romance

VERY seriously. There were themed snacks. There were costumes. There was a cardboard cutout with hand-drawn abs. I've never felt more at home.

Speaking of home, meet my new fluffy overlord roommates:

I pull back from the laptop. "Okay, orange cheeseballs, photo time! Look cute for the internet!"

Chonkarella, of course, immediately turns her back to me. The kittens scatter like I've announced bath time.

"Really? You were all over me two seconds ago!" I chase one kitten around the coffee table, nearly tripping over my own feet. "Come back! I need content!"

Finally, I manage to catch all three near their empty food bowls, the one place they'll hold still. I email myself the photo and hop back onto my laptop, attaching the image, then I'm into my blog once more.

Meet Chonkarella (the CEO) and her two minions, whose names are TBD because I'm taking suggestions. Current front-runners are Chaos and Mayhem, for obvious reasons.

But let's talk about what you REALLY want to know: the cowboy situation.

Deep breath.

So... I may have gotten to know one of them a bit better. Maybe too much better? Like, definitely crossed some professional boundaries better.

Here's the thing—when a six-foot-three cowboy looks at you like you're water in the desert, maintains proper consent while pressed against you in a very small space, and kisses like he's trying to prove a point to God himself... what's a girl supposed to do? Say no? I'm only human! An

Omega human with WORKING HORMONES, thank you very much.

Am I ashamed? Should I be ashamed? Because mostly I'm just tingly and trying to figure out how to keep my damn head around three stupidly hot cowboys who smile like sin and talk like trouble.

(I'm kidding. Sort of. Okay, I'm not kidding at all. Judge me. I deserve it.)

You know what? Because right now, outside my window, I can see infinite stars. And there's this one cowboy who stands looking up at them like they hold all the answers. He's the mysterious one, all distant and brooding silence. People keep mentioning an accident that changed him, but nobody says what.

Is it wrong that I want to know? That I want to stand out there with him more and learn what else he sees in all that darkness and the constellations?

(Don't answer that. I already know I'm in trouble.)

Tomorrow's goal: Actually help around the ranch instead of just swooning at inappropriate moments. Wish me luck.

But more importantly, send name suggestions for these kittens.

City Omega out. (Still in the country. Still in denial about feelings. Still slightly wine-drunk.)

PS: If you're my mother reading this, I'm JOKING about the cowboy thing. Totally joking. Complete fiction.

PPS: If you're not my mother, I'm totally not joking. He tasted like heaven and promises. Send help.

I hit publish before I can second-guess myself. My followers are going to have a field day with this one. The comments will probably range from *Get it, girl* to *This is better than the demon book* to my personal favorite type: all-caps declarations of lust, feral emojis, and key-smash battle cries like SKDJSKDJSHD I'M ASCENDING.

The cats have arranged themselves on my bed again in a perfect orange gradient, Chonkarella in the middle, kittens flanking her like tiny bodyguards.

"You guys have the right idea," I tell them, finally heading for the shower. "Claim your space and don't apologize for it."

The hot water feels incredible, washing away the evening's wine and discussions of demon anatomy. But it can't wash away the memory of Walker's hands, his mouth, the way he devoured me in the dressing room.

Or the image of Ridge under the stars, searching for something in all that vast darkness.

Or Cash's easy smile hidden behind country-boy charm.

Three Alphas. One temporary Omega. What could possibly go wrong?

Everything, my brain supplies helpfully.

But as I fall into bed, surrounded by purring cats and the kind of quiet that only exists far from city lights, I can't bring myself to care about potential disasters.

Tomorrow I'll work on being sensible. Tonight, I'm just a city girl with a blog, three cats, and a kiss-bruised heart trying to figure out how three months suddenly feels like forever.

The last thing I think before sleep claims me is *I wonder what constellation Ridge was looking at tonight.* Then I'm gone...

The early sun paints everything golden as I stand in my doorway, coffee mug warming my hands, three orange shadows weaving between my legs. Montana mornings are nothing like they are in Chicago. Here, the air tastes clean and crisp. Birds sing conversations in the trees, and the barks of dogs come from somewhere in the distance.

Yet, I can't stop staring at the paddock that sits maybe thirty yards from my cottage. The other night it was lost in the darkness, but now it's very much visible. As is the shirtless cowboy currently working a horse inside it.

Cash.

Sweet merciful God.

He's wearing worn jeans that sit low on his hips, scuffed boots, and a black hat. That's it. The whole outfit. The sun turns his skin bronze, highlighting every ridge and valley of muscle as he moves with the horse, a beautiful paint with patches of white and chestnut that catch the light.

The horse is clearly green, still learning, tossing its head and moving sideways whenever Cash commands something new. But Cash just moves with it, patient and fluid, like they're dancing rather than fighting. His muscles flex with each movement, sweat already making his skin glisten despite the early hour.

I should go inside. I should definitely not stand here ogling him like some romance novel heroine.

Instead, I take another sip of coffee and lean against the doorframe, settling in for the show.

The way he moves is graceful and powerful. When the horse tries to buck, Cash rides it out like he's rocking in a chair, one hand on the reins, the other relaxed at his side. His abs contract with the movement, and I nearly drop my mug.

How long have I been standing here? Five minutes? Ten?

Time seems irrelevant when presented with this particular view.

"Okay, enough," I mutter to myself and the cats. "Get dressed and be a functional human being."

Chonkarella meows what sounds suspiciously like disagreement, but I force myself inside.

I dress in the clothes Walker bought me—comfortable jeans that actually fit properly, boots that don't pinch, and a T-shirt that hugs in all the right places without being too revealing. Looking in the mirror, I barely recognize myself. I look... like I belong here.

Dangerous thought.

I head out, determined to make myself useful, just as Cash exits the paddock and comes my way along a narrow path in the lawn. He's dusting his hat against his thighs in that unconscious way cowboys do, sending little puffs of dirt into the air. The movement draws my attention to said thighs and...

He glances my way and winks. Actually winks. Like he knows exactly what he's doing to my blood pressure.

"Morning, ma'am," he drawls, and I swear my knees consider giving out.

"I'm a ma'am now?" I call back, proud that my voice sounds steadier than my pulse.

"Would you prefer *little lady*? *Sugar pie*? *Darlin'* with a heart over the *i*?" His grin is pure evil.

I laugh despite myself. "Let's stick with *Sophia*."

He saunters closer, and it's definitely a saunter, all long-legged confidence. "That outfit suits you. Real well."

"Thanks," I manage, trying desperately not to let my gaze trail down his bare chest. I fail. Spectacularly.

God, he's only ten feet away now, and the man is basically a walking anatomy lesson. Muscles I didn't know had names are on full display, still glistening with perspiration from his workout. There's a dusting of hair across his chest that trails down to disappear into his jeans, and I need to look literally anywhere else before I combust.

"So, what's on for the day?" he asks, oblivious to my internal crisis. Seemingly.

"I want to help around the ranch," I say, forcing my eyes back to his face. His knowing, amused face. "Pull my weight, you know?"

He tilts his head, studying me for a moment, then slaps his hat back on. "All right, I accept the challenge."

I raise an eyebrow. "Didn't know helping out came with that much drama."

"Oh, sugar, everything's a challenge when you're involved." The way he says it makes heat pool low in my belly. "Can you ride a horse?"

"Does the carousel at Navy Pier count? Or those carnival pony rides?"

He laughs, a rich sound that makes my toes curl in my new boots. "Not really, but at least you're not scared. That's a start. Come with me."

I follow him toward another paddock, trying not to notice how his back muscles move as he walks. Failing at that too.

"We'll start you easy," he's saying. "Ranch this size, we use horses to check the property, bring in strays, help with the training school we run. You'd be perfect for that."

"Like horse-riding lessons?" I perk up at something I might actually be useful for.

"Yeah. Got a group of kids coming in this morning, actually."

We round the corner of a barn and emerge in a small arena set up with obstacles, two people already working with horses, and yes, a yellow school bus pulling up in the distance.

"You're not going to put on a shirt?" I ask, aiming for casual and missing by miles.

He chuckles, low and knowing. "Does it bother you?"

"No, why would it?" I shrug, but my face is burning, and we both know I'm lying.

"Good to know." He's definitely smirking now. "Wouldn't want to make you... uncomfortable."

The way he draws out that last word makes me think of other kinds of discomfort. The kind that involves needing a very cold shower.

"I'm fine," I lie.

"'Course you are." He leads me to where a horse stands in the shade, already saddled. "This is Junebug. Don't let the name fool you, as she's steady as they come."

Junebug is a pretty bay mare, smaller than the one he was working with earlier but still intimidating when I'm standing next to her. I reach out tentatively to pat her neck, and she turns to nuzzle my hand.

"She likes you," Cash observes. "Good sign. Now, put your left foot in the stirrup..."

He talks me through mounting, and I'm stupidly proud when I manage it on the first try, swinging up with only minimal awkwardness.

"Natural," he says, grabbing the lead rope at the bridle.

I settle my hands on the split reins, trying to look like I know what I'm doing.

"Let's see how you do moving."

He starts walking, leading Junebug and me down a path toward the open meadow. The motion is strange at first, a rolling gait that makes me grip the reins probably harder than necessary.

"Relax," Cash suggests without looking back. "She can feel if you're tense. Horses are like that—they read emotions better than most humans."

I try. I really do. But the view? Let's just say riding behind Cash was a mistake. Every shift of his muscles, every glint of sunlight on his skin, makes it harder to breathe. And don't even get me started on how his jeans ride low enough to tease things I have no business imagining this early in the morning.

My thighs are tense, my pulse is out of control, and I swear if this horse senses one more of my *emotions*, we're both going down.

The silence stretches. My skin is hot, and it's not from the weather. I need a distraction, fast, or I'm going to combust and take the horse with me.

"So... I hear you were at the diner last night," I say, blurting it out. "Funny how you three would go there and not even come say hi."

He chuckles. "We were there for dinner, not to get in your way. You think we'd stalk you?"

"Well..." I draw the word out, trying to sound innocent.

He shoots me a side glance, sin dancing in his eyes. "Uh-huh. Real subtle."

We ride in silence for a few more steps, the clink of tack and the soft thud of hooves the only sounds between us. The open range stretches out around us like a damn postcard, lush green fields kissed by wildflowers, golden hills rolling toward a backdrop of hazy blue mountains in the distance. It's breathtaking. Peaceful. Dangerous, too, in the way it makes me think I could maybe belong here.

Then I catch the flicker of a grin tugging at his mouth, sly, knowing, and I just feel that trouble is coming.

"Heard you had a fun time shopping with Walker," he says casually, like he's commenting on the weather.

My face flames instantly. "Oh my God, shut up. Please tell me he didn't tell you."

He turns fully now, walking backward with the confidence of someone who clearly owns every inch of this land. The motion makes his abs flex, and I nearly slip sideways in the saddle.

"Whoa there." He's beside me in an instant, steadying

me with hands on my waist. "Can't have you falling off on your first ride."

"I'm fine," I squeak, very aware of his hands still on me.

"Mm-hmm." He steps back but keeps those knowing eyes on me. "And cowboys don't kiss and tell, sugar. That's the code."

I narrow my eyes. "God, you're a good liar. Almost had me there. But he told you, didn't he?"

He shrugs and turns back around to lead Junebug again, and I'm pretty sure my face is the color of the tomatoes.

"Look," I say to his back, "sometimes people do things they shouldn't."

"So you regret it?" His voice is casual, but there's something curled beneath it. Something sharp.

"I didn't say that."

"Then what are you saying?" He stops again, turning just enough to catch me with those sharp blue eyes. "He's not your type? Or were you just curious?"

"What? No! I'm not—"

His grin curves, slow and wicked. "So you do want him. Was it a one-time thing? Or just a you-and-him thing?"

I narrow my eyes. "I'm not playing this game with you, Cash. I'm here for three months. That's it. No strings, no mess."

"Not even if the mess shows up anyway?" he says softly, like it's not just a question but a warning.

"What's that supposed to mean?"

He shrugs again like he didn't just drop a grenade. "Life's rarely tidy, sugar. Even when you try to keep it that way." And then he's walking again, leaving me tangled in a hundred new questions.

Is he talking about Walker? About the ranch? About all three of them watching me like they already decided I belong here?

"You're doing good with the walk," he calls over his shoulder. "Think you're ready for the next level?"

I eye him suspiciously. "I'm good right here, thanks."

That grin is back. All trouble and temptation. "C'mon. Trust me?"

"Cash, don't you—"

Too late. He lifts Junebug's reins over her head and hands them to me so I'm suddenly holding both sets. Then he swings up behind me like it's the most natural thing in the world, settling in against my back with all that shirtless chest pressed along my spine.

Oh. Oh, hell no. Or maybe... oh, hell yes.

His heat is searing through my T-shirt like it's made of tissue paper. His chin hovers near my shoulder, breath whispering across my neck. I've forgotten my name, my purpose, possibly how to breathe.

His arms come around me, reaching for the reins, and suddenly we're wrapped up in each other like this was always inevitable.

"We'll hold them together," he murmurs, his voice a low rumble that vibrates against my spine. "So you can feel my commands."

"Right," I croak. "Commands. Like I'm one of your animals that needs a collar."

I feel him smile against my shoulder. "We don't do collars here, sugar. But I could show you what it means to be claimed... if that's what you're into."

The words are soft, dangerous, and said straight into my ear like a secret too filthy for the daylight. My body goes molten. There's no denying that I'm wet. Right here. On a horse. With Cash molded to my back like sin itself. It's mortifying. It's criminal. And when he inhales deeply, chest expanding against me like he's trying to commit my scent to memory, I nearly come undone.

He hums low, gravel and heat. "You feel that?" His hand shifts just slightly on the reins. "That little hitch in your breath, that tight little tremble? That's what happens when an Omega meets an Alpha who knows exactly what she needs."

I swallow hard. "Geez, do you ever shut up?"

He chuckles. "Not when I've got this view." He shifts slightly behind me, just enough to make my whole body go rigid. "And this close."

I choke on my own breath. "We should—uh—probably head back."

He makes a soft clicking sound with his tongue. "If you insist."

And just like that, he takes the reins, turns the horse, and starts leading us back toward the barn, leaving me praying that no one notices the wreck I've become.

His laugh is all grit and gravel. "Hold on tight."

He clicks his tongue again, and Junebug surges forward, not walking anymore but bouncing into something faster, something that makes every part of me jolt against every part of him.

My heart leaps into my throat, fear squeezing me.

Cash's arms bracket mine, and there's no escaping the contact or my breasts brushing his forearms with every bounce, and I swear I hear his breath hitch.

"God, you're loving this, aren't you?" I mutter, not even sure if I'm accusing or confessing.

"You have no idea," he rasps, rougher now, his teasing edge traded for something darker. Needier.

I do my best to concentrate on staying upright instead of on the solid wall of bare muscle pressed against me... or how every little bounce creates friction in places that are already screaming *Mayday*.

"You're doing great," he says, all warmth and amusement. "Natural rider."

"If I die from this, I'm haunting you," I warn, bouncing about, air through my hair.

"There are worse ghosts to have." I hear the grin in his voice, that signature drawl curling every word. "But if you haunt my house, sugar, you'd better come ridin' in on a full moon with spurs and sass."

We finally reach the barn again. Cash swings down in one smooth, unfairly sexy motion, like he was born in a saddle. He ties Junebug to the fence and gives her a fond pat.

I attempt to dismount with the same confidence. *Attempt* being the key word. I get both legs over to one side, and then... gravity betrays me. My foot slips, my balance vanishes, and I'm plummeting toward the dirt like a very uncoordinated sack of potatoes.

Except I never hit the ground.

Strong arms catch me mid-fall, spin me in a dizzying arc, and suddenly I'm chest to chest with Cash again. His grip is firm, his heat unmistakable, and his breath brushes against my ear like a secret.

"I'm always here to catch you," he murmurs. "Don't forget that."

I blink up at him, heart hammering like a runaway horse. I don't know if he's talking about riding lessons or something much, much deeper.

Before I can figure it out, I pull away, cheeks burning hotter than the Montana sun. And that's when I spot Walker leaning against the barn, arms crossed, watching us with an unreadable look that shoots straight through me.

Images flash—his mouth between my thighs, the dark hunger in his eyes, the rough sound of my name when I came apart in his hands.

I tear my gaze away, pulse stuttering.

Next to me, Cash chuckles low. "Well, I'll be damned. That cowboy stare could start a brush fire."

I glance at him, mortified.

He grins, eyes dancing. "Don't look so guilty, sugar. Ain't no shame in gettin' a little saddle sore from one and weak in the knees for another."

"Stop talking," I groan.

"What? I'm just sayin', you're settin' off sparks all over this ranch. Might wanna giddy-up before someone else catches fire."

"Cash," I hiss, even as I'm trying not to laugh.

He winks, then tips his hat. "Don't worry, sugar. I've got my fire extinguisher ready."

God help me, I think I actually like this mess.

"Come on," he insists, breaking the charged moment with a grin. "Let me introduce you to the training team. They're always looking for help organizing events and getting the word out. Other ranches have riding schools, but we want ours to be *the* school."

Relief floods me. Yes. This. This I can handle. This doesn't involve riding double with a half-naked cowboy and rethinking my entire existence.

"Oh, so you want me to crush the competition and steal their clientele?" I smirk, slipping back into my comfort zone.

He laughs, loud and genuine. "Now we're talkin'. I knew there was a reason I liked you."

We walk toward what looks like an office annex built onto the barn. A yellow school bus has parked nearby, and the high-pitched squeals and excited chatter of kids float through the morning air. It feels fresh. Normal. A reminder that I might actually have something real to offer here, something besides being a complication with great legs.

This I'm good at.

But as we move, Cash's hand occasionally finds the small of my back, casual, warm, completely unhurried, and every time it happens, my heart stutters like a skipped track. He's not trying to claim me, not yet. Just guiding. Grounding.

Then, as we reach the barn door, he leans in, his breath warm against the shell of my ear.

"You walk like you don't know that every man in a hundred-mile radius is already watching," he murmurs, voice low and slow like molasses. "But I see it. And if you were mine, sugar... I wouldn't let you forget it for a second."

My breath catches. My knees might actually give out. There's an inferno flooding every inch of me. He says it like a promise. Like a threat. Like a fantasy I'm one wrong move from making real.

I tilt my head just enough to meet his gaze, heart pounding like it's trying to make a break for it. "You keep saying things like that, and someone is bound to fall for you."

His grin deepens. "Is that a promise?"

I lift my chin, forcing a smirk. "Oh, you think I'm talking about me?"

I brush past him toward the barn, tossing my hair back like it's nothing. "You're not my problem, cowboy."

But his grin only grows, like he sees straight through me.

I keep walking, pretending I'm brazen. Brave.

Inside, I'm anything but because my body is already choosing. Already craving. Already giving in. And it scares me that what I'm starting to feel reminds me a bit too much of my heat.

Not good when I'm supposed to leave in three months. When my life, my job, my friends, my entire identity, is hundreds of miles away.

The question now isn't whether something will break.

It's *who*.

And what pieces will be left behind when that happens.

14

SOPHIA

My laptop screen glows in the afternoon light as I stare at the email I've been drafting for twenty minutes. Thirty days' notice to my Chicago landlord. I need to do this. If I'm stuck here for three months to satisfy the will requirements, I can't afford to pay rent on an empty place. Not with the insurance deductible hanging over my head and my freelance income being what it is.

Dear Mr. Peterson,

This email serves as my thirty-day notice to vacate apartment 4B as of...

I calculate the dates. If I send this today, I'll need to have everything out by the end of next month. Most of the furniture came with the place, one of those *furnished* situations that cost extra but meant I didn't have to buy a couch or a bed. Just my clothes, some books, personal items. Manageable.

I fill in the date and sign it off, then hit Send before I can second-guess myself. Next, I pull up my messages with Meredith and start typing.

Me: *Hey, so I'm giving notice on my apartment. I can't afford to pay Chicago rent while living here. Going to move out, figure out what comes next after the 3 months. Might need your help if the landlord wants me out quickly and I can't get back in time.*

Meredith: *Girl, you know I'll help.*

Me: *Maybe we can do it together if I can get away for a weekend?*

Meredith: *Just tell me when. So... how's ranch life going?*

I pause, fingers hovering over the keyboard. How do I explain that this place is nothing like I expected? That I wake up looking forward to each day instead of dreading it? That I have constant butterflies in my stomach around the cowboys.

Me: *It's... different than I expected. And don't freak out, but I think I kind of like it here.*

Meredith: *I'm not surprised. Does it have anything to do with three hot cowboys? Been reading your blog... I NEED DETAILS!*

Me: *There may be some details to share.* *We need to have a proper phone call. Maybe tonight if you're free?*

Meredith: *Ugh, I have that stupid work event. The one where we pretend to like our clients?*

Me: *Oh right, the quarterly schmooze-fest.*

Meredith: *But tomorrow for sure. I want EVERY detail.*

Me: *Deal.*

A knock at my door interrupts me. I glance at the clock, six on the dot. Dinnertime at the ranch, and I'd been planning to bring a full plate back here and keep working on this social media campaign.

Me: *Someone's at the door, talk tomorrow! Good luck tonight.*

Meredith: *It's totally the cowboys, isn't it? GET, IT GIRL!*

I close my laptop with a laugh and head to the door, expecting maybe Cookie with a dinner reminder.

I'm not expecting Cash and Walker looking like they stepped out of a country lifestyle magazine.

They're both in crisp button-down shirts, the kind that

look like someone actually ironed them. Walker's is a deep forest green that makes his brown eyes look impossibly warm. Cash chose navy blue that sets off his perpetual tan and those sinful eyes. Clean blue jeans that fit just right, not the work-worn ones from this morning. Their good boots, polished to a shine. And, of course, their hats, not the everyday ones but what I'm learning are their *going out* hats.

"Well," I manage, gripping the doorframe because my knees have forgotten their job. "Don't you two clean up nice. What's the occasion? Hot date with some cattle?"

Walker's chuckle rumbles through the evening air.

"There's a rodeo about an hour out," Cash explains, and that grin of his should require a warning label. "Thought you might want to come with us."

"A rodeo?" I try not to sound as intrigued as I am. "Like, an actual rodeo with cowboys and horses and extremely dangerous activities?"

"That's the one," Walker confirms with that sexy deep voice. "They've got good food too. Best corn dogs in three counties."

"You're bribing me with carnival food?"

"Is it working?" Cash asks, leaning against my doorframe in a way that makes the simple pose look like art.

I glance between these two men who showed up at my door looking good enough to eat, inviting me to something that sounds both thrilling and terrifying. The smart thing would be to politely decline, finish my work, and eat alone.

"Maybe," I admit. "But this feels very..."

"What?" Walker prompts when I trail off.

"Formal? Like you're properly asking me out or something."

They exchange one of those looks, the ones where entire conversations happen in a glance. It's annoying and oddly endearing.

"Perhaps," Walker says slowly, watching my reaction, "it could be."

"If you wanted it to be," Cash adds, and there's something serious under his usual playfulness.

"Both of you?" The question slips out before I can stop it.

"Is that a problem?" Cash asks.

Yes, my brain supplies. Because I'm already confused enough about my feelings without adding official dates to the mix. Because dating multiple people might be normal but I've never done it. Because these aren't just any men—they're my scent matches, and that terrifies me.

"I don't... I mean..." I gesture vaguely at them, at myself, at the general situation. "Wouldn't that be complicated?"

"Everything worth doing usually is," Walker says simply.

The way they're studying me has my stomach fluttering and my resolution wavering.

"I should change," I say, easily giving in and glancing down at my leggings and oversized shirt. Three cats weave between my legs, meowing their opinions about the interruption to their evening routine. "Can't go to a rodeo looking like I've been hunched over a laptop half the day."

"We'll wait," they say together, and I flee before I do something ridiculous like invite them in while I change.

I race to my bedroom, cats trailing behind like fuzzy assistants, and tear through my new wardrobe. What does one wear to a rodeo? Jeans seem too casual after seeing them dressed up. Then I spot the dress Walker bought, hanging like a temptation. Navy with silver stitching that catches the light, hitting just above my knees, with spaghetti straps and a low neckline that's flirty without being scandalous.

I shimmy into it, the skirt part flowing, and I'm grateful again for June's insistence on getting me basic toiletries yesterday before dinner. My hair gets a quick brush until it falls in soft waves. Lip gloss that tastes like strawberries. A spritz of perfume that probably won't mask how nervous I am. My new boots complete the look.

When I check the mirror, I barely recognize myself. The girl looking back fits here, like this cowgirl aesthetic was hiding under my Chicago exterior all along, waiting for the right moment to emerge.

That thought should scare me more than it does.

I hurry back out, finding them leaning against Cash's truck. It's a massive black thing with chrome details and only a bench seat in front. No back seat. Which means...

"Where's Ridge?" I ask, trying not to think about the seating logistics. "Isn't he coming?"

Something passes over Walker's face, a tightness around his eyes. "Ridge doesn't do rodeos anymore."

"Oh." There's clearly more to that story, but the way Walker's jaw sets tells me now isn't the time to ask.

"He's fine," Cash assures me, but there's something careful in how he says it. "Come on, sugar. Let's show you some real Montana entertainment."

Walker opens the passenger door and helps me climb up. The dress rides up as I slide across the bench seat despite my attempts at grace, and I catch both of them noticing. The bench that looked reasonably sized from outside becomes impossibly small once we're all in. I'm sandwiched between them, my thigh pressed against Walker's solid warmth on my right, Cash's shoulder brushing mine on my left every time he moves.

Cash turns the key, and the engine rumbles to life. The radio comes on, some country station playing a song about back roads and summer nights. With the doors shut, their scents smother me in the enclosed space. Not subtle or ignorable, but overwhelming, making my head swim until I'm drowning in Alpha pheromones. I'm suddenly hot and breathing quickly.

"You okay there?" Cash glances at me as he shifts gears, speeding away from the ranch. "Looking a little flushed."

"Just warm," I manage, nudging Walker and gesturing for him to roll down the window a crack. The cool evening air helps, but not much when I'm pressed between two men who smell like everything my biology is programmed to want.

We drive in silence for a few minutes, the landscape rolling by outside. The sun is still up but starting its descent, painting everything golden. I watch fence posts blur past, trying to focus on anything besides the heat radiating from both sides.

"Never been to a rodeo," I say, needing conversation to distract me from how aware I am of every point of contact.

"You'll love it," Walker explains. "Though I bet it's pretty different from Chicago entertainment."

"Everything here is different from back home." The truck hits a pothole and I bounce, pressing harder against Walker. "Sorry."

"Don't be." His hand comes up to steady me, warm on my bare arm, and doesn't immediately let go.

"Cash takes the corners like he's racing," Walker explains, thumb brushing my skin in what might be an accident but feels deliberate.

"I drive with enthusiasm," Cash defends, taking the next turn at a speed that has me sliding the other direction. My hand lands on his thigh for balance, and I sense his muscles tense under my palm.

"Enthusiastically trying to kill us," I mutter, but I don't move my hand right away.

"Never had a complaint before." Cash grins, shifting gears in a way that flexes the muscles under my palm.

"That's because everyone's too terrified to speak," Walker says dryly.

We settle into easier conversation after that, but the

awareness never fades. Every bump in the road shifts us closer. Every turn has me leaning into one or the other. Cash's hand brushes my knee when he shifts gears. Walker's arm ends up along the back of the seat, not quite around me but close enough that I feel its warmth.

"So," I say as we pass a sign announcing the rodeo five miles ahead, "you two really went all out tonight. Ironed shirts and everything. Should I be impressed?"

"Cash even showered, and used soap," Walker says solemnly.

"Revolutionary," I agree. "What's next, using actual shampoo instead of a bar of soap on your hair?"

"Let's not get crazy," Cash protests. "Baby steps."

"Is that why you smell so good?" I ask before my brain can stop my mouth. "The soap upgrade?"

They both go still for a heartbeat.

"Do we smell good to you, sugar?" Cash's voice drops lower, teasing.

My face flames. "I mean... objectively. You smell like... clean. Clean is good."

"Clean," Walker repeats, and I can hear his smile. "That's what we smell like?"

"Stop fishing for compliments," I mutter, slouching lower in the seat, which only presses me more firmly between them.

"Can't help it," Cash says. "Not often that a pretty Omega notices how we smell."

"Pretty sure every Omega in three states notices how you smell," I correct. "I'm certain you are noticed everywhere you go."

"But we only care about one Omega's opinion," Walker says quietly, and I catch my breath.

Before I can figure out how to respond to that, we're pulling into the rodeo grounds, passing a huge sign with the words *Thunder Creek Arena*.

The parking area is a field converted to rows of vehicles, trucks as far as the eye can see. Some beat-up work trucks, others shiny and new. People mill between them, some tailgating from their truck beds.

"Wow," I breathe as Cash finds a spot. "This is like a pickup-truck convention."

"Welcome to a night out in Montana," Walker announces. "Trucks, horses, and delicious food."

"Don't forget the beer," Cash adds, cutting the engine. "Lots of beer."

They come around to help me down, and I'm very aware of my dress as Cash's hands span my waist. He lifts me like I weigh nothing, setting me gently on the ground but keeping his hands on me a beat longer than necessary.

"Ready for your first rodeo?" Walker asks, and something about how he says those words leaves my stomach burning up.

"That sounds like a line from a bad pickup attempt," I inform him.

"Is it working?" He grins, hand finding the small of my back to guide me through the crowd.

"Jury is still out."

They flank me as we make our way to the entrance, close enough that their heat engulfs me. The crowd is thick, filled with families and kids, groups of teenagers trying to look cool, older couples in matching Western shirts. But I notice the looks we get, specifically from women who track Cash and Walker with hungry eyes before landing on me with considerably less warmth.

One brunette in particular actually stops mid-conversation to stare.

"Friends of yours?" I ask sweetly.

"Just admirers," Cash says, steering me past them with a hand on my elbow. "Hazard of being devastatingly handsome."

I burst out laughing. "Your humility is inspiring."

"I'm very aware of my best qualities," he agrees.

Walker pays for us at the entrance, and we stroll into the arena. It's set up like a small stadium with metal bleachers forming a horseshoe around a dirt-covered oval. Gates at one end lead to what I assume are holding pens. Barriers line the arena edges, and everything smells like dirt and animals and fried food.

"This is incredible," I say, taking it all in, smiling at experiencing something new. "It's like stepping into a movie."

"Wait'll you see the actual events," Walker says, guiding me up the bleacher steps. His hand hovers near my waist, ready to steady me if I wobble in my boots.

We find seats about halfway up, a perfect view of the arena without being too close to the dust. The metal bench is narrow, keeping me pressed between them even here. Cash immediately volunteers to get food and drinks.

"Corn dogs?" he asks with a wink. "As promised?"

"And beer," Walker adds. "The large ones."

"On it." Cash bounds down the steps with energy that makes several women turn to watch.

Alone with Walker, I'm even more aware of his presence. He shifts to face me slightly, arm along the back of the bench, creating a private bubble in the crowded space.

"You really do look stunning," he murmurs with a voice low enough that only I can hear. His gaze tracks over me slowly, taking in the dress, the boots, the effort I made. "That dress..."

"You liked it when I tried it on," I remind him.

"It was perfect on you just as it is now." His fingers brush my bare shoulder, light as air. "Been thinking about you in it since yesterday."

"Just *in* it?" The flirty question escapes before I can stop it.

His eyes darken. "About you out of it too. Couldn't sleep

last night. Kept remembering how you felt, how you tasted…"

My breath catches hard in my throat.

"Tell me you thought about it too," he insists, voice low, leaning closer until the warmth of him is like a sun I shouldn't get too close to. "Tell me you remember how perfectly you fit against me."

"How could I forget?" I whisper, almost without meaning to.

"Good." His hand slides down my arm, fingers trailing heat and raising goose bumps in their wake. "Because I plan to make a lot more memories you can't forget."

"That's very confident of you."

"I know what I want, Sophia." The way he says my name wrecks me a little. Like it belongs to him now. "Question is, do you?"

I should pull back. I should rein this in before I dive so deep I forget which way is up. But instead, my body leans into his like it's not mine at all. Maybe it isn't around him. Being this close to Walker does something to me. It makes me feel braver, bolder. Like maybe I could be the kind of woman a man like him wants, strong and shameless and certain.

Before I can say anything crazy, movement in my peripheral vision saves me. Cash is heading our way, somehow balancing three beers, corn dogs, nachos, and what looks like fried Oreos like a one-man county fair.

"How are you carrying all that?" I ask, grateful for the interruption, and a little disappointed too.

"Talent," he states, grinning as he hands things off to us. "Plus I sweet-talked the girl at the stand into giving me a carrier box."

"Of course you did," Walker mutters, settling beside me again but not quite touching.

We dig into the food just as the announcer's voice

booms over the speakers, welcoming everyone to the weekly rodeo series. I bite into my corn dog—delicious, obviously—but it's not enough to distract me from the simmering heat still clinging to my skin.

And the way Walker keeps looking at me like I'm already his.

The gate clangs open, and the first bronc rider bursts into the arena like a cannonball with legs. The horse bucks wildly, twisting and snapping its body like it's trying to launch the cowboy into the stratosphere. The crowd erupts around us, and I jolt in my seat, pressed tighter between two very solid cowboys.

Walker leans in, voice low against my ear. "Eight seconds. That's all they need to stay on and not be disqualified. Only one hand is allowed to hold the rope. The other can't touch the horse or themselves."

"That sounds kind of doable," I murmur, but I'm already watching with rapt attention.

"Wait and see," Cash says beside me, close enough that his thigh brushes mine with every shift. I glance over. He's watching the ring, but I don't miss the little smirk tugging at his mouth.

The buzzer sounds just as the crowd shouts, "Eight!" and I realize I've been holding my breath.

"Holy shit," I breathe. "That was intense."

Walker grins. "That was a good one. Sometimes they don't even last three seconds."

I tear my eyes from the arena to find both men still close, Walker's arm still draped behind the back of my seat and Cash's knee resting firmly against mine. It should feel claustrophobic, but somehow it doesn't. Somehow it feels as though they're anchoring me like the three of us make up a closed circuit that hums when we're together.

We watch several more events—riding, barrel racing, roping—with the crowd whooping and cheering as riders fly through patterns or cling to chaos. I'm halfway through my beer, cheeks flushed from adrenaline and attention, when a shadow falls over us.

I glance up to see a blonde. Barbie-shaped. Walking like she owns the floor under her boots. Her eyes lock on Cash.

Jeans so tight I'm surprised she's breathing, and a top that's doing less work than my napkins. She leans over me like I'm not even here, letting her perfume, something aggressively floral, invade my space as she plants a hand on Cash's shoulder.

"Cash," she purrs. "Haven't seen you around lately."

"Brittany," he states politely, his smile thinner now. He doesn't move any closer. Doesn't even blink. But he doesn't back away either.

Meanwhile, Walker's fingers tap once against the back of my shoulder.

My jaw's already tight, my skin flushed, and I can practically feel the irritation fizzing beneath my ribs like shaken soda. Not jealous. Just... highly observant. Of everything. Like the way Brittany is practically climbing over me to get to Cash and blocking my view of the arena.

I shift slightly in my seat, resisting the urge to elbow her away, or at least hand her a map labeled *Personal Space, Learn It.*

She doesn't take the hint, because of course she doesn't. Instead, she leans in even closer, kneeling between us to get to him, whispering something against Cash's ear while her hand trails slowly down his arm like she's auditioning for a soap opera. Whatever she says earns a polite nod from him, but that's it.

"That's Brittany Carson," Walker murmurs against my ear, sounding way too entertained. "She's had a one-track mind about Cash since he moved into town. Real determined type. Like a dog with a bone."

"Persistent," I mutter, working hard to keep my voice

even. My now-empty beer cup creaks in protest from how tightly I'm gripping it.

"Easy there, killer," Walker says, nudging my side. "No one's stealing your man."

"He's not my man," I whisper and gain myself a sneer from Brittany. I already dislike her.

"Sure. So you're just strangling your beverage because hydration's a serious business?"

I glance down. My knuckles are white against the cup. Damn it. "Shut up."

He grins, thoroughly enjoying himself. "Just sayin', it's kinda hot. You getting all fire-eyed and bitey like that."

"I'm perfectly calm."

"Sure you are," he says, voice dipping low as he leans in again, breath warm against the shell of my ear. "And if I looked under that little dress, would *calm* be the word I'd find?"

I nearly choke on my beer. "Walker."

"You have no idea how hard it is not to stare at your legs." His voice is a rough whisper, meant for me and only me. "Or to imagine what they'd feel like wrapped around me."

The heat in his voice makes me reckless. Bold. Dangerous, even. And I want to make him squirm as much as I am.

"Probably doesn't help that I forgot to put on underwear."

He goes still. Stone still. "You what?"

I smirk. "Oops?"

"Sophia—"

"Guess you'll just have to keep wondering."

He shifts in his seat like it physically pains him, then leans back with a groan. "That's just mean. Are you serious?"

"I don't know," I say lightly, fluttering my lashes. "How serious is your reaction right now?"

He mutters under his breath, just loud enough for me to hear, "Jesus, I'm gonna wreck you."

The words punch low in my stomach and coil heat through my core like a lit fuse.

"And I'm about two seconds from dragging you back to the truck to check for myself," he adds.

"Better be quick, cowboy. I'm slippery."

His eyes flare, and I know I've won this round. He's suffering, and I feel spectacular about it.

That's when Brittany chooses to finally flounce off, hips swinging like she's in a country music video, flipping her hair in a full one-eighty that nearly smacks a passing toddler.

Cash shifts in his seat and glances over just in time to find me watching him like he's personally responsible for my unraveling.

"What?" he says, brows raised. "Why do you both look like I kicked your dog?"

"Just admiring your people skills," Walker says cheerfully. "Hell of a talent. But you missed out on something way more interesting."

I shoot him a warning look, instantly suspicious.

He ignores it. "Turns out our girl here forgot something kind of essential when she got dressed today."

"Walker." I say it low. Dangerous. But not nearly deadly enough, apparently.

Cash narrows his eyes, suddenly very focused. "Forgot what?"

Walker leans in even closer. "She's not wearing anything under that dress."

Cash's gaze snaps to me, slow and sharp. "Is that right?"

His hand starts to reach for the hem of my dress, fingers brushing close to my thigh.

I swat him away without hesitation. "Don't think so."

He chuckles, low and dark. "Can't blame a man for trying. But is it true?"

"I-I'm not—this is not up for public debate," I stammer, my entire body going thermonuclear.

Walker smirks. "Pretty bold, though, if it is true. Coming out in a crowd like this, nothing between you and that little sundress but fresh air and confidence."

"I call her bluff." Cash leans in, just enough to invade my space in that maddening way he does. "You jealous of Brittany because I didn't pay you attention or because she got to stand close and you didn't?"

"Neither," I lie with the strength of a thousand liars. "Why would I be jealous? There's nothing going on here."

"Oh?" Walker repeats with mock thoughtfulness. "That's funny. Because last I checked, we're scent-matched. All three of us."

"And don't forget," Cash adds, his smile going slow and wicked. "I still owe you a lesson in what it means to be claimed."

My brain exits stage left. My thighs press together on reflex. And still, my mouth, traitor that it is, fires back, "You two really need to learn the meaning of *boundaries*."

Walker laughs softly. "We're cowboys, darlin'. We never did take kindly to fences."

"Can we please watch the rodeo?" I plead.

"Whatever you desire, sugar," Cash agrees easily, but his hand finds my knee, thumb brushing the bare skin just above where my dress ends.

The next event is bull riding, and any thoughts about scent matches fly out of my head as I watch cowboys try to stay mounted on animals that look like they're made of pure muscle and rage. And I thought Brutus was terrifying.

"This is insane," I say as one rider gets thrown after only two seconds, barely rolling away before the bull's hooves hit where he'd landed. "Why would anyone do this?"

"Adrenaline," Walker says. "Glory. Money, if you're good enough."

"Ridge was the second-best bull rider in the country and close to taking the first spot," Cash adds quietly. "Could ride anything they put him on."

The mention of Ridge makes my chest tight. "I remember Belle telling me he was once a big rodeo star but had an accident?"

Walker nods. "Yeah. Bull riding. Three years ago."

We watch in silence as another rider explodes out of the chute, clinging to a beast three times his size. Now that I know Ridge used to ride those monsters, I see the whole thing differently. It's not just a sport anymore. It's a gamble with your life.

I picture Ridge in that ring. That quiet, brooding man I've seen with a whiskey glass and a thousand-yard stare, once flying out of a gate with nothing but grit and rope to keep him from being crushed. My throat tightens.

"He must have loved it," I say softly. "To be that good. To risk that much."

"It was his life," Cash confirms, eyes on the ring. "Everything to him. Making it to the pro circuit, ranked nationally... he was right there."

"Then one bad ride changed everything," Walker adds. "Six point nine seconds that went sideways."

My stomach twists. That's all it took to tear down a dream, to change the course of someone's entire life. I can't stop imagining Ridge getting thrown, hitting the dirt, not getting up right away. The panic. The pain. The silence that must've followed.

It makes sense now why he keeps to himself, why the rodeo is off-limits. Every second of this must feel like a memory that won't stop replaying.

"I should talk to him," I murmur. "When we get back."

"Maybe," Walker says, thoughtful. "Ridge is... complicated about it. Sometimes talking helps. Sometimes it just makes the ache louder."

We fall quiet again, watching the rest of the show. Calf roping. Team roping. More barrel racing. But my mind keeps circling back to Ridge, to what he lost, to how easily something you love can break you.

By the time the rodeo ends, floodlights drape the arena in stark shadows. The crowd starts to thin, people buzzing about their favorite rides.

"That was incredible," I blurt as we get up and start making our way toward the truck, the noise fading behind us. "Terrifying. But amazing."

"Glad you enjoyed it," Cash states, his palm settling on the small of my back like it belongs there. "Wasn't sure it'd be your kind of thing."

"I'm discovering I like a lot of things I didn't expect to," I admit, glancing between them.

They exchange one of those loaded looks again, and Walker grins. "That's good to know."

Back at the truck, we're inside in no time, and Cash is driving us home already. I'm pleasantly buzzed from the beer and the excitement, pressed between them in the truck's cab like I belong there. About halfway home, Cash pulls off at a scenic overlook sign we pass.

"Ice cream stop," he announces. "Can't have a proper date without dessert."

The ice cream shop looks like it hasn't been updated since the 1950s, all chrome and neon and checkered floors. The selection is impressive, though, with dozens of flavors in old-fashioned glass cases. And it's a drive-through.

"Rocky road," Cash orders.

"Vanilla with fudge," Walker adds.

I scan the options. "Mango," I decide out loud. "With rainbow sprinkles because I'm an adult who makes excellent choices."

"All in cones," Cash says and then pays.

With our cones in hand and slurping up the goodness, we are off again. But instead of heading home, Cash drives to another overlook, one where we're alone up here. The valley spreads below us like a painting with only the moonlight bringing it life.

"Stunning," I say, trying to eat my ice cream before it melts entirely in the warm evening air.

"Beautiful," Walker agrees. He's not looking at the scenery but at me.

"Cheesy," I inform him, fighting a smile.

"You like cheesy," Cash counters, licking his rocky road like it owes him something. It shouldn't be distracting. It really, really shouldn't.

"You know," he adds, "things have felt different since you showed up at the ranch."

"How so?"

"Lighter," Walker answers. "Like someone flipped the switch and everything stopped feeling so... gray."

"The hands noticed too," Cash says. "Said we've been walking around like we've caught something contagious."

"Lovestruck idiots," Walker corrects. "Cookie's exact words were *moon-eyed fools*."

"That's..." I pause, blinking down at my melting cone. "A lot. We barely know each other."

I watch them both devour and finish their ice cream in several bites, while I'm still licking mine.

"Know enough," Cash says without hesitation. "Know your laugh sticks in my head longer than it should. Know you walk around like you've belonged here all along. Know your scent wrecks me in ways I'm still not recovered from."

A drop of mango ice cream escapes down my knuckle. I lick it off quickly, cheeks flushed, only to realize both of them are watching me as if I just performed some sort of indecent ritual.

"Missed a spot," Walker notifies me. He catches my wrist, slow and gentle, and brings my hand to his mouth. His tongue traces a line from the base of my palm to the pad of my thumb, hot and unhurried.

My breath hitches so sharply I swear I stop existing for a second.

"You're dripping, sugar," Cash murmurs, voice low and too close.

I look down. A golden smear of mango has landed just above the neckline of my dress. Right over my heart.

"I'm a mess." I laugh, but the sound is nervous, breathy.

Walker's eyes darken. "Let us clean it up."

The way he says it has my pulse tripping over itself, my dress feeling thinner, the air heavier. I can't decide what's more dangerous—the suggestion in his voice or how badly I want to say yes.

I should say no. Should clean myself up with a napkin like a responsible adult. Instead, I find myself nodding.

Walker leans in first, pressing soft lips to my collarbone where some of the ice cream landed. His tongue follows, warm against my skin, and I gasp at the sensation. Cash mirrors him on the other side, and I'm caught between them, melting faster than the ice cream.

"You taste sweet," Cash murmurs against my throat.

"That's the ice cream," I manage, breath hitching.

"No," Walker disagrees, lips brushing my pulse point. "That's all you."

Another drop lands lower, just above the neckline of my dress. They both follow it, hands gently sliding the straps down my shoulders to access the spot. The cool evening air makes me shiver, or maybe that's the heat of their mouths.

Then Cash's hand slides up, cupping my jaw, turning my face toward him. There's a moment where the world narrows to the dark glint in his eyes, the faint rise and fall of his chest, and then his mouth claims mine. It's deep and consuming like it's been building between us since we met, all burning fire and possession. His lips are firm, tongue coaxing mine in a slow, devastating pace that has me melting in my seat.

He doesn't rush, but every second is intense, the kind that makes me forget where I am, who I am. When he finally pulls back, my breath spills out in shallow bursts, my lips tingling. He grins that sexy smile while sweeping a thumb over my lower lip, his gaze dropping there before flicking back to meet mine.

"Sweeter than any ice cream." He lowers himself to my neck, taking long strokes, joining Walker.

"We should stop," I whisper, then lick my dripping ice cream that is going everywhere.

"Are you sure?" Cash asks, pressing kisses along my shoulder.

"Because… because…" I lose my train of thought as Walker's teeth graze my collarbone. "I can't think when you do that."

"Good," they say in unison.

My ice cream is melting faster now, forgotten in my hand. A thick drop slides down the side of the cone, landing on the upper swell of my breast, slipping under the dress. Then another. The sound they both make is low and rough, less human, more instinct.

"Can we?" Walker asks, his fingers hovering near the neckline of my dress. His voice is tight, like he's holding himself together by a thread.

I nod, breathless, already trembling.

Their hands move in sync as they peel the top of my dress down inch by inch. The fabric slips over my shoulders and pools at my waist, leaving me bare to the evening air and the scorching heat of their gazes.

They both go completely still.

"Fuck me," Cash breathes, his voice pure grit. "You're unreal."

Walker's hand grazes the underside of one breast, thumb brushing gently, like he's trying to prove to himself that I'm real. "So soft," he murmurs. "So goddamn perfect."

Cash takes my other breast into his large palm, and at this stage, I don't know how I'm still breathing.

My nipples are already puckered from the chill and the sheer anticipation. I shiver under their attention. They're looking at me like they've uncovered something sacred and forbidden all at once.

Walker meets my gaze, a teasing smile tugging at the corner of his mouth. "Pink," he says approvingly. "I wondered."

"You wondered about my—" I start, then pause, eyes narrowing. "You talked about this?"

"Might've come up," Cash says, completely unrepentant.

Before I can respond, his mouth closes over one aching nipple. I gasp, body jerking at the sudden heat, and then Walker claims the other with equal hunger.

Their mouths are hot, wet, relentless. Tongues swirling. Teeth grazing just enough to make me cry out. They suck and tease, learning what makes me whimper and what makes my legs shake.

"God, look at her," Cash mutters, his voice hoarse with awe. "Fucking angel. And we've barely started."

I don't know where to put my hands, so I grab one of their shoulders with my free hand, nails digging in as the men devour me, worship me. Walker slides a hand around to the small of my back, holding me steady as I arch into them.

"You're shaking," he murmurs, pressing a kiss above my heart. "Still want this?"

"Yes," I breathe, not even hesitating.

Cash takes the forgotten ice cream cone from my hand,

the mango melt now sticky along his fingers. He catches a drop with his thumb and smears it on my nipple, then licks it clean, eyes locked on mine the whole time.

"Waste not..." Cash murmurs, voice thick with heat.

Instead of letting it drip, he presses the cold tip of the ice cream cone directly to one of my nipples, swirling it slowly, coating my breast. The shock of cold makes me cry out, spine arching, hips lifting like I can escape the sensation, but there's nowhere to go.

"Fuck, that's gorgeous," Walker breathes, and before I can recover, he takes the cone from Cash and does the same to the other side, coating my skin in sticky sweetness. My nipples pebble impossibly tight, a fresh shiver racking my entire body.

Then their mouths are on me.

Hot tongues chase the cold trails of ice cream. Their mouths are everywhere, sliding, tasting, groaning against me like I'm something decadent they've waited too long to have. I feel teeth nip gently at the undersides, lips wrap around each tight peak until I'm squirming, my hands fisting in their shirts.

They each grab a thigh to hold me still, and it only makes me feel more exposed, more owned. Their low growls vibrate against my skin as they feast on me like men starved.

"Sweetest fucking thing I've ever eaten," Cash groans against my breast.

Walker lifts his head for a breath, his lips slick. "You're gonna ruin us. And I'm not even sorry."

"Let us wreck you a little," Cash adds. "You're already halfway there."

I can't speak. I can barely breathe.

Fingers brush the undersides of my breasts, thumbs circle my nipples, and I'm gone, completely unraveling. Pressure builds, sharp and electric, crawling under my skin until it bursts.

My orgasm slams into me so fast I don't even get a warning. One second I'm melting under their mouths, and the next I'm arching between them, crying out like I've lost my damn mind. Everything tightens, shudders, then breaks open in the best possible way, heat and pressure exploding out in waves that won't stop.

It's too much. Too good. Too filthy. I definitely can't believe this is happening in a truck with melted ice cream running down my chest.

Their mouths don't stop. Cash is still sucking gently, teasing like he's got all the time in the world, and Walker brushes slow, soothing kisses across my skin.

I tremble between them, every inch of me hypersensitive, gasping.

By the time I come back to myself, I'm slumped between them, and someone, probably Cash, has eaten the rest of the damn ice cream. The cone is gone, but his grin says it wasn't wasted.

I don't even have the strength to roll my eyes. Not yet, anyway.

Cash pulls back slightly, gaze wide. "Did you just...?"

Walker huffs a stunned laugh, wiping a trail of melt from my skin with his knuckle. "Damn. That was just dessert."

I hide my face in my hands. "Oh my God, I can't believe that happened. From just... I'm so embarrassed."

"Don't be," Walker says, tugging my hands away gently. "You have no idea how beautiful you looked just now."

Cash touches my cheek, his thumb brushing beneath my eye like I might break. "You felt like fire in our arms. Every sound you made, every reaction, it was like watching the stars come out."

A nervous laugh slips out of me, unsteady. "You two are going to be the death of me."

They help me pull my dress back up. Their hands linger,

soft and reverent, but neither pushes. It's oddly tender, considering what just happened.

"We should probably get back," I manage once I'm decent again. "Before someone stumbles on this and we all end up on the county's gossip page."

"In a minute," Walker murmurs. He draws me into his side, strong and steady like he could shield me from the world. "Just let us hold you. You've earned a second to breathe."

I lean into them. Cash slides an arm around my waist from the other side, pressing a kiss to the top of my head like I'm something precious. It should be overwhelming, but all I feel is calm.

"My brain is fried," I admit quietly. "None of this makes sense, and yet it feels… safe. Which makes even less sense."

Cash pulls me in tighter. "You don't have to understand it tonight."

"I don't know what I'm doing," I say, eyes fixed on a distant spotlight. "This thing between us, I've never felt anything like it. It's fast. Intense. And it scares the hell out of me."

Walker's hand slides down my arm. "That makes all of us."

"I had only Nolan," I continue. "Thought he saw me. Made me feel like I mattered until one day I didn't. Like someone flipped a switch and I stopped being enough." My voice falters. "It broke something in me. And I'm still not sure I ever fixed it."

Walker shifts so I'm facing him. His voice is low but fierce. "He didn't break you. He just never deserved you in the first place."

I search his expression, half expecting pity. I don't find any. Just unwavering certainty.

"How do I know you won't do the same?" I ask. "Fall in

love for the version of me you think I am, then leave when it turns out I'm just... ordinary."

"You're not ordinary. You're our match," Cash says over my shoulder. "I've spent my whole damn life feeling like something was missing, and then you showed up and the world stopped spinning sideways."

Walker nods slowly. "I looked for years. Thought maybe it wasn't meant to happen for me. That I wasn't meant to have a scent match. But then you walked in, glaring at all of us, and suddenly everything made sense."

"It's a lot," I whisper. "The way you look at me. The way it all feels. It's too much, too fast."

Walker presses his forehead to mine. "Then we slow down. No pressure. Just time."

I nod, not because I'm sure, but because I want to believe him.

They don't push. Just stay close as I breathe through the chaos in my chest.

Eventually, we gather ourselves, and Cash starts to drive us home.

Walker holds my hand while Cash drives, his thumb brushing soft, absent-minded circles against my palm like he's memorizing every inch of me. The silence isn't awkward, yet it's full of everything we're still too raw to say out loud.

When we pull up to the guesthouse, they both get out and walk me to the door. I pause on the porch, not quite ready to let go of the quiet cocoon we've built around us tonight.

"Thank you," I say, voice low. "For tonight. For not pushing. For letting me fall apart and not making me feel broken."

"You're healing. There's a difference," Walker says without hesitation.

Cash nods beside him. "And we're not going anywhere. You set the pace; we'll match it."

They leave me with a kiss to each cheek, then one to my forehead so soft it steals my breath. I don't move until their footsteps fade back into the dark.

Inside, three cats launch a coordinated guilt-trip ambush.

"Okay, okay," I mutter, stepping out of my boots and grabbing their dinner. "I'm late. Sue me."

Chonkarella gives me a withering glare and headbutts the cabinet for emphasis.

I feed them on autopilot, my thoughts miles away, back in the truck, back in the arena, back with those two cowboys who look at me like I'm worth waiting for.

Two scent matches. Two men who hold space for me instead of trying to fill it. Two hearts wide open, even knowing mine is still covered in cracks.

And somewhere in the big house, a third cowboy nursing something deeper than physical scars. One who doesn't look at me like I'm a miracle, but like I'm a threat to the protective barriers he's built.

"Why is it that every time I make a plan, I immediately do the opposite?" I ask the cats.

One of the kittens meows like she's just as baffled. Chonkarella dives face-first into her food. The second kitten yawns.

"Tomorrow," I promise, though it feels weak even as I say it. "Tomorrow I'll be smart. I'll keep some distance, take it easier, and let myself deal with a scent match. I'll get a grip before I run away, terrified I'm rushing things."

But even as the words leave my mouth, I know I'm lying.

Because what I want isn't distance.

It's them.

All of them.

And that might be the bravest, or dumbest, thing I've ever admitted.

15

SOPHIA

Confessions of a City Omega

What They Don't Tell You in Omega Ed

Dearest Diary,

Being in close confines with ice cream and two cowboys can lead to a very happy ending.

There. I said it. Judge away.

God, I can't believe tonight. Every day I wake up promising myself I'll be rational, figure out what I actually need, keep some professional distance. And every day I somehow dig myself deeper into this sweet, complicated mess. Someone send a ladder. Or a shovel. At this point, I'm not sure which direction I'm trying to go.

Let's talk about something they definitely didn't cover in those clinical Omega education classes we all had to sit through in high school.

Remember how they said we'd *feel drawn* to compatible Alphas? That nice, sanitized phrase that made it sound like a gentle pull, like magnets on a refrigerator?

LIES. ALL LIES.

What they should have said was, "Your body will stage a full coup against your brain. You will lose any semblance of control you thought you had. Your perfectly reasonable life plans will go up in flames while your hormones dance on the ashes."

With my first Alpha? Never felt anything close to this. I thought I was broken, honestly. Thought maybe those textbooks were exaggerating or I was somehow defective. Turns out I just wasn't with the right Alpha.

Here's what they don't tell you about true compatibility:

The Scent Thing Is Real

And by "real," I mean overwhelming. It's not just "Oh, he smells nice." It's "I would follow that scent into traffic." Your Omega brain completely bypasses all logic and goes straight to MINE, MINE, MINE.

Your Body Becomes a Traitor

Thought you had control over your reactions? Adorable. Your body will do whatever it wants, whenever it wants. Blushing, trembling, other things we won't discuss in a public forum.

Distance Doesn't Help

You think you can just avoid them? Maintain professional boundaries? Your Omega instincts laugh at your cute attempts at self-preservation.

And tonight I discovered that ice cream can be a dangerous weapon in the wrong hands. Or the right hands. Depends on your perspective.

But here's the real lesson, my fellow Omegas: When you find yourself in a situation where your biology is screaming one thing and your brain is desperately trying to maintain some dignity, remember that it's okay to be scared. It's okay to want to run. It's okay to feel like you're losing yourself.

Because you're not losing yourself. You're just discovering parts you didn't know existed.

(That doesn't mean you should make major life decisions while under the influence of Alpha pheromones. Learn from my mistakes.)

To all my Omega Readers:

Those dealing with their own Alpha situations, you're not broken if you don't feel the pull. You're not weak if you do. And you're definitely not alone if you're currently hiding in a barn, googling, *How to maintain rational thought around scent matches.*

We're all just out here doing our best with biology that has its own agenda.

Tomorrow's goal: Actually stick to the plan. Work. Cats. No cowboys.

(Place your bets now on how long that lasts.)

City Omega out. (Still in the country. Still learning. Can't look at ice cream again without having feelings.)

16

RIDGE

The whiskey burns less than the knowledge that they were at the rodeo without me.

I sit on my usual stump, glass in hand, staring up at stars that used to mean something more than just a way to pass sleepless nights. The Big Dipper mocks me tonight, that bear forever circling the sky, never quite catching what it's after. Story of my fucking life.

They invited me. Of course they did. Cash with his grin, Walker with that way he asks without pushing. "Sure you don't want to come?" Like I'd suddenly decide that watching other men live my dream sounds like a good time.

Three years since I've set foot near a rodeo. Thought I'd buried the worst of it. Not the physical pain, a dull echo I've learned to ignore—that's just part of the job now. No, this ache is different. Has nothing to do with bulls or broken ribs.

It's knowing she was there.

Sophia.

Laughing in the stands, wide-eyed at the rides, probably gripping her drink with both hands and asking a hundred questions. And I wasn't the one beside her. Didn't get to see her first reaction. Didn't get to explain the rules or tease her about city-girl boots in arena dirt. That should've been me.

Goddamn, I'm losing my head over her.

Didn't I already promise myself I wouldn't? That I'd keep my distance? Let her find her way without dragging her into my mess?

And yet... that twist in my gut won't quit. Like I missed something important. Something I won't get back.

She deserves better than this. Better than me.

So why the hell do I want to be the one who shows her everything?

I take another sip, letting the heat of the drink distract me from darker thoughts.

That's when I hear the sound of footsteps on gravel, pulling me from my spiral. I don't turn, but I know who it is before she speaks. Something about the way she moves, lighter than the boys but determined.

I smirk as her silhouette comes into view, hair like copper fire, that dress fluttering around her knees.

"Lost your cat clan again?" I ask as she steps into view, moonlight catching the edge of her smile. She's fucking beautiful.

She gives a soft laugh, the kind that hits somewhere low in my gut. "Nope. They're currently starfishing across my bed like royalty. I've been demoted to the floor."

I smirk. "Sounds about right. Cats got a solid union going."

She stops a few feet away, wrapping her arms around herself like the night's chill just caught up to her. "You always sit out here alone?"

"Most nights." I nod toward the sky. "Good view. Quiet."

Her gaze lifts, scanning the stars. "Anything happening tonight? Cosmic fireworks? Star-born prophecies?"

I grunt a laugh. "Nah. Just the usual. Scorpius rising. Orion slacking off."

She grins, and something about the way she looks at me tightens my rib cage. Then she gestures to the spot next to me on the stump. "Mind if I join?"

I shift over without a word, making space. She hops up beside me, legs dangling, hands bracing behind her on the wood. Her knee presses lightly against mine, radiating heat I can feel through my jeans.

And I can't even smell her.

Damn broken senses. That part still guts me. Knowing I'll never get her scent the way Cash and Walker do.

"You all right?" she asks.

I glance at her. "Yeah."

She tilts her head, studying me. "You looked... far away for a second."

"Was just thinkin'," I say, keeping it vague. I don't need her knowing how close I am to losing it when she's near.

She swings her feet lightly, the motion brushing her leg against mine again. "The rodeo was amazing tonight. Terrifying too. Like, some of those riders? Insane."

I nod, biting back a smile. "Yeah. Gotta be a little crazy to climb onto the back of a pissed-off animal bred to throw you."

She glances at me for a long moment, then says, "Cash said you used to ride bulls, those giant monsters."

"Eight seconds at a time, or at least I tried," I answer, and there's a flicker of pride there. Still is. "They say you're not a real cowboy 'til you've eaten dirt with a mouthful of regret."

Her brows rise. "Were you scared?"

I glance at her, then back at the stars. "Not at first. When I was young and stupid. It was a rush. Power. Crowd screaming. Felt untouchable."

"Cash and Walker told me... what happened. About the accident. And that's why you didn't come with us to the rodeo."

The words hang between us, quiet but loaded.

I don't look at her. Just track a slow-moving star across the sky and take a sip of whiskey.

"It wasn't the rodeo," I say finally. "That's not what got to me."

She waits, giving me space.

"It was knowing you were there," I add, the words barely audible. "And I wasn't."

Her brow furrows slightly. "Why does that matter?"

I shake my head, half a laugh escaping. "Forget it."

"No," she says, voice gentle. "I want to understand."

I risk a glance at her. Moonlight hits her cheek, that soft, open expression. She's not pushing. Just... asking. Curious and kind in a way I'm not used to.

But there are some things I'm not ready to lay bare. Not yet.

"Maybe some things are better left in the past," I murmur. "Doesn't mean I want to talk about them."

Her face falls a little, and I instantly hate myself for putting that look there.

"I'm not trying to pry," she says. "I just, when I heard, I felt like an idiot for enjoying the night so much while you were—"

"Don't." My voice comes out rough. "You didn't do anything wrong."

Silence stretches between us again. Her fingers shift slightly on the wood beside mine, not quite touching, but not quite pulling away either.

"I'm sorry," she says again, softer now. "For whatever that night meant for you. And for bringing it up."

I nod, eyes back on the sky. "Not your fault."

She leans in a little, like she's testing the weight of what we are. What we're not.

"You don't have to talk," she whispers. "But if you ever want to, I'll listen. No questions. No pressure."

My throat tightens. I don't answer, just let the silence settle again. Let her words echo somewhere in the parts of me I keep closed off.

Eventually, she shifts her weight, and her shoulder brushes mine—light, warm, grounding.

We sit like that for a while. No more talking. Just stars. Just stillness.

And the quiet ache of wanting something I don't know how to hold.

I move slightly, the memory I hate crawling back in detail. But I don't look away.

"Bull was called Diesel Rage. Rode him before. Thought I knew his patterns, but I lost focus, my own fucking fault. Just for a second. Doesn't matter now." I shrug and stare into the shadows around us.

Her hand brushes against mine on the stump. Barely a touch. But it grounds me enough to keep going.

"He felt me lose my focus and balance for that split second. Next thing, I went airborne. Landed headfirst into the rail. Hip's been off ever since. Docs said I was lucky I didn't break my damn spine."

Her breath catches. "Jesus, Ridge."

"I used to measure my worth by what I could do on a bull," I say, voice gravel-thick. "Eight seconds. Crowd screaming. All eyes on me. That was my whole world."

She doesn't interrupt, just listens, her body quiet beside mine.

"After the fall," I continue, slower now, "I had to learn how to be a man off one. Off the adrenaline. Off the dream. Without the noise and the spotlight. And I also lost my damn sense of smell in the accident."

That last part strikes harder than I want it to. I didn't mean to say it out loud. But there it is, raw and unvarnished, hanging in the dark like a bruise.

Sophia shifts closer, and this time the contact is full, her thigh brushing mine, the press of her shoulder warm and grounding. Then, without hesitation, her hand finds mine. Fingers lace like it's the easiest thing in the world.

"You don't smell me," she says softly. Not a question. Just the truth.

I nod once. "Inner ear got wrecked. Skull fracture did the rest. Docs said it was a miracle I didn't lose more."

She hesitates. "Do you... feel anything now? Around Omegas? Around... me?"

Her voice dips on the last word like she's not sure she should ask. Like she's already half regretting it.

I don't look at her right away, just keep my gaze on the horizon. Stars flicker across the sky, quiet and distant. I wish I could smell her. Wish I could say yes with certainty. But I can't lie about what I've lost.

"Not scent," I admit. "But... that's not the whole story."

She turns, her body angled toward me now. "What do you mean?"

"I mean I may not pick up on instinct," I say slowly, "but I'm not exactly unaffected either."

She blinks. "So you do feel... something?"

"Plenty of things," I say, finally looking at her. "Just not in the way an Omega like you deserves."

Her brow pinches slightly. "You don't think I get to decide that for myself?"

"I think you should have the full picture," I state. "That's all. No scent, no bond. Not in the way you'd get with Cash or Walker. And maybe that's fine right now. But down the line?"

She doesn't answer right away. Just watches me, lips pressed tight like she's weighing every possible reply.

"I'm not even sure what I want tomorrow," she says eventually. "Let alone down the line."

"Fair enough."

Silence stretches between us.

"You said you still feel things. What kind?" she murmurs.

I huff a quiet breath. "Things that make it real damn hard to sit this close to you and pretend I'm unaffected."

She gives a small smile at that, then glances down at our hands.

"Guess that makes two of us," she whispers.

My jaw tightens, but I don't pull away. "Probably not the smartest idea."

"No," she agrees. "But it doesn't stop me from thinking about it."

We fall quiet again, but it's a different kind of silence now. Not avoidance. Just... charged, like the air before a summer storm.

She tips her head, studying me. "You really don't smell anything? Not even a hint?"

"Nothing," I say, rubbing the back of my neck. "It's like... radio static. I know there's supposed to be something, but all I get is fuzz."

She glances over, watching me closely.

"But you?" I let out a slow breath. "You're not static. You're loud. Sharp. The kind of noise that keeps a man up at night."

Her lips twitch. "Loud, huh?"

I nudge her boot with mine. "Not always a bad thing. Just means I walk into rooms and miss the smell of burned coffee or food but somehow still notice when you're near. Go figure."

She laughs, warm and unguarded, and it settles something in my chest.

We fall into silence again. Not awkward, but just full. The kind of quiet that hangs heavily between two people carrying more than they say.

She hasn't pulled away from me. Hasn't made an excuse to leave. That surprises me more than it should. Most people look at me too long and decide they've seen enough. But not her. She's still here. Still warm at my side. Still leaning in like maybe I'm worth staying for.

She clears her throat softly. "My ex did the same to me," she says. "Different circumstances, but same result. Ripped my life away without my say."

I don't respond. Just wait. Sometimes silence does more than words ever could.

"I was forced into a match with him. Family arrangement. He wasn't my scent match, but our families thought we were perfect on paper. Good for business, good for bloodlines." Her voice goes bitter. "My family kept blaming me for not making him happy. Kept saying I wasn't trying hard enough, wasn't Omega enough."

"Sounds like they were assholes."

She huffs a dry laugh, but there's no humor in it. "I really thought at first it would just take some time, as he was kind initially. Then, after several months together, I was convinced he'd reject me officially. Let me go. Instead, he kept me around to save face. To the world, we were the perfect couple. Behind closed doors? I was a ghost. He barely spoke to me, didn't touch me after the first few times. I was just... there. Existing but not living."

My jaw tightens. Something cold and angry rises in my chest, sharp enough to make my fingers twitch. Knowing the bastard is already in the ground doesn't make it easier. Doesn't stop the anger from curling in my gut. Can't hurt him now, but that doesn't kill the urge. She doesn't need revenge, though. She needs someone who actually sees her. Someone who stays.

"Fuck." The word slips out anyway, low and guttural.

"Sometimes I wonder why he left me this ranch in his will. Was it some twisted final gesture? Or did he set it up when we first got together and just forgot to change it?" She turns her face into my shoulder. "Probably the latter. I was always forgettable to him."

I set my glass down on the ground and shift, tugging her closer to me. Her body molds against my side, soft and heartbreakingly real, and I wrap my arms around her before the fury gets the better of me.

"He was a fucking idiot," I murmur. "Had no idea how lucky he was to have you."

She sinks into the embrace, and for a second, everything else disappears. Just the two of us and the night, and the pieces of our pasts we're finally letting someone else see.

My body notices every inch of her pressed against me. How could it not? But I shut it down. This isn't about wanting her. Not right now. This is about her needing someone to prove she's not invisible.

After a long moment, I point to a patch of stars just above the tree line. "You know what constellation that is?"

Her head lifts slightly. "Which one?"

"Andromeda," I say, lifting my hand to trace the pattern in the sky. "See those four stars in a curved line there? That's her torso. The ones branching out mark her arms, chained to the rock. The rest trails off toward Pegasus."

She squints up at the night sky, following the lines I draw in the air. "Huh. I wouldn't have guessed those looked like a woman chained to a rock."

"Most people don't." I glance at her, then back at the stars. "But the story sticks."

She settles closer, cheek brushing my chest again. "What's that?"

I let out a slow breath. "Andromeda was a princess. Her mother bragged that she was more beautiful than the sea nymphs. Gods didn't like that. So they punished the whole kingdom by sending a sea monster to wreck everything. To stop it, her parents chained her to a rock as a sacrifice."

She exhales. "Cheerful."

"Wait for it." I rest my chin lightly on top of her head. "Perseus saw her there. Chained. Alone. And he didn't keep walking. He fought the monster, freed her, and made her his queen."

Silence lingers between us, heavy and quiet. I stare at the stars, but I feel her watching me.

"Sometimes," I add, voice lower now, "we have to be chained to the rock before we find what we're really meant for. Until we find that answer or... person."

She pulls back slowly, and when our gazes meet, her expression is softer than I've ever seen it. In the moonlight, her eyes are vivid green.

"You shouldn't hide that romantic streak under all that brooding," she says, almost a whisper. "You're an amazing guy, Ridge. So easy to talk to and..."

Her gaze flicks down to my mouth. Lingers.

For a second, I think she's going to close the space between us. My heart stumbles. Every instinct says to lean in, to taste her, to take just one moment for myself.

But she looks away. The space stretches out again, and the moment is gone.

Of course.

Why would she want the broken one when she already has two perfect matches?

Without scent, sure, we could be together. Plenty of couples make it work. But what if that's not what she wants after her first Alpha wasn't a scent match? And that turned out fucked up.

And I'd always know it.

I turn to stare at her again, heart thundering against my ribs. That's when a growl slices through the quiet, low and close enough to twist something cold in my gut.

Sophia startles, but before she can speak again, I'm already moving. I shove her gently behind me, body snapping to attention, instincts taking over.

"What was that?" Her voice is tight, barely more than a breath.

"Coyotes, I think," I say, scanning the dark tree line. "Or wolves." My attention catches the shift of movement slinking low in the shadows not too far to our left. Close. Too close.

She presses into my back, her hands gripping the fabric of my shirt like she needs something solid to hold on to. Fuck, I love that. That she trusts me to protect her. That she seeks me out when it counts.

"We need to move. Stay close," I mutter, bending to grab a thick fallen branch, long as a bat, dense and weighty in my grip. I take her hand with my free one and start toward the house to our right, keeping her tucked into my side, shielding her with my body.

"Shit," she breathes. "It's moving again."

"Yeah," I say, the branch gripped tightly in my hand. "Stay behind me. Eyes on the guesthouse."

"Do they usually come this close to the house?"

"Not unless they're hungry," I mutter. "Real hungry."

Her breath catches. I don't need to see her face to know she's scared. I can feel it in the way she clings to me, the way her steps falter.

Two shapes peel out of the shadows. Lean, ragged coyotes, eyes catching the moonlight like glass. Hungry. Starving. Unpredictable.

"Don't run," I say low, firm. "Whatever you do, stay behind me."

She nods, her fingers locking around mine. Her pulse thumps through that one point of contact. Hell, maybe mine is just as fast.

I stop walking and slam the stick hard against the ground. The sound echoes like a gunshot in the stillness. "Back off!" I bark. "Go on!"

They flinch but don't bolt. Just prowl lower. Closer. Eyes never leaving us.

"Ridge…" she whispers, pressing even tighter against my side now. I feel her body tremble, and something raw, something ancient, rises up inside me. A possessive fury that coils tight in my chest. Mine.

"Almost there," I grit. Ten more feet. Just ten.

Then the larger one lunges.

"Go!" I bark, shoving Sophia toward the steps. "Get inside, now!"

She stumbles but doesn't argue, racing up the porch. I hear the door creak as she grabs it.

I pivot, swinging the branch wide in a warning arc just as the animal closes the distance. I don't want to hurt it. I really don't. But I won't let it get near her. I plant my boots and bare my teeth right back at the fucker.

"Not tonight," I snarl. "Not her."

The smaller one tries to dart past me. I block it with a hard sweep, slamming the stick into the dirt right in front of its path. The thud vibrates all the way up to my shoulders, but the coyote gets the point.

Both animals hesitate, whining low.

"That's right," I growl. "Nothing here for you. Move the fuck on."

They retreat slowly, shadows slipping back into the tree line. I wait until I can't see their eyes anymore before I turn.

Sophia's standing in the doorway, hand clutching the doorknob, chest rising and falling like she just ran a mile. Her eyes meet mine, wide, wild, and then she's flying down the steps.

Straight into my arms.

I catch her without hesitation. She buries her face in my chest, clinging to me, and I feel the last of the adrenaline burn off like smoke in the air.

"You okay?" I murmur into her hair.

She nods, but her voice wobbles. "You didn't even hesitate."

"I wasn't about to let them get near you."

"You were..." She pulls back just enough to look at me, her eyes searching mine as I walk us onto the porch. "That was the manliest thing I've ever seen."

My lips twitch, but I'm still riding the edge of that protective high. I cup her jaw gently. "Are you okay?"

She nods, staring up at me.

I hold her against me like she's mine.

Because for those few terrifying minutes, she was.

And I'm not sure I ever want to let her go.

I carry her the whole way back into the guesthouse, arms tight around her, like putting her down too soon might invite those coyotes to try again. She doesn't argue. Just leans into me, her cheek against my chest, warm breath feathering through my shirt.

I kick the door shut behind us, and only then does she squirm gently. "You can put me down now," she mumbles, clearly flustered.

I do, slowly and carefully, trying not to think about the softness of her against me. But it's already burned into my skin. The feel of her breasts pressed close. The way her breath caught when I lifted her. The quiet tremor I wasn't supposed to notice.

She flicks on the hall light, brushing back her hair, and starts toward the living room. I follow, more out of instinct than invitation. It's been months since I've set foot inside the guesthouse. Since it was just a quiet shell for temporary stays.

But now?

Now it looks like someone lives here.

Her boots are kicked under the side table, jacket tossed over a chair. A mug with the words "I Do What I Want" sits beside an open book, bookmark wedged in at an angle. The barn cats trail her like ducklings, meowing their complaints. She hums under her breath—off-key, relaxed. Like this place belongs to her now.

And hell, maybe it does.

I pause as I pass the library nook, something drawing my eye.

She'd just stepped in to grab something, but it's what she's built in there that stops me cold.

The hanging chair is nestled in the corner, but it's not empty. Blankets piled high, pillows arranged with care, a perfect dip in the center like a hollowed-out nest. Two side tables dragged close, one with water bottles and tissues, the other with snacks and books stacked high. A battery-powered lantern glows a soft amber in the corner, casting everything in a warm, golden hush.

Textbook nesting.

She turns and catches me looking. "What?" she asks, feigning casualness. "It's just cozy."

I cock a brow. "It's a nest."

Her blush is immediate. "It's not. I just like being comfortable. And the cats like the blankets."

"Mm-hmm." I lean against the doorway, trying not to grin. "They teach you to lie that badly in the city?"

She huffs, marching over to retrieve her laptop. "Do you want a drink, or are you just here to judge my interior decorating? I've got water, juice, maybe coffee."

I don't answer. I'm still staring at the space she's carved out, instinctively or not. My chest tightens.

Her heat is coming. Probably sooner than she realizes. And that knowledge settles like a hot brand in my gut.

Because it won't be me she turns to when it happens.

"I'm serious," I say finally. "You're nesting, Sophia."

"I'm not," she insists again, but softer this time. Less sure. She marches into the living room, fluffy cats on her heels.

I push away from the doorway, shaking my head, joining the trail. "You don't have to pretend. I get it."

She flops down onto a couch, and something flickers in her expression. She watches me for a moment, then sets her laptop down and leans on the edge of the couch's arm, bare feet tucked under her, hair falling loose over one shoulder.

No words exchanged.

That damn nest flashes in my mind. A cozy, perfect mess of comfort and instinct. No matter how many times she denies it, the truth is right there in front of me. Her body knows what's coming. She's preparing.

Not that anything I say will change her mind tonight. She's stubborn as hell. I admire that about her, just not when it's working against me.

But it's not my place, is it?

"You gonna join me?" she asks suddenly, chin tilted with a hint of challenge. "Or are you going to keep lurking in the doorway like some cowboy-shaped shadow?"

A smile pulls at the corner of my mouth, helpless and unwanted. "I should let you rest," I say, voice lower than it should be. "You've had a long night."

She arches a brow but doesn't argue.

I take a step back. Then another.

And still, it guts me to leave.

I'm fooling myself, thinking I can keep this distance. Thinking I can watch her build a life here, watch her nest, watch her laugh, watch her turn to someone else when the fire hits, and just smile through it.

But what choice do I have?

She deserves the absolute best. A match who can scent her needs before she speaks them. One who can anchor her in the storm she doesn't even realize is coming. Not someone who's already broken. Who won't ever be able to offer her that bond.

Even if I want to. More than I've ever wanted anything.

"Night, Sophia."

I leave her there on the couch in a tangle of cats, a little uncertain and a little beautiful and absolutely not mine.

And still, I'd fight the world to keep her safe.

As I step off her porch and the door clicks shut behind me, I realize something strange—my hip doesn't ache. Not the usual tight pull in my joints, not the dull throb that follows me like a shadow. It's just... gone. Like I'm walking on air instead of scar tissue. I pause at the edge of the path, glancing back toward her window, the soft light glowing inside. I woke up this morning the same way—no pain, no stiffness. Just a calmness in my body I hadn't felt in three years.

The orgasm rips through me before I'm even fully awake, my hips grinding against the mattress as waves of pleasure crash over me. My fingers clutch the sheets, back arching while I ride out something so intense my vision goes white at the edges.

"Oh, fuck. Oh, fuck," I gasp into my pillow, thighs clenching around nothing while my body spasms. The dream is still there, fragments of it... Walker's mouth between my legs, Cash's hands on my breasts, Ridge whispering filthy things in my ear while they take me apart piece by piece.

When the aftershocks finally stop, I flop onto my back, chest heaving. My tank top clings to my skin with perspiration, and my underwear is absolutely ruined. Again.

"What the hell is wrong with me?" I whisper to the ceiling, one hand pressed to my racing heart.

This is the third morning in a row I've woken up while coming my brains out. My body has apparently decided that sleep is the perfect time to torture me with X-rated dreams about three cowboys who smell good enough to eat.

Sunlight streams through the window, painting golden

stripes across my rumpled bed. For a moment, I just lie here in the afterglow, body humming with satisfaction. Chicago never gave me morning orgasms. Chicago gave me alarm clocks and anxiety.

But that's dangerous thinking. This isn't my life. This is temporary. Three months of playing ranch girl before I sell this place and go back to reality.

I've managed five whole days of keeping my distance from them since the rodeo. Days of polite conversation at meals before fleeing to safety. Of pretending my hormones aren't staging a rebellion against my common sense.

Shit. I haven't updated my blog in days. My followers are probably thinking I've been murdered by cowboys. Or worse, that I'm too busy getting railed to write.

Still, it hasn't been a total loss. I actually finished *Infernal Temptation*, the book club pick I borrowed from June. Dark magic, sexy demons, and a heroine who isn't afraid to bite back... That was the kind of distraction I needed.

I grab my laptop from the nightstand, settling against my mountain of pillows. Time to check in on messages, let the internet know I'm alive, and then overwrite just enough to keep them guessing.

Confessions of a City Omega

Houston, We Have a Problem

Dearest Diary,

Is it normal to wake up mid-orgasm three mornings in a row? Because your girl is starting to worry she's broken. Or blessed. Honestly can't decide which.

I've been SO GOOD lately. Keeping my distance from three certain cowboys, being professional, focusing on work. Gold star for me, right?

Wrong.

Apparently, my subconscious didn't get the memo about boundaries, because I've been having dreams that would make that demon romance book from the book club look like a children's story. We're talking full HD, surround sound, scratch-and-sniff-level vivid dreams.

And the worst part? I wake up already... you know. DURING. Like my body couldn't even wait for me to be conscious before betraying me.

Is this what happens when you stay away from your scent matches? Some kind of biological uprising? "Oh, you won't let us near those Alphas? Fine, we'll just imagine them in explicit detail until you cave."

Can't blame my heat, as that's still over weeks away, according to my app with its aggressive flower emojis. (Why flowers? Why not warning sirens? Skull and crossbones? Something that accurately represents the chaos about to hit?)

In other news, ranch life continues to be suspiciously delightful.

Example: Yesterday I witnessed one of the cowboys practicing pickup lines. On his horse. Full conversation, complete with pauses for the horse's responses.

Him: "Are you a parking ticket? Because you've got 'fine' written all over you."

Horse: *sneezes directly on him.*

Him: "Yeah, okay, that was pretty bad."

I hid behind a barn wall, giggling. The thing is... it was adorable. When did I start finding terrible pickup lines endearing? This place is doing something to my brain.

Today's Omega Advice Corner: Based on the approximately forty-seven messages asking about maintaining boundaries...

Here's the truth: Boundaries are like diet plans. Great in theory, total disaster when someone waves chocolate cake in your face. Or in this case, when three cowboys walk around looking like snacks.

The key is being honest with yourself. Are you avoiding them because you genuinely need space? Or because you're scared of how much you want them? Both are valid, but knowing which one helps you make better choices.

Stay strong out there, dearest Omegas. Or don't. I'm not your mom.

City Omega out. (Still not a ranch girl. Still pretending I might be.)

I close my laptop just as my phone rings. Meredith's face fills the screen, already looking suspicious. So I quickly answer.

"Finally! I was starting to think the cowboys had murdered you and buried you under a cactus."

"We don't have those kinds of cacti in Montana," I inform her, heading to the bathroom. "And they wouldn't murder me. They need me alive to sign papers."

"Uh-huh. So everything's totally normal? You're being good?"

I prop the phone against the mirror, grabbing my toothbrush. "Define *good*."

"Really?"

"I'm trying! But my body has developed its own agenda that involves very detailed dreams and morning... situations."

Her eyes light up. "Are we talking about what I think we're talking about?"

"I plead the Fifth."

"Oh my God, you're having wet dreams about cowboys! This is better than Netflix!"

"Can we focus on the actual reason you called?" I beg. "Please?"

"Fine, spoilsport. I can help you move your stuff this weekend, as my brother has a van from work we can use."

"Yeah, no," I say quickly, pausing my brushing. "I'm worried about anyone seeing me leave the ranch. Someone might use it against me with the will stuff. I really need this inheritance money, Mer."

"And the cowboys?" Her voice gentles. "You planning to just leave them behind after the three months?"

The question sits heavily between us. I quickly fill my mouth with water to rinse it out. "I don't know," I admit finally, cleaning my toothbrush. "I'm trying not to think about it."

"Very healthy. Denial always works great."

"Says the woman who pretended she wasn't in love with her boss for two years."

"We don't talk about that." But she's smiling. "Seriously, though, maybe see how things play out? You've got time."

"Yeah. And honestly, I don't have much stuff. Can you store my boxes in your garage?"

"Of course! What are friends for if not enabling questionable life choices and storing your crap?"

"You are amazing, and you know I love you."

"And don't forget, you owe me big," she states.

I laugh. "Always. Anyway, I'd better get ready."

After we say our farewell and hang up, I shower quickly and dress in work clothes—jeans that actually fit properly, thanks to Walker's shopping trip, and a T-shirt covered in some cat fur. I feed my three orange rascals, let them out for the day, and head out toward the sanctuary.

Rounding the corner of the main barn at a good clip, I slam directly into what feels like a warm, muscle-covered wall.

"Oof!" The impact sends me stumbling backward.

Strong hands catch my waist, steadying me. "Whoa there, gorgeous. Where's the fire?"

Walker. Because of course it's Walker, looking unfairly good in a gray Henley that clings to every ridge of muscle. His hair is slightly mussed, and is that a hint of stubble? My fingers itch to touch it.

"No fire," I manage. "Just heading to work."

His hands are still on my waist. I should probably mention that. Or step back. Instead, I'm focusing on how his thumbs are making little circles against my sides through the thin fabric of my shirt.

"Missed you," he murmurs, voice dropping to that point where my knees weaken. "Been hiding from us?"

"Nope. Working. Very different things."

"Uh-huh." His gaze tracks over my face slowly, lingering on my mouth. "You know you've got a..." He reaches up, thumb brushing the corner of my lips. "Toothpaste."

I did not have toothpaste there, the sneaky bastard. I wipe frantically at the corner of my mouth, nevertheless.

"Thanks," I breathe, very aware we're still standing too close.

"You've been working hard. You should take it easy sometimes. All work and no play makes Sophia a dull girl."

"I'm playing," I protest. "With cats. Very safe, noncomplicated cats."

His grin is slow and devastating. "We're not that complicated."

"You're the definition of chaos. You're like... a calculus problem wrapped in a crossword puzzle dressed up as a cowboy."

"That's the nicest thing anyone's ever said to me." His hands finally drop from my waist, and I pretend I'm not disappointed. "Have dinner with us tonight? Main house, six o'clock. Just food and conversation, Scout's honor."

"Were you actually a Scout?"

"Nope. But the invitation stands."

I should say no. Should maintain this distance that's

been keeping me marginally sane. But his eyes are so warm, and he smells so good, and my dream from this morning is still fresh in my mind...

"Okay," I hear myself say. "But just dinner."

His smile could power the entire state. "Yep," he agrees, but the heat in his stare suggests he's thinking about dessert.

18

The rest of the day crawls by. Every time I check the clock, it's moved approximately thirty seconds. By five thirty, I've changed outfits three times, finally settling on denim shorts that showcase my legs and a button-up shirt with the sleeves rolled to my elbows. Casual but cute. My flip-flops complete the *I definitely didn't spend an hour getting ready* look.

Standing outside their door at six on the dot, I feel stupidly nervous. It's just dinner. With three men who feature prominently in my morning orgasm dreams. Totally normal.

Cash opens the door, and my mouth immediately goes dry. He's wearing dark blue jeans that fit him perfectly and a black button-down that has his blue eyes practically glowing. His hair is damp and pushed back, and dear God, he smells amazing.

"There's our girl," Cash grins as he pulls the front door wider, stepping aside. "Come on in, sugar."

The smell crashes into me first, something rich and savory, warm bread and herbs.

I enter the home, the creak of old wood beneath my flip-flops grounding me. I quickly take them off near the door and continue barefoot. The ranch house is massive with wide hallways, vaulted ceilings, and antique rugs underfoot, but there's a lived-in comfort to it.

My fingers brush along the edge of a hall table as I move through the space, nerves fluttering like they do on a first date. Voices drift from the kitchen, low and teasing, and then—

Walker rounds the corner, and my breath catches as it had earlier today. He's wearing a forest-green T-shirt that hugs his shoulders, sleeves rolled just enough to expose strong forearms. His hair is slightly tousled like he ran his hand through it in frustration, or maybe nerves, and there's flour smudged along the side of his neck.

"Evenin', darlin'. Been waitin' on you." Then he ducks back into the kitchen.

Behind him, Ridge leans against the far wall in a dark navy shirt, auburn hair pulled off his gorgeous face. His posture is relaxed, arms folded, but the way his gaze tracks me tightens my stomach. He doesn't just look at me. He *sees* me.

"You all look…" My voice fails for a second as heat climbs my throat. *Edible. Dangerous. Like a buffet I want to sample one at a time.* I swallow and recover, barely. "Really nice."

"And you're beautiful," Ridge says simply.

Not flirtatious. Not coy. Just *real.* And that undoes me more than anything clever ever could. His voice wraps around me like velvet, rough at the edges, and I have to look away or I'll combust.

The dining room is just off the open living space, cozy but elegant. The table is set like they're expecting company, not just me. Real plates, actual napkins folded into triangles, and wildflowers spilling out of a mason jar in the center like someone cared *a little too much.* That someone being them.

It's sweet. And so alarmingly domestic that something

aches deep in my chest. I can't remember the last time someone made dinner for me just because they wanted to. Not out of obligation. Not for optics. Just... to see me smile.

"Walker's cooking," Cash explains, appearing at my side with a glass of lemonade I didn't even ask for. "Ridge handled the music. I'm here for my sparkling personality."

"And modesty," I murmur, lips curving despite myself.

He flashes me that cocky grin, all dimples and hotness, and my thighs clench. *God help me, I'm in trouble.*

Country music drifts through the space, something easy and warm that fills the air. I wander, letting myself absorb the scent of garlic and rosemary, the flicker of candles on a side table, the sound of Walker humming low under his breath in the kitchen. It's *too much.* Too good. Too tempting.

That's when I spot a photo on the mantel.

My smile fades.

It's Rose, seated on the porch of the guesthouse, her grin wide. And beside her, a much younger Nolan. My first Alpha has his arm around her shoulders, chin tilted just right to show off his best angles. Even in still life, he manages to suck all the air from the room.

My stomach knots. The sight of him, that easy smile and confident stare, pulls me straight into a memory I didn't ask for.

"Jesus, Sophia, do you have to be so emotional about everything?"

"No, you can't take that job. What would people think?"

"I've already decided. Discussion over."

"You're lucky I put up with you."

A wave of cold washes through me. I wrap my arms around my stomach without thinking, trying to breathe past the tightness.

Ridge appears at my side. "Rose was an incredible woman. Kind, generous. Treated everyone like family."

I nod, throat thick. "Shame her grandson was a walking dumpster fire," I manage.

Ridge huffs out a dry laugh. "That's insulting to dumpster fires. At least they provide warmth."

"And light," I add, grateful for the distraction.

"Occasionally cook food."

"Serve a purpose in society."

"Unlike the Alpha who never deserved that title," he finishes.

Our eyes meet, and something warm sparks between us. But it's his grin that really gets me. It softens all his edges and has me forgetting that when I was with Nolan, I didn't think I'd ever feel safe laughing.

And right now, I'm standing in a home that smells delicious and welcoming, with three cowboys who have nothing but open arms for me.

I drift into the open kitchen doorway, the scent smothering me in the best possible way. Rich, buttery, savory, and my stomach practically growls in response.

"That smells incredible," I breathe, stepping in farther.

Walker is pulling out a massive roast from the oven, arms braced as he sets it gently on the stovetop.

"Wait 'til you try it."

The kitchen is chaos, though. Steam curling up from mashed potatoes glistening with pools of butter. Green beans sautéed with almonds. Fresh cornbread stacked high. Roasted vegetables, two kinds of salad, and mac and cheese that definitely isn't from a box.

"Holy shit," I say, eyes wide. "Did you cook for the entire county?"

He wipes his hands on a towel and glances up at me, a little color rising to his cheekbones. "Didn't know what you liked," he says, shrugging. "Figured I'd make a little of everything. Cover my bases."

"A *little* of everything?" I arch a brow.

His mouth tips in a lopsided smile. "Used to watch my mom make Sunday roasts. Every damn week, like clockwork. She'd hum while she worked, made it look easy. Taught me all her tricks before I hit high school."

I step closer, unable to stop myself from inhaling again. "If this tastes half as good as it smells, I might propose."

That gets a real smile. "Careful what you promise."

"Still a better offer than my last relationship."

That earns me a low, amused sound from his throat. Then he tilts his head toward the counter. "Want to help carry things out?"

"Sure."

We load our arms with dishes, moving around each other. Our hands brush once. Then again. The third time, my fingers linger too long on a bowl of roasted carrots, and I glance up to find Cash and Ridge watching us. Something warm and electric crackles between us.

"Sit here," Cash says, pulling out a chair between him and Ridge at the round table.

"Not even letting me pick my spot?"

"Strategic placement," Walker calls as he brings in the roast. "Keeps the conversation interesting."

"Or keeps the flirting even," I mutter under my breath, only half joking.

Before I can even lift a serving spoon, Cash and Ridge are already loading up my plate. Mashed potatoes, cornbread, salad, vegetables, generous portions of everything. I watch in amused horror as the mountain grows.

"I can't eat all this," I protest.

"Try," Walker suggests, sliding in across the table with his own plate. "You need your strength."

"For what?" I ask, too late in realizing the trap.

Three sets of eyes lock on mine. The air thickens with something darker, heavier, and a not-so-innocent smile tugs at Cash's mouth.

Ridge just grins my way, that tempting, impossible-to-resist smile that gets me every time.

I take a bite of the mashed potatoes and groan. "Okay, that's ridiculous."

Walker glances over, clearly trying not to smile. "Too much salt?"

"Too much *perfect*," I mumble around another forkful. "Like, I'm offended. Why does it taste this good?"

Cash snorts. "Because he's a show-off. Did you count how many side dishes he made? He's compensating."

"For *what*, exactly?" Walker drawls, raising a brow. "Because I've got a ten-pound roast and the confidence to serve two salads. Sounds like I'm thriving."

"You made two kinds of salad," I say, pretending to be scandalized.

Walker leans in slightly. "You said you liked options."

Ridge clears his throat. "Some of us just wanted to eat dinner without a pissing contest."

"It's not," Cash states, reaching for another roll. "I already won."

"With *what*, the personality of a golden retriever?" Walker deadpans.

"They are beloved," Cash points out. "You, on the other hand, are broccoli. Useful. Occasionally impressive. But no one *craves* you."

"Speak for yourself," I mutter, immediately regretting it as three sets of gazes swing my way.

Heat rushes up my neck, and I stab a green bean. "I meant the broccoli. Obviously."

Walker's low chuckle is warm against my skin. "Uh-huh."

"Try the cornbread, Sophia. It's Rose's recipe." Ridge, mercifully, changes the subject.

I don't waste time and help myself, nodding with

approval as I take a mouthful. "Tastes like Sunday mornings."

For a second, no one speaks, just the soft clink of silverware and the quiet strum of country music from the speaker on the counter. It's warm. Comfortable.

Until I glance toward the mantel and see *him*.

Nolan stares back at me from the photo like a ghost. It's the face of a man who made me feel like I never quite measured up. Who made me feel invisible, even while I sat right beside him. Who kept me as his possession for show only.

Walker is staring at me. Of course he is.

He stands abruptly, crossing to the mantel. "You know what? This needs to go somewhere else." He takes the photo, disappearing into the hallway.

"Interior decorating phase?" Cash teases. "What's next, feng shui?"

"Scented candles," Ridge suggests. "Maybe some healing crystals."

"Those little signs that say *Live, Laugh, Love*," I add to join in on the fun.

"I can hear you assholes," Walker calls from the hallway.

But when he returns, he catches my attention and winks. He noticed. He fixed it. Such a simple thing, but my throat tightens.

I return to my food, and we're all silent for a while, enjoying this incredible feast until I'm ready to burst.

Cash suddenly stretches in his chair, arms behind his head like he doesn't have a single shameful bone in his body. "Been sleeping well lately, Sophia? Like, real deep sleep? Waking up full of energy, feeling... satisfied with life?"

I pause mid-bite of cornbread, one brow lifting. "That's oddly specific."

Across the table, Ridge is suspiciously invested in refilling his glass of sweet tea, mouth twitching at the corners. Walker's smile is pure innocence, which makes it absolutely criminal.

"Just making conversation," Cash shrugs, grabbing another spoonful of mac and cheese. "Sleep's important. Found a whole article about it on the internet. Said it affects mood, hormones, even your scent."

Okay, *now* they're being weird.

"Sure," I say slowly, chasing a green bean around my plate with my fork. "Sleep's great. Love it. Big fan."

Walker clears his throat, failing miserably to hide a grin. "Dreams been... vivid, by any chance?"

I blink. "Excuse me?"

"Dream recall," Ridge chimes in like he's a damn expert. "Can say a lot about your subconscious."

"Right," I say, eyeing all three of them. "So we're just casually chatting about dreams and hormone cycles now? That's our dinner topic?"

"Very modern of us," Cash says cheerfully.

I shake my head and go back to eating, but they keep side-eyeing each other with smirks so smug it's like they're in on a private joke. My brain starts flipping through possibilities.

Wait.

This morning.

And yesterday morning.

And the morning before that.

Oh my *God*.

They *couldn't* have heard—

No. No way.

Except... there *was* that open window.

But they wouldn't just *spy* on me. Right?

Oh, *shit*.

The blog.

My blog.

My very detailed blog post about waking up during an orgasm.

Which, apparently, the cowboys have read.

Here's the thing—I've never *advertised* this blog. I only ever told Meredith about it, and she swore on her collection of designer heels to keep it secret that it's me writing it. But I guess if someone were, say, googling *Omega and cowboys*, they might stumble across *Confessions of a City Omega*. And if they read even one post? Well. I don't exactly hold back.

It wouldn't take long to connect the dots. Especially if they recognized the specific details about rural Montana, barn cats, and being annoyed by how hot your scent matches are while also kind of wanting to bite them. And then me arriving here from Chicago...

So, yeah. That mystery is solved.

They found the blog.

And now I have to live with the fact that three infuriating, perfect Alphas have read my posts about them.

Cool, cool, cool. Totally fine. Not spiraling at all.

My fork freezes halfway to my mouth as it all comes together like a horror montage in my head. I stare at them. They're still chatting like nothing's wrong, but I *see* it now. The amused glint in Ridge's eyes as he picks at roasted carrots. Walker's suspiciously attentive chewing. Cash, grinning like a hyena who just found the snack stash.

"Are you—" I start, voice rising before I cut myself off. No. Don't give them the satisfaction.

"Everything okay?" Cash asks, completely faking concern. "You've gone a bit pink. Need us to crack a window?"

"Choking on a green bean," I snap.

"No shame in that," Ridge offers, the picture of politeness. "Happens to the best of us."

"Oh, I bet it does," I mutter.

Walker stands abruptly. "Dessert!" he announces, like

he's just pulled the fire alarm to evacuate a burning building. "Tiramisu. Made it this morning."

Walker collects the empty plates. Like he's not fazed at all. Like he didn't just watch me connect the dots between my blog and their smug little performance. Ridge helps without a word, stacking dishes as though this is just another night. Cash hums something under his breath that sounds suspiciously like a victory song.

Soon, we're all back at the table, staring at a delicious tiramisu. The scent of coffee-soaked ladyfingers and cream fills the air as Walker cuts me a generous slice, plates it like a damn chef, and slides it toward me with a small bow.

"Enjoy."

I do. The first mouthful is so rich and creamy that I forget to be embarrassed for a full three seconds. The mascarpone melts on my tongue, velvety and just sweet enough to make my toes curl. The coffee hits next, and this is beyond addictive. I don't just taste it; I *feel* it, like this dessert is trying to ruin me in a whole new way.

Then I moan. Like, an actual out-loud *moan*.

All conversation dies.

"Jesus," Ridge murmurs, ears visibly reddening.

Cash coughs into his napkin and mutters, "Guess she *really* needed that sugar."

Walker grins so hard he has to look down at his plate. "Glad you like it."

"Walker," I say, glaring at my tiramisu like it personally betrayed me. "This is amazing. You're a menace."

He leans in a little. "Full of surprises, remember?"

"I need a drink," I mumble, and Ridge is already filling my glass with sweet tea.

"Hydration's important after intense activity," Cash adds helpfully, eyes twinkling.

I grab a roll and throw it at him. He dodges and catches it in midair like he's been waiting for it.

"I'm fine, by the way," I lie. "Completely fine."

"Mm-hmm," Ridge hums, calm as ever. "Just checking. Wouldn't want our guest overheating."

"I *hate* all of you," I say sweetly, biting another forkful of tiramisu like vengeance can be achieved through dessert.

But the worst part?

I can't stop smiling.

We migrate to the living room after dinner, with my glass of sweet tea in hand, sprawling on the massive sectional. I end up between Ridge and the arm of the couch, hyperaware of every inch of my distance from them.

"Movie?" Ridge suggests.

"Don't let him pick," Cash warns immediately. "His collection is... specific."

"I have normal movies," Ridge protests.

"You have a whole shelf of documentaries." Walker makes air quotes. "Very educational documentaries. About anatomy."

Oh. *OH.*

They're talking about *porn.*

Ridge has a porn collection.

My glass freezes halfway to my mouth. My face goes nuclear as the realization hits, heat creeping from my neck straight into my scalp. I glance at him, half expecting denial. But Ridge doesn't even flinch.

"I also have regular movies," he says smoothly, though the tips of his ears are definitely pink. "Y'know. With plots. Dialogues. Occasionally even a budget."

"Sure you do," Cash drawls, the picture of innocence as he leans back in his chair. "Filed alphabetically, right between *Cowgirls Gone Wild* and *Rodeo After Dark.*"

Ridge chuckles low. "You mean the two you borrowed last month and never gave back?"

That gets Cash. His mouth opens. Shuts. Opens again.

He stares at Ridge like a cat caught mid-pounce, and the silence lasts a full two seconds longer than usual.

Walker snorts into his glass. "Well, now the silence is suspicious."

"Was research," Cash mutters, then perks up. "Character development."

We all lose it. Even Ridge's low laugh rumbles from his chest, and I bite my lip because I'm sitting way too close to him to not feel *everything*. The heat, the vibration, like I belong here.

"You got a collection too, sugar?" Cash turns to me, eyes twinkling with mock curiosity. "For science, of course."

"A lady never tells," I say primly, lifting my chin after setting my glass down on the coffee table.

Ridge raises an eyebrow. "That sounds like a yes."

"And the good kind," Walker adds. "Bet hers are alphabetized *and* have a color-coded rating system."

"Hotness scale from one to burn the sheets." Cash grins.

I shake my head, trying not to laugh. "You three are *ridiculous*."

"Ridiculously curious," Cash fires back. "Just sayin', we'd be open to suggestions if you got any personal favorites."

Ridge turns to me, eyes glinting in the firelight. "So... what's your take? Story-driven? Or straight to the good stuff?"

My face flames. "I'm not answering that."

"You *are* blushing," Walker notes smugly. "Like, bright red. Kinda cute, actually. But hey, we support self-care in this house."

I roll my eyes, trying for unaffected, but my cheeks are on fire. "You three really are the worst."

Ridge just chuckles, low and amused. "Didn't hear a denial, though."

I shoot him a glare, but his smile only deepens, like he's

reading something I'm not saying out loud. My stomach does a little flip I pretend not to feel.

I reach for my glass of sweet tea on the coffee table, suddenly desperate for a distraction. But even with the space between us, Ridge's attention clings to my skin like a touch I can't shake.

And maybe, just maybe... I don't mind it.

"Let's play a game," Ridge suggests quickly. "Found this online. Cowboy phrases."

He explains the rules where we each say a phrase and everyone gets one guess at the meaning. If you're right, you can demand something from the person who said it. If everyone's wrong, the phrase-sayer gets to dare someone.

"I'll go first," Cash volunteers, that troublemaker grin in full force. "Hotter than a goat's butt in a pepper patch."

"That cannot be real," I protest.

"Is too! Anyone want to guess what it means?"

"Something about spicy food?" Walker tries.

"Temperature in hell?" Ridge suggests.

"A really unfortunate farming accident?" I offer.

Cash laughs. "All wrong! It means it's extremely hot outside. Goats eat peppers, so their butts would be—"

"That's disgusting," I interrupt. "Who comes up with these?"

"Farmers with too much time," Ridge adds. "So Cash owes a dare. Who's it gonna be?"

Cash's eyes lock on mine, of course. I swallow hard. "Sophia. You have to sit on Ridge's lap for the next round."

I stiffen, fire bursting through my chest. "That's not fair!"

"Them's the rules, sugar."

Ridge pats his thigh, and that simple gesture shouldn't make my mouth go dry, but here we are. "Come on. I'll behave."

"It's not you I'm worried about," I mutter, but I move to his lap.

I try to perch on his knee, keeping some distance, but Ridge wraps an arm around my waist and tugs me back against his chest.

"Might as well be comfortable," he murmurs in my ear.

Comfortable. Right. I can feel every hard plane of his chest against my back, his arm solid around my waist. And is that... yes, that's definitely his erection pressing against my ass. My body temperature spikes about a thousand degrees.

"My turn," Walker says, and his voice has gone deeper. "Slicker than deer guts on a doorknob."

"Why are they all gross?" I complain, trying not to squirm on Ridge's lap. Squirming would be bad. Squirming would create friction. Friction would make Ridge's situation more obvious and my situation more desperate.

"It means slippery," Ridge guesses, his breath fanning against my neck.

"Dangerous?" Cash tries.

"Something about hunting?" I manage, proud that my voice doesn't shake.

"It means very slippery or sneaky," Walker confirms. "Ridge got it. What's your demand?"

Ridge's arm tightens slightly around me. "Tell me about the last dream you had."

Walker doesn't hesitate. "It was about a certain Omega. In my kitchen. Wearing nothing but my apron while I cooked breakfast."

My whole body goes still.

Cash lets out a low whistle. "Don't hold back now. What happened next?"

I lift my head off Ridge's shoulder just enough to shoot them both a warning look. "We don't need the details."

Walker grins at me like I just dared him to go on.

"I mean, could've been any Omega," Ridge adds dryly, like he's trying to toss me a lifeline. "Doesn't mean it was you."

But I stiffen anyway.

Walker's smile sharpens. He leans forward, resting his forearms on his thighs. "She was standing barefoot on the cool tile, apron tied at the back, and nothing else. I kept cooking while she leaned over the counter, watching me. Every time she shifted her weight, I could see more of her. Every curve. Every inch I wanted to taste."

Ridge's breath hitches behind me.

"She turned around, lifted herself onto the island," Walker continues, voice a little lower now. "That apron fell just enough for me to see everything. And I couldn't help myself. I laid her back on the cold marble, peeled that apron off her slowly, and—"

"Okay!" My voice comes out an octave too high, my cheeks blazing. "We got it. You made breakfast."

Walker raises a brow. "Did I?"

Cash is laughing quietly, and Ridge's fingers flex slightly where they're resting at my hip. His breath is warm on my neck, and I swear his thickness nestled against my ass just throbbed, getting harder. No one says anything for a long moment, but the tension in the room thickens like honey, slow, golden, and impossible to ignore.

Still flushed, I shift on Ridge's lap, suddenly all too aware of how warm his body is beneath mine. I clear my throat and slide off, trying to be casual about it. Yet they're all watching me.

"It was only one round," I mumble, smoothing my shorts as I settle on the cushion beside him. My thighs brush his for half a second, and I feel his stare on me like a touch. He doesn't say a word, but his gaze slowly, deliberately drags down my legs like he's trying to memorize the length of them.

I tuck one leg beneath me and pretend not to notice. Pretend I'm not imagining how his hands would feel, gripping my bare thighs instead of just looking.

Walker stretches out, clearly still smug from his dream reveal. Cash cracks his knuckles like he's resetting the mood, leaning forward with a grin.

"All right, next one's mine," Ridge announces, dragging his attention back to the group. "Let's see who's got real ranch smarts."

He rests an elbow on his knee and looks around the circle, his voice low and playful. "What does it mean when a cowboy says he *rode the fence until the cows came home, but still ended up knee-deep in goat shit?*"

Cash snorts. "Means he worked hard and still got screwed."

"Means he was chasing tail and got the wrong species," Walker offers, grinning.

I scrunch up my nose.

Ridge shakes his head. "Wrong. And wronger."

They both glance at me. I blink. "Hmm. It means he tried to keep everyone happy and ended up with a mess anyway."

All three of them stare.

Walker lets out a low whistle. "Damn."

Cash tips his imaginary hat. "She's been studying Cowboyese."

Ridge's mouth twitches, pride flickering in his expression. "That's right."

I smile, trying not to glow too obviously, seeing as I completely guessed that.

"All right," Ridge says, leaning back with a gleam in his eyes. "Winner picks the next dare. Anyone in the room."

I sit up a little straighter. Oh. Power. Dangerous in the wrong hands. Even more dangerous in mine.

My gaze drifts slowly across the three of them. Cash, lounging with his arms spread across the back of the couch like he owns the place. Walker, sprawled at the other end, still smirking. And Ridge, silent and intense, watching me.

God, which one of them do I dare?

And what would I make them do?

I toy with my empty glass, trying to buy myself time, before I put it down on the table.

They're all watching me. Waiting. Three pairs of eyes. Shit. What do I say?

The power is mine. I could pick something harmless. Silly.

But some wicked part of me wants to see them squirm. Wants them to feel the heat I've been drowning in for days.

I shouldn't. God, what am I thinking—

"What would you do to me?" I blurt. "If we were alone?" My breath catches. "Whisper it. In my ear."

The room goes still. Then—

Cash lets out a low whistle. "Whew, sugar. Going straight for the throat, huh?"

"Damn," Walker mutters, leaning forward with a grin so wide it makes me blush. "I love that one. Can I answer too?"

I laugh, a little breathless. "Nope. This one's all up to Ridge."

He hasn't moved. Just watches me. Heat blooming behind his eyes. Then he shifts slowly in his seat, turning until he's fully facing me, knees brushing mine.

The closeness tightens something in my chest. I shouldn't have asked. Not like this.

I made a mistake. A beautiful, terrible mistake.

The others are watching me, waiting for my reaction like it's dessert.

Ridge leans in. One hand finds the back of the couch behind me.

"I'd tie your wrists to the headboard so you can't stop me," he growls in my ear, voice dragging over my spine like smoke and sin. "Spread you wide and feast like a starving man, slow at first, just to hear you beg. Then rough. Until you can't remember your own name, only mine. And when your thighs are shaking and your voice is hoarse from screaming, I'd slide in deep and stay there. Let you feel just how long I've been dying to ruin you."

My entire body flushes. A soft gasp escapes before I can stop it.

My legs press together instinctively, and I swear I hear Cash groan.

Walker runs a hand over his mouth, eyes locked on me like I'm the main course.

"Whatever he said," Cash mutters, voice hoarse, "I second it. Hell, I'll make it a group project."

"I third it," Walker says, eyes hungry.

I blink fast, trying to get my heart to slow down. It's pointless. Ridge is still close, eyes locked on mine.

And I know, without a shadow of a doubt, this game just got dangerous. And I took it there...

The silence after Ridge's whisper is obscene. My pulse is in my ears, my thighs pressed tighter.

He leans back, smug, unreadable, but I *see* him. For all the times he's pulled back, all that careful brooding... he's just as hungry as the others. Maybe more. He watches me like he wants to consume every inch and leave nothing untouched. And I'm no better. Around them, my self-control slips like sand through fingers. Every brush, every look, sends my body spiraling toward something dangerous.

The kind of desire that doesn't just burn; it *ignites*.

"Well then," Cash finally says, his voice thick. "It's Sophia's turn."

I blink back to the present, struggling to remember what game we're even playing. The living room feels too warm, the couch too soft beneath me, the air too heavy with their scents, with everything that just passed between us.

I clear my throat. "Fine. Here's mine." I let the words drip from my lips, teasing. "Rode hard and put up wet."

Walker groans like he's in pain. "Now that's just cruel."

"Means she's had a real long day," Ridge explains, still watching me with that molten gaze.

Cash grins. "Or a real long night. But I'll bite. Was I close?"

"Not close enough," I smirk, swirling the last of my drink. "It means someone looks worn out. Used up. Like they've been pushed too far and never given the rest they needed."

Three sets of eyes are still locked on me. And the irony of that phrase hanging in the air doesn't go unnoticed.

"So now..." I say, standing slowly, smoothing my hands over my thighs just to *do* something. "I get to pick a dare."

Cash sits forward like a kid at Christmas. "Please let it involve me and rope."

Walker's grin is feral. "Or licking. I vote for licking."

Ridge just raises a brow, silent. Waiting.

But I can't. *God,* I want to. If I stay, I know exactly where this ends. The fireplace still crackles low, casting gold across skin and shadows. If I give in, if I so much as brush against Ridge, I'll cave. And we'll end up tangled on this rug, my clothes gone, their mouths on me, and I'm not sure I'd ever recover.

And worse?

I'm starting to worry. My body's been heating steadily since arriving at the ranch, the slow kind of build that always comes just before the crash. My next heat isn't due for weeks, but something's wrong. Or *right.* That's the terrifying part. Because if it happens here, without warning, without meds, without a clinic? With *them?*

I might not survive it.

So I smile, sweet and sinful, and say, "Walker."

He perks up like he just won a prize. "Yeah?"

My heart pounds. "Walk me home."

A pulse of stunned silence. Then—

"*That's* your dare?" Cash looks personally offended. "Boo."

"Cop-out," Ridge mutters, but his voice is hoarse.

Walker is already standing, eyes dark with understanding. "You got it."

I laugh like it's no big deal, but it is. I clutch that illusion of control with both hands as I head for the door, every step screaming with want. Behind me, I feel their eyes, hear the soft disappointment they don't even try to hide.

They wanted more.

So did I.

But tonight, restraint wins.

Just barely.

Walker walks me to the door, the others staying behind in the soft glow of the living room. I glance back at them once before stepping out onto the porch, then turn and offer a small, warm smile.

"Good night, boys."

They smile and say their good nights, then I'm out before I change my mind.

Walker lingers beside me as we head down the path toward the guesthouse. We don't talk at first, the gravel crunching underfoot the only sound. It's a beautiful night, cooler now, the stars scattered across the sky like secrets waiting to be told. And beside me, Walker strolls like a shadow, steady and unshakable.

"It was amazing having you with us tonight," he says eventually, voice softer than the breeze. "You brought the house to life."

I bite my lip, unsure how to respond. "It felt... right. Being there."

He glances sideways. "Then why do you sound so uncertain?"

"Because the more right it feels, the more terrifying it becomes," I admit. "Like I'm slipping too far into something I can't undo."

Walker stops walking and faces me. "Then don't undo it."

I look away, heart hammering. "That almost sounded like a proposition."

He doesn't smile as I glance his way. "We want you closer, Sophia. The guesthouse is nice, sure. But it's too far from us."

"I like my space," I say, though the words sound thinner than I meant them to.

"You'd still have it. Your own room. Your own quiet. But you'd be near if you needed us." His tone gentles. "Ridge said you've been... nesting."

My eyes narrow. "It's not a nest. It's a highly organized comfort zone."

He chuckles. "It sounds like a nest. A gorgeous, soft, perfectly you nest. But if you go into heat out here alone..."

I hesitate, the warning in his voice threading straight through me. He's not wrong.

"I'm not due anytime soon, so don't worry," I say, softer now. "But... I'll think about it."

Walker doesn't push. Just steps in closer, the air between us going tight. "We're patient, Sophia. But you're our scent match. And when your heat hits for real, you won't want to be out here alone. You'll need us."

His voice is low. And I hate having this discussion like my heat dictates my life.

My breath catches, heart stuttering. I know I should step back, say good night, make it easier. But I don't. Not yet.

He leans in, brushing his knuckles down my arm in a touch so gentle it undoes me. My skin prickles, heat blooming deep and low. His fingers trail to my wrist and linger there, his eyes fixed on mine like he's waiting for a sign, a permission, a crack in my restraint.

I give it to him.

The space between us vanishes as our mouths crash together, all heat and hunger and tension that's been building since the moment we met. His hands cup my face, tilting me up as his lips move over mine, soft at first, then deeper, rougher, like he's starving. I melt into him, fingers fisting the front of his shirt, wanting more, needing everything.

The world blurs. There's only the taste of him, the feel of his body against mine, the low sound he makes when I whimper against his mouth.

When we finally break apart, I'm breathless. Shaky. My lips are swollen, my heart pounding, my whole body aching with need. I want to drag him inside, lock the door, and never let go.

But he's already stepping back, eyes dark with something dangerous. Something barely held in check.

"Sleep well, gorgeous," he murmurs.

And then he turns, striding off into the dark and leaving me trembling in the doorway, still tasting him on my lips.

Inside the guesthouse, the soft mewling chorus of ginger cats greets me. Chonkarella winds around my legs, purring like an idling engine, while the two kittens leap between couch cushions. One knocks over a throw pillow. The other skitters across the floor, chasing dust motes only he can see.

I feed them, then retreat to the small library nook, my sanctuary, and sink into the hanging chair suspended from the ceiling. The cocoon of blankets and pillows welcomes me.

I still taste Walker.

My lips tingle, my skin thrums where he touched me, and the memory of his mouth on mine unravels my carefully built restraint. It would've been so easy to ask him in. Too easy. The heat between us had flared so fast, so hot, that I'm still reeling.

And it's not just him. It's all three of them. I keep thinking what it would be like if I stayed with them tonight.

If I gave in.

If I stopped pretending I wasn't already theirs.

But instead, I'm here, tucked away in my not-a-nest like a coward. Because if I go to them now... I might not come back.

And part of me doesn't want to; part of me is terrified of how it might end.

So, I pull my laptop into my lap, staring at the blank screen.

The evening plays over and over in my head, the way they moved around me like I already belonged.

And then I remember the sleep conversation. The pointed questions. The smug looks.

I groan, covering my face. They read the blog.

Dirty dogs.

Well... two can play that game.

I grin, flex my fingers, and start typing.

Confessions of a City Omega

Does Size Really Matter?

Dearest Diary,

Let's address the python in the pants, shall we?

I've been blessed (cursed?) with three specimens of prime Alpha real estate. And while they're all impressive in their own ways, one of them is packing some SERIOUS heat. Like, how-do-you-find-pants-that-fit level of impressive.

I've been dreaming about it. Wondering how it would feel in my hands. My mouth. Other places that would make this blog for adults only.

But what about the others? Should I feel guilty for

comparing? Is it wrong that I spent time sneaking glances at certain areas for research purposes?

The thing is, they each bring something different to the table (or bed, hypothetically speaking). One has technique that could probably make me come from kissing alone. Another has stamina that suggests he'd keep going until I begged for mercy. And the third? Well, let's just say he's got the equipment to reach places I didn't know existed.

Tonight's Omega Wisdom: Size matters less than enthusiasm. Less than caring about your partner's pleasure. Less than taking the time to learn what makes them fall apart.

But when you find someone with size AND skill AND the desire to worship you like a goddess? That's when you spend time wondering if your legs will ever stop shaking.

Had dinner with certain someones tonight. Played games that revealed way too much. Remembered what it's like to be wanted just for being myself.

So maybe what really matters isn't what's in their pants, but what's in their hearts. Maybe the real treasure is finding Alphas who take down photos that hurt you without being asked. Who cook feasts just to find out what you like. Who build sanctuaries for broken things and see beauty where others see damage.

(But also, seriously, HOW does one like that find jeans that fit?)

City Omega out. (Still comparing. Still curious. Still absolutely shameless about it.)

I hit publish with a wicked grin, scooping up the nearest kitten, who then purrs against my chest.

Game on, cowboys. Game absolutely on.

19

The morning sun streams through the dining room windows, painting golden rectangles across the hardwood floor. I'm nursing my second cup of coffee, appreciating the rare quiet moment. Ridge sits across from me, absorbed in the local paper, occasionally making disgusted noises at whatever political nonsense they're reporting today.

That peace shatters when Cash crashes through the door with all the subtlety of a spooked mustang.

"Christ, did you read Sophia's latest blog?" He's practically vibrating, phone clutched in his hand.

Ridge doesn't even glance up from his paper. Just rolls his eyes hard enough to strain something. "You enjoying your daily dose of Omega gossip?"

"You'd be surprised what you can learn between the lines," Cash shoots back, then swings his attention to me. "Walker, back me up here."

I lean back in my chair, taking another slow sip of coffee. "Maybe back off on the cyberstalking of our scent-matched Omega."

Cash grins wickedly. "You hearing yourself? As her scent

matches, we should be hunting her down, making her live with us, in our bed. But sure, let's keep giving her space while you pine from a distance. And worse yet, the rest of us have to suffer the same."

"Nobody's pining," I say, though the memory of last night's kiss is burned into my brain. The way she melted against me, the little sound she made when I pulled her closer...

"Right," Cash draws out the word. "That's why you spent twenty minutes arranging wildflowers in that mason jar last night for dinner."

"Those were already there."

"You measured the stems with a ruler."

Ridge finally sets down his paper, staring at me.

Cash barks out a laugh. "Well, you're gonna want to read this one. It's about us. Directly."

"Bullshit," Ridge mutters, but there's definite interest flickering in those eyes now.

"Scout's honor." Cash holds up his phone. "The title? 'Does Size Really Matter?'"

The dining room goes dead silent. My coffee mug freezes at my lips. Ridge's hand stops halfway to his water glass.

"You're making that up," I say, already reaching for my phone. No way she'd write something that bold.

"Read it and weep, gentlemen." Cash's grin could light up half of Texas.

We pull out our phones simultaneously. The only sounds are screens tapping and Ridge's sharp intake of breath. I scan through Sophia's latest post, trying to keep my expression neutral even as heat crawls up my neck.

I've been blessed (cursed?) with three specimens of prime Alpha real estate. And while they're all impressive in their own ways, one of them is packing some SERIOUS heat. Like, how-do-you-find-pants-that-fit level of impressive.

Jesus. She's been checking us out. Really checking us out.

The thing is, they each bring something different to the table (or bed, hypothetically speaking). One has technique that could probably make me come from kissing alone. Another has stamina that suggests he'd keep going until I begged for mercy. And the third? Well, let's just say he's got the equipment to reach places I didn't know existed.

My jeans suddenly feel too tight. The memory of her pressed against me last night, the way she sighed into my mouth, the heat of her body... Fuck.

"She's fucking with us," I manage.

"Or," Cash drawls, pushing off from the wall. "Maybe you and Ridge have already gone far enough with our little Omega that she's gotten herself a real good look at your weaponry."

Ridge chokes on air. "Did you just—"

"What? We're all thinking it." Cash starts pacing, energy crackling off him. "Tell me you haven't thought about showing her exactly what you're working with."

"Every damn day," I admit, because what's the point in lying?

"Look, all I'm saying," Cash continues, "is that she paid very close attention to us and came to the obvious conclusion that I am the Alpha she's been dreaming about."

"Jesus Christ, you're delusional," I tell him, though I'm already rereading the blog post. That line about "stamina that suggests he'd keep going until I begged for mercy" has my chest puffing up. That's gotta be about me. Has to be.

"The real question is," Ridge says, "which one of us has the equipment to reach places she didn't know existed?"

We all go quiet.

"I mean, she did stare when I was chopping wood the other day," I offer. "Watched for a solid ten minutes."

"She was reading on the porch," Ridge counters. "You just happened to be in her line of sight."

"Shirtless. Sweating. Flexing with every swing."

"That's called manual labor, not a strip show."

Cash laughs. "Meanwhile, she actually asked me about my belt buckle collection. Wanted to know all about my biggest trophy."

"I doubt that," I say.

Cash's eyes gleam. "She asked if I had anything else that impressive to show her."

"She did not," Ridge adds.

"She might as well have. The way she was looking at me..."

We're all talking over each other now, voices rising as each of us stakes our claim on Sophia's supposed interest. Three grown men, successful Alphas, reduced to bickering like teenagers over a blog post.

"There's only one way to settle this," Cash announces suddenly.

He starts unbuckling his belt with purpose.

"Whoa, what the hell are you doing?" Ridge demands.

"Getting proof." Cash's fingers keeps working on his buckle. "She put it in a public forum. Half this gossip-driven town is probably reading it right now, placing bets. We need to set the record straight."

"By doing what exactly?" I ask, though watching him, it's pretty damn obvious where this is heading.

"Measuring. Right here, right now. Winner takes bragging rights."

"That's the stupidest thing you've ever suggested," Ridge says flatly. "And you once tried to train a raccoon to fetch beer."

"That almost worked." Cash's belt is fully undone now. "Come on, boys. Unless you're scared she got it wrong?

Scared you're not the one packing the heat she's talking about?"

"I ain't scared," Ridge mutters, but damn if he isn't standing up too.

"This is insane," I state, but I'm already on my feet because if these two idiots are doing this, someone needs to witness it. For... documentation purposes. "We're grown men. Ranch managers. We have employees who could walk in."

"Ground rules," Ridge says, all business now. "Are we talking about fully ready for action or just everyday carry?"

"Either way works for me," Cash grins. "I'm impressive in all states."

"Christ Almighty," I mutter, but my competitive side is kicking in. "If we're doing this, we're doing it right. No exaggerating, no creative measuring angles."

"Agreed." Cash is already heading for the hallway. "Let me grab that measuring tape from the toolbox."

"For fuck's sake," Ridge mutters, but his hands are on his belt buckle.

"You know what?" I find myself saying. "Sure. Let's settle this. Because I'm tired of you two strutting around here acting like God's gift to Omegas when we all know who she was really writing about."

"You?" Cash scoffs. "Mr. Slow and Steady? She wants passion, not a relationship counselor."

"Better than whatever the hell you think you're offering," I shoot back. "Stalking her blog isn't foreplay, Cash."

"At least I'm showing interest instead of brooding in corners like Ridge here."

Ridge snorts a laugh.

Cash vanishes down the hall and returns, measuring tape held high. "Gentlemen, prepare to be humbled."

"Hold up," I say. "Are we seriously about to whip our dicks out in the dining room?"

"You got a better location?" Cash asks.

"Literally anywhere else?"

"Kitchen's too risky. Living room has too many windows. My bedroom's too far and might give the wrong impression."

"As opposed to the right impression of three Alphas comparing cock sizes in the dining room?" Ridge asks incredulously.

"When you put it that way, it sounds weird," Cash admits.

"It *is* weird," I point out.

"But we're still doing it," Ridge says, and it's not a question.

"Hell yeah, we are," Cash confirms.

That's when a soft creak comes from the hallway. We all freeze, heads whipping toward the open doorway.

Sophia stands there, hands in the pockets of her denim shorts, smirking so wide her face might split. Her red hair is pulled up in a messy bun with tendrils framing her face, and she looks absolutely delicious.

More importantly, she looks like she's been standing there for a while.

"Don't let me interrupt. Please, continue with your... measurement party." Her voice drips with amusement.

Cash still has the measuring tape extended. Ridge's hands are frozen on his belt buckle. I'm pretty sure my face is red enough to brand cattle.

She bursts out laughing. Not a polite giggle or a shocked gasp. Full-bodied, bent-over, tears-streaming-down-her-face laughter. She has to grab the doorframe to stay upright, and the sound fills the room, warm and rich and completely uninhibited.

"I KNEW IT!" she gasps between breaths. "Oh my God, you actually... you were going to—" She dissolves into giggles again, one hand pressed to her stomach.

"How long have you been standing there?" Cash demands, his face matching mine in color.

"Long enough to witness the Great Dick Duel of Wild Hearts Ranch," Sophia says. "I know you've been reading my blog."

Ridge freezes. Cash pauses mid-step. I don't move. I just watch her, waiting to see how she plays it.

Sophia stands in the doorway like she owns the damn room, eyes sharp, lips twitching, fire in her posture. "Don't blame me," she says sweetly. "Blame your fragile egos. You read my recent blog posts and then, over dinner, tried to bait me with those not-so-subtle questions about how I've been sleeping, waking up, dreaming…"

I grin because of course she knew what we were doing. Hard not to, after she wrote about waking up mid-orgasm from dreams about us.

She lifts a brow, cocking her hip. "So, naturally, I followed up with a little blog post to teach you a lesson… and found you all about to measure yourselves like teenage boys in a locker room."

I shrug. "You drop something that spicy online, you're gonna start a fire. That's just how it works."

Sophia blinks, mock-serious. "And? The verdict?"

"Still pending," Ridge mutters.

Cash leans in slightly, eyes gleaming. "Unless you want to be the final judge."

Sophia bursts out laughing. That sharp, wicked sound of hers. Her grin turns downright dangerous. "Oh, I cannot wait to write the follow-up: 'Why Men Shouldn't Own Tape Measures.'"

Cash circles her like a wolf scenting a challenge. "Tell you what, sugar. We'll make it worth your while. A proper demonstration. All three of us. Line up for inspection."

She gasps, but the sound is laced with laughter.

"Imagine the traffic to your blog," I add, stepping closer,

drawn in without even trying to resist. *"Local Omega Reviews Three Alpha Cowboys.* You'd break the internet."

"Stop it!" She laughs again, biting her lower lip, flushed and glowing from the attention. "You're all absolutely terrible."

"For what it's worth," Ridge adds, "we could always settle it another way."

Sophia turns to him, still catching her breath. "What do you mean?"

"You could just admit you were playing us on your blog," he says, meeting her gaze. "That post? Those comments last night? You knew we'd read it. You were waiting to see what we'd do."

She lifts her chin, unbothered. "Guess that's one option."

The smile on her lips is still spirited, but something in the air shifts.

And just like that, we're standing on a fault line.

It would be so easy to keep going with this game, teasing, circling like it means nothing. We're all good at it. Too good, maybe. But I can feel it, deeper than the banter, under the surface, tension pulsing like a second heartbeat. And we're all thinking the same thing. This thing between us? It's not a joke.

We're walking a tightrope, and if we don't start grounding this in something real, it's going to burn us.

She's *ours.* We feel it. We know it. But she hasn't said the words. Not yet. And maybe that's what's holding us back from crossing the line we all keep pretending isn't there.

So, yeah. Time to stop circling.

I clear my throat, voice dropping. "Sophia. Let's sit. We need to talk."

Her eyes narrow, still playful. "That sounds ominous. Are we measuring something else now?"

I smirk, placing a light hand on the small of her back as I guide her toward the living room. "Just honesty."

The others follow. Sunlight spills in through the wide windows, casting a golden wash across the couch where she settles between Ridge and Cash like it's the most natural thing in the world. I sit across from her, on the coffee table, needing to see her face. Every reaction. Every flicker of emotion that passes through those gorgeous, guarded eyes.

This isn't a game anymore.

Not really.

Not for me.

"About last night," I begin, and I see her stiffen, just slightly. Her gaze flickers to me, then away. "What I said about moving in with us, I meant every word."

She exhales sharply through her nose. "We've talked about this—"

"Hear me out," I cut in, leaning forward, elbows on my knees, keeping my voice steady and low. "Your body is already responding to us. The scent matching—"

Ridge clears his throat.

"All of us," I amend, glancing at him with a dry look. "Whether certain stubborn Alphas want to admit it or not. You're fighting something that's natural. Something that's meant to be."

"Just like our Ridge here," Cash adds, nudging her arm with playful warmth. "Pretending he doesn't feel the pull too."

Sophia doesn't smile. Her arms curl tighter around herself, her legs shifting slightly where she sits between them. She's retreating, not physically, not yet, but it's in the way her shoulders rise, how her voice drops low.

"I've managed my heats alone for years," she says quietly.

And just like that, the room shifts.

Something about the way she says it, flat, like a fact, like an apology, has my breath catching in my throat.

"Even when I was rejected during one."

The air leaves my lungs in a rush. Cash's hands clench at his sides. Ridge doesn't move, but his entire body goes rigid —too still, the kind of stillness that feels dangerous.

We knew bits of her past. Enough to piece together her pain. But not the way she says it, like it's just another detail. Like it didn't shatter something inside her.

"Sophia," Ridge murmurs, and his voice is lower than I've ever heard it. "That should never have happened to you."

She tries to brush it off with a forced laugh. "It's fine. I'm fine. I handled it."

But her knuckles are white where she grips her thigh. Her shoulders are too square, too still. She's holding it in like it doesn't still echo.

"You shouldn't have had to," Cash murmurs, the flirt gone from his voice. He turns to her fully now, hand gently settling on her knee. "No Omega should ever go through that. Especially not during her heat. That's... that's sacred. That's when an Alpha should be at his most devoted."

"It wasn't that bad—" she starts.

"Stop." The growl escapes me before I can catch it. "Stop minimizing what he did to you."

Her eyes snap to mine, wide with surprise.

"You deserved better," I say, slower now, gentler but no less firm. "You deserved an Alpha who saw you for what you are. Who worshipped you. Who made you feel safe. Protected. Who *stayed*."

She's quiet for a moment. "It wasn't the first time he rejected me. Just the last."

My chest aches with the need to pull her into my arms. To protect, to soothe, to erase every cruel second that bastard carved into her. If he weren't already six feet under,

I'd find a way to make him hurt. Slowly. Quietly. Permanently.

But right now? That doesn't matter.

She does.

"You've been so strong for so long, Sophia," Ridge says quietly, and it's the tenderness in his voice that nearly undoes me. Not the rough edge, not the grit. Just the gentle way he says her name like it matters. Like *she* matters. Like he's finally gotten over his damn brooding.

His hand finds hers. Large, calloused, careful. He doesn't grip; he cradles. Like she's something fragile.

"There's nothing weak about letting your guard down," he continues. "Nothing wrong with letting someone else carry the weight now."

She doesn't speak. Doesn't move. But her fingers curl into his.

Cash shifts beside them, slower than usual, all that easy charm stripped back to something steady. Intentional. He places his hand over both of theirs, anchoring the moment with quiet strength.

"Let us carry the load for you," he says. "So you don't have to keep pretending you're fine if you don't want to. So you never feel forgotten again. Never feel less than the absolute treasure you are."

Her breath hitches.

And just like that, the cracks show.

Her jaw trembles first. Then her lips press tight like she's trying to fight it, but her eyes betray her. Glimmering, glassy, one blink away from shattering.

And then... she does.

A single tear slips free, trailing slowly down her cheek.

I feel it like a punch.

Because this isn't a woman trying to manipulate or perform. She's been carrying too much for too long and doesn't remember what it feels like to be held.

I rise from the coffee table and kneel in front of her, one hand resting on her knee, grounding her. We've surrounded her without planning to, like instinct. Like gravity.

"You don't have to do this alone anymore," I tell her. "Let us be the walls around you. So nothing ever hurts you again."

A soft sob breaks from her lips. Then another. No gasping, no theatrics. Just silent tears falling one after the other, her entire body folding in as if she's finally safe enough to unravel.

Cash moves first, pulling her gently against his chest, arms wrapping around her like she's precious. Ridge leans in from her other side, pressing his forehead to her temple, hand still wrapped tightly in hers.

I stay where I am, on my knees in front of her, both hands now holding her legs as if to remind her that I'm here too. We all are. We're not going anywhere.

And she fits, so perfectly, in the center of us. Like she was carved from the space between us. Like every inch of her was meant to be held like this.

"I'm sorry," she whispers eventually, hiccuping through the tears. "I don't usually get like this. It's... embarrassing."

Ridge shakes his head, lips near her hairline. "You don't have to apologize for being human."

Cash rubs slow circles into her back. "You've been holding too much. This was bound to spill."

"You don't need to pretend around us," I add. "We'll figure it out. All of us. Together."

She nods, but her shoulders tense—just a little. That subtle pullback. Her body trying to rebuild walls even as we hold her.

We've pushed her hard. Too fast. She let go for a moment, but she's clearly afraid of what it means to *stay* open.

I gently squeeze her knee. "Hey," I say, voice quiet. "It's

okay. We're not rushing anything. We're not going anywhere. You take all the time you need."

Her eyes lift, red-rimmed and cautious, and I offer her the softest smile I can.

"We've got nothing but time, Sophia. And it's yours."

She pulls back slightly, wiping her eyes with the back of her hand. Her breath still trembles on the exhale, but there's clarity in her expression now. Calm after the storm.

"You guys..." Her voice cracks, and she clears it, but she doesn't retreat this time. "Thank you. I don't think I've ever... had that. Not like this. Not from anyone."

Ridge squeezes her hand, silent and steady beside her. Cash rubs her back, waiting without pushing. I don't speak. I just hold her gaze, grounding her.

"I don't know what to do with it yet," she admits, voice soft. "I want to be here. I want to try. But right now, I just... I need a little space to breathe. To sort out what's mine and what's fear talking."

"No pressure," I say gently. "Take all the time you need."

"We're not going anywhere," Cash adds.

Sophia smiles—small, but real. "I know."

She stands slowly. Her legs brush mine as she rises, and she pauses, glancing down at all three of us like she's seeing us fully for the first time.

"I just need some time," she says, voice steadier now. "Before this turns into something even bigger than it already is."

She walks to the door, and just before stepping out, she looks back.

"Thank you for not making me feel weak for needing someone."

And then she slips outside, the door closing softly, leaving behind silence that hums with possibility.

20

The afternoon sun beats mercilessly on my shoulders as I work the fence line near the animal shelter section. The posts have been sagging for weeks—probably from the goats using them as their personal scratching posts. The throb in my hip is there, quieter than usual. Three years since the accident, and I still move like an old man some days.

I've got my toolbox spread out, new wire coiled at my feet, trying to focus on something other than the Omega who's been haunting my every thought. Yet my gaze keeps drifting to the pen beyond the fence I'm repairing, where she's attempting to feed the rescue goats.

She's completely swarmed, clearly out of her element. Not a ranch girl—that's obvious from how she holds the feed bucket like it might explode. But there she is, boots planted uncertainly in the mud, wearing jeans and a shirt, and that red hair fluttering in the breeze as she tries to fend off eager goat heads.

"Harold!" Her voice carries across the field, sharp with exasperation. "Back it up. I see you, and no, my shirt is NOT a snack for your face!"

Harold, our biggest and most stubborn billy goat, butts against her hip with enough force to make her stumble. The bucket tilts dangerously in her grip.

"Oh, you think you're tough?" She plants a hand on her hip, staring him down with more courage than sense. "I've dealt with Chicago rush-hour traffic, buddy."

I pause mid-hammer swing, something dark and possessive stirring in my chest. She's arguing with them like they understand every word, and maybe they do. Harold tilts his head, considering his options, before making another grab for her pocket.

"That's it!" She backs up, holding the bucket high above her head. "Y'all had better be glad you're cute, or I'd be filing workplace harassment charges. This is a hostile work environment! I know my rights!"

I chuckle to myself.

Mabel, our escape-artist doe, sneaks behind her and starts nibbling at her calf through her jeans.

"OW!" Sophia jumps, spinning around so fast she nearly loses her balance. "What kind of evolutionary advantage is that supposed to be? Darwin would be appalled!"

I'm fighting not to laugh out loud now. The way she moves, all that untamed energy, that mouth that never stops, it makes me want things I shouldn't want. Dark things. Things that would probably scare her if she knew the thoughts running through my head.

"Listen up, you mangy lot," she announces, attempting to pour feed into the trough while using her knee to block Harold's advances. "Form an orderly line, or I swear I'll turn every last one of you into stew. Don't test me. I have recipes. Google is free, and I'm not afraid to use it!"

The goats surge forward in complete chaos, ignoring her threats entirely. She squeals, laughing despite herself, and the sound shoots straight through me like lightning. I'm grinning like a fool, watching and listening to her.

I turn back to the fence post, gripping the hammer harder than necessary. Need to focus. Can't spend all day watching her like some kind of stalker. That's Cash's job. Just need to secure this last section.

When I look back up, not even ten seconds later, she's gone.

The bucket is on its side, feed scattered everywhere.

Every single goat is perched along the natural rise in the ground, necks craned as they peer over the edge at the five-foot drop into the deep riverbed below.

Ice floods my veins, colder than any winter storm.

"Sophia!" I call out.

Nothing. Just the wind through the grass and my own blood roaring in my ears.

I drop everything and vault over the fence line into the pen, boots sliding in the mud as I race to the edge. The slope is nearly vertical here in this section, all loose dirt and exposed roots, and below—

The river is moving fast enough to take down a full-grown steer. The banks are sheer clay walls with nothing to grab on to. If you go in, you don't come out without help.

I can't see her. Just ripples. A disturbance in the current that could be anything.

A sound, so faint I might be imagining it, then a splash. Maybe her voice, cut off by water.

That's all it takes.

I launch myself down the slope without thinking, half sliding, half falling until I hit the water like a sledgehammer. The cold knocks every thought from my head except one: Find her.

The current immediately tries to claim me, pulling me downstream toward the rapids. I fight against it, diving under, eyes burning in the murky water. Can't see more than a foot in front of me. My hands sweep through nothing but silt and branches.

I surface, gasping. "SOPHIA!"

Just the rush of water that suddenly sounds like mocking laughter.

I dive again, deeper this time, lungs already protesting. The water is so dark it could be midnight down here. My hands search, finding nothing, nothing, nothing—

I breach the surface and spot hair floating like silk ribbons in the current.

My heart squeezes.

Frantically, I swim over and grab her, hauling her against my chest as I kick desperately for the edge of the river. I'm gasping. She's limp in my arms, a rag doll.

"Don't you dare," I call out. "Sophia, do you hear me?"

The current fights me for her, trying to tear her from my grip, but I'll die before I let go. I fight to get us up the bank, using strength I didn't know I had left to haul us both up the muddy slope. All I can see is her face, too pale, too still.

I lay her on the grass, hands shaking as I tilt her head back, check her airway. She's breathing... Just.

I drop to my knees beside her. "Don't you dare do this to me."

Her eyes flip open, wide and unfocused. She coughs violently, water sputtering from her mouth as her chest heaves like her lungs can't decide whether to work or give out.

I push the wet hair from her face. "Sophia, hey. Look at me. You're okay. Just breathe."

She wheezes in another breath, then coughs again, deep, racking, like it's clawing its way up from her ribs.

I shift her onto her side, steadying her with one hand on her shoulder, the other rubbing circles on her back. "That's it. Let it out. You're safe now."

Her fingers clutch the grass, nails digging in. She's shaking all over.

"You hit your head?" I ask, gently running my hand over

her scalp, checking for anything bleeding or swollen. "Sophia. Talk to me."

She flinches at my touch but doesn't pull away. Just coughs again, slower this time. Less frantic.

"Why didn't you swim?"

She doesn't answer. Maybe she can't. But she's breathing now, chest rising steadily beneath her soaked shirt, and it's the only thing keeping me from falling apart completely.

"R-Ridge?" Her voice is barely there, scraped raw.

"I'm here. Not going anywhere."

Terror and guilt twist in my gut like barbed wire being pulled tight. One second she was there, laughing, threatening to turn my goats into dinner, and the next she was gone. I'd looked away. Just for a moment, but it was enough. Almost enough to lose her.

"I-I don't know how to swim," she gasps, cheeks flushing.

God. She could've drowned. Right here on my land. Because I didn't know. Because I didn't think.

I cup her face gently, trying to steady both of us. Her skin is cold and slick with river water, but her cheeks are burning with embarrassment.

"Hey," I say softly, brushing a soaked strand of hair from her face. "You didn't do anything wrong, all right? This isn't your land; you couldn't have known how steep it gets there. But you scared the hell out of me."

Her lashes flutter, water clinging to them. She looks so damn vulnerable that it tears at something deep inside me.

"I'm going to teach you how to swim, sweetheart. Personally. Okay? And get that fence up there damn fast too."

"Okay," she whispers back. "I'd like your lessons." She blinks slowly, her eyes struggling to focus. "The goats... Harold pushed me..."

A weak, watery cough cuts her off.

"Harold's going on a diet after this," I tease, but it cracks like dry timber. "Actually, forget the diet. He's getting turned into curry."

A faint ghost of a smile curves her lips, and she's laughing lightly.

"Ridge... I need to tell you—"

"No." The word rips out of me, too sharp. I try again, gentler. "No deathbed confessions. You're not dying. I've got you."

"I know," she agrees softly, coughing again. "Just... need you to know..."

Something in her voice makes everything inside me still.

"Know what?"

"I feel it. The pull. The... connection to you, as strong as it is to Cash and Walker."

Her voice is hoarse, but her grip on my hand is steady. Stronger than it should be after what just happened.

"Been fighting it since I got here," she adds, her gaze flicking between my eyes like she's afraid of what she'll find there.

I've spent all this time convincing myself she didn't feel it for me the same way. That whatever was happening between her and the others... it didn't include me.

"I think we're scent matches," she whispers.

The words nearly stop my heart.

I glance down at our hands, trembling, hers so small wrapped around mine like it's the only thing keeping her tethered here. And maybe it is.

"I can't scent you," I admit. The confession tastes bitter after holding it down so long. "Some days I think I'm losing my damn mind."

Her fingers curl tighter, staring at me.

"I didn't think it could happen for me anymore. Not after the accident. Not with all the ways I came out of it...

wrong." My voice cracks on the last word, yet I push through. "But I think there were signs I've been too scared to look at."

She blinks up at me.

I pause, swallow hard. "The pain in my hip, three years of living with it every single day, every step like broken glass under my skin. But since you got here..."

I search her face, needing her to understand.

"It's like my body forgets to hurt. Like it eases just by being around you. You... soften it. You soften *me*."

Her breath catches, eyes shining with what looks an awful lot like a realization.

"I didn't want you to pity me," I say, quieter now. "Didn't want to be the one you felt obligated to bond with. Not just because you were a match with Walker and Cash."

"Then don't think for a second I feel sorry for you." Her voice is rough, shaky. "You pulled me out of that river, Ridge. You saved me. Broken or not, you were the only one I wanted when I thought I was slipping under."

A noise escapes my throat, half laugh, half sob. Like she cracked me open, a part of me I didn't know was still breakable.

And even drenched and shivering, she's still the most beautiful damn thing I've ever seen.

Tears mix with river water on her cheeks. She's trying to say something but can't get the words out between the coughing and tears.

She pushes herself up, facing me fully. Her eyes blaze with fierceness despite how she's trembling.

"You'd better not ever drown on me again," I say. "That's an order. Now, do you need me to give you some mouth-to-mouth?" I grin.

A weak smile tugs at her lips. "Maybe you should. Might have been worth drowning for."

My laugh comes out strangled. "Don't tempt me."

I stand, lifting her into my arms. She weighs nothing, feels too fragile.

"Where—"

"Getting you warm and dry. No arguments."

She doesn't protest, just burrows closer, and I feel that purr starting in her chest. Faint, but there. A sign of trust that threatens to undo me completely.

I carry her straight to my room, kicking the door shut behind us. My bathroom is bigger than the entire guest-house bedroom, with a huge claw-foot tub and enough towels to dry a small army. I set her on the counter, her legs dangling, and grab towels from the cabinet.

"Let's get you out of these wet clothes," I say, turning to give her privacy by facing the door.

Her hand suddenly grabs my wrist. "Don't leave me. Please."

The raw fear in her voice stops me cold. This isn't about modesty or propriety. This is terror, bone-deep and real.

"I'm not going anywhere."

We stand in silence for a moment.

"Nolan tried to drown me once," she admits softly.

The words come out in a rush, like she's been holding them back with a dam that just broke. Her whole body starts shaking violently, teeth chattering.

"Fucking bastard." I step nearer, wrapping my arms around her so she's closer to my body, my warmth.

"In our pool," she continues. "He... he held me under. Said maybe he'd be better off getting rid of me. Make it seem like an accident so he didn't have to look at me anymore."

Her lips pinch to the side like she's trying to fight off sorrow, and my heart is shredded to hear her words.

"He said I was embarrassing. That I didn't deserve to be his Omega. That the sight of me made him sick. And then he pushed me under and held me there until I stopped fighting."

Rage floods through me, hot and violent enough to burn away any remaining cold. If that asshole wasn't already dead, I'd kill him myself. Slowly. Make him suffer every second of fear he gave her.

"He pulled me up just before I passed out," she says, voice breaking. "Laughed. Said he was just kidding, that I needed to learn to take a joke. But I never learned to swim after that. The water... every time I'm near deep water, I hear his voice. Feel his hands on my head, pushing me down."

"He's gone now," I say softly, trying to keep my voice level when all I want to do is tear through time and rip his throat out. "He can't hurt you anymore."

She nods faintly, but then her lips tremble. "I know. But when I went under today..." Her voice cracks. "All I could think was that he was right. That I was going to die alone in the water just like he said I deserved."

Something sharp splinters inside me. Not rage. But helplessness laced with grief that she ever believed that. That someone carved those words into her like truth.

"You're not alone," I say, stepping between her knees, cupping her face gently. My thumb brushes a tear from her cheek, then another, and still they come. "You'll never be on your own again. I swear to you, Sophia. Not as long as I'm breathing."

Her shoulders quake, and she folds into me without warning, pressing her soaked face into my neck. I hold her tighter, closer. I don't care that we're both dripping.

Gradually, her breathing evens out. The sobs soften into quiet trembles, then stillness, her fingers curling gently into the fabric of my shirt. She pulls back just enough to look up at me, eyes red-rimmed but clearing. Her lips twitch, and then a small laugh escapes.

"God," she says, voice scratchy but lighter. "You must think I'm a total mess."

I brush my thumb over her cheek, not smiling but not

serious either. "I think you nearly drowned. I think you were terrified. And I think you're still standing, even if it's with help. That doesn't make you a mess. That makes you strong."

Her eyes shimmer again.

She huffs out a breath and looks down, plucking at the wet hem of her shirt. "Guess I should get out of these clothes before I freeze." Her fingers move to the first button, struggling a little with the tremble still in her hands.

But she doesn't get far.

"Help me?" she whispers, almost too quiet to hear. "I can't... my fingers won't work right. Everything's numb."

"I've got you."

I ease her gently from the counter like she weighs nothing. She leans into me, half standing, and her hands quiver at the hem of her shirt, fumbling.

So I reach for her hands, cover them with mine, and slowly lift the wet fabric over her head. I try to be clinical. Gentle. Detached. But nothing about her feels clinical to me, not the way her breath hitches, not the way her skin prickles under my touch, not the way she looks at me like I'm the only thing holding her together.

She's shivering in just her soaked jeans and a thin, white cotton bra now, goose bumps breaking out across skin I've only ever imagined touching.

And fuck me, she's stunning.

The bra clings to her like a second skin, translucent from the water, revealing the soft swell of her breasts and the perfect curve of her cleavage, those delicious pink nipples. My gaze flicks there before I can stop it. I want to bury my face in that softness, kiss my way down every inch, feel her arch under my mouth.

Pale, perfect skin scattered with faint freckles, like stars someone tossed across her shoulders. A soft dip at her waist

I want to memorize with my mouth. She's exquisite. Vulnerable. Mine.

But I don't let myself linger.

Not now.

Not when she's trusting me to help, not devour her. Later, maybe. When she's ready, when she's begging. But right now, I shove the hunger down deep and try to breathe through it.

She fumbles with the button of her jeans, fingers trembling too badly to get it undone. "Stupid wet denim," she mutters, cheeks flushed, not just from cold anymore.

"Let me," I say roughly, kneeling before her.

Her breath hitches as I undo the button and slowly pull down the zipper of her soaked denim jeans. I take my time, careful not to tug too hard, careful not to look too long at the way her hips shift to help me. My knuckles brush her thighs, and she shivers.

I slide the jeans down inch by inch, over her hips, past the curve of her thighs, her soaked panties sticking to the denim and slipping down with them. She doesn't stop me. Just breathes, slow and shallow, her hands still braced on my shoulders, her legs slightly parted to help me.

By the time I reach her ankles and tug the whole mess off, she's bare. Somewhere between removing her top and me peeling those jeans and panties away, she must have ditched her bra too.

She's completely naked. Wet. Shivering. Glorious.

And I can't look away.

She's all soft curves and pale, lightly freckled skin, flushed from cold and adrenaline. Her nipples are tight from the chill, and God, her breasts are bouncy and perfect. Full and high and made to be held, to be worshipped. A line of red curls leads down between her thighs, and just the sight of it makes my vision darken around the edges.

My mouth waters. My cock throbs so hard it's painful. And still I don't move. Not unless she asks.

Her voice is barely a whisper. "Your turn."

"You don't have to—"

"I want to." Her fingers reach for the buttons on my shirt again as I get to my feet. "Please. I need... to feel warm. To feel alive. To know this is real."

The hunger in her voice urges me on.

I let her unbutton my shirt, helping when her fingers falter. Every brush of her hands on my skin is electric, every second I spend standing still takes a Herculean effort not to drag her into my arms and bury myself in her warmth.

She pushes the shirt from my shoulders, and her hands don't fall away. Instead, they slide across my chest, fingers tracing the pale scar down my ribs, then the puncture mark on my side. She's memorizing me. Not flinching. Not pitying.

"Jesus, Sophia," I rasp. "You're gonna break me."

She looks up at me, still damp, still flushed, completely naked and entirely the most beautiful thing I've ever seen in my life.

"Then break," she whispers.

My jeans are next, and I have to help with the belt, the button, everything. Her hands are too unsteady. I take it all off, kick them aside. When I'm standing there in nothing, she steps closer, pressing against me, skin to skin.

The contact lights up every nerve ending. She's ice cold but warming quickly, and I wrap my arms around her, trying to share my heat.

"You're so warm," she murmurs against my chest.

I grab a towel, starting with her hair, trying to focus on the task instead of how perfectly she fits against me. The towel moves down her shoulders, her back, and she makes this small sound, not quite a moan, not quite a sigh, that goes straight to my cock.

"Turn around," I murmur. "Let me dry you properly."

She turns, and I have to bite back a groan. The curve of her spine, the perfect roundness of her ass, the way her hair falls wet down her back. She's going to be the death of me.

I run the towel down her back, across her hips, trying to be thorough but gentle. When I kneel to dry her legs, I'm eye level with perfection, and my control starts to crack.

"Ridge?" Her voice is soft, uncertain.

"Yeah?"

"I've been aching for someone to touch me and make me feel wanted and alive." She turns to face me, and I'm still on my knees, looking up at her like she's a goddess. "Will you?"

My control doesn't just crack; it shatters completely.

I surge to my feet, capturing her mouth in a kiss that's all desperation and need. She responds immediately, opening for me, her tongue sliding against mine as she presses closer. She tastes like river water and sweetness underneath, and my head spins.

My hands tangle in her wet hair, angling her head to deepen the kiss. She makes a sound—half whimper, half moan—that has me pressing closer with need.

She gasps against my lips. "Please. I need—"

"I know what you need," I growl, walking her out of the bathroom and into my bedroom. "The question is whether you can handle what I want to give you."

The corners of her lips curl upward. "Try me."

The challenge in her voice triggers that primal side of me. The same rush I used to get right before the gate opened, eight seconds of adrenaline waiting on the other side. Except this time, I plan to last a hell of a lot longer.

"You have no idea what you're asking for," I tell her. "I'm not gentle. Not soft. I take what I want, and right now, what I want is to make you scream until your throat is raw."

Instead of fear, heat flares in her eyes. "Then why are you still talking?"

Brave little Omega. She'll soon meet the beast she's provoking.

I spin her around, pressing her face-first against the wall beside my bed. She gasps, hands splaying against the wood, and I cage her in with my body.

"You sure about this?" I murmur in her ear, giving her one last out. "Because once I start, I won't stop. Not until you're marked, claimed, and so thoroughly mine that you'll feel me for days."

She pushes back against me. "Stop threatening and start delivering, cowboy."

That's all I need.

I grab the rope from my gear bag in the corner, not the rough stuff I use for the ranch, but the soft cotton rope I've had since my rodeo days. I always keep it close. Some habits die hard, and the need for control is one of them.

"On the bed," I order. "On your stomach."

She moves immediately, crawling onto my bed with a grace that leaves me drooling. The sight of her, all that pale skin still damp, hair falling like wet silk around her shoulders, it's enough to drive a saint to sin.

And I'm no saint.

"Wrists," I command.

She extends her arms toward the headboard, watching as I loop the rope around one wrist, then the other, securing both to the headboard with enough slack that she can move but not escape.

"Why do you like this?" she asks.

I run my hand down her spine, feeling her shiver. "Because you're mine to pleasure. Mine to worship. Mine to wreck." My hand reaches her ass, squeezing hard enough to leave marks. "And because you trust me enough to let me."

She moans, dropping her head between her arms, lifting her ass so she's on her knees. "I do trust you."

"Good." I move behind her, spreading her thighs wider

with my hand. "Because I'm about to ruin you for anyone else."

The sight of her like this, open, vulnerable, trusting, it feeds something dark in me. The same part that used to crave the adrenaline of riding bulls, the knife-edge between control and madness.

"You're already so wet," I observe, running a finger through her folds. She jerks at the contact, a whimper escaping. "From being at my mercy."

She gasps. "Everything. You."

I drop to my knees behind her, the sight of her all flushed, trembling, dripping with slick, burns into my brain. My hands grip her hips, thumbs stroking the soft curve where her ass meets her thighs. She's shaking, not from cold now, but from anticipation that hums between us.

I part her slowly, deliberately, my thumbs coaxing her lips open until I can see every swollen, glistening inch of her.

"Look at you," I murmur, my voice low and rough. "Perfect little Omega pussy, wet and ready for me."

She lets out a breathy whimper, her fingers tightening on the bed blanket, knuckles pale.

I lean in and drag my tongue over her, from the very bottom of the swollen bud of her clit up to the slit, tasting her, savoring the shiver that runs through her. When I circle my tongue there, she cries out, hips jerking, but I hold her still, my grip firm.

"Stay right there," I tell her, my mouth brushing her as I speak. "You move, and I'll start over. And you don't want me to start over, sweetheart."

"Oh my God... Ridge..." Her voice breaks into a moan as I seal my mouth over her and suck gently, then harder, until her thighs start to quake.

I explore her with my tongue like I've got all day, because I do, mapping her with deliberate strokes. I find the exact pressure that makes her moan louder, the rhythm that makes her writhe faster.

"That's it," I growl against her. "Let me hear you. Louder."

I slip two fingers into her, gradually at first, just enough to feel her squeeze around me. She's so tight, so wet, it's almost painful not to be inside her yet.

Her moan turns desperate, broken. "Please... more."

The plea punches right through my control. I add a third finger, stretching her open inch by inch.

"Fuck, your pussy holds on to me like you're scared I'll stop," I rasp, pumping into her. "I'm not stopping, sweetheart. Not until you're shaking so hard you can't even say my name."

Her head tips back, releasing a needy cry.

"You're going to come for me," I tell her, dragging my tongue over her clit while my fingers fuck her steadily. "Again. And again. And again. Just like that filthy demon book you wrote about in your blog. Seven times, right?"

Her eyes fly open, cheeks flushed. "You... read—"

"I had to buy and read the book after you recommended it." My mouth curls into a wicked smile against her. "Now I know exactly how to ruin you."

"Oh, fuck..." she breathes, and I feel her clench around me at the words.

"That's right. You want someone who'll worship your body until you can't take any more. You're going to get it, Omega."

I work her faster, harder, curling my fingers with every thrust until she's trembling so violently I have to hold her steady. Her moans turn into frantic gasps, the wet sound of my fingers working her filling the room.

Then she breaks, her whole body locking up before she comes around me, crying out my name like it's the only thing keeping her tethered.

I draw my fingers out slowly, watching her collapse against the bed, panting.

"That was..." She's still catching her breath, voice wrecked. "That was intense."

I grip her hips, move forward, and lie over her so my mouth is at her ear, my chest pressed against her bare back, and slide my cock along her slick folds. The heat of her against me blurs my vision.

"We're just getting started," I promise, letting the head of my cock nudge against her entrance, teasing her with the threat of what's coming.

Her hips shift under me, the curve of her back arching just enough for her to glance over her shoulder at me.

"You're... so big," she breathes, eyes wide with something between want and doubt. "I don't know if—"

"You'll take me," I cut in, my voice low, certain. I press the tip deeper into her, slow, deliberate. "Every inch. You were made for me."

The first push draws a gasp from her, her arms outstretched, wrists tied up. She tenses, so I still my hips. "Breathe," I say. "Let me in, beautiful."

She exhales shakily, and I pull back and start to move again, inch by inch, feeling her body stretch around me. The sight nearly undoes me. My grip on her hips tightens, holding her steady as I sink deeper.

"That's it," I coax. "Good girl. You're taking me perfectly."

By the time I'm fully inside her, my pulse is pounding in my ears. She's trembling.

"Move," she whispers, almost pleading. "Please, Ridge... move inside me."

"Careful what you ask for," I warn, but I draw back and thrust in again. The bed creaks beneath us, her soft sounds spilling into the room with every push.

She presses back into me, giving as much as she takes,

and my control frays fast. I grip her hips hard enough that she'll feel it tomorrow and drive into her like I've been waiting my whole damn life for this moment.

Her body bows, a strangled cry ripping from her throat, and she clenches around me so tightly with her orgasm, hitting so fast, so intense. I have to grit my teeth at how hard she grips my cock.

"That's two," I growl against her shoulder. "Five more to go."

She shakes her head weakly. "I can't—"

"You will," I tell her, already pulling her hips back to meet mine again. "And when I'm done, you'll be begging me for more."

Her thighs start to shake, her knees threatening to give way, but my grip on her hips is iron. I keep her right where I want her, my body slamming into her. I keep at it, living a dream, thrusting in and out, each plunge taking me into Nirvana. I lose track of time, lost in my own heaven.

"Oh, fuck—" she cries, the words splintering into a scream as she comes again, her body locking tightly around me.

"That's four to go," I grit out, not easing up, fucking her through the aftershocks until her moans break into ragged little sobs of pleasure. Her body is trembling beneath me, slick and perfect, but I'm nowhere close to being done. "Next ones will be on your back."

Before she can catch her breath, let alone protest, I pull out, then flip her. The rope at her wrists has enough give to let her turn without biting into her skin, bringing her arms closer together above her head. She gasps at the sudden movement, her hair tumbling over flushed cheeks, eyes hazy with lust and a touch of surprise.

God, she's stunning like this. Face soft with pleasure, lips swollen from biting them, pupils blown wide. I could spend hours just watching her like this, but I want more. I want her wrecked.

Her legs part for me without thought, showing me her glistening pussy, spread for me. Instinct takes over, and I press closer between her thighs, lining myself up. One hard thrust and I'm buried inside her again, her cry breaking against the quiet.

Her hips lift to meet mine, like she can't decide whether she's trying to escape or pull me closer.

"You're so deep," she gasps, her voice a raw, breathless confession. "I can feel you everywhere."

"Good." My hand slides up her body, wrapping gently but firmly around her throat, my thumb pressing in the hollow just enough to feel the rapid thud of her pulse. "I want you thinking about me every time you walk. Every time you try to sleep. Every time you touch yourself. I want you to be mine."

Her eyes flutter shut, a needy whimper spilling from her lips as I pound into her, the headboard thudding in rhythm. The sight of her head tipped back, mouth open, hair sticking to her damp temples, burns itself into my brain.

Her body tightens around me again, and I sense the rush building in her before she even cries out. I don't stop. I don't slow. I hold her exactly where I want her and slam into her one final time, driving her over the edge until she's screaming my name like it's the only word she knows.

I lean forward, pressing my forehead to hers as she shakes beneath me. "Three more, sweetheart. And I'm still not finished with you."

"God, Ridge, I can't," she gasps, her voice breaking. "Let's save it for a bit later."

I smirk at how fucking adorable she is, still trembling, still panting, still rolling her hips against my cock even as she swears she can't take another. "You're saying no with your mouth, but your body's begging for more."

I shift my weight, keeping myself buried inside her, and slide my hand between us. My thumb finds her clit, swollen, slick, throbbing, and I work it in slow, tight circles. Her breath catches instantly, her hips jerking despite herself. When I pinch lightly, she lets out a strangled cry, her hands tugging at the rope above her head.

"That's it," I growl. "Give it to me. I want to feel you fall apart again."

She shakes her head like she's trying to fight it, but her thighs are trembling. I keep her pinned exactly where I want her, fucking her slow and deep while my thumb never stops its relentless rhythm.

"Ridge, oh my God—" Her voice splinters as the pleasure takes over, her body tightening around me in hard, desperate pulses. She's gasping now, eyes squeezing shut, legs locking against my hips as if she can hold me inside forever. I hiss at her strangling me, but it's fucking bliss.

"Two to go," I say when the tremors finally begin to ease, but I don't let her catch her breath. I grip her hips, roll her under me, and thrust again, deep enough to make her arch off the bed with a sharp gasp.

Her chest heaves with each breath.

"You're so beautiful like this," I tell her.

She's moaning, smiling. "This might actually kill me."

"But what a way to go," I tease, and she laughs even with me buried to the hilt inside her. The sound melts into a desperate moan as I work out and in, hitting that spot that makes her thighs tighten around me.

I feel the flutter start inside her that suggests she's close. "That's it," I encourage, my voice low and rough. "Give me another one, sweetheart."

She comes with a scream that could probably reach the ranch hands' quarters, her whole body seizing under mine. I have to freeze, gritting my teeth so I don't lose control and follow her over.

"That's six," I pant, leaning down to press my lips to hers. "One more and you've lived your demon fantasy." I grin, to which she is smiling and laughing. "But we can stop if you want—just say the word. Anything you need, I'll do it."

Her eyes are glazed, her lips trembling, and I smooth a hand over her hair. She makes this sound in her throat, low, needy, almost a purr, that goes straight to my cock.

"I know I said I couldn't," she breathes, "but God... when you stop, the ache comes back. The hunger. I really want to feel your knot, Ridge... please. Keep going."

That's all I need to hear. I cup the back of her neck, force her to look at me. "You're sure?"

"Yes." It's barely a whisper.

I start again, slow, deep, grinding into her. She gasps, and I let the pace build until she's making those sweet, helpless sounds that tell me she's gone again. I work her clit with my thumb, pinning her in place as her body bows beneath me.

She cries out, shuddering just as my knot swells, stretching her even more, and she groans louder, eyes wide as the full pressure locks me inside her.

The sensation is almost too much, her gripping me like her body is trying to keep me forever. I'm as deep as I can go, and the knot locks tight. Her scream of pleasure turns into a long, broken moan as she comes, the seventh orgasm ripping through her in waves.

I lean over her, spilling into her in hard, relentless pulses. My cock throbs inside her, pumping her full. I hold her through every shudder, every aftershock, keeping her pinned against me like she might somehow slip away if I let go.

"Mine," I growl against her damp skin, my lips brushing the frantic beat of her pulse. "My Omega. My mate."

Her whole body tightens at the words, a sob tearing

from her throat as she arches into me, desperate for even closer contact despite the knot holding us flush together. "Yours," she gasps, the word breaking on a moan. "Always yours."

I reach up, fingers working at the knot in the rope until it loosens. Her wrists come free, and I take them gently, bringing each one to my mouth. I kiss along the tender skin where the bindings held her, lingering there like I can erase every mark.

She just watches me like she's completely smitten, and I fucking love her staring at me that way.

She makes a soft sound when I roll onto my side, taking her with me and maneuvering her so her leg isn't trapped beneath me. She hooks the other leg over my hip, pulling me in closer. We're still locked, my knot buried deep, keeping me inside her, and the position presses her breasts flush against my chest, skin to skin, both of us breathing hard.

My knot is... unlike anything else. It's more than just the physical stretch. It's the way it binds her to me, the way her body clenches and pulses around it, milking every drop I give her. I can feel the faint tug every time her hips shift, the deep, slow throb of her muscles around me. It's primal. Claiming. Like the universe carved us to fit only this way.

Her forehead rests against mine, her lips parting as she drags in shaky breaths. I study every flicker of sensation on her face, the pleasure still washing through her in waves, the warmth spreading between us from where we're touching. My hand curves around her jaw, my thumb brushing over her lower lip before I kiss her, unhurried.

"You feel it, don't you?" I murmur against her mouth, smirking. "The way you can't get away from me even if you tried."

Her eyes are heavy-lidded, pupils wide. "Yes. Oh, yes. I like it like this."

I smile, but it's sharp, possessive. "Good. Because I'm not letting you go. Not now. Not ever."

Her breathing starts to slow, lashes fluttering as exhaustion tugs at her. I smooth a damp strand of hair from her cheek, keeping my arm locked tightly around her waist.

"Rest," I whisper. "I've got you."

Her lips curve in a drowsy, wicked little smile. "I still can't believe you made me come seven times. I feel like an Olympic champion."

A low laugh rumbles in my chest. "Gold medal performance, sweetheart. You're getting a trophy. Hell, I'll build you a damn podium."

She lets out a soft snort before her head finds its place on my outstretched arm, her body molding perfectly to mine despite the heat still simmering between us.

I hold her there, feeling her breathing deepen. And as she drifts, I realize I've never known this kind of peace, never known the kind of bone-deep happiness that comes from having an Omega in my arms, trusting me enough to fall asleep right here, still connected.

And I know, without a single doubt, I'm never letting her go.

21

SOPHIA

I wake up in a large bed alone, and for a moment, I can't remember where I am. Then it all crashes back—the river, the drowning, Ridge pulling me out, his confession, and then... oh God. Everything that happened after.

My body feels like it's been thoroughly claimed. The ache between my thighs is deep and satisfying, a reminder that Ridge made me come seven times. Seven. Like he was proving some kind of point about rodeo stamina. My inner muscles clench at the memory, and I can still feel the phantom stretch of him inside me.

But underneath the satisfaction, a different kind of heat stirs, low in my belly. Not arousal, though that's there too, but something more primal. More urgent than it should be for pre-heat.

"No," I whisper to the empty room, pressing my hand to my stomach. "This can't be happening."

My heat isn't due for weeks. I calculated it carefully before coming here, made sure I'd have time to figure things out before dealing with that particular complication. But my body doesn't seem to care about my calendar.

I stretch, trying to ignore the growing warmth, and roll

onto Ridge's pillow. His scent of cedar wood, cinnamon bark, and fresh mountain air wraps around me like a blanket. For a moment, it soothes the building fire in my veins, makes everything feel safe and right.

But I need to get up. Need to figure out what to do.

I shift to swing my legs out of bed, expecting to feel the sticky reminder of our activities. I glance down at the sheets, preparing to see evidence of what we did, but there's only a small spot where we were joined. Confused, I reach between my thighs and don't find myself in a mess.

My fingers come away only slightly damp.

"What the..." I touch my inner thighs. Clean. Completely clean, like someone took a warm cloth and carefully...

"Oh my God. He cleaned me. While I was sleeping."

The thought of Ridge—gruff, brooding Ridge—gently cleaning me while I slept makes my heart twirl. That's so intimate, so caring, so unlike what I expected from the damaged rodeo star who ties women to his bed.

"Get it together, Sophia," I mutter, but my voice comes out shaky.

The heat in my belly pulses stronger, spreading through me. And I know this feeling... It's pre-heat just before it hits hard. The warning signs that usually give me a few days to prepare, to get to a clinic or stock up on suppressants.

My stomach clenches, not with arousal but with anxiety. I'm in pre-heat, naked in an Alpha's bed, on a ranch with three Alphas who are all my scent matches. I don't know how to feel. Excited? Scared? Anxious?

I look around for my clothes, but they're gone. Of course, they were soaked with river water. But there on the armchair is a neat pile of fresh clothes. A soft flannel that has to be Ridge's, jeans that look too small to be any of theirs, and canvas sneakers.

My hands shake as I dress. The flannel smells like him, and wearing it feels too intimate, like a claim I'm not ready for. The jeans are loose but stay up. The shoes fit well enough.

I need to get out of here before anyone sees me. Need to reach the guesthouse and figure out what to do.

I crack open Ridge's bedroom door, listening. Voices drift up from downstairs—multiple people, not just my three cowboys. Great. Company. Just what I need when I'm sneaking out after the best sex of my life while going into pre-heat.

I creep down the hallway, wincing at every creak of the floorboards. The old ranch house seems determined to announce my presence. At the bottom of the stairs, I pause again, trying to make out the voices.

Business talk. Something about horse prices and feed costs. Two voices I don't recognize, older-sounding men, probably ranchers or suppliers. Then Walker's laugh, low and warm. Cash making some joke.

And then, a feminine giggle that makes my blood turn to ice.

"Oh, Cash, you're so funny!"

I know that voice. Fucking Brittany from the rodeo. The blonde who was all over Cash.

My hands grip the banister so hard my knuckles turn white. What is she doing here? Why is she in their house?

I creep closer until I can peer around the corner into the living room. What I see makes my vision go red.

Brittany is draped over Cash's arm, wearing a dress so tiny it might as well be a belt. Her legs go on for miles, spray-tanned to perfection, and she's tossing her platinum blonde hair while pressing her breasts against Cash's bicep.

He's not pushing her away.

He's smirking, talking to one of the older men, probably Brittany's father, now that I look closer. They have the same sharp features, the same calculating eyes. Walker and Ridge are right there, chatting with the other man like nothing is wrong. Like it's perfectly normal for Cash to have another woman hanging all over him after I slept with Ridge.

My rational brain tries to intervene, reminding me that there must be an explanation. But the pre-heat is making everything worse. Every emotion is amplified, turned up to eleven. The jealousy that floods through me is volcanic, mixing with the heat already burning in my veins until I can't tell where one ends and the other begins.

My heartbeat pounds so loud in my ears that I can barely make out their words. Something about land development. Investment opportunities. Brittany's father mentioning his connections in Dallas.

Then another wave of pre-heat pain slices through my abdomen, sharp enough that I have to bite my lip to keep from gasping. I wrap my arms around my middle, doubling over slightly.

That's when Brittany's giggle cuts through again, crystal clear.

"Oh, Cash, I knew you were a sweetheart! And I have our seats ready for us at the auction next week. Front row for the bull riding exhibition. You always wanted to see Dakota Jones ride, didn't you?"

I hold my breath, waiting for Cash to shut her down. To tell her he's not interested. To mention that he has a scent match, an Omega who needs him.

"That's tempting," he says instead.

Tempting.

The word slams into me. Here I am, going into pre-heat, needing my Alphas, and he's calling another woman tempting?

The room spins. My chest feels like it's actually on fire, not from heat but from rage. Every protective instinct I have is screaming at me to march in there and rip her off my Alpha. But I can't. Because maybe he's not really mine. Maybe none of them are.

Just like Nolan never really was.

The thought sends me spiraling. They got what they wanted—Ridge had his fun, proved his point about being the biggest, claimed me thoroughly—and now they're moving on to business. Once they get the ranch situation sorted, they'll find a way to push me out. They'll take what Rose left me and leave me with nothing.

Just like Nolan would have, if he'd lived.

I glance back at the group. They're all absorbed in conversation, Brittany now showing Cash something on her phone while her father talks to Ridge about property values. None of them notice me watching.

I dart across the doorway while they're distracted, practically diving for the front door. My hands shake as I turn the handle as quietly as possible. The door opens with a soft click that sounds like a gunshot to my paranoid ears, but no one calls out.

Then I'm outside, and I run.

My feet pound against the dirt path to the guesthouse, kicking up dust. Tears blur my vision, making me stumble. I feel so stupid. So naive. I let Ridge in, let him see me vulnerable, let him claim me, and for what? So he could clean me up like a responsibility and leave me alone while Cash entertains other women?

"Stupid, stupid, stupid," I chant with each step.

The rational part of my brain tries to argue that Ridge was probably letting me sleep, that Cash is probably just being polite to business associates, that there's probably a reasonable explanation. But that voice is drowned out by the roar of hurt and heat.

I burst into the guesthouse to find Chonkarella and the kittens waiting by the door, meowing plaintively.

"I know, I know," I sob, dropping to my knees to pet them. "I'm late with breakfast. I'm a terrible cat mother on top of everything else."

My hands quiver so badly I can barely open the cat food. I spill half of it on the floor, but the cats don't seem to mind, descending on it like they haven't eaten in days instead of just since yesterday.

"At least you guys want me around," I tell them as Chonkarella purrs against my leg. "Even if it's just for the food."

One of the kittens climbs up my leg with those tiny claws, and I grab him in my arms while sliding down to sit on the kitchen floor with them. The little one starts kneading its claws into my thigh.

"Ow, buddy. I'm already in enough pain."

But I don't push him away. I sit there for a moment, surrounded by purring cats, trying to get myself under control. The pre-heat is getting worse, making my skin feel too tight, too hot. I need to do something. Need to think.

My nest. I'll go to my nest, surround myself with comfort things, and figure out a plan.

I stand on shaky legs and head to the library, to my sanctuary. The suspended bamboo chair is piled with soft blankets and pillows, my little tables nearby holding chocolate and biscuits from Cookie's care package. This is my space, my safe place where—

Yet, all I can see is green.

Jealous, venomous green coloring everything. Brittany's manicured nails on Cash's arm. Her perfect smile. Her father's money and connections. Everything I'm not and never will be.

The first pillow flies before I even realize I've grabbed it. It hits the wall with an unsatisfying thump.

"Not enough," I growl, snatching another. This one I tear at, but the fabric is too strong. "Why won't you rip?"

I throw it anyway, then reach for the blankets from the chair, yanking them free with violent jerks. The chair swings wildly on its chain, creaking in protest.

"Stupid nest!" I kick at the pile of blankets on the floor. "Stupid Alpha pheromones making me nest in the first place!"

The side table goes next. I sweep my arm across it, sending chocolate bars and cookies flying. They scatter across the floor with satisfying crashes and thuds.

"Tempting," I spit, getting the books from the shelves and hurling them. "She's TEMPTING, while I'm dying here!"

I'm full-on ugly-crying now. Then I take another pillow, this one finally giving way under my assault. Feathers explode everywhere, floating through the air like snow. I sneeze, which makes me cry harder because even my own destruction is turning against me.

"Can't even destroy things properly," I sob, kicking at the feathers. They just flutter away, some sticking to my tear-wet face. "Pathetic. No wonder Nolan didn't want me. No wonder they don't really need me either."

A kitten appears in the doorway, surveying the destruction with typical cat judgment.

"Don't look at me like that," I tell him, sinking to the floor among the chaos. "You'd lose it too if you saw some perfect blonde draped all over your Alpha."

He meows and picks his way through the debris to curl up in my lap again.

"Okay." I wipe my nose with the back of my hand. "Phone. Need my phone and an action plan."

I stand, stepping carefully around the mess, and head to the living room. My handbag is where I left it this morning, before the river, before Ridge, before everything went to hell.

In my desperation, I grab it too roughly. The whole thing tips over, contents spilling across the floor.

"Perfect!" I cry out, fresh tears flooding my eyes. "Just perfect! Could this day get any worse?"

My lipstick rolls under the couch. Receipts flutter like

moths. Change scatters in every direction, coins spinning across the hardwood. A tampon escapes and rolls away.

The heat cramp that follows my rhetorical question nearly brings me to my knees. It's like my uterus is trying to claw its way out of my body.

"Okay, okay," I gasp, dropping to the floor to gather my things. "Message received, universe. Things can definitely get worse."

I'm roughly shoving items back into my bag when my fingers close around a small plastic container. My heart stops.

I pull it out, hardly daring to hope. One pill rattles inside. One single suppressant, probably from my last heat months ago.

"Oh my God." I clutch it like a lifeline. "Universe, I take it back. You don't completely hate me."

I immediately swallow the pill dry, nearly choking in my haste. Then I remember what they taught me at the heat clinic. Cold showers. Lots of them. The pill should kick in within half an hour, and the cold water will help manage my symptoms until then.

I stumble to the bathroom, stripping off Ridge's flannel. It smells so much like him that it makes my heart ache. I throw it in the corner.

The shower is freezing. I gasp as the cold water hits my overheated skin, but I force myself to stand under it. Let it numb everything, the heat, the pain, the image of Brittany's perfect body pressed against Cash.

I stay under the spray until my teeth chatter and my lips probably turn blue. When I finally emerge, I feel marginally more human. The suppressant is starting to work, pushing back the worst of the pre-heat symptoms. My thoughts are clearer, less clouded by hormones and rage.

But I need more suppressants. One pill won't last long, and I can't risk being caught without them. The drugstore in town should have the over-the-counter ones for pre-heat. They're not as strong as the prescription pills, but they'll help.

I dress quickly in my own clothes—can't wear Ridge's shirt, not now—and head outside. A ranch hand is loading feed into a truck nearby. Jake? Jay? Something with a *J*.

"Hey!" I call out, trying to sound normal and not like my world is imploding. "Any chance you could give me a ride to town? Please? You don't need to stay. I'll get a ride back."

He looks uncertain, glancing toward the main house. "I don't know, miss. The bosses might—"

"Please." I know I sound desperate, but I am desperate. "It's an emergency. Female emergency."

His face goes red, and he nods quickly. "Oh. Oh! Yeah, sure. Of course."

The ride to town is torture. He tries to make small talk at first, but I can barely string two words together. I stare out the window, watching the ranch disappear behind us, trying not to think about what Cash and Brittany might be doing now. Planning their date to the auction? Laughing at how easy it was to distract the poor city Omega while they make their real deals?

"You okay, miss?" the ranch hand asks as we pull up to Front Street.

"Fine," I lie, already opening the door. "Thanks for the ride."

"You sure you don't need—"

"I'm good. Thanks!"

I practically bolt from the truck, heading for the drugstore. My head stays down, eyes on the sidewalk, focusing on holding myself together until I'm out of sight.

My shoulder crashes into someone rounding the corner, jolting me into the glass of a storefront.

"Watch where you're—" The words die in my throat.

The man in front of me is maybe five-eight, with black

hair combed back in a style better suited to a boardroom than Front Street. His suit is sharp, tailored, the kind of expensive that doesn't get dirt on it. Gray eyes study me with a cold curiosity, as if he's deciding whether I'm worth his time.

Then his mouth twists. "If it isn't the gold-digging whore."

The insult snags me mid-breath. My stomach tightens. "Excuse me?"

His hand shoots out, gripping my upper arm with a pressure that warns me not to pull away. "You know exactly who I am."

"I don't," I snap, trying to twist free.

Before I can step back, he drags me into the narrow alley between the drugstore and the hardware shop. My shoulder slams into rough brick, the chill seeping through my jacket.

He leans in close, whiskey heavy on his breath. "Ronan Blackwood. Rose's actual grandson. Her blood."

The name is familiar immediately. The lawyer told me he'd tried to contest the will.

I glance toward the street. No one's looking. No help.

"Let go of me." I keep my voice steady, but my pulse is pounding.

His lips curve into something almost amused. "That ranch isn't yours. It's mine. I'm family. You're just some desperate Omega that an Alpha tossed aside."

Anger burns away a sliver of fear. I lift my chin. "If Rose wanted you to have it, she would've left it to you. She didn't. Probably because she knew exactly what kind of man you are. The kind who—"

His hand clamps around my throat. My breath stops. My nails dig into his wrist, but he's stronger than he looks. The brick at my back feels like it's pressing in on me, the edges of my vision going dim.

"Don't worry," he hisses. "Things are going to be fixed

soon. Then you can get out of my town. You and that rancid scent stinking up the place."

He actually gags, like the idea of my pre-heat body disgusts him. His grip loosens just enough for me to move.

I don't think. I drive my knee into his groin.

He curses and his hold breaks.

I run. Air scorches my throat as I gulp it in, boots hammering the pavement. His voice follows me down the street, sharp and furious, but I don't look back. I just keep moving, searching for anywhere, anyone, that might be safe.

There, the real estate office. A painted sign swings in the breeze. *Sweetwater Creek Realty*. June's family business.

I burst through the door, bell chiming frantically, and immediately lock it behind me.

"Sophia?" June looks up from her desk, and I can see she's been crying. Mascara smudged, eyes red. But her own problems vanish the second she sees me. "Honey, what happened?"

I stand there shaking, hand at my throat, trying to find words.

"Sophia, are you hurt? You're crying and—is that a hand mark on your throat?"

That's all it takes. I break down completely, ugly-sobbing as I collapse into the vintage chair across from her desk. The office smells like vanilla candles and old paper, comfortable and safe, but I can't stop shaking.

"Breathe," June says, rushing around the desk. "Just breathe. What happened?"

"You first," I manage, gesturing at her tear-stained face, trying to regain my own composure. "You've been crying too."

"Just my parents being assholes." She waves dismissively. "They called to lecture me again about selling the agency and moving to Dallas. That someone like me should get a job with my cousin's investment firm and work in an office. Because, apparently, preserving the town's history and helping people find homes isn't important enough."

"That's awful," I say, momentarily distracted from my own drama.

"It's fine. I'm used to it. But you, Sophia, what the hell happened?"

The whole story pours out in a jumbled mess. I start with waking up in Ridge's bed, the pre-heat beginning, seeing Cash with Brittany.

"That bitch," June interrupts. "She's been trying to get her claws into those cowboys since they arrived. Her daddy wants to buy their land for some development deal."

"Well, they all looked pretty chummy," I say bitterly.

"Men are idiots," June says firmly. "But I doubt your boys are interested. I've seen the way they look at you."

"Yeah, well, it felt pretty real when she was draped all over him and nobody cared." I continue with the story, about destroying my nest, finding the suppressant, and then Ronan.

"He grabbed me," I explain, touching my throat where I can still feel his fingers. "Said things were being fixed soon. That I'd be leaving town."

"That bastard!" June's face goes red with anger. "I'm calling the sheriff right now—"

"No!" I grab her hand. "Please. I can't deal with that right now. And what if it makes things worse? What if he comes after me again?"

"Then I'm calling your cowboys. They'll handle him—"

"Hell no!" The words come out louder than intended. "I can't see them right now. Not after... I just can't."

June stares at me for a long moment, then nods. "Okay. Okay. But we're reporting this eventually. Ronan is bad news. Always has been. Rose cut him off for good reason." She grabs tissues from the box on her desk, pressing them into my hands. "And no way Cash would be walking away from you."

"You really think he isn't interested in Brittany?"

"Whatever you think you saw, or didn't see, it's probably not what your brain is telling you," June says. "Those three are crazy about you. I can feel it. And I'm an expert in these things."

I shake my head. "It's not about what I saw; it's just... the way it felt."

"Mm-hmm." She gives me a look. "You're spiraling. And you just got manhandled by a jackass. We're not doing the spiral thing today."

"I'm trying not to," I protest, even though I kind of am. "I just—"

"Soph, Ronan didn't just talk. He grabbed you. That's not small. You're allowed to be shaken."

The memory flashes hard and fast. "I just need to get my suppressants and make it through my pre-heat. I can deal with him later."

She stands and grabs her handbag. "Right, we'll go to the drugstore, but we're also heading to the café. You need hot chocolate and the largest slice of chocolate cake I can find. Maybe the whole cake. And I'll help you eat it, because I'm selfless like that."

I laugh, loving how at ease she makes me feel.

"No arguments. Chocolate first, plotting revenge later. The drugstore will still be there in an hour." She loops her arm through mine. "And if your boys happen to walk in while you're mid-bite, you get to make them grovel in front of everyone. Which, frankly, is a public service."

A reluctant smile tugs at my mouth. "That does sound... satisfying."

"See? My plans are flawless." She starts toward the door, then pauses to check the street through the glass. "Coast is clear. No creeps around here."

"Thanks," I say, my voice catching a little. "For... all of this."

She bumps her shoulder against mine. "Please. Who else is going to make sure you survive murderous relatives and questionable Alpha behavior?" She squeezes my arm.

"That's what friends are for," I say.

We reach the café, and June holds the door open for me. The familiar scent of coffee and warm sugar draws me indoors, and my stomach growls in protest at being ignored all morning.

"Corner booth," June directs.

We slide into the worn vinyl seat of the circular booth, and before the waitress even makes it over, June fixes me with a look. "You've been reacting to everything, Soph. Inheriting the ranch, the three Alphas, now Ronan and Brittany. You've been playing defense since the day you got here. How about, just for once, you start playing offense? Take control before someone else does it for you."

Her words settle in my chest, heavier than I expect. She's right. I've been letting things happen to me, letting other people dictate the pace, the choices, the outcome.

"I still... I still want them," I admit quietly. "They're my scent matches. That hasn't changed. But I can't just... let myself be swept along anymore. I need to be sure. I need to know where I stand, and they need to show me."

"That's the spirit," June says, raising her fork like it's a glass of champagne. "To taking control."

I tap mine against hers. "To taking control."

And for the first time all day, I feel a flicker of steadiness under my ribs. With a friend like June in my corner, I might just be okay.

Even if it means I'll have to murder a few more pillows along the way.

22.

The front door finally closes behind the Carson family, and I slump against it like I've just survived a stampede. Two hours. Two fucking hours of Brittany draped over me like a cheap blanket while her father dropped hints about buying our land for his latest development scheme.

"Well, that was painful to watch," Walker says, grinning. "How's it feel being the sacrificial lamb?"

"Like I need a damn shower and a priest," I mutter, heading for the kitchen and the whiskey I know Ridge keeps hidden behind the flour.

"Brittany did seem extra handsy today," Walker observes, following me in. "What was that thing she did with your belt buckle?"

"Don't remind me." I pour three fingers of whiskey, then think better of it and add another. "The woman has octopus tendencies. I swear she grew extra arms just to grope me better. I feel fucking dirty after that."

Walker laughs, stealing my glass before I can drink. "Come on, it wasn't that bad. You maintained business relations with our biggest horse buyers. Carson's operation in Texas alone accounts for thirty percent of our sales."

"Doesn't mean I have to like his daughter climbing me like a tree." I pour another glass, guarding it from Walker's grabby hands as Ridge stalkers closer, so I collect a glass for him as well. "Besides, you two weren't exactly helping. Just stood there chatting about feed prices while she practically marked me with her perfume."

I'm leaning against the counter with a glass of whiskey I hand to Ridge, then start to pour my own.

He swirls his glass like he's got all the time in the world. Then takes a sip before saying, "Sophia's upstairs."

Walker glances over his shoulder. "Upstairs... doing what?"

Ridge takes another drink, lets the pause drag. "Sleeping. In my bed."

I stop mid-pour. "The hell she is."

"Oh, she is," Ridge says easily. "But before you get your hearts in a twist, you should know, this morning, she damn near drowned in the river by the goats' pen."

That rips my attention clean away from the smug grin. "What?"

"Fell in the river. Harold knocked her in. Current took her under." His jaw ticks, and for a moment, that cocky glint is gone. "Scared the hell out of me. Thought I'd lost her before I even had her."

My heart is thundering to just be hearing about this. "And you didn't fucking tell us this earlier, why?"

"Didn't exactly get a chance when we had the Carsons pop over unexpectedly."

"And you pulled her out?" Walker butts in.

"Dragged her out as she was choking for breath," Ridge says. "Got her inside, warmed her up. We talked. She was still shaking, still looking at me like I was the only thing holding her here. And then..."

He tips an invisible hat, grin sliding back into place. "She told me what she wanted. She made it real clear. And I'm a cowboy who answers an Omega's call."

Walker narrows his eyes. "You telling me you fucked her?"

Ridge leans in. "Not just fucked her. I knotted her. And Christ Almighty, she was perfect. Tight, dripping, screaming my name like she'd been waiting her whole damn life for it."

My grip tightens on my glass. "Years you've been pining, and you go and—"

"When she bent over in bed—fuck—it took everything I had not to lose it right there. Watching her take me, knowing I was filling her so deep she wouldn't forget me if she tried..." He shakes his head like he's reliving it.

I'm grinding my jaw at his bragging, at the hunger inside me to be the one to finally make her mine.

Walker swears under his breath, turning back to the sink like that'll hide the way his breathing is deepening.

"She's still upstairs?" I grind out and throw back all the whiskey in my glass before putting it down on the counter.

"Curled up, sleeping like a baby." Ridge smirks.

"I think her heat's coming. Within days," Walker suggests. "And when it hits, she's gonna need all three of us."

"Then she needs to move in with us immediately," Ridge states. "Today. We can't have her alone in that guesthouse when it hits."

"Agreed." I set down my glass, already thinking logistics. "We'll set up the spare room for her nest. It's got the best light, and it's between all our rooms."

"She'll need supplies," Ridge adds.

"We're really doing this," Walker interrupts, a grin spreading across his face. "All three of us. Finally finding our Omega."

"And we're not letting her go. Ever," I add.

"Right," they both confirm simultaneously.

"Then let's go tell her the good news." I head for the stairs first, eager to see her, taking them two at a time.

We reach his room, and I knock softly before opening the door. The bed is empty, sheets rumpled, his scent heavy in the air mixed with jasmine and arousal.

"Bathroom?" Walker suggests.

Ridge checks. "Not there. But the clothes I left for her are gone."

A prickle of unease runs down my spine. "Maybe she's checking out the house?"

We tear through the main house, calling her name, checking every damn room—bedrooms, kitchen, pantry, even the mudroom—and nothing. Ridge swears under his breath. Walker's jaw is tight. And an unease curls under my rib cage.

"Guesthouse," Walker states, already moving.

We take the steps two at a time to cross our property. My boots thud against the porch boards, and I pull the door open as we push into the guesthouse. The air is stale. Quiet. Too quiet. Then we spread out, searching different rooms.

"Library," Ridge calls from the hall after barely moments of arriving.

I follow the sound of his voice, Walker close behind, and step into the small room Rose built years back, her own cozy retreat with the built-in shelves and big windows.

I stop dead.

The place looks like a storm tore through it. Books scattered everywhere, spines cracked. Pillows shredded wide open, feathers plastered to everything. Blankets tossed, chocolate and packets of biscuits all over the place.

It's her nest. Or what's left of it.

My chest knots tightly. She built this space for comfort, safety. And now? It's not just a mess; it's destruction.

"Something set her off," Walker says, his voice low.

If she walked out of our house... she'd have had to pass through the living room. My stomach drops.

Ice threads through me. She would've seen that fucking Brittany was draped across me.

Shit.

And the memory comes back of how Sophia went sharp as a blade at the rodeo when Brittany approached me.

I rake a hand over my face. "I think she saw Brittany all over me. And she must have lost it."

Walker nods grimly. "If she's in pre-heat, her hormones are all over the place. Possessive instincts, emotions swinging hard... it wouldn't take much to push her over."

"Hell," Ridge states, scanning the wreckage. "If it were me, I'd have tossed a few things too."

We don't waste another second. We split up, scouring the ranch. Walker heads for the stables, Ridge toward the back pastures. I hit the barn, checking every stall, feed room, and tack closet, asking every hand I pass. No one has seen her.

I'm heading back toward the yard when I spot Jarrod climbing out of his truck, carrying a coil of rope.

"Jarrod!" I jog over. "You seen Sophia?"

His expression goes guilty fast. "Yeah, uh... sorry, boss. She flagged me down, asked if I could run her to town for... y'know, girl stuff. She looked upset. Desperate, even. I didn't think—"

"When?"

"Maybe half an hour ago. Little less."

"Where?"

"Dropped her near the drugstore. She barely said two words the whole drive. Just stared out the window like she might cry. Is everything okay?"

"I hope so." Then I grunt my thanks and already have my phone out, texting Ridge and Walker. *Found her. Town. Meet me at the truck.*

They come at a run. Ridge's face is carved from stone, Walker's eyes hard.

"She got a lift into town," I tell them. "Let's move."

We pile into my truck, the bigger cab, more seats, and I throw it into reverse. Gravel sprays up as we spin around, then I gun it toward the road, not giving a single damn about the speed limit.

"Easy," Ridge mutters, bracing one hand on the dash and the other gripping the door handle as I take a corner sharp enough to send more gravel skittering. "Won't help her if we wind up wrapped around a fence post."

"She's in pre-heat," I snap, my knuckles white on the wheel. "Alone. In town. Upset enough to rip her damn nest apart. I'm not going easy."

Walker shifts in his seat. "We need to make it up to her. Should've told her that Brittany is nothing but a handshake and paperwork."

"You don't dip your pen in the company ink," I mutter.

Ridge makes a face. "You and your sayings."

"But accurate," I fire back, swinging us into another turn. The tires protest, squealing. "Brittany's been sniffing around me for years. If I cut her off too clean, her daddy might take his horse contracts somewhere else. But that's gonna come to an end now."

"She's our Omega," Ridge says. "And she needs to know she is the only one for us."

My attention locks on the road. "And we're fixing this. Today. She's moving into the blue room. Her nest gets rebuilt from scratch. We'll prove she belongs with us."

"If she'll let us," Walker says quietly.

"She will." I yank the wheel to pull into town, my jaw set. "She has to." I won't be able to take it if she rejects us.

I nose the truck into a spot in front of the drugstore, parking a little too hard. We pile out fast, boots hitting pavement. Inside, the place smells of antiseptic and old wood.

"Seen a red-haired Omega come through in the last hour or so?" I ask, leaning on the counter.

The pharmacist frowns, thinking. "Nah. Been quiet all morning. Haven't had many customers in the last couple hours."

Back outside, we work our way down the street. The general store, empty. The post office has just one customer. The real estate office, CLOSED sign swinging in the window, door locked tight. I was hoping she'd come here to see June, but no luck.

"Where else would she go?" Ridge asks, scanning the storefronts.

The street is busier than usual, kids darting between cars, two women chatting outside the florist, someone unloading a crate of apples from the back of a truck. I spot Mrs. James across the way, already angling to flag me down. Probably to complain about something we did wrong. I ignore her. My attention is locked on one thing: finding Sophia.

"Café," Walker says suddenly, like the thought just snapped into place, and he's already crossing the road. Ridge and I follow him.

I push open the door to Wildflower Bakehouse & Café, and the warm blast of coffee, cinnamon, and sugar nearly knocks me sideways. The bell overhead chimes.

Every head turns. The lunch rush is still trickling out, but the room is full enough that our entrance pulls every gaze our way.

"Afternoon, boys," Kitty calls from behind the counter, drying her hands on her apron. Her smile is friendly enough, but her eyes are already trying to figure out why we're all here together. "What can I get you?"

"We'll know in a minute," I tell her, already scanning the booths.

Tucked into the far corner in a circular booth, June's

curls bob as she turns her head, eyes going wide when she spots us. And next to her... Sophia.

She's hunched slightly, shoulders drawn in. Ridge sees her too; I can hear the breath leave him. Walker doesn't say a word, but his whole stance shifts, angling toward her like instinct alone is pulling him in.

We've found her. Now we just have to make sure we don't lose her for good.

My chest loosens and tightens all at once. She's here, safe, but her face is blotchy from crying, and she's stabbing a fork into chocolate cake as though it personally wronged her.

June leans in and murmurs something to Sophia that earns the tiniest twitch of a smile from her.

The café hum quiets to a low murmur, small-town quiet, where every single person is pretending not to watch while absolutely watching.

I stop at the edge of their table. "Afternoon, ladies." My voice comes out lower than I meant, the words directed at Sophia and June but pitched so the whole damn room could hear. "Mind if we join you?"

Sophia doesn't look at me, just keeps cutting her cake into smaller and smaller bites. "I don't think there's enough room."

The dismissal lands like a kick to the ribs. Ridge shifts beside me, restless, but I hold my ground. "Then we'll stand."

June tips her mug toward us, her gaze flicking between all three of us like she's weighing the entertainment value. "Soph's got cake and I've got caffeine. You boys sure you want to do this here?"

"We're not here to cause a scene," Walker says, calm but steady, his hat shadowing his eyes. "Just to clear the air."

Sophia finally glances up at him, and the ache in my

chest sharpens. She's guarded, braced for a fight. "If this is about Brittany, I don't want to hear it."

"You deserve to hear it," I explain before she turns away again. "And you deserve the truth from us, not pieces of it, not when it's convenient. The Carsons buy more horses from us than anyone in the state. Brittany's been circling me for years, and I've been tolerating it for the sake of keeping her father's business."

Her jaw tightens, but she doesn't interrupt.

"That's not an excuse," I add quickly. "It's a mistake. A bad one. I should've shut her down harder, and I should've told you exactly who she was after the rodeo."

"We all should've told you," Walker adds, his voice rougher than mine. "You shouldn't have had to find out while—" He cuts himself off, glancing at her hands on the table.

"I shouldn't have left you alone this morning. I thought our catch-up with the Carsons would be quick," Ridge adds.

"You were scared," I say quietly, studying Sophia. "That's the only reason you'd tear up your nest like that. And I get it. We made it worse."

Sophia exhales slowly, but her eyes stay on the cake, not on us.

"We're not here to crowd you," Walker says, letting his voice drop lower so only the five of us can hear. "Just to tell you, we want to fix this. However we can. However you'll let us."

The café hum picks up again, chairs scraping, cups clinking, but I barely hear any of it. All I see is Sophia, silent and unreadable, the fork still in her hand.

I drop to one knee beside her booth.

The scrape of my boot against the tile is loud enough to draw a few curious glances, but when I lower myself down, it's like someone hit mute on the whole café. Forks freeze halfway to mouths. Conversations die mid-sentence. The espresso machine cuts off like the damn thing is holding its breath. Even June is gasping.

"Cash—" Sophia's voice stutters over my name, caught somewhere between shock and... I don't know.

I don't get time to figure it out before Ridge sinks down next to me, his big frame casting a shadow over the table, his hat tilted low. Walker follows, slower, like he's committing to something irreversible. Three grown men on their knees in the middle of Wildflower Bakehouse & Café.

I keep my eyes locked on hers. If I look away, even for a second, I might lose her.

Her knuckles are white. And all I can think is *Don't pull away from me, sugar.* Not now. Not after the way we left things.

"Sophia," I say, making my voice steady when my chest is anything but. "You are our scent match. Our Omega. Something we've wanted for so long that we'd almost stopped believing it could happen."

Her breathing changes, slowing, deepening, but her face is careful. Guarded.

"We thought we were doing right by you," Walker explains, his voice low. "Giving you room. Letting you settle without pressure from us."

"And in doing that," Ridge adds, "we left you in the dark. Made you think perhaps you weren't our choice." His jaw works like he hates the words as much as I do. "That's on me, on us."

I swallow hard. "You're not just our choice. You're the only one who's ever felt like *home.*"

I want to touch her, take her hand, push her hair back, anything, but my hands stay braced on my knee. Because if she's not ready, I won't force it.

Her lips part like she's about to speak, but she doesn't. Instead, she looks at me the way she did that first night she arrived at Wild Hearts Ranch. She's measuring us as though weighing whether we're worth the risk.

Ridge leans in, his voice rough like gravel. "You're it for us, Sophia. Our Omega. Our home. The only star in the damn sky worth following."

Walker nods, his eyes never leaving hers, steady and unblinking like she's the only thing in the room worth seeing. "You're not just someone we want, Sophia. You're the center of all of it. The reason we get up in the morning, the reason the ranch even feels like a home. Without you..." He shakes his head slowly. "Without you, all of this is just land and chores and empty nights."

I feel the weight in my chest twist tighter, the words spilling out before I can stop them. "Will you forgive us? I swear, Sophia, you'll never have to deal with Brittany again. Or any other woman who thinks she has a claim on us. Because there is no other claim. There's only you." My throat goes tight, but I push through. "We've built our lives on dirt and sweat and stubbornness, but none of it means a damn thing without you in it. Without you, we lose the purpose. The fight. The... us."

"You're our universe, darlin'. Everything orbits around you," Ridge murmurs.

I meet her eyes. "The only one we will ever want is you. The only one we will ever fight for is you. And if it takes the rest of our lives to prove that... we'll do it."

Something cracks in her expression, just a hairline fracture, but I catch it. Her fork slips from her fingers, the metal clinking against porcelain.

"I... needed to hear that." Her voice is quiet, almost lost under the hum of the refrigerator case.

Walker's gaze sharpens. "So you forgive us?"

Her mouth curves, but it's not quite a smile. "Not that easy, cowboy." She swipes under her eye, the movement quick like she doesn't want anyone to see. "My pre-heat is making me a little crazy, I'll admit. But I guess…" Her gaze drags from Ridge, to Walker, to me. It's like she's searching for a reason not to trust us, and not finding one. "I guess I'd already chosen you three as mine. I was just too scared to say it. Afraid you'd hurt me like—"

"Never," we say together.

"We're not him. We'll *never* be him," I admit, holding her stare, needing her to know we mean every damn word.

She studies me, really studies me, and I let her. If she needs to see every fault line I've got, I'll stand here and let her examine the whole damn map.

Finally, she grins so sweetly that my insides melt. "You three gonna join us in the booth already?"

Her grin isn't big, but it's real, as is the acceptance in her forgiveness, which eases something sharp in my chest.

June scuttles out from her side of the booth, sliding past Ridge with a muttered "Let me get out of the way before things get all Hallmark in here."

I take her spot, going in beside Sophia. Not too close, but close enough to feel the warmth radiating from her thigh, the subtle shift of her breathing. Walker slips into the other side, boxing her in gently, while Ridge takes the spot beside Walker.

Sophia exhales, just the smallest lean toward us, and my lungs finally start working again.

"Well," June says. "Guess I'd better go order some celebration cake before this turns into a full-on group cuddle."

The room slowly resumes its chatter, but for me, it might as well be empty. Sophia's here. She's forgiven us. And even if we've still got a long way to go, she's ours.

June heads for the counter, already calling to Kitty about the biggest, most decadent cake she's got.

As soon as she's out of earshot, we all lean in. Sophia's smile is so wide it has me grinning too.

"I'm sorry too," she says, her voice softer now. "For

making such a big deal out of this. I know it's my hormones and emotions, but I just—" She exhales slowly. "I just got so worked up when I saw her with you. It felt like... like I was already losing you before I even had you."

"You're never losing us," Ridge says, his voice steady.

"You have no idea how good it feels to know you came for me," she continues, eyes flicking to each of us in turn. She reaches out, one hand on my forearm, another on Walker's knee, and Ridge reaching over to her. "All of you." She gives a little tug, pulling us closer like she can't stand the space between us.

I lower my head until my forehead almost touches hers. "You're ours, Sophia. Always."

Walker leans in from the other side, murmuring something low in her ear that makes her lips twitch in a barely there smile. Ridge's thumb brushes the back of her hand.

"Speaking of sweet things," Walker says. "We need to talk about moving you into the main house."

She tilts her head, the beginnings of that stubborn look in her eyes. "I don't know—"

"Your nest is destroyed," Ridge cuts in gently. "And your heat is coming. You need somewhere safe. With us."

"We've got the blue room picked out," I add. "Best light in the house. It's right between all our rooms. Plenty of space for your things."

She bites her lip, and I can see the hesitation. I don't believe it's because she doesn't want to, but because it's a big step.

"We're making you a new nest," Walker says.

"And," I add, "I can't bear to be so far away from you."

Her eyes search ours for a long moment, then she leans back, the faintest smirk curling her mouth. "Only if I still get my privacy."

"Deal," I respond immediately with a grin.

"That was too easy," she mutters, but I notice the pleased flicker in her eyes.

That's when June returns, balancing an entire hummingbird cake made with pineapple, banana, and cream cheese frosting, which is piled high and swirled into perfect peaks. Kitty follows with plates, forks, and a knife.

"Well, if we're celebrating, we're doing it right," June declares, sliding into the circular booth next to me and setting the cake down in front of her. "Figured there's no such thing as too much cake," she adds, grabbing the knife and making the first cut.

June is laughing, and we're all eyeing this sinful cake she's cutting up.

"Careful," I say, smirking. "That's sacred territory you're slicing into."

"I'll be gentle," she deadpans, handing me a plate with a wedge big enough to feed two people.

"You're so lucky, Sophia," June says while passing out big slices. "Three cowboys willing to grovel in public? That's straight-up romance novel material."

"Careful," Ridge says with a half smile. "Don't say it too loud, or someone from the bookstore might start scribblin' notes for their next release."

That gets a quiet ripple of laughter from the booth, the kind that draws a few curious glances from nearby tables.

Walker eyes Sophia's plate. "You gonna eat that whole thing, or—"

"Touch her cake and I will cut you," June warns without missing a beat, sending Sophia into a cute giggle, drawing the plate closer to herself.

I chuckle. "And here I thought cowboys were territorial."

"You have no idea," June says, already taking a giant bite. She chews, swallows, and then adds, "I need to find guys who will grovel for me."

They all laugh, but I'm barely hearing them. My attention is locked on Sophia as Walker offers her a forkful of cake. She rolls her eyes but opens her mouth anyway, accepting it like it's no big deal... and somehow it still squeezes my chest.

I lean in, my voice low enough for only her. "You really had me scared earlier." The truth comes out rough. "I can't ever lose you."

Her gaze catches mine, something soft and certain in it. "I feel the same," she whispers. "And today... for now... everything's perfect."

For now. The words stick in my head even as she takes another mouthful of cake and smiles like the weight is finally off her shoulders. I should just enjoy it, let the laughter around us carry me, but I can't help wondering exactly what she means by *for now.*

23

CASH

The truck rumbles along the road back to the ranch, windows cracked just enough to let in the afternoon air. The radio plays something low and country, that new Chris Stapleton song Walker's been obsessed with lately. I keep stealing glances at Sophia in the passenger seat as I drive, watching how the sunlight catches the red in her hair, turning it to fire.

She's been quiet since we left the café, but it's clear she's still processing everything in the way she drums her fingers against her thigh. Her gaze is fixed somewhere far beyond the windshield, and she's distracted, almost worried.

"Everything okay?" I ask, glancing at her, keeping my voice low enough to not make it sound like an interrogation.

She exhales. "Ronan," she says finally, her voice tight. "Rose's grandson. He cornered me today in an alley in town. Said I didn't belong here or deserve the ranch. That things were being... fixed for me to leave town soon." She swallows, her hands curling in her lap. "He grabbed me by the throat. Wouldn't let go."

Everything in me goes molten-hot in an instant. My hands tighten around the steering wheel until the leather creaks. The air in the truck shifts, and Walker and Ridge both go deathly still, the kind of still that only means trouble for whoever is on the receiving end.

I keep my eyes on the road, but my jaw is locked so hard it aches. "He put his hands on you?"

Her gaze flicks to mine, and it's the faint tremor there, the quick flash of uncertainty, that takes my fury and sharpens it into something lethal.

"Yeah," she says quietly. "And I didn't know what he meant, about... fixing things. But I believed him when he said he could make me leave. It... scared me."

I glance at her again and see that fear she's trying to hide, but I notice the way she keeps her shoulders tight, her voice smaller than normal.

"Not fucking happening," Ridge says from the back. "Not today. Not ever."

Walker leans forward between the seats, his eyes like dark steel. "We'll handle Ronan, gorgeous. Don't you worry."

"Handle?" I growl. "I'll bury him if he so much as looks your way again." My free hand leaves the wheel long enough to press against her thigh, grounding her, grounding me. "You're ours. That means you don't walk alone, not until this is sorted. He comes near you again, you tell us. Immediately. You have my word, *our* word, Sophia, that he'll regret even breathing your name."

Her lips twitch in the smallest, weary smile. "I hate to say it, but that makes me feel better."

"It should," Ridge mutters. "He doesn't know what he's just signed up for."

"Because it's three on one," Walker says. "And we don't lose when we're protecting what's ours."

She nods, some of the tension in her shoulders loosening, and for a moment, I let myself breathe, though the fury is still coiled tight inside me.

Then she shifts in her seat with a little groan. "Oh, crap, I never made it to the drugstore. I need more suppressants. I only had the one I already took and—"

"You don't need them," Walker pipes in.

She turns to look at him. "Pretty sure I do, unless you want me going into full heat in the next day or two."

"You have us," I say. "We're the natural remedy for your heat. That's how it's supposed to work—Alphas helping their Omega through it."

"Suppressants just make it worse anyway," Ridge explains from the back in a matter-of-fact way. "They delay the heat, build it up. When the inevitable happens, the ache and hunger are sharper, harder to control. More painful."

Sophia exhales through her nose, the corner of her mouth pulling down. "I know. I can already feel it more this time, like my skin is too tight. Every sound, every smell... It's just louder. If I skip them completely, I'm not sure I can keep a handle on myself."

Ridge leans forward, bracing his forearms on the backs of our seats. "I helped you earlier today when things got intense." There's a glint in his eye, dark and possessive. "And I'll do it again. And again. Seven times each time if that's what it takes." His grin is slow and wicked, like he's picturing it right now.

I glance between them, my brows pulling together. "Seven? What the hell am I missing here?"

Sophia's cheeks flare crimson instantly, her gaze darting out the window. "Nothing. It's... nothing."

Ridge makes a sound that's somewhere between a chuckle and a satisfied growl. "Not nothing. Our gorgeous Omega came seven times earlier." He says it with enough pride to fuel a damn parade.

The truck lurches a little as my grip on the wheel slips, gravel pinging the undercarriage when I jerk us straight.

"Wow, seven, I'm damn impressed." Heat rushes into my chest.

Walker's head whips toward Ridge, eyes wide. "In one session?"

"Every. Single. One. Earned," Ridge states smugly, settling back with the air of a man who knows he's stirred the pot good and proper.

Sophia groans, covering her face with her hands. "Why would you even—"

"Because," Ridge says, leaning forward again so his voice is right in her ear, "I like reminding you what we can do for you. What we will do. Every time your heat gets to be too much, we'll be there. All of us."

Her hands slip down to her lap, and I catch the faint, guilty smile she's trying, and failing, to hide, and my stomach tightens. Not with jealousy. With the bone-deep need to make damn sure I'm part of the next seven.

"You know," she says suddenly, eyes flicking to Ridge. "In that demon romance book, he had to give her seven orgasms over time. Not all at once."

Ridge's grin turns slow and smug, like he's been waiting for this opening all along. "I know. That's why I had to do one better than that demon."

I can't help it; I bark out a laugh. "Ah, I'm caught up now. Y'all are talking about Sophia's blog post about the demon book. I think we might need to all read this one together. You know, for... ideas."

"Okay, challenge accepted," Walker declares.

"Hell no," Sophia says quickly. "This is not a competition. My body is not a scorecard."

Her cheeks go pink, but her smile only widens, and the heaviness from earlier feels lighter.

"Everything's a competition with us," I add. "Last month they competed to see who could muck out stalls faster."

"Walker cheated," Ridge protests.

"Boys," Sophia interrupts, but she's fighting a smile. "Can we please not turn my orgasms into a rodeo event?"

"Too late," I mutter, pulling up to the main house and parking the truck. "Ridge already set the bar. Seven is the number to beat now."

"Cash!" But she's laughing as she climbs out of the truck. "Well, I guess I have some packing to do."

"We'll get your room ready," I call out. We watch her stroll toward the guesthouse, and yeah, she's definitely adding extra sway to those hips. Knows exactly what she's doing to us.

"Fuck," Walker breathes, adjusting himself not so subtly.

"Seven times," I mutter, still processing.

"The benefits of being thorough," Ridge answers smugly.

"We need to fix her room," Walker says suddenly, snapping us out of our trance. "Now. Before she gets back."

We head into the house like the place is on fire. I take the stairs three at a time.

We skid to a stop in the guest doorway, nearly crashing into each other. The room is beautiful but basic—king-size bed with navy sheets, empty dresser, bare walls, hardwood floors with one simple rug.

"This won't work," Walker states, running his hand through his hair. "It looks like a hotel room."

"A nice hotel," Ridge defends.

"But still a hotel. She needs a nest. To feel like home. Comfortable. Safe."

"Soft things," Ridge adds. "Lots of pillows, blankets. Textures she can burrow into."

"Snacks," I contribute. "Easy access to food and water is crucial."

We stand there for a moment in silence. I can practically see the gears turning in their heads.

"I'll handle the snacks and drinks," Walker states, already heading toward the door.

"All the soft stuff is my domain. Different textures— some smooth, some fuzzy." Ridge is backing out of the room.

"I'll grab some of our clothes," I say, mostly to myself, already picturing her curled up in here surrounded by our scent. My mind is spinning with ideas, hell, maybe too many ideas, but the second the picture forms, I'm moving. Out the door, across the yard to the storage shed, rummaging through boxes until my fingers hit the prize.

Rose ordered it before she passed. Said it'd be perfect for reading on summer evenings. I grin, because I can see Sophia in it already, bare legs tucked under her, hair spilling over her shoulder, eyes half lidded while she loses herself in a book. Or in us.

As I'm hauling the item back upstairs, I catch voices from the spare room.

"That's too many pillows," Walker barks, sounding like he's losing patience.

"There's no such thing as too many pillows for an Omega," Ridge fires back, his tone dead serious, like he's quoting the goddamn Bible.

I chuckle under my breath.

"She needs to be able to actually get in the bed," Walker argues.

"She can move them if she wants," Ridge shoots back.

I shoulder the door open and drag my prize inside. "Quit arguing about pillows and help me with this."

Walker's eyes light up. "Tell me that's a sex swing."

"It's a hanging chair, you pervert."

Ridge cocks his head, already scanning the ceiling. "Could serve dual purposes."

"It sure could. Let me go grab my tools," Walker mutters, but he's already heading for the hallway closet.

It takes all three of us to get the hook mounted, mostly because we keep arguing over where to put it.

"Higher," Ridge insists, holding the chair steady while I drill. "She needs to curl up completely, tuck her feet under."

"Lower," Walker says. "Easier access for... reading."

"Reading. Sure," I mutter. "That's definitely what you're thinking about."

"Like you weren't picturing the same damn thing," Walker shoots back.

Truth is, he's not wrong. I've been picturing her here the whole time in one of our shirts, smelling like sex. I can't stop thinking about her.

We finally get the comfy chair hung at the perfect height —high enough to swing, low enough that she can step in without climbing. It faces the window, angled just right so she gets the mountain view and the best of the afternoon light.

"Try it," Walker states.

"Why me?"

"You're the smallest."

"Fuck you," I grumble, lowering myself into the chair. But the second it sways under me, I'm grinning. "Okay, yeah... this is nice. Damn nice. Even better than the one in the guesthouse."

"Get out. That's Sophia's spot," Ridge says, already fussing with throw pillows like he's nesting himself. I'm chuckling at how intense they've become.

By the time we're done, the whole room has transformed. The bed is layered with blankets in cream and pale blue, piled with enough pillows to make a fort. Mini fridge stocked. A few of our shirts tucked into the bedding, not obvious, but enough for her to feel us close. Books stacked on the nightstand, wildflowers in a vase. And that hanging chair... already looking like it belongs to her.

I stand back, hands on my hips, and something in my heart squeezes. This isn't just a room anymore; it's a promise. A safe place. Her place.

Ridge glances out the window. "She's on the porch, got boxes there. Looks ready. We'd better go help her, then."

We step back, surveying our work one more time.

"Think she'll like it?" Walker asks, and there's vulnerability in his voice.

"She'll love it," I assure him, though my own nerves are jangling.

"Hello?" Sophia's voice carries up from downstairs. "Little help? I've got precious cargo!"

We thunder down the stairs, probably looking way too eager, like kids on Christmas morning. But when we see her standing in the doorway, cradling three ginger cats while only one bag so far sits at her feet, my lips pull into the happiest grin.

"Oh, they're coming too?" Ridge asks, though his tone is more amused than annoyed.

"Of course! They're mine now, so they need to move in too. Package deal—take me, take my cats."

"Welcome, fur babies," Walker states, already reaching out to pet Chonkarella, who eyes him suspiciously before allowing one chin scratch.

"Well, I guess we can accommodate three cats," I say, trying to sound put-upon but probably failing completely. "As long as they don't scratch the leather furniture."

"They're perfect angels," Sophia explains, then whispers to the cats. "Don't listen to him. Scratch whatever you want."

We help her upstairs, the cats immediately scattering to explore their new territory. One kitten goes straight under the bed, another jumps on the windowsill, and Chonkarella claims the hanging chair before anyone else can.

"Chonky, that's my spot!" Sophia protests, but she's laughing.

Then she really looks around the room for the first time, and her mouth falls open.

"You did this for me?" Her voice is barely a whisper, and I swear she's tearing up. She walks slowly into the room, touching everything, running her fingers over the soft blankets, testing the chair's swing after relocating Chonkarella, opening the mini fridge to laugh at the amount of chocolate inside. "Just now? In the time it took me to pack?"

"We move fast," Walker admits with a wink, rubbing the back of his neck.

Her eyes go wide, and her hand flies to her mouth. "Oh my God," she whispers. "You're going to make me cry."

I want her to know exactly how far we'll go to make her feel safe here.

"This is…" She turns slowly. "This is everything."

When she reaches the window, the one facing the mountains, she stops dead, palm pressed to the glass. The view of the mountains is spectacular. "It's perfect," she murmurs. "No one has ever… I've never had anything like this."

The invisible armor she's worn since the day she set foot on this ranch, the steel in her spine, the walls around her heart… all of it softens in one tiny, unguarded moment. I hear it in her voice, and it's beautiful.

My chest pulls tight, like somebody is cinching a rope around it, only this time it's not from anger—but sheer happiness.

Before Ridge can so much as twitch, I'm already crossing the space and wrapping her up in my arms. She melts against me, soft and warm, and I swear I could stand here all day just breathing her in. "Then you'd better get used to it, sugar," I whisper into her hair. "This is just the start."

She tilts her face up to me, and whatever she sees there must be enough, because her lips part, her eyes soften, and she lets me close that last inch.

Her mouth tastes like chocolate cake and tears. Her fingers curl into my shirt, holding me there. I kiss her slowly at first, then deeper, until I'm tasting every little sound she makes, every shiver. I've kissed her before, but this... this feels like claiming.

By the time I pull back, she's breathing like she just ran the ridge trail, cheeks flushed, pupils wide.

"That's how you say thank you," I tell her, my thumb brushing over her jaw.

Her laugh is shaky, but it's real. "Guess I'll have to thank you all a lot, then."

"Count on it."

Ridge steps in, all sharp edges like he's daring me to stop him. He spins her to face him and curls a hand into her hair, tilting her head just enough to take her mouth like it's his by right. His kiss is rough, deep, the kind that steals the air from the room, and when she fists his shirt in return as well, he makes this low, satisfied growl.

I can see her shiver from where I'm standing. Hell, I can feel my own hands clenching because watching them is its own kind of torture.

When Ridge finally pulls back, her lips are kiss-swollen, her breathing uneven, and Walker is already there. He slides in with the kind of steady confidence that sneaks up on you, his palm cupping her jaw, thumb brushing over the damp curve of her bottom lip before he leans in. His mouth meets hers softer than Ridge's, coaxing instead of taking, but it doesn't stay that way. The second she makes that needy little sound in the back of her throat, his arm tightens around her waist as I hold her from behind, and the kiss turns hungry, his body pressing her back just enough that her toes leave the floor for half a breath.

By the time they're done, she's flush-faced and unsteady, looking between all three of us like she's trying to remember how to breathe. And then her gaze lands back on me, like maybe she already knows I'm not letting her walk away without another taste. I lean in and steal that kiss that has me captivated. Her lips are soft, her mewls delicious.

She's breathless, leaning into all three of us now.

One of the kittens launches himself onto the bed and bats at a pillow tassel like it's his mortal enemy.

"I think he approves," Sophia says with a watery laugh, scooping him up. She buries her face in his fur for a second, probably so we won't see the fresh tears in her eyes. "This is way better than the guesthouse, isn't it, baby?"

"Everything's better now," Ridge says, but he's looking at her, not the cat.

And I get it. I look around at my pack because that's what we are now—a real pack—and it smacks me square in the gut. I've been restless for years, never settling anywhere. But this feels like setting down roots. Like maybe I finally found the place I was meant to land.

"So," I say, letting a slow grin spread across my face. "You want to really test out that hanging chair? Make sure it's properly installed?"

She laughs, wiping her cheeks. "Is that all you think about?"

"No," I say, dead serious. "Sometimes I think about that desk in my office. Very sturdy. Great height. Perfect for—"

She swats me in the arm, laughing now, cheeks pink, while Ridge and Walker both snort like I've just said something saintly instead of filthy.

"What? I'm just saying a girl ought to know her options. Variety is the spice of life."

"You're impossible," she says, but she's smiling the way she did back at the café—open, lit up from the inside.

"Yeah," I say, tugging her in as Ridge and Walker press close from either side, surrounding her with warmth and scent and promise. "But I'm yours. We all are."

"Always," Ridge murmurs into her hair.

"Forever," Walker adds against her shoulder.

And standing there in her new room, cats claiming the bed, our Omega in our arms, I know exactly what I'd fight for. What I'd kill for. What I'd die for, if it came to it.

Tomorrow, we'll deal with Ronan. Tomorrow, we'll figure out the logistics of keeping her safe through her heat. Tomorrow, we'll face whatever storm is rolling in.

But today?

Today, we made her a home.

And that's everything.

24

SOPHIA

Confessions of a City Omega

Plot Twist: I Live Here Now

Dearest Diary,

This one is short because I'm exhausted and emotionally drained and possibly having an out-of-body experience.

After a day of drama and misunderstandings (involving a certain blonde who shall remain nameless but rhymes with Twittany), I am now officially moved into the main house with my three cowboys.

Big move. BIG.

Am I excited? Yes. Am I terrified? Also yes. Am I moving too fast? Probably. Do I care? Jury is still out.

Here's the thing… They're my scent matches. All three of them. And I can't keep running from that, no matter how much my trust issues scream at me to flee into the night.

Your girl has somehow, through all the trauma and terrible life choices, actually found her Alphas.

(I'm still processing this. It might take years. Or therapy. Or both.)

But TODAY they didn't just move me into their house.

They built me a nest. An actual, perfect, made-with-love nest. And yes, I might have cried. Sue me.

It has:

- Every soft thing in existence
- A mini fridge stocked with chocolate (they KNOW me)
- Their scents everywhere (swooning)
- A HANGING CHAIR because they remembered I loved the one in the guesthouse

I mean, LOOK AT IT.

They did this in the time it took me to pack. Three Alpha cowboys literally speed-built me a sanctuary because they wanted me to feel at home.

I can't even.

Tonight's Omega Wisdom: Sometimes it's okay to believe things might actually work out. Even when your whole history suggests otherwise. Even when every instinct screams that happiness is temporary and disaster is imminent.

Sometimes three cowboys will surprise you with a perfect nest and make you believe in fairy tales again.

City Omega out. (Still can't believe this is my life. Still waiting for the other shoe to drop. Still... happy?)

<h1 style="text-align:center">25</h1>

For a moment, I forget everything except how perfect this glorious morning feels in the main house. My room. The hanging chair sways gently in the breeze from the cracked window, and Chonkarella has claimed it as her throne, orange fur glowing in the light.

I stand at the window, a coffee mug warming my hands, taking in the view that still doesn't feel real. The valley stretches out in the distance, huge mountains rising. Down below, the driveway curves up from the main road, disappearing into morning shadows cast by the oak trees. To the left, I spot the animal shelter, the barns, the life of the ranch in motion.

This is home. After everything—Nolan's cruelty, his death, the uncertainty—I have a home with three men who actually want me here. Who moved heaven and earth yesterday to make me a perfect room. Who kiss me good morning and good night like it's essential to their survival.

God, I'm getting sappy. Must be the pre-heat hormones making me all emotional and—

Movement catches my eye near the front gate in the distance. Large, black, and absolutely where it shouldn't be.

"Oh, for fuck's sake," I mutter, pressing closer to the glass. "Brutus the bull."

The bull is just standing there near the main gate into the property, massive head lowered, pawing at the gravel like he's preparing for battle. The same bull that destroyed my rental car on my first day here, the rental I'm still paying off in pathetic monthly installments that barely cover the interest.

My phone buzzes with a payment confirmation from my latest freelance client. Web design for a boutique in Denver. The payment barely makes a dent in what I owe, but it's something. At this rate, I'll be paying off that destroyed car until I'm eighty.

Now that things are starting to feel solid between me and the cowboys, we're going to have to figure out what happens with the ranch, how we handle ownership, payment... if we even put a price on it at all. It's not just land and buildings anymore; it's a future home. Gosh, I can't believe I am even saying those words. Things happened so fast.

Another flash of movement catches my eye through the window. A deep blue SUV turns into the driveway from the main road.

I gasp, watching Brutus's head snap up, focusing on the vehicle.

The bull snorts, a cloud of hot breath visible in the cool morning air. He scrapes one hoof against the ground, tears up a chunk of our recently repaired lawn, and I swear I can see him calculating distance and trajectory.

"Don't you dare, you oversized hamburger."

Brutus charges.

The SUV driver must see him coming because the engine roars, tires spinning as they floor it. The vehicle shoots forward just as Brutus reaches where it was, his horns missing the bumper by inches. He skids to a stop in a cloud of dust and gravel, snorting its head into the air in displeasure at the missed target.

The SUV continues up the drive at a much more cautious pace now. Brutus watches it go, then turns and ambles back toward the main road like he didn't just attempt vehicular homicide.

Behind me, Chonkarella yawns dramatically from the hanging chair while both kittens sprawl across my bed, clearly exhausted from their 3:00 a.m. zoomies session that had them racing from one end of the room to the other like tiny, furry tornadoes.

"Oh, sure, now you're tired," I tell them. "After keeping me up half the night with your parkour practice."

I turn back to the window, figuring I'd better tell the guys about Brutus before he actually manages to gore someone. Or something. Again.

I hurry downstairs in my jeans and T-shirt, no shoes. The kitchen is empty. The guys must be out working or checking the damage from last night's barn leak that had them all running out after dinner.

There's a knock at the front door.

Walker appears at my side as I reach for the handle, sliding his arm around my waist and pulling me in for a quick kiss that makes my toes curl.

"You look gorgeous this morning," he murmurs against my ear, and I feel his smile.

"I look like I haven't brushed my hair yet," I counter, but I'm smiling too.

"Gorgeously disheveled, then."

These small moments, these casual touches and compliments, I still can't believe this is my life now. That I get to have this every day.

I open the door, and we're faced with two men in business suits who look deeply uncomfortable in the morning heat. They're already sweating through their jackets, ties slightly askew.

The older one, mid-fifties with silver at his temples, attempts a professional smile that fails. The younger one behind him clutches a leather portfolio and looks like he'd rather be anywhere else.

"Mornin', ma'am. Sir," the older man greets, his voice carrying a warm, rural Texas drawl softened by a faint lisp on his *s*'s. "Name's Jim Matthew, Matthew and Johnson Law Firm." He tips his head toward the man beside him. "And this here's my associate, Brett Yeaman."

Walker doesn't move from the doorway, his body language shifting from relaxed to protective. "Can I help you gentlemen?"

The older man steps forward, adjusting the brim of his hat before speaking. "I'm lookin' to speak with a Miss Sophia Hollis."

"That's me," I say, straightening even though my pulse has already picked up.

He tips his hat politely, then removes it, revealing a neatly combed patch of thinning gray hair. "Mind if we speak in private for a spell?"

"My mate Walker will join us," I reply firmly, leaving no room for discussion. If Ronan's name is anywhere near the reason these men are here, I'm not facing it alone.

Jim's attention flicks between us, but after a beat, he nods. "Fair enough, ma'am."

Walker's jaw tightens, but he steps aside. "Living room's this way."

We settle on the couch, Walker's hand finding mine immediately. The lawyers sit across from us, Brett pulling out a notepad and an expensive-looking pen. My knee starts bouncing involuntarily, anxiety crawling up my spine like cold fingers.

Walker's hand moves to my knee, steadying it, but I can feel the tremor running through my whole body.

"What can we help you with?" Walker's voice is carefully neutral, but I can feel the tension coming off him in waves, with his tight shoulders, jaw working like he's grinding down the words he really wants to use.

Jim clears his throat, the sound dry and papery, before pulling a worn folder from his briefcase. His suit has seen better days, the cuffs frayed and a faint coffee stain darkening the lapel, but there's nothing uncertain about the way he handles those papers. "Well now," he begins, slow and deliberate. "This ain't the kind of news I like deliverin', but here we are. Seems Mr. Blackwood took out a substantial loan over a year ago while his grandmother, Rose Martinez, was still alive. And used her as a guarantor."

I am hooked on his every word, waiting for the bomb to drop.

Walker doesn't even blink. "Sounds like *his* problem." His voice is flat, but I can hear the sharp edge under it... One wrong word and he'll cut with it.

My stomach is already starting to churn, acid pooling in my throat. This is what Ronan meant yesterday. This is his plan. My palms start to sweat, and I curl my fingers into fists to hide the tremor.

"Well now, that's where it gets complicated." Jim's blue eyes shift to me, and I swear they glisten like a predator who's just found the weakest animal in the herd. "See, Miss Hollis, the bank needs payment on that loan. Mr. Blackwood's got no assets to claim to pay back the loan."

"Get to the point." Walker's voice comes out lower now, a growl building in his chest.

Jim licks his lips, the faint hiss of that lisp curling around every *s*. "The point is, with Rose's passing and the ranch assets now under your name, Miss Hollis, that burden falls to you. That's how this guarantor loan was set up, I'm afraid."

For a second, the room tilts. My pulse hammers in my ears, drowning out everything else. The weight of those words is too heavy to process all at once. *Me.* Not Ronan. Me.

"How much?" My voice is thin, almost unrecognizable to my own ears.

"Three million dollars." Jim doesn't hesitate, doesn't soften it.

"Fuck!" The word rips out of me before I can stop it. "Three million. Three *fucking* million." My throat feels raw just saying it.

"The bank is giving you a four-week window to settle the debt," Jim goes on, like he's reading off the weather report instead of upending my entire life. "After that, they'll foreclose on the ranch. Already got a buyer lined up, from what I hear."

"You can't do this," I manage, but it sounds weak, the protest of someone already losing ground.

"Wish it were different, ma'am," Jim says, flipping a page in his folder. "Rose signed the papers, put up the ranch as collateral. Now it's yours, so is the debt."

Walker is on his feet before the last word leaves the man's mouth, pacing the length of the room like a caged animal. His hands flex at his sides, dangerous and barely contained. "This is a fucking joke. Ronan set this up. That weasel planned this whole damn thing."

Brett, the younger associate, shifts awkwardly, eyes darting between us like he's not sure if he should be taking notes or bracing for a fight. I catch the faintest smirk on Jim's face before it's gone, replaced by a bland mask of legal politeness. It makes my skin crawl.

And all I can think is *Ronan is winning.*

"Can't speak to anyone's intentions," Jim says as he stands, the old leather of his briefcase creaking. Brett is on his feet fast, like he's desperate to escape the thick tension in the air.

Jim offers a single sheet from the folder, a business card tucked into the corner, and then holds out the rest of the file. "Here's our card, along with all the bank documents, loan agreement, contact information, payment schedule. Everything the bank sent us."

"Is there any legal way to fight this?" Walker demands, his voice hard enough to cut steel.

Jim's gaze meets ours for a moment. He shakes his head slowly, hat clutched to his chest like a shield. "Afraid not. It's all legal and above board. Rose's signature is clear as day. Notarized, witnessed... every box ticked."

"You can leave now," Walker snaps, the words cold enough to frost the air.

But Jim doesn't take the out. He glances toward the door just as it swings open, and Cash and Ridge step inside, both covered in mud, shoulders squared from a long, grueling cleanup in the barn.

"What's going on?" Cash asks, eyes scanning the scene, the lawyers, Walker stiff as a board, me on my feet, fighting the tears burning hot in my eyes.

Jim tips his head toward them but keeps his tone matter-of-fact. "One last thing, ma'am," he says, staring down at me. "You can't sell any assets from the ranch to raise the money. That'd violate the terms of the agreement. No sellin' property, no sellin' horses, no sellin' land. Has to be outside capital."

"Get out," Walker repeats louder. "We've heard enough."

They take the hint, shuffling toward the door in silence. I don't even bother reminding them to watch out for Brutus in the yard. If that bull destroys their shiny SUV, I'll consider it cosmic justice.

The second the door shuts, my body caves in. I collapse

into the couch cushions, my vision blurring as the first sob breaks loose. Walker starts talking, filling Cash and Ridge in with clipped, furious words.

"Motherfucker!" Cash snarls, slamming his fist into the wall hard enough to leave a crater.

"That fucking asshole." Ridge almost growls the words, his voice darker than I've ever heard it. "He planned this. Must have moved his assets months ago so the bank couldn't touch him."

"Probably hid everything," Cash mutters, pacing. "Made himself judgment-proof."

"He knew Rose wouldn't leave him the ranch," Walker snaps. "So this way, he made sure whoever did get the place would lose it."

Their voices are a storm with rage, cursing, threats of retribution, but all I can hear is the pounding rush in my ears. It's not my fault. I know it isn't. Ronan set this trap long before I was even in the picture. But knowing that doesn't stop the heat stinging my eyes or the ache building in my chest.

"It's not fair," I choke out, my voice cracking. My hands cover my face, trying to hide the tears, the shaking. "He's taking everything from you. From us. And I can't stop it."

Then they're there, solid and warm, their presence closing in around me like a shield. Strong arms, familiar scents, the grounding weight of them pressing the chaos back.

"Hey," Cash says firmly, catching my wrists and pulling my hands away so I'm forced to look at him. His eyes burn with the kind of honesty you can't fake. "This isn't on you. You didn't put us here—he did. And all of us will handle it together, okay?"

Walker is there next to me. "This is our home. All of ours. And we're not letting that dick take it. Plus, I'm reaching out to our lawyers to review the bank contract and also find out exactly what Ronan did with his assets."

"What are we going to do?" I hiccup, looking between them. "Three million dollars in four weeks? God, I feel sick just thinking about that much money."

"We have some saved," Ridge says quietly. "We've been putting everything aside to eventually buy the ranch properly."

"How much, if you don't mind me asking?" I question.

They exchange glances.

"Two and a half million," Cash admits.

My heart sinks. "We're still short by half a million."

The silence that follows is heavy. We're so close but still impossibly far. Half a million dollars might as well be ten million.

Then Cash straightens, that determined glint in his eye I've come to recognize. "When you're being stampeded, you can either lie down and get trampled, or you can get up, dust yourself off, and find a way to run faster than the herd."

We all stare at him.

"That's..." I start.

"Weirdly applicable?" Walker finishes.

"Wait." I sit up straighter, an idea forming. "What if we could raise the money? We can't sell ranch assets, but we could bring in outside income. The horse rides, the animal shelter visits. I could promote on my blog, ask for donations. I have over fifty thousand followers. If even a fraction donated..."

"Would it be enough, though?" Ridge asks, but I can see him thinking.

"The blog alone won't do it," I admit. "But combined with events? Fundraisers? I'm certain some in town will help."

Ridge starts pacing. "We need an attraction. Something

big that'll make people need to attend. Something they'll pay serious money for."

We all watch him, and even in the middle of this crisis, I can't help noticing how gorgeous he is when he's intense like this. The way his jaw sets, how his green eyes go dark with concentration.

"You have an idea, spill it," Walker states.

He stops pacing, turns to face us, and the serious look on his face makes my blood run cold.

"A rodeo," he says simply. "Where Ridge Colter returns to the arena for the first and final time. *Come see the champion reclaim his eight seconds.*"

I stiffen. "Ridge, no."

"Absolutely fucking not," Cash says immediately.

"Hell no," Walker's voice is sharp. "You're still in pain. Still recovering."

"You almost died," I say, grabbing his hand and pressing it to my chest so he can feel my racing heart. "And you haven't trained. You can't risk your life. I would rather be homeless with you alive than lose you trying to save this place." I clutch his hand harder, afraid to let him go. The thought of him riding one of those bulls again terrifies me.

"Listen to me," Ridge says, crouching in front of us, his voice steady, but my eyes are burning with tears. "A comeback ride from a champion who nearly died? People would pay hundreds for those tickets. Thousands for VIP access."

"It could be suicide," Cash shoots back, his jaw flexing. His voice cracks on the last word, and he swallows hard, like he can't even bear the thought.

"It's eight seconds," Ridge counters. "I've done it a thousand times."

"Not in three years," Walker points out. "And your hip—"

"It's been better since Sophia arrived," Ridge interrupts, glancing at both of them. "I may not be able to scent her, but something about her... it quiets the pain. Makes me feel like I can move the way I used to."

"That's not—Ridge, please," I whisper, my throat tight. The thought of him climbing onto a bull again makes my stomach knot so hard it hurts. My mind flashes back to all the ways a ride can go wrong, the crush of hooves, the snap of bone, the impossible stillness that follows. I grip my knees to stop them from shaking, but it doesn't help. "You could die."

He takes my hands in his. "We charge premium prices. Get the arena owners to donate their cut. If they won't, we do it here on the ranch. Build stands, keep every dollar. We can raise what we need in one night if we make it big enough."

Cash still looks unconvinced, arms crossed tight, but there's a flicker in his eyes, calculating. "Publicity would be huge," he admits reluctantly. "Ridge Colter's comeback ride to save his family ranch? Press would eat it up. Even the rodeo circuits might want in."

Walker shakes his head. "Sponsors, maybe. We could reach out to some old contacts. Tie it to the town's fall festival, get them to donate a cut."

"Exactly," Ridge says, turning to them. "We make it impossible for anyone to ignore. This isn't just a ride; it's a stand. It's telling Ronan he can't take this from us."

Cash's jaw loosens as he starts running the numbers out loud. "Tickets plus donations... corporate packages, VIP meet and greets, behind-the-scenes tours..." His tone shifts —less resistance, more momentum.

Walker exhales through his nose. "We'd need security, medical teams, sponsors lined up. But if we pull it off..." He looks at Ridge and then at me. "It could work."

"This is insane," I say, my voice breaking. But they're all exchanging that silent, wordless agreement they've perfected over the years. I can feel the tide turning, and it terrifies me.

Ridge pulls me into his arms, holding me so close I feel the thump of his heartbeat against me. I cling to his shirt, inhaling cedar and cinnamon. "I don't want to lose you," I whisper, hating how small I sound.

"Sophia, my sweet," he murmurs, brushing a hand over my hair. "This is our home. I'll do anything to protect it from that bastard. If it takes eight seconds to keep this place, then that's what I'll give."

Cash rests a hand on my shoulder, his voice low but certain. "We'll make it massive. You work your magic, reach out to every reader, every follower, every person who's ever set foot on this ranch. We're gonna make sure this fight is ours."

I pull back from Ridge and turn to Cash and Walker, heat prickling my skin. "How are you both okay with this? This is madness. He could get killed." My voice shakes from the raw, ugly fear that's clawing its way through my chest.

Cash meets my gaze, leaning in closer. "Sugar, we're not okay with it," he says plainly. "But we know Ridge. He's the strongest man we've ever known, and when he says he can do something, he means it. If we tell him no, he'll find a way to do it anyway, without us. And that's more dangerous. At least this way, we can help him train, keep him sharp, keep him alive."

Walker leans forward, his elbows on his knees. "If he pulls this off, we keep the ranch. If he doesn't, we lose it. All of us. And I'm not just talking about land and barns, Sophia. This place..." He gestures toward the window, toward the pastures that stretch into the horizon. "It's our history. Our blood is in that soil. Every fence post, every hoofprint, every laugh we've had here—it's part of us. Rose made it that way."

Cash nods. "We could go start over somewhere else.

Find another ranch, rebuild. But why the hell should we let that snot-faced bastard kick us out of the place Rose spent her life building? She wanted this in the hands of people who loved it, people who would protect it. That was her wish, and Ronan is spitting on it."

My throat tightens.

"It's Rose's legacy. And we'll be damned if we let anyone take it without a hell of a fight."

"I'll contact the arena management today," Ridge says. "Lock down a date."

"I'll reach out to our business contacts," Walker adds. "Every ranch that's bought horses from us, every supplier we've worked with."

"Media blitz," Cash says. "Local news, sports channels, documentary crews if we can get them. And we need to start your training. I'll bring out the mechanical bull you used to practice on."

They're all talking at once now, planning and strategizing, and I'm swept along in their determination.

"We're really doing this?" I ask, glancing between them. My voice wavers, my stomach churning. It feels like I'm standing at the edge of a cliff, watching them get ready to jump.

"We don't have a choice," Walker says, then softens, leaning forward just enough for his eyes to catch mine. "But we're in it together, right?"

I laugh and cry at the same time, overwhelmed, my emotions tangling. "I can't believe I'm agreeing to this. Ridge, God, if anything happens to you—"

"Nothing will happen," he says firmly, holding my gaze like it's an anchor. "I promise I'll train. I'll do my absolute best. But I don't see another option that brings in this much money this fast."

"Eight seconds," I whisper, my throat tight.

"Eight seconds to save our home," he confirms, and

there's a glint in his eyes, a tiny quiver of his chin, a grin on his lips.

"We'll need a marketing campaign. Posters, social media, the works. That's your forte, right, sugar?" Cash says, leaning forward with a spark that has nothing to do with the crisis and everything to do with the thrill of a challenge.

"I can design those," I answer automatically, my mind already flicking through layouts, headlines, taglines, anything to keep my hands busy and my thoughts from spiraling into fear.

"Merchandise," Walker adds, his voice sharpening with focus. "T-shirts, hats. 'Save Wild Hearts Ranch,' branded everything."

"Or 'Save a Bull and Ride a Cowboy,'" I joke, and all three of them freeze for a second before exchanging a look that's equal parts heat and wicked amusement.

"Careful, sugar," Cash drawls, his grin slow and full of trouble. "We could print that and make you wear the shirt." He winks sexily.

"'Eight Seconds Isn't Enough,'" Walker suggests, his tone deadpan but his eyes glinting with challenge.

Ridge chuckles, shaking his head. "'Cowboy Up or Go Home.'"

"'Ride Hard, Hold Tight,'" Cash adds, shooting me a sly glance.

"This could actually work," I breathe, the first small flicker of hope lighting in my chest. It's fragile, but it's there.

"It has to work," Walker says, shoulders squared, appearing proud.

And as I look at my three cowboys, my Alphas, I realize the shift that's happening. The fear is still there, coiled tight in my stomach, but it's being met with something else. Their energy is contagious, pulling me into their orbit. They're already seeing the arena lights, hearing the crowd, smelling the dust and leather.

We sit there for a moment, the four of us tangled together on the couch, processing the enormity of what we've just decided. The cats wander downstairs, oblivious to the life-changing gamble about to unfold, and one of the kittens jumps into Ridge's lap, purring like it's any other morning.

"'Ridge's Last Ride,'" Walker says suddenly, the words landing heavily in the room. "That's what we call it."

"Morbid," I protest, my nerves flaring again.

"Dramatic," he counters. "Sells tickets."

"Fine, but I'm adding a subtitle," I say, forcing my mind into the part I can control. "'Eight Seconds to Save Everything.'"

"Perfect," Ridge answers, standing and pulling me up with him. His grip is warm, solid. "Now, let's go save our home."

And despite the ache in my chest, I start to believe him. Ronan thinks he's won, thinks he's backed us into a corner we can't escape.

He's wrong.

We're going to save this ranch. Ridge is going to ride again. And I'm going to document every second of it for the world to see.

"Hey," I say suddenly. "What about Brutus? He's loose again. Nearly gored the lawyers' SUV."

They all exchange glances.

"Good," Cash says simply. "Hope he got them on the way out."

"We should probably—" Walker starts.

"Later," Ridge interrupts. "Let him have his fun for a few more minutes."

And despite everything, the debt, the fear, the impossible task ahead, we all laugh. Because that's what we do. We face the stampede together, and we find a way to run faster.

Four weeks. Half a million dollars. One ride.

We can do this.

We have to.

Confessions of a City Omega
When the Universe Decides You've Had Enough Happiness

Dearest Diary,

Remember yesterday when I was floating on cloud nine? When I thought I'd finally figured this whole life thing out?

Yeah, well.

The universe just called to inform me that my subscription to happiness has expired, and no, I cannot renew at this time. Would I like to sign up for the Suffering Plus package instead? It comes with bonus anxiety and a free side of financial ruin!

Just when I thought my life was finally coming together, that the shit was behind me, and I could move on, start fresh with my three scent matches who actually want me around, the universe pulled the ultimate "SYKE!"

Here's what happened in bullet points because if I write it in paragraphs, I'll cry:

- Someone from ex-Alpha's past has orchestrated revenge
- Said revenge involves three million dollars I don't have
- If I don't find it in four weeks, I lose everything
- Including the ranch that was supposed to be my fresh start
- And the home my Alphas just made perfect for me

Three. Million. Dollars.

That's the price tag on my happiness, apparently.

For context, I'm still paying off a rental car that got destroyed by a bull. Three million might as well be three billion.

But here's the thing:

My Alphas aren't giving up.

And neither am I.

We're planning something huge. Something that might just save everything. I can't share all the details yet (still working them out while trying not to hyperventilate), but I'm going to need you. All of you. Every single reader who's been following this disaster of a journey.

Because if there's one thing I've learned, it's that sometimes the family you choose, including the virtual one reading your chaos online, is stronger than the assholes trying to tear you down.

So stay tuned. Share this blog. Tell your friends about the Omega who's about to fight back against the universe's bullshit.

We're going to need:

- Donations (every dollar counts)
- Word of mouth (tell EVERYONE)
- Good vibes/prayers/whatever cosmic juice you believe in
- Maybe someone who knows a billionaire with a heart of gold?

Details coming soon. Like, really soon. Like, we-only-have-four-weeks soon.

Tonight's Omega Wisdom: Happiness comes with terms and conditions. Fine print. Hidden clauses that activate just when you think you're safe. But you know what?

Fuck the fine print.

We're rewriting the contract.

The person who orchestrated this thinks he's won. He's probably sleeping soundly tonight, dreaming of our failure.

But he forgot one thing. I've got three Alpha cowboys who'd ride through hell for me. And apparently, one of them is about to ride something almost as dangerous.

(More on that terrifying development later. I need wine first. Or whiskey. Or both.)

Meanwhile, I'm here trying not to let them see how scared I am. Trying to be strong when all I want to do is curl up in that hanging chair they installed for me and pretend none of this is happening.

But that's not how life works, is it?

You don't get to opt out of the hard parts.

You don't get to skip to the happy ending.

Sometimes you just have to saddle up and ride the damn bull.

Even if it might kill you.

(God, I really hope that's just a metaphor.)

City Omega out. (Still fighting. Still terrified. Still asking the universe, WHAT THE ACTUAL FUCK?)

PS: If any of you know how to organize a massive fundraising event in four weeks, slide into my DMs. I'll trade you homemade cookies and eternal gratitude.

PPS: Or if you just want to donate to the "Save Sophia's Sanity and Also Her Ranch" fund, that works too.

PPPS: Seriously, though, we're going to pull off something incredible. Stay tuned. It's about to get WILD at Wild Hearts Ranch.

26

SOPHIA

Three days of nonstop planning, phone calls, and design work for the fundraiser. My fingers are cramped from creating promotional materials, posters, social media graphics, donation trackers. My voice is hoarse from coordinating with vendors, sweet-talking local businesses into sponsorships, explaining over and over why this matters. I even managed to publish a detailed blog post to my followers, laying out exactly what the event is, why we're fighting so hard, and how they can get involved. But we're making progress. The event is coming together piece by piece, and for the first time since the lawyers showed up with their devastating news, I feel like we might actually pull this off.

The house is quiet, too quiet. The kind that makes every small sound echo. The guys left this morning before dawn to pick up a mechanical bull from a ranch over two hours away. The one Ridge had been planning to practice on, the one Cash swore was in working condition, turned out to be broken beyond repair. Rusted through at the joints, hydraulics shot, dangerous enough that even looking at it wrong might cause tetanus. So all three of them piled into

Cash's truck with the trailer attached, promising to be back by evening.

Perhaps I should have gone with them, as I miss them terribly. But someone needed to stay and manage the social media campaign preparations. Respond to donation inquiries. Answer the phone. Keep everything moving forward because we have limited time to make this a success.

I'm in my room, my nest, arranging and rearranging the pillows for the hundredth time. It's a nervous habit I've developed, this compulsive need to perfect my space. The sun streams through the windows, lighting up the room. The hanging chair sways gently in the breeze from the cracked window, and Chonkarella and her kittens are running around somewhere in the house.

My laptop is open on the bed, showing the donation tracker we set up. We've raised eight thousand dollars in three days. It's good, but nowhere near enough. I refresh the page obsessively, watching the number tick up in five- and ten-dollar increments. Every donation feels like a tiny victory, but the mountain we need to climb is still impossibly high.

A sudden ache flutters low in my belly, different from menstrual cramps, different from hunger, different from anxiety. It's deeper, primal, spreading through my core like someone lit a match in my bloodstream. My skin suddenly feels too hot, like I'm burning from the inside out.

Then comes the gush of slick, warm and sudden, soaking through my underwear and pajama shorts in an instant.

My hand flies to the wall for support, knees already trembling. The laptop slides off the bed, hitting the floor with a crack I barely register.

"Fuck. No. Not now. Not fucking now."

I know this feeling. Know exactly what's happening

when my heat charges forward—it's not approaching anymore. It's here. Full force. No warning. No gradual buildup like usual. Just zero to a hundred in seconds.

My phone. Where's my phone?

I fumble for it on the nightstand, knocking over a book in the process. It hits the floor with a thump. A moan escapes as another wave of need crashes through me, this one strong enough to bring me to my knees.

My fingers shake so badly I can barely unlock the screen. The numbers blur, swimming in and out of focus. Last number called. Walker. Thank God.

It rings once. My thighs are trembling, more slick pooling between them.

Twice. I'm panting now, short, desperate breaths that do nothing to cool the fire.

Three times. By the third ring, I'm on my knees properly, forehead pressed to the cool hardwood floor, phone clutched in a death grip.

"Hey, darlin', everything okay? Did the donation site crash again?"

His voice, warm and steady, breaks something in me.

"Walker," I whimper. "Heat. It's here. Now. Full heat."

I hear his sharp intake of breath, then muffled cursing as he must have pulled the phone away. I hear him telling the others.

"Sophia, baby, we're coming. We're on our way already. Right fucking now."

"Why did you leave?" The words tear from my throat, irrational and desperate. I know it's not their fault, but my Omega brain doesn't care about logic. "I should have gotten suppressants. I knew it was close. God, it hurts so much."

Another wave hits and I cry out, phone slipping from my sweaty palm. It clatters across the floor, but I can still hear voices. Someone else picks up.

"Sugar? Sophia, talk to me. Keep talking to me," Cash says.

I reach for the phone, every movement sending sparks through my oversensitive skin. "Cash," I sob, finally grabbing the device with trembling fingers. "Please. I can't—I need—"

"How bad is it, scale of one to ten?"

"Eleven. Twelve. Fuck, I don't know!" My voice breaks on a moan as another wave crashes through me. "It's never been this intense. Never this fast. How long until you're here?"

There's a pause that feels like eternity. I hear the truck engine roaring louder, tires squealing, Cash telling Ridge to drive faster.

"Less than an hour, sugar. Maybe forty-five minutes if Ridge keeps this pace. We're doing ninety with a fucking horse trailer, but we don't care."

I whimper, and I hate how pathetic I feel. How needy. How desperate. "That's forever. I need someone now. Need Alpha. Need touch, need knot, need—"

"I know, baby. I know. God, I'm so sorry we're not there." His voice is wrecked, and I can hear Walker and Ridge talking in the background, their voices low. "Listen to me. Cold shower. Right now. It'll help take the edge off until we get there."

"Can't move," I protest, but I'm already trying to crawl toward the bathroom.

"You can do this. You're strong. Strongest Omega I know."

"Don't feel strong," I admit, using the bed frame to pull myself up. Standing makes my head spin, my vision going white at the edges. "Feel like I'm dying. Like I'm burning alive."

"You're not dying. Your body's just calling for us. We're

coming, sugar. Ridge is about to blow the engine, he's pushing so hard. We're coming."

Part of me wants to beg them to drive safely, but my body just wants them here NOW. Wants their hands on me, their knots in me, their teeth in my neck.

"Cold shower," Cash repeats. "Deep breaths. Think about... fuck, I don't know, think about how good it's going to feel when we get there. How we're going to take care of you."

There's a shuffle with the phone on their side again, and someone might have growled. "Whatever you need. However you need it," Walker states in a hurried tone.

I end the call and drop it before I crawl to the bathroom. My legs won't support me properly, muscles trembling with need, with the biological imperative to present, to submit, to be filled.

The heat clinic had taught me about this. About managing the waves when they hit. They'd inject Alpha pheromones directly into your bloodstream to trick your body, take the edge off just enough to function. Not enough to satisfy, nothing but an actual Alpha could do that, but enough to survive.

Then you'd go to the red room with soft surfaces every-where, sex toys of every size and shape, everything an Omega might need to ride out the heat alone. The walls were soundproof because the screaming could get intense. They'd check on you every hour, bring water and protein bars, even offer an Alpha staff member if you wanted to hire an Alpha for the session. They had a whole roster of profes-sional heat partners, clean and certified and willing.

I never could bring myself to accept. Not when I had Nolan. Even though he didn't want to touch me, the thought of another Alpha felt like betrayal.

God, what I wouldn't give for those pheromone injec-tions now. Just something to take the edge off this burning.

I manage to turn on the shower, cranking it to the coldest setting. Then I drag my shirt over my head and toss it aside. My pajama shorts are next, then my underwear, every movement slow and clumsy, like my own body is working against me.

The shock of cold water makes me gasp, but it helps. Marginally. Like throwing a cup of water on a house fire, but at least it's something.

I crouch low in the shower, letting the icy water run over my heated skin. Every drop feels like tiny needles, sharp and clarifying, but it's better than the burning. My nipples are hard and aching, oversensitive to even the water's touch. Between my legs throbs with emptiness, clenching around nothing, desperate to be filled.

Time becomes fluid. I don't know how long I've been here. Minutes? Hours? The water has turned my skin pink, then pale, then almost blue. I'm shivering and burning simultaneously.

I try to remember the breathing exercises from the clinic. In for four, hold for four, out for four. But every breath brings another wave of need, another gush of slick that the shower immediately washes away.

My hands wander without my permission, one sliding between my legs to try to ease the ache. But my own touch isn't enough, could never be enough. I need Alpha hands. Alpha cock. Alpha knot.

Another wave hits and I moan, the sound echoing off the bathroom tiles, loud and desperate and animalistic. My vision blurs, goes dark at the edges. The bathroom tile is cold against my heated forehead as I press against it, seeking any relief.

When I open my eyes, there's someone in the doorway.

For a moment, my heat-addled brain sees Nolan. That cruel smile, those cold eyes that looked at me with such disgust during my heats. "You're pathetic," he used to say. "Like an animal."

I flinch back, a whimper escaping, pressing myself into the corner of the shower.

But as my vision clears, it's not Nolan.

It's worse.

It's Ronan.

I scream, hands flying to cover myself, pressing back against the shower wall in a crouching position.

"Could hear you moaning like a cow from outside," he says, leaning against the doorframe with casual cruelty. His eyes roam over my naked form, taking in every detail with a sneer. "Your cowboys aren't here to help you. Why would they be? They're probably halfway to Mexico by now, leaving you to deal with your mess alone."

"Get the fuck out!" I manage to yell, though my voice cracks on another wave of need. "How did you even get in here?"

"Door was unlocked. Very careless for an Omega in heat." He takes a step into the bathroom, and he's swaying just a bit like he's drunk. "Came to tell you to stop wasting time with this stupid fundraiser. Heard all about it. Your little 'save the ranch' campaign? You really think you'll raise enough?" He laughs, ugly and sharp. "In your dreams. I'll make sure no one in this town helps you. Already talked to the Carsons and they're pulling their support."

"GET OUT!" I scream again, and it turns into a sob as another wave of heat crashes through me. My body betrays me, more slick pooling despite my terror.

He steps closer, into the bathroom properly now, and my stomach revolts. The sight of him makes me gag.

"I mean, if you need an Alpha that badly, I could lower myself," he says, eyes dark with something that has my skin crawling. "You're not much to look at, but a hole's a hole when you're desperate enough."

I gag. Actually gag. The thought of him touching me, his scent anywhere near me, his hands on my body, draws bile to rise in my throat.

"You're disgusting, and I'd never let you touch me," I manage to spit out, but I'm trapped. Naked, vulnerable, in the worst possible state. The shower is still running, cold water streaming over me, and I can't even stand properly.

He reaches for the shower door handle, fingers wrapping around the metal.

"Come on, don't be difficult. I'm trying to help you out here. Your cowboys abandoned you. I'm all you've got."

"I'd rather die," I snarl, but my voice is weak.

"That can be arranged too," he says casually, pulling on the door and ripping it open out of my grasp.

I cry out, hoping someone will hear me while recoiling in the corner, shaking, terrified.

That's when a blur of motion crashes into the room. The next second, Ronan's flying sideways, his body slamming against the bathroom wall with a sickening thud. Walker is on top of him like a bear, fist connecting with his face, over and over.

"You fucking think you can lay your eyes on her, let alone touch her?" Walker's voice is unrecognizable, more animal than human. Another punch, blood spattering across the white tiles. "I'm going to rip your fucking eyes out so you never see a thing again." Another hit, this one to Ronan's ribs. "Threatening our Omega?"

Ronan tries to protest, but his words are lost in the gurgle of blood from his broken nose. Walker is beyond reason, every hit looking devastating. I cringe each time I glance over at the blood, hear Ronan's cries.

"Walker's going to kill him," I whisper, not sure if I care, but I don't want him charged for murder.

Then Cash is there, towel in hand, turning off the shower and stepping in with me fully clothed, boots and all.

"Hey, sugar, hey, I'm here. We're here. Don't look at him. Don't worry about him. Just look at me."

He wraps the towel around me with infinite gentleness, a complete contrast to the violence happening three feet away. His hands are shaking too, but from rage, not heat. I can feel it radiating off him.

"You're safe," he murmurs, pulling me against his chest. "We've got you. He's never touching you. Never coming near you again."

Ridge is in the doorway, making way for us, then rushes to Walker. "Enough. Walker, enough. We need him alive."

It takes physical effort, but Ridge manages to haul Walker off Ronan, who's groaning and bleeding and possibly missing some teeth.

"You come near Sophia or our farm again, and we're hauling your sorry ass straight to the cops," Walker growls. "But if I have to warn you one more time to stay the hell away from her... you won't survive it."

"Help me get him out," Ridge snarls at Walker. "Now. Before I finish what you started."

Together, the pair drag Ronan out by his arms, his protests cut short when Ridge's hand closes around his throat. I hear them in the hallway, their threats low and vicious.

"We mean it. You come near her again, you're dead," Ridge snaps.

"This was your last mistake, Ronan. Your very last," Walker warns. "You think you've won with your lawsuit? We'll bury you."

Cash lifts me into his arms like I weigh nothing, carrying me away from the bathroom. My room feels safe again with him here, his scent engulfing me.

"I've got you," Cash murmurs, settling me on the bed while keeping me wrapped tightly in the towel like he can hold me together if I start to fall apart. "You're safe. We're here now. We're never leaving you alone again."

I clutch at his shirt like I could crawl inside his chest and hide there, my face pressed against his throat, breathing him in. His scent is a lifeline, steadying me against the storm inside, the fear from what just happened, the humiliation of being found like that, and the unbearable heat pulsing low and deep.

"He's never coming near you again," Cash says, voice vibrating against my cheek. "Ridge and Walker are making sure of that. And if he tries, if he even thinks about it, we'll end him."

The memory of Ronan, his hands on my bathroom door, his voice, the invasive way he looked at me leaves me feeling sick. I whimper, the sound small but needy, because even with the fear still fresh, the heat is crawling back in, dragging every nerve toward desperation.

"Cash, I need... please, I can't—"

"I know, sugar." He cups the back of my head, pressing a kiss to my hair. "We're going to take care of you. All of us. You're not alone. Never alone again."

The slam of the front door is so loud that the bed frame vibrates. Heavy boots pound up the stairs. Walker and Ridge appear in the doorway, both with bloody knuckles, their chests rising fast. Walker's shirt is streaked with blood, Ridge's is clinging to his chest with sweat, and both of them look like they'd happily finish what they started.

"He's gone," Walker says flatly. "Thrown off the property with a promise of worse if he comes back. Might have a few broken ribs. Definitely a broken nose."

"Should've killed him," Ridge mutters darkly, flexing his injured hand. But his gaze flicks to me, to the way I'm pressed into Cash, the Omega scent no doubt heavy in the room. The shift in him is instant. "Should've ended him for even looking at you."

"Later," Cash says, his voice low but firm. "Sophia needs us right now."

They don't come to me immediately. Instead, they head for the bathroom, the sound of the sink running filling the room as they scrub their arms and face. I see them in there, shirts being pulled over heads, boots hitting the tile. Broad shoulders rolling, chests bare, muscles shifting under sun-darkened skin. A faint trail of hair runs down from Ridge's chest, disappearing into the low waistband of his jeans, and my mouth goes dry. Walker's chest is a solid wall of muscle, a small scar bisecting his left pec.

My fingers twitch with the need to touch, to feel that heat under my palms.

They return a moment later, knuckles cleaned, the faint scent of soap clinging to them under the sharper bite of their hypnotic scents. Ridge kneels beside the bed, his rough hand finding mine and threading our fingers together. Walker takes the other side, his bloody knuckles now cool against my cheek as he brushes my hair back.

"We've got you," Walker murmurs, pressing a kiss to my forehead.

"Always," Ridge adds, his thumb stroking across the back of my hand.

"Forever," Cash promises against my temple, then pulls back and rips off his shirt and kicks off his boots, my gaze locked on that toned chest, the light dusting of hair, and I'm squeezing my thighs.

The heat flares so hard that it's almost pain, and my eyes sting with everything—the shock, the relief, the want. My gaze sweeps over their bare chests again before I can stop it, my body moving without thought as I reach out, my finger-tips brushing over Ridge's sternum, then skimming the hard plane of Walker's ribs.

"Please," I whimper, my voice wrecked.

"We know, darlin'," Walker whispers, already leaning in, the promise of what's coming burning in his eyes. "We're going to take such good care of you."

27.

The air in my bedroom is thick with need, heavy like the moments before a thunderstorm. My three cowboys stand before me, shirtless in just their jeans, and the sight is mesmerizing. The sunlight streaming through the windows turns their skin golden, highlighting every muscle.

Ridge's auburn hair falls across his shoulders, his green eyes dark with promise. Walker's chest rises and falls steadily, but I spot the tension in his jaw, the way his hands flex at his sides. Cash leans against my dresser, trying for casual, but the bulge in his jeans and the way his eyes track my every movement betray his need.

The heat is consuming me from the inside out, each wave stronger than the last. My skin feels too tight, too hot, like I might burst from the pressure building inside me. The towel wrapped around me is damp with sweat, clinging to my overheated skin.

"Please," I whisper, breaking on the single word. "I need... God, I need..."

"What's that, darlin'?" Walker asks, taking a step closer. "Tell us."

"Keep your cowboy hats on. I need... I need my cowboys. Need to see you as you are."

They exchange glances, and despite the intensity of the moment, despite the heat raging through my body, soft chuckles escape them. The sound warms something in my chest even as another wave of need crashes through me.

"Now that's a request I can handle," Cash murmurs, reaching for his worn brown hat on the dresser. He settles it on his head, the brim shadowing his blue eyes.

Walker grabs his from where he must have placed it earlier on the bedpost. "Anything for our Omega," he whispers, his voice dropping into that dark, velvet register that makes my thighs clench.

Ridge just reaches over to my nightstand, fingers brushing the brim of his black hat. He sets it lower on his head, angling it back so nothing blocks his view of me sprawled beneath him. The man looks like sin incarnate, every inch a cowboy carved out of desire and muscle.

"Anything else you crave?" Ridge asks, eyes locked on mine.

Emotion clogs my throat. "I missed you," I confess, trembling fingers reaching for him. "Missed all of you. Even when you were gone just a few hours, it felt like pieces of me were missing."

"We're here now," he promises. "Not letting go. Not again." His head dips as he leans in closer to me, that hat tilting as if even it bows to the moment, and then his mouth claims mine.

The kiss is nothing like before. Ridge kisses me like he's starved and I'm the only salvation left. His tongue presses past my lips, tangling with mine, demanding and devastating. Heat pours through me, and I moan into him, dragging him closer with my hand around his neck, like I can fuse us together if I just try hard enough.

His hand trails down my collarbone and lower still, tugging at the towel around me, unwrapping me.

He completely peels it back from my body, and the air is cool on my skin. Yet he never breaks our kiss as his hand trails over the curve of my breasts, slow enough that my pulse stutters and my nipples tighten under the weight of his attention. His fingers don't just touch; they linger, tracing, teasing, making me feel bared in more ways than skin-deep.

By the time he reaches my stomach, I'm trembling. His fingers slide over the hair between my legs, and my thighs press together in reflex, but Ridge only growls low in his chest, that deep cowboy rumble that vibrates straight through me.

"Wider," he orders against my mouth, then keeps kissing.

Heat floods me, shame and need colliding. I hesitate only a heartbeat before obeying, parting my legs.

"More, gorgeous," he says, pushing at my inner thighs, spreading them further. Cash's sharp inhale cuts through the room, and Walker is clearing his throat.

Ridge strokes the inside of my thigh, every pass closer, slower, until I'm nibbling on his lip. My hips twitch toward him without permission, desperate and helpless, all while he kisses me, making it impossible for me to see Cash's and Walker's reactions. But I know they're there, watching, seeing it all.

"Already dripping for us," Ridge murmurs, his thumb brushing the slick heat between my legs before slipping a finger through my soaked lips. He licks my mouth, and I take his tongue in, sucking on it, writhing at the attention.

When his fingers finally slide inside, it's torturous, agonizingly slow, curling just enough to make me gasp, then withdrawing and pressing in again until my walls clench around him.

"Oh God—" My voice fractures, embarrassment lacing with raw pleasure as my body arches.

"Look at me," Ridge commands. My eyes snap open, meeting his under the brim of that tilted hat. His stare pins me there mercilessly. "You love being spread out like this for us? Knowing they're watching me finger you?"

My cheeks burn at the dirtiness of his words, but my body betrays me, more slick dripping out, thighs trembling as he pushes a second finger into me.

Walker swears under his breath. Cash's groan is hoarse, broken. And I can't stop, can't hide, can't be anything but his writhing, desperate Omega as Ridge plays me, slow, steady, relentless.

He finally drags his mouth from mine, his fingers sliding free from my body with a wet sound. I whimper at the loss, but then he brings his hand to his lips, tongue flicking out to taste me. His eyes stay locked on mine as he sucks his fingers clean, hungry, deliberate, like he's savoring every drop.

The sight steals the air from my lungs. My legs stay spread wide on the bed, trembling, and I can't even think to close them. My body is caught between shame and pure need, every nerve buzzing as if I'm still stretched around his fingers.

When I glance past Ridge, Cash and Walker are at the end of the bed, watching me like wolves about to jump me. Cash's grin is gone, replaced by something possessive, his chest rising and falling fast like he's barely holding himself back. Walker's jaw is tight as if it's taking everything he has not to climb onto the bed and claim me right now.

"Greedy little Omega," Cash finally says, voice hoarse but laced with affection. "Don't worry, sugar. We're going to give you everything you desire."

"Come here," I plead, reaching for them with my free hand, still holding myself wide open for them. My voice cracks with desperation. "I must have all of you."

They move together, Cash and Walker stepping closer while working at their belts and zippers, the metallic sound filling the room. My mouth waters, anticipation winding so tight it hurts.

"We're yours," Walker promises, shoving his jeans down. My breath stutters when I see him—thick and hard, the heavy length of his cock straining forward, the tip already glistening like he's been waiting for this as long as I have.

"Forever," Cash adds, following suit. His fingers are slower, more deliberate as he unbuckles, almost taunting me with every movement. When his jeans and boxers drop, my vision swims. He's impossibly big, jutting forward with a slight curve to the left, thick veins ridging the shaft in a way that makes my thighs press tighter together. He catches my stare and smirks, like he knows exactly what kind of mess that sight is making me.

Next to me by the bed, Ridge pushes his belt loose and drags his jeans down as well, and I nearly choke on my breath, remembering very well the beast in his pants. He's large, though heavier at the base, the blunt head flushed a deep red, promising to stretch me in ways I can hardly imagine. His hand curls around himself as if testing his own restraint, and his eyes flick up to mine with a heat that pins me in place.

Three men, three cocks, each different, each terrifyingly perfect, and all of them mine. My body clenches at the thought, slick heat dripping out as lust and desperation battle inside me.

"I was so wrong in my blog," I whisper, staring between them with wide eyes. "You're all... God, how am I supposed to—there's no way I have enough room for all of them."

Cash grins, wicked and sure. "You can take it. You were made for us, remember? Your body already knows what it needs."

"What is it about cowboys being so fucking huge?" I mutter, half in awe, half panicked.

They all chuckle, the tension twisting tighter instead of breaking.

"Good breeding," Walker admits, completely straight-faced, which only makes me choke out a helpless laugh.

"Plus all that time in the saddle," Cash adds with a wink. "Builds stamina too."

"Stop bragging and get over here," I demand, the ache in my body erasing any hint of embarrassment.

"Bossy little thing," Ridge rumbles, still smirking.

"Out of my way," Cash growls, shoving Walker aside. "You've both had a taste. Now I'm going in first. I want her sweetness all over my face."

My breath catches as he drops to his knees at the edge of the bed, tugging my thighs and dragging me toward him over the bed, then pushing my thighs over his broad shoulders. The cowboy hat stays tilted low, shadowing his eyes, forcing my legs wider, and the sight of him between my legs in that damn hat sears itself into my memory forever.

"Cash, I—"

"Shh, sugar. Let me take care of you."

He uses his fingers to spread me open, his eyes grinning like he's on his knees before some sacred altar. The air is cool on my skin, but his stare burns hotter than anything I've ever felt.

"So fucking pretty and pink," he murmurs, and then his mouth is on me. The first stroke of his tongue has me jerking on the bed like I've been shocked.

"Oh God!" I cry, my fingers digging so hard into the blanket that I hear a seam pop.

Walker climbs onto the bed beside me, pressing his lips to my collarbone before kissing his way up to my ear. "That's it, darlin'. Let him taste you. Let him drown in you." His voice is smug, almost taunting, but his hand cradles my face like I'm fragile. "You taste so fucking sweet. Like honey drippin' straight from the comb... only dirtier."

I whimper, half from his words, half from the heat pooling in my belly.

"Can't wait to be inside you," he whispers, his breath hot against my ear. "Been thinking about it for days, how tight you'll be, how you'll milk me dry when my knot swells inside you."

The filth sends another wave of slick gushing between my thighs. Cash groans against me, licking greedily, like I just proved Walker right.

Ridge settles on my other side, his big hand cupping my breast before his mouth latches onto my nipple. His tongue circles once, twice, before he scrapes it lightly with his teeth, and I scream again, caught between all three of them.

I gasp. My body is a live wire, every nerve begging for more.

Ridge rumbles against my skin. "You're doing so well. Taking everything we give you. Our perfect Omega."

Cash's tongue flicks harder, faster, then slows just enough to drive me insane. His finger teases lower, circling my other entrance.

I force myself to relax, though my heart hammers frantically. When his finger presses inside, my pleasure detonates. My body convulses, a scream tearing out of me as the orgasm crashes through, slick gushing down my thighs, coming out of nowhere...

"Holy fuck," Walker breathes, voice gone raw. "What a beautiful mess you're making."

Ridge groans, low and guttural. "Don't stop, Cash. She looks so gorgeous when she falls apart like this."

Cash pulls back, face wet with me, grinning like he just claimed some kind of prize. "Prettiest sight I've ever seen. And, sugar, that's just the start. Next time, it won't be your slick dripping out of you."

Walker's laugh is wicked. "Nah. Mine's stayin' put. I'm not lettin' a drop escape once I lock inside."

Despite the intensity, I choke out a laugh, half delirious. "You three are... highly entertained."

"Entertained?" Cash smirks, dragging his mouth up my thigh, his chin gleaming with me. "We're fucking obsessed."

Ridge flicks my nipple again, making me yelp. "We're starved. Can't believe we went this long without devouring you."

"And now you're stuck with us," Walker drawls, pressing a kiss under my jaw. "Poor little Omega, chained to three bastards who won't get enough of fucking you."

God help me. I *love* that they bicker over me. That they each can't get enough of devouring me.

Walker's eyes go dark, and he's moving immediately, positioning himself onto his back on the bed, his cock hard and sticking upright. My mouth is salivating, which is crazy.

"Come here, beautiful. Let me see those perfect tits while you sit on my cock."

My body obeys before my brain catches up. With their help, I straddle him, trembling as the blunt head of his cock nudges against me. The need is unbearable, my skin buzzing, my womb aching, my body begging to be filled.

"I can't wait," I whisper, the words slipping out raw, needy, unguarded. "To have you inside me."

Walker smirks like he's been waiting years to hear that. He steadies my hips, holding me just above him. "Easy, sweetheart. Don't rush it. Rub that pretty pussy over me first, get me slick so you don't split yourself in half from my size."

I shiver, heat crawling up my throat. "I think I got this."

Cash laughs low. "He's actin' like you aren't already drippin' all over him."

Walker's grin is wicked. "Maybe I just like watchin' you grind on me slowly."

Ridge leans close, his breath brushing my ear. "Do it, gorgeous. Rock your hips, make him lose his patience. Let him feel how bad you need it."

I gasp as Walker drags the thick head of his cock against my clit, a bolt of pleasure stealing the strength from my arms. "Oh God. That—"

"Again," Walker groans, fingers digging harder into my skin. "Do that again."

Cash presses his hand to the small of my back, steadying me as my legs threaten to give out. "Grind on him 'til you can't stand it anymore. We'll hold you right here."

I whimper, rubbing myself over him, slick coating his length as the friction builds and my thighs tremble. "You're killing me," I pant. "I need you inside me."

Walker's jaw ticks. "Then take me, sweetheart. Inch by inch. Show us how good our girl can ride."

I brace my hands on his chest, trembling as I start to lower myself, the thick head nudging past my entrance. My breath stutters, caught between arousal and the impossible stretch. The pressure builds, sharp and sweet all at once, and a cry slips out before I can stop it.

"Fuck, you're big," I gasp, panic and bliss tangling in my voice.

"You can take it," he assures me, voice husky but calm, grounding me. His hands hold my hips, firm but not forcing. "You're made for me, darlin'. Made for all of us."

Cash is behind me in a heartbeat, his breath hot on my shoulder. "Got another hole beggin' for attention, sugar. Think you can handle bein' stuffed like our perfect little toy?"

"Yes," I whimper, no hesitation, no shame. My body is past the point of denial. "Want it. Please. Want all of you."

Walker's groan vibrates through me. "Hear that? She's beggin' for it. Our desperate little Omega."

Cash chuckles darkly, sliding his fingers between my cheeks, which are already covered in slick. "Never done this before, huh?"

I shake my head frantically. "Never."

"Good girl." His praise is a rumble in my bones. "Then I'll make it so sweet you'll never forget it."

Instead of pushing inside right away, a finger circles the tight ring of my ass, and I jolt, a startled moan ripping from my throat. My body wants to fight it, every instinct tensing until the heat burning through me claws louder, screaming for *more*.

"That's it, sugar," Cash croons, pressing a kiss between my shoulder blades as his fingertip teases. "Breathe. Let me in."

Walker palms my breasts, rolling my nipples between his thumbs, breaking my resistance. Cash pushes his finger past the stubborn ring. The stretch makes me whimper, torn between the ache and the fiery rush of desire flooding me.

"Too much?" he murmurs, though he already knows the answer from the way I grind back against him.

"Not enough," I pant, the words spilling out. "Please— more."

He groans, working that single finger deeper before sliding out, only to push two back in, scissoring me open. The pressure steals my breath, a sharp ache that melts into heat until I'm trembling, rocking shamelessly against his hand while squeezing Walker, who's hissing beneath me, catching his breath.

"There she is," Cash mutters, voice dark with approval. "So ready for us she doesn't know what to do with herself."

Walker chuckles low in my ear. "She knows. Look at her taking you. Can't get enough, can you, sweetheart?"

I can't answer. My nails bite into Walker's chest as Cash twists his fingers just right, and the sharp edge of the stretch makes me cry out. The ache is unbearable and perfect all at once, and still it isn't enough. Not nearly enough.

Cash withdraws his fingers, slick with my arousal, and positions himself at my entrance. The head of his cock nudges against me, the pressure enough to draw another loud moan from my throat.

"Easy," he murmurs, voice rough, steady hands braced at my hips. "Gonna take my time with you. Make sure you're good and ready."

He pushes forward an inch, then stills. The stretch burns, overwhelming, and I gasp, clenching around him. My head drops forward onto Walker's shoulder, a helpless sound breaking from me.

"That's it," Walker soothes, kissing my brow as Cash eases another inch inside.

"Doing so damn good," Ridge murmurs.

I'm trembling, a mix of strain and pleasure spiraling tighter with every slow push. I feel myself opening around him, my body yielding even as it shudders from the effort.

"Cash—" My voice fractures, half plea, half moan.

"I know, sugar." His thumb strokes circles into my hip, anchoring me. "You want more, don't you?"

"Yes," I breathe, raw and shaky. "Please."

He gives me what I beg for, driving deeper until he's fully sheathed. The fullness knocks the air from my lungs, every nerve alight. He holds still, letting me adjust, letting me fall apart around him.

Walker presses his lips to my temple, his voice a low rasp. "Look at her, taking every inch. Our girl's perfect."

Cash groans, forehead dropping between my shoulders. "Tight as sin. Like she was made for us."

The world tilts, blurs, pleasure spiking hot and relentlessly through my veins. I'm full, stretched, dizzy with it, and yet, even like this, I can't stop craving more.

That's when Ridge steps up, looming over us, hand tangling in my hair. His cock is right there at my lips, thick and flushed.

"Don't forget about me, gorgeous," he growls.

"I couldn't," I pant, licking my lips, the ache in my body twisting into sharper need. "Want you too."

"Open for me," he orders. "I want to feel that sweet mouth."

I part my lips willingly, taking him in. My moan vibrates around his thickness as Cash and Walker do small thrusts in and out of me. The triple assault is almost too much, heat swallowing me whole, body stretched to breaking, mind short-circuiting.

"Fuck," Walker groans beneath me, his hips jerking. "She's clenching like a vise. You like this, sweetheart? Like bein' stuffed full by your Alphas?"

I try to answer, but it comes out garbled around Ridge's cock, a broken moan that makes them all laugh in hungry delight.

Ridge's grip in my hair tightens, his thrusts shallow, teasing. "Not born for it. She *chose* it. Chose us. Didn't you, baby?"

I manage a muffled *yes*, tears pricking the corners of my eyes from the overwhelming fullness.

Walker grits his teeth, hips bucking harder. "Shit, Ridge. She's squeezin' me so hard I'm about to lose it."

"Don't you dare," Cash growls, biting at my shoulder. "She's not done with us yet."

Walker thrusts as Cash drives in behind, Ridge letting me take him deeper at my own pace. My body is fire, nerves overloaded, every sensation spiraling me higher.

And the worst part? I *want more, and harder.*

"So damn beautiful," Walker says, staring at me. "Never seen anything more perfect than you fucking us."

Their rhythm builds with every thrust of their cocks. Grunts, growls, moans, the song is just perfect, and that earlier pain has softened, replaced by an excitement that overrides everything. It's hypnotic and all-encompassing.

Cash's fingers circle my clit, and the pressure detonates inside me like wildfire. That's when an orgasm rips through me, sharp and bright, my cry muffled around Ridge as I convulse helplessly between them.

I barely come down before they push me higher again, Walker's pace unrelenting beneath me, Cash grinding into me from behind, Ridge's grip tightening in my hair as he feeds me his cock. I can't tell where one sensation ends and the next begins; it all blends into a feverish haze that has me sobbing with pleasure, clawing for more even as I climax again.

Walker's knot swells first, catching at my entrance before driving deep. The lock steals my breath, a brutal, exquisite stretch that feels like surrender and possession all at once. He groans against my neck as he cranes his head up more, his mouth hot and claiming on my skin as he buries himself to the hilt. Then he's pumping his cum into me.

Cash follows, his thrusts growing shorter, rougher, until his knot catches too. The pressure of being stretched in both places nearly undoes me, so full I don't know how my body takes it, only that it does and that the sensation tilts me into delirium. He buries his face in the back of my neck as he sinks home, his growl vibrating through my spine, his seed flooding me.

Pinned between them, my body clenches and spasms, the intensity tipping me into another orgasm that feels like a free fall. I groan around Ridge, trembling so violently I think I'll come apart entirely. It's also when Ridge growls and I sense his cock pulsing in my mouth, then he's coming, and I'm working my throat to swallow him. To take all of him.

Ridge finally pulls free of my mouth, eyes burning down at me while I gasp for air. His hand stays in my hair, steadying me, guiding me through the storm as though he knows I've gone beyond thought into pure sensation.

Every nerve feels stripped bare. I float in the heat of them, suspended between the knots locking me tight and the weight of Ridge's body hovering close, the three of them surrounding me until there's no escape, no air, no self. Only us.

Ridge lowers his mouth to the softness just below my shoulder, his breath hot against my skin. His teeth graze the spot before he sinks them deep, claiming me with a growl that vibrates through my bones. My gasp turns to a cry, sharp and shattering, as pleasure lances through the pain.

Walker's lips follow the curve just above my collarbone, his teeth snapping in a warning growl before he bites hard, sealing his mark. My body jerks around him, the sting sparking through the haze of heat until I'm shaking, trapped on his knot and begging for more.

Cash claims the other side of my neck, his bite deliberate, drawn out, his tongue soothing the wound even as his teeth lock down until tears blur my vision. "Ours."

Three sets of teeth, three burning marks. My body thrums with it, tethered by more than knots now. Their scents mix with mine, binding me in a way deeper than flesh, deeper than bone.

Cash shifts carefully, rolling us onto our sides. I'm still impaled on Walker and Cash, every pulse of them inside me sending aftershocks through my oversensitized body. Ridge stretches out beside Walker, fingers reaching over him and tracing my arm, all of us gasping for air.

I'm overwhelmed, marked, filled, owned, and it's bliss. I never imagined possession could feel like floating.

I'm sprawled between them in a messy tangle of limbs and heartbeats. My throat is raw from moaning, my skin painted with their marks, but my body continues to hum with want.

"God," I pant, still trembling. "That was—I don't even have the word for it. But my body is already sparking again. Does that make me broken?"

Walker's lips graze the mark he left on my neck, his voice warm against my skin. "Makes you ours. Heat's got nothing on how good you feel and taste right now."

"Not broken," Cash says from behind me, voice gravel-edged and steady. "Just greedy. Which happens to be my favorite thing about you."

Ridge leans in, brushing hair from my cheek with the back of his knuckles. His gaze softens in a way that always melts me. "Greedy works. We'll match you, however long it takes."

Walker huffs a laugh, half wicked, half tender. "Could be days, darlin'. You sure you can handle three cowboys deter-mined to ruin you?"

"Try a week," Cash adds, tone low and matter-of-fact.

My breath catches. "A week? You're kidding. I'll end up crawling out of this bed in pieces. And the rodeo—"

"Rodeo can burn for all I care," Walker cuts in, fierce. "You're first. Always."

Ridge's hand finds mine, lacing our fingers. "We'll figure out the rest. You're not carrying that weight alone."

Cash presses a kiss between my shoulder blades. "Right now, you worry about this." His hand slides down my belly in emphasis. "The rest can wait."

My throat tightens. "You don't get it—I love this ranch. I love you. All of you. I'm terrified I'll lose both."

Walker's lips press against mine, his words hot and certain: "You're not losing us. You're stuck with us. And fuck, I love you so much too."

"Forever, I love you," Ridge says simply. No drama, no hesitation, just truth.

Cash tilts my head back against his chest, his eyes burning into mine. "Storm, fire, stampede, we go through it together, my Omega. Love you so much."

Emotion swells until I can barely breathe.

Walker smiles against my mouth.

Ridge's thumb strokes my palm like he's memorizing me.

Every thump of Cash's heartbeat syncs with mine.

Walker groans low, his knot swelling harder, pressing me full until I swear there's no part of me left untouched. "Hell, darlin'," he rasps, forehead slick against mine. "You're gonna keep us trapped here all day and night."

I laugh, shaky, raw, already trembling from how much they've wrung from me. "And that's... a problem?"

Cash answers with a rough chuckle that vibrates against my skin. "Not for me. Feels like heaven. Just means round two's already started, whether you realize it or not."

The thought alone has me clenching, my body desperate, answering him without words.

Walker shifts his hips just enough to make me gasp, the thick swell of his knot grinding deeper. "See that? Ready again," he adds with a grin, though the sweat dripping down his temple betrays just how much this is wrecking him too.

"Brag later," I manage, my voice a hoarse whisper, rolling my hips despite the ache, the impossible stretch. "Prove it."

Ridge smirks, leaning over Walker to move toward me, his hand tangled in my hair as he closes in, lips brushing my ear. "Careful, gorgeous. You tempt us like this, and we'll never leave this room."

My pulse skitters, my body answering before my mouth can. "Good," I breathe, desperate and delirious. "Don't stop. Don't ever stop."

And they don't. Not for minutes. Not for hours. Not until

time itself loses meaning and the edges of the world dissolve, leaving only the weight of them, the unrelenting knots binding me to them.

Because this isn't just biology or heat—it's *us*.

If this is what heat is, then I never want it to end.

28

SOPHIA

Confessions of a City Omega
Emerging from the Heat Haze (Or: Your Girl Just Had a Religious Experience)

Dearest Diary,

Taps microphone Is this thing on? Can anyone hear me?

I'm asking because I'm pretty sure I just lost four days of my life to the most intense heat I've ever experienced. Four. Entire. Days.

I'm writing this from my nest, wrapped in approximately seventeen blankets that smell like my Alphas, and I'm not even sorry about how sappy that sounds.

So. Heat with actual Alphas versus heat at a clinic. Let's discuss, shall we?

Things Nobody Tells You About Heat with Your Scent-Matched Alphas:

- It lasts SO MUCH LONGER. My usual heat? Two days, max, at the clinic with their synthetic pheromones. This time? FOUR DAYS.
- You'll forget your own name. Also the day of the

week. Also how to form complete sentences that aren't *please* and *more* and *right there.*

- Three Alphas means three times the... everything. Math has never been my strong suit, but even I can calculate that equation.
- You'll consume your body weight in water and protein bars because apparently marathon sex is an Olympic sport, and I've been training without knowing it.
- Your marks will have marks. I look like I've been mauled by very affectionate bears. With cowboy hats.
- The emotional intensity is INSANE. We're talking declarations of love, promises of forever, the whole romance novel package but in real life.

For My Omega Readers Still Using Clinics:

Look, no judgment. I used them for years. The controlled environment, the medical support, the ability to just handle your heat and move on, I get it. I really do.

But if you find your actual matches? Your scent-matched Alphas?

Baby, it's a WHOLE different universe.

The clinic injects you with synthetic pheromones that trick your body into thinking an Alpha is nearby. It takes the edge off, makes it manageable. Like taking ibuprofen for a migraine, it helps, but the pain is still there, just dulled.

Real Alphas? That's like... okay, I can't even think of an analogy because my brain is still scrambled. It's like the difference between watching fireworks on TV versus being inside the actual fireworks. It's overwhelming and intense and absolutely life-changing.

Also, they made me FOOD. Like, actual food. They cooked between... sessions. Brought me fresh fruit. Fed me chocolate. Try getting that at a clinic.

The Emotional Whiplash:

Here's the thing nobody prepared me for: the vulnerability. When you're in heat with Alphas who love you (THEY SAID THEY LOVED ME!!!), you can't hide. You can't put up walls. You're just... raw. Open. Theirs.

And they see all of it. The needy parts, the desperate parts, the parts of yourself you don't know exist until you're begging for something you can't even name.

They said they loved me. All three of them. Multiple times. In multiple ways.

Your girl is SWOONING. Still. Probably forever.

But Back to Reality:

Clears throat

Okay, so while I was busy having my world rocked (literally), we lost four days of fundraiser prep. We now have twenty-one days to raise half a million dollars, or we lose the ranch.

No pressure.

BUT, and this is where I get emotional, you guys are INCREDIBLE.

My inbox is flooded with messages from readers wanting to help. People offering to donate, to spread the word, to attend the rodeo. Some of you are planning road trips just to be here.

I'm not crying, you're crying.

For everyone asking: YES, there will be tickets available! We're finalizing the details now (or we will be once I remember how to walk properly). VIP packages, general admission, even camping spots for those traveling from far away.

And for my international readers or those who can't make it, I PROMISE I will livestream the ride on the blog. You'll have front-row seats from wherever you are.

(Yes, I convinced three growly Alphas that livestreaming is essential. Yes, it took some convincing. No, I will not share my methods, but they may have involved the strategic removal of clothing.)

Current Fundraiser Status:

- Amount Raised: $47,000 (YOU GUYS!!!)
- Amount Needed: $453,000
- Days Remaining: 21
- Anxiety Level: DEFCON 1
- Optimism Level: Surprisingly high
- Number of Times Ridge Has Practiced on the Mechanical Bull: 0 (we were... busy)

Tonight's Omega Wisdom:

Sometimes life gives you lemons. Sometimes it gives you a massive debt, a dangerous rodeo challenge, and three Alpha cowboys who look at you like you hung the moon.

When the latter happens, you hold on tight and don't let go. Even if it means spending four days in heat-induced delirium where you may or may not have promised to name your future children after various ranch equipment.

Thank you all for your support, your messages, your donations, and for following this absolutely insane journey. We're going to save this ranch. Ridge is going to ride that bull. And I'm going to document every terrifying second of it.

But first, I need about seventeen more hours of sleep and possibly a donut. Or twelve.

Kitten Name Update:

Before I pass out, a quick kitten update. I received so many amazing suggestions for naming the two adorable ginger kittens currently terrorizing my laundry room. After much debate (and one shredded curtain), I've decided on names that popped up a few times and just fit.

Please welcome Crumb and Beans to the family.

Huge thanks to @moonlitreads and @alphaaddict88 for

the perfect suggestions! You officially have naming rights. Chonkarella has approved their names (by not hissing when Crumb tried to boop her tail and Beans crash-tackled her). I'll take that as a win.

City Omega out. (Still marked. Still claimed. Still can't believe this is my life.)

PS: To the reader who asked if cowboys really are better in bed: Yes. Next question.

PPS: Ticket sales go live tomorrow at noon. Set those reminders!

PPPS: If anyone knows how to cover hickeys that look like you've been attacked by a very passionate vampire, please advise. I look like a walking advertisement for turtlenecks, and it's ninety degrees outside.

29

I breathe in deeply as I step out of the main house, the air clean and crisp with that after-rain smell I never knew existed in Chicago. The ranch spreads out before me, puddles reflecting the sky like scattered mirrors, and I can't help but giggle at myself that city girl Sophia actually looks forward to feeding goats.

Who would have thought? Months ago, I was navigating Chicago traffic and dealing with nightmare clients who wanted their websites to *pop more* without any actual direction. Now I'm walking across a ranch in my pale green sundress and muck boots, heading to feed animals that have somehow become mine.

This feels more like home than my Chicago apartment ever did. More real. More... everything.

The guys were up and gone before I woke, which is saying something since we've been sharing a bed—two king-sizes pushed together to accommodate all four of us— and usually at least one of them lingers for morning kisses. But with the fundraiser happening in eleven days, everyone is pulling double duty. Ranch work doesn't stop just because we're trying to save said ranch.

I check my phone as I walk. The fundraiser tracker shows $237,000. We're halfway through our time, including tickets sold for the rodeo so far. My stomach clenches with anxiety. We need $263,000 more in eleven days. The math isn't looking good, but I refuse to give up hope. We've come too far.

Since Ronan's last unwelcome visit, where he ended with Walker rearranging his face, he hasn't shown himself on the property. But we've heard through the town grapevine that he's been spreading poison, telling anyone who'll listen that we're scamming people, that Ridge can't really ride anymore, that the whole thing is a desperate grab for money we don't deserve.

Some people believe him. But more believe in us. At least, I hope they do. I have June and the book club ladies pushing bake sales and asking for donations. They are amazing, and I tear up thinking about their kindness. Even Belle, who I first met on arriving at the ranch, is now donating half of her earnings from the cowboy calendar to our cause.

The crunch of gravel comes from behind me, and I turn, expecting to see one of the ranch hands arriving for the day. Instead, a black Mercedes pulls up near our house, so out of place on our dusty ranch that it might as well have landed from space.

The door opens, and out climb legs that go on forever, mini shorts that barely qualify as clothing, boots, and a shirt tied up just below breasts.

Brittany Carson!

"Fucking hell," I mutter under my breath. "What does she want now?"

She spots me immediately, of course. She starts toward me with that runway walk that probably takes years to perfect. Her presence can't be good news.

"Sophia!" she calls out. "You got a sec?"

I force a smile that probably looks more like a grimace. Can't be too rude, seeing as her family's money could still save us if they decide to support us again and not listen to Ronan.

"Brittany. What brings you out here so early?"

She stops just far enough away to avoid any actual ranch dirt. "Oh, be a doll and point me in the direction where I can find Cash?"

"He's working," I say, proud of how level my voice stays. "And even if he weren't, I don't think he'd want to see you. We've been pretty clear about boundaries."

"Don't be all upset with me," she begins, examining her manicured nails. "I'm actually here to help. My family has decided to extend quite a generous offer."

"What are you talking about?"

She smiles. "Well, I convinced Daddy to donate enough to ensure you win this little fundraiser of yours. All in exchange for Cash taking me as his Omega."

My hands tighten on the feed bucket until my knuckles go white. "Excuse me?"

"It's a small price, really. You have the other two men, and everyone's happy. Isn't that fair?" She tilts her head, blonde hair catching the sunlight. "You taking all three is rather greedy, don't you think? Some might even say selfish."

The rage that floods through me is volcanic. "Greedy?" I set the bucket down carefully because I'm afraid I might throw it at her perfectly contoured face. "Let me explain something to you, Brittany. Cash isn't a prize to be bought. He's not property your daddy can purchase with a big enough check. He's a person, an Alpha who chose his mate. Me. His scent-matched, true mate. Not some fake wannabe in expensive boots who thinks she can buy her way into his bed."

Her face goes red under her spray tan. "You don't know who you're messing with. My family—"

"Your family can take their money and their threats and shove them where the sun doesn't shine," I interrupt, my Chicago street kid coming out in full force. "Cash is mine. Ridge is mine. Walker is mine. And I'm theirs. That's not greed, sweetheart. That's fate. That's biology. That's love. Something you wouldn't understand if it bit you on your surgically enhanced ass."

"You little—"

"Mind you, I'm being polite compared to what Cash would say if you approached him with this bullshit. He'd probably laugh in your face. Actually, no, he'd probably just feel sorry for you. Because it must be exhausting, constantly chasing after men who don't want you."

Brittany's mouth opens and closes like a fish. "You're making a huge mistake. When your little ranch is foreclosed and you're homeless, don't come crying—"

"Leave." My voice drops to something dangerous. "Now. Before I forget my manners entirely."

She spins on her designer boots with a huff. "You'll regret this, you backwater little—"

That's when I grab the bucket and open the goat pen, shaking my head.

Suddenly, Harold charges out like he's been shot from a cannon.

"Harold, no!" I call out, but there's probably not enough conviction in my voice.

He's already reached Brittany, that goat head low, and connects with her ass with the precision of a guided missile. She shrieks, arms windmilling, and goes face-first into the largest mud puddle on the entire ranch, the one that's been growing for three days since the rains started and is now the consistency of chocolate pudding.

I shouldn't laugh. I really shouldn't.

But I'm chuckling anyway.

"You BITCH!" Brittany screams, struggling to get up but slipping back down, now covered head to toe in mud. Her hair is brown, her outfit is ruined, and I think I see tears cutting tracks through the mud on her face. "You did that on purpose! You made that feral beast attack me!"

"Harold's not feral," I say, walking over to grab his collar while trying to hide my grin. "He's just not a fan of intruders on our ranch."

She finally manages to stand, mud dripping from everywhere. "I'm going to sue! I'm going to destroy you!"

"Good luck with that," I call as she squelches to her car, leaving muddy footprints. "Hard to prove assault by goat!"

She peels out, sending gravel flying, and I turn to Harold, who's looking tremendously pleased with himself.

"Good boy," I tell him, scratching behind his ears. "Extra treats for you today."

He butts my hip gently, and I swear he's smiling.

After securing Harold back in the pen and actually feeding the goats, I head to the main barn. We've transformed it into a training facility, complete with professional-grade equipment. My boots echo on the concrete as I slip through the side door.

The space opens up before me, impressive even after seeing it every day. Soft landing mats surround the mechanical bull in the center, weights and strength training equipment line one wall, and there's even a reaction time board that Ridge has been using to sharpen his reflexes.

And there he is.

My hunk.

My Alpha.

Ridge is on the mechanical bull, wearing only jeans, boots, and a hat, his chest bare and glistening with sweat. One hand grips the rope while the other is high in the air, perfect form even on a machine. The bull spins and bucks, but Ridge moves with it fluidly, like the machine is an extension of his own body.

I stand frozen, mesmerized by the play of muscles across his back, the way his thighs grip, the sheer power and grace of him. He's spectacular. Beautiful. Mine.

The mechanical bull makes another violent turn, and that's when he spots me. His concentration breaks for just a second, but it's enough. He has to grab on with both hands to keep from falling and hits the stop button with his knee.

"Enjoying the show?" he asks, grinning as he climbs off.

"Just checking on my champion," I tease, walking closer.

He meets me halfway, and despite the sweat and the fact that he probably needs water and rest, he pulls me against him immediately. His kiss tastes sweet, and I melt into him like I always do.

"You look absolutely delicious today," he murmurs against my lips, hand sliding down to pat my ass. "This dress will get you into so much trouble."

"It's just a sundress," I protest, but I'm pleased.

"On you, nothing is *just* anything." He pulls back to really look at me, and I take the opportunity to do the same.

There's a new bruise on his ribs from yesterday's practice, purplish green against his tan skin. His jeans hang low on his hips, and I can see the V of muscle that disappears beneath the denim. Even after three years away, his body remembers what it was built for.

"How's training going?" I ask, trying to focus on anything other than how much I want to drag him to the nearest hay bale.

His expression shifts, becomes more serious. "Good. But I need to lift my game. Not much time left, and muscle memory only goes so far." He pauses. "I'm going to the arena tomorrow. Practice on real bulls."

My stomach drops. I knew this was coming, but

knowing and accepting are two different things. "Real bulls."

"Have to. The mechanical bull is good for form, but it's predictable. I need the unpredictability. Need to remember how to read an animal, not a machine."

I nod, forcing myself to be supportive even as fear claws at my throat. "Just... please be safe. Wear a helmet. So many riders do now. And a mouth guard."

He cups my face in his hands, thumbs stroking my cheekbones. "I adore how much you care about me."

I laugh, but it comes out shaky. "Ridge, I'm terrified. Every time I think about you on a real bull, I see all the ways it could go wrong. I see you unconscious in the dirt. I see another accident that you don't walk away from."

"Hey." He draws me closer, forehead resting against mine. "I'm not the same cocky kid who thought he was invincible. I'm older, smarter. I know my limits."

"Do you, though?" I pull back to search his eyes. "Because sometimes I see that look, that rodeo champion confidence, and I worry you'll push too hard."

"I have too much to live for now." He kisses me again, deeper this time, like he's trying to prove his promise through touch alone.

"You'll be amazing," I murmur when we break apart, and I mean it even as my heart races with worry. "I know you will. You're a legend."

He grins, predatory and perfect. "Anyway, training can wait ten minutes."

"That's all?"

"Twenty if you stop talking."

"Thirty if you're lucky," I tease. "Then I'll tell you something funny that just happened."

"Deal." He's already walking me backward until the backs of my knees hit a stray bale of hay near the main entrance. Before I can catch my breath, he hooks an arm around my waist and hauls me down with him. We land in a soft explosion of straw, laughter breaking free of me even as I end up sprawled across his chest.

His hat is gone, his hair mussed, and that wicked grin is aimed straight at me like I'm the only thing worth looking at.

"You planned that," I accuse, half breathless.

"Maybe." His voice is rough silk. "Maybe I just wanted you right here."

And then he kisses me, hard, hungry, the kind of kiss that tilts the whole world sideways. My palms press against his solid chest beneath me, hay sticking in our hair, and still I can't bring myself to care.

This shouldn't be real. It feels too much like the kind of dream I'll wake up aching from. But the scrape of his stubble against my skin, the heat of his body caging me close, the sound of him groaning my name, none of that is a dream.

When he finally breaks away, his lips hovering a breath from mine, I whisper the only truth that matters.

"I don't ever want to wake up."

And from the way his arms tighten around me, neither does he.

30

SOPHIA

Thunder Creek Arena buzzes with pre-event energy as Walker parks his truck near the loading docks. It's late afternoon, the heat of the day starting to break, and everywhere I look, there's movement—vendors marking their spots for next week, workers testing sound equipment, and those posters...

God, those posters I created are everywhere.

Ridge's image stares back from every surface, captured mid-ride, one hand high, body arched in perfect form as a huge bull bucks beneath him. It's from his championship days, all raw power and grace. *RIDGE'S LAST RIDE* blazes across the top in bold red letters, with my addition underneath: *Eight Seconds to Save Everything.*

The date, nine days away, seems to scream at me. At the bottom is *One Champion. One Chance. One Ranch Worth Fighting For.*

"Still think Ridge's Last Ride sounds like a funeral?" Walker asks, catching me staring at one of the gigantic banners they're hanging across the main entrance.

"Maybe a little," I admit. "But it sells tickets, right?"

"That's my practical girl." He comes around to my side of the truck, and I drink in the sight of him. Worn jeans that hug him in all the right places, a blue Henley that stretches across his chest, hat tilted just enough to reveal those brown eyes that never fail to turn me on.

"See something you like?" he teases.

"Always," I say, not even trying to hide it anymore. We're past that. Past pretending we don't affect each other, past the careful dance of new lovers. His hand finds mine immediately, fingers interlacing like they belong there.

"Come on," he suggests, tugging me toward the loading area. "Bulls are arriving for next week. Want to get a look at what Ridge might be up against."

"They don't know which one he'll ride yet?"

"Random draw, day of the event. Fair for everyone, all the riders coming to support Ridge get the same chance at an easy or hard bull. But I want to see what's in the pool, get a feel for their temperaments."

We walk past trailers where cowboys are unloading enormous bulls, and my heart rate kicks up. These aren't like the cattle at our ranch. These animals are pure muscle and attitude, bred for one purpose. The thought of Ridge on one of these tightens my chest.

"Jesus," I breathe, watching a particularly large brindle bull slam against the side of his pen. "Ridge is actually going to climb onto one of these?"

Walker squeezes my hand. "You okay?"

"My heart is racing, and he's not even here. How am I going to survive the actual event?"

"With us holding your hands," he says simply. "Come on, let me check these boys out, then I'll show you around while it's still quiet."

He guides me to a raised platform overlooking the holding pens, where someone with a clipboard is taking notes. Walker joins him, and they start discussing the bulls below, their stats, their tendencies, their rankings. I tune out the technical talk and just watch Walker work.

His forearms flex as he points to different bulls, and I remember how those arms felt around me last night when I fell asleep. How his hands—

"Darlin'?"

I blink. He's looking at me with amusement. "Sorry, what?"

"Asked if you wanted to see the behind-the-scenes area."

"Oh. Yes. Sure."

He grins like he knows exactly where my mind went. "Come on, space cadet."

The other man chuckles. "That your Omega? The one with the blog?"

"That's her," Walker confirms, pride evident in his voice.

"My wife is obsessed with your posts," the man tells me. "Says you make ranch life sound romantic instead of just hard work and cow shit."

"Well, it helps when you've got three cowboys making it interesting," I say.

"I'll bet it does."

Walker steers me away, hand possessive on my lower back, a huge grin on his face.

The arena is massive from down here, empty seats rising up like ancient amphitheater walls. The dirt under our boots is soft, and the smell of earth and sawdust floods my lungs. I turn in a slow circle, imagining what it'll be like filled with people, all screaming, all watching Ridge.

"It's intimidating," I admit. "Being down here. How did Ridge do this for years? All those eyes on him."

"He damn loved it," Walker states, moving closer. "The adrenaline, the challenge. Some people are just built for the spotlight."

"Not me. I'd throw up."

"You're doing pretty well with all your blog followers reading your every word."

"That's different. They can't actually see me."

He brings me in him, and I melt into his warmth. "I see you," he murmurs against my ear. "Every morning when you steal all the blankets. Every time you think we're not watching and you dance in the kitchen. Every face you make when you're writing and something's not working."

"Stalker."

"Devoted." His hands slide down to my hips. "Completely fucking devoted to every inch of you."

A couple of workers pass by, and one whistles low. "Get a room, you two!"

"Get your own Omega!" Walker states, but he doesn't let go of me.

"Yours is prettier anyway," one of them calls out, continuing on.

"Damn right she is," Walker replies, loud enough for them to hear. "And she's all mine."

"All yours?" I raise an eyebrow. "Pretty sure I've got two other cowboys who might disagree."

"Right now, in this moment, you're mine." His voice drops to that register that makes my knees weak. "And I'm going to show you around our world."

He walks me through the arena, pointing out the chutes where riders mount up. The narrow metal passages look like cages, barely wide enough for a man to squeeze in beside a two-thousand-pound bull.

"Ridge will enter here," he explains, showing me the system. "Bull gets loaded, he climbs on from above, gets his rope wrapped just right. Then, when he nods, that gate swings open and the eight seconds start."

I run my hand along the cold metal, imagining Ridge

here, preparing for those crucial seconds that will determine everything. "What if something goes wrong?"

"That's why we have safety riders, medical crew, everything planned down to the second." He turns me to face him. "Every preparation is being arranged."

I nod, gnawing on my lower lip.

"I can promise we'll do everything possible to keep him safe." His hands cup my face. "And afterward, when he's victorious and high on adrenaline, we're going to celebrate."

"Oh yeah?"

He backs me against the fence, and my breath catches. "Want to know what I've been thinking about all day?"

"Walker, there are people around—"

"Let them look." His thumbs stroke my cheekbones. "I've been thinking about you in that white sundress you wore yesterday. How the sunlight made it almost transparent. Could see every curve, every shadow."

Heat floods my cheeks. "You didn't say anything yesterday."

"Was too busy planning all the ways I wanted to peel it off you." He leans closer, breath hot against my ear. "Been thinking about having you against the wall in the barn. Your legs wrapped around me, those pretty sounds you make when you're trying to be quiet."

"You're going to make me blush."

"Love how you sound so flustered." His lips brush my neck, barely a touch but enough to make me shiver. "Love how pink your skin gets. Right here." He traces a finger along my collarbone. "And here." Down between my breasts. "And especially here." His hand stops just above my heart, feeling how fast it's racing.

"You're being very inappropriate for a public place." I'm breathless.

"Just being honest about how my Omega affects me. How

I can barely concentrate when you're around. How every time I see you, I remember how you taste. How you feel. How perfect you are when you cry my name in my arms."

Before I can respond, he kisses me. It's not gentle. It's claiming, possessive, his tongue sliding against mine until I'm gripping his shirt to stay upright.

"WALKER!" someone shouts from across the arena. "Boss man's looking for you!"

"Damn," he mutters but doesn't move immediately. "Rain check?"

"On public indecency?"

"On showing you exactly how much I want you." He backs away slowly, that predator's grin making my stomach flip. "Don't go anywhere. I'll be right back."

I lean against the fence, trying to catch my breath while he jogs toward whoever called him. My lips still tingle, and the heat between my thighs is an inferno.

"You must be the famous Sophia," a male voice says.

I turn to find an older man in expensive Western wear approaching. He's probably sixty, with silver hair under a pristine white hat and boots that shine even in the dust.

"I'm Tom Garrison." He extends his hand. "I own Thunder Creek Arena."

"Mr. Garrison." I shake his hand, trying to compose myself. "Thank you for hosting our event."

"My pleasure. Ridge was magic to watch back in the day. Shame how his career ended."

"He's been training hard," I say, a defensive instinct kicking in.

"I'm sure he has. But three years changes a body. Especially after the kind of injury he sustained." He rocks back on his heels. "You know the statistics on comeback rides after that long away?"

"No, and I don't want to."

He chuckles. "Fair enough. Rose would've liked you. She always appreciated a woman who spoke her mind."

"You knew Rose?"

"Everyone knew her and her Wild Hearts Ranch. She was a fixture at these events, back when her husband was still alive. Used to bring cookies for all the riders." His expression softens. "It's a damn shame what Ronan is trying to do to her legacy." He tips his hat. "For what it's worth, I hope you win. Wild Hearts Ranch is exactly the kind of place this town needs, not some shopping development. But if this doesn't work, his people are already lined up to grab it from the bank."

My stomach twists so hard I think I might be sick. It shouldn't surprise me, not with the way Ronan operates, but the knowledge still burns, sour and hot. Fury crackles through me. How dare they treat the ranch like some prize to be stolen, like all the blood and sweat poured into it means nothing? My fists clench, nails biting my palms, and all I can think is that I'll fight tooth and nail before I let them take it.

He walks away, leaving me with mixed feelings—gratitude for his support, anxiety about his comments on comeback statistics, and fury toward fucking Ronan.

"Making friends?" Walker reappears at my side. "Tom's a good guy."

"He said something about comeback statistics of a returning bull rider I refused to hear."

Walker flips his arm around my waist. "Good. Don't need those numbers in your head."

"Are they that bad?"

"Doesn't matter. Ridge isn't a statistic."

We walk through the rest of the arena, Walker showing me the judge's booth, the timer's station, and so much more.

Before long, we're heading back toward the truck, but I

pause at one more poster. Ridge's face stares back at me, frozen in that moment of perfect control.

"Nine days," I murmur.

"Yep," Walker confirms, wrapping his arms around me from behind. "You scared?"

"Terrified."

"Me too," he admits quietly. "But not of Ridge riding. Of what happens if we don't raise enough. Of losing the ranch. Of watching you lose your home."

"It's your home too."

He turns me in his arms to face him. "Home is wherever you are. The ranch is just land and buildings. You're what makes it home."

"When did you become such a romantic?"

"When a sassy city Omega crashed into our lives and turned everything upside down."

"Best accident ever," I murmur, pulling Walker down for another kiss, only for his phone to buzz between us.

He grabs it from his pocket, frowning. "It's Cash."

Walker opens the message, and his whole expression lights up. "Holy hell. Listen to this. 'Some country music fan page shared Soph's blog, and donations are flooding in. We're at three hundred grand. Site crashed twice. Phones ringing off the hook. We might actually pull this off.'"

My breath catches, tears burning hot in my eyes. "Three hundred thousand?" I whisper.

Walker grins widely, spinning me up off my feet before I can blink. "We're over halfway there!"

I'm laugh-crying into his chest now, clutching him tightly. "This is real. We can do this."

He kisses my temple, still grinning like a fool.

"Come on," I say, tugging his hand toward the truck. "Let's get back to the ranch."

As we drive away from Thunder Creek Arena, I look back

at those posters one more time. Nine days. One ride. Two hundred thousand to go.

We have to make this work.

Because failure isn't an option when you've got three Alpha cowboys willing to risk everything for their home.

Even if it means watching the man you love climb onto a dangerous bull.

God help us all.

31
SOPHIA

Five Days Later

The parking lot of KMTN Rural Radio is nearly empty when Cash drives his truck into a spot near the entrance. We're close to over half an hour outside our town, in Raven Hill, because apparently this tiny station broadcasts to half of Montana despite looking like someone's converted garage.

Cash cuts the engine but doesn't move to get out. His fingers drum against the steering wheel.

"You okay?" I ask, though seeing my usually confident Alpha anxious is oddly endearing.

"Just... not used to this." He gestures vaguely at the building. "Talking on the radio. Being interviewed."

I laugh. "Cash, you literally charm every person you meet."

"That's different. That's one-on-one, not thousands of people listening."

I pull out my phone, showing him my latest blog post. "Speaking of thousands, I told my followers we're going live at two. They're already commenting about setting reminders to tune in."

He groans, letting his head fall back against the headrest. "Well, hell, sugar... no pressure."

"They already love you," I explain, reaching over to poke his side where I know he's ticklish. He squirms away, catching my hand. "Remember when I posted that photo of just the back of you fixing the fence? Shirtless? I got three hundred marriage proposals for you."

"You got what now?"

"Oh, did I not mention that?" I grin innocently. "My personal favorite was from someone who offered to trade her prize-winning cow for one date with you."

"A cow?"

"A prize-winning cow. Apparently, she's worth quite a bit."

Despite his nerves, he laughs, bringing my hand to his lips. "Only prize I want is sitting right here."

"Smooth talker."

"Learned from the best." He kisses each knuckle slowly, deliberately, and my stomach does that familiar flip. "You sure about this? We could still leave. Tell them I got food poisoning."

"From my cooking?"

"I'd never blame your cooking. Maybe Walker's. Remember that experimental chili?"

"The one that made Ridge cry actual tears?"

"That's the one."

We're both laughing now, the tension easing. This is what Cash does—deflects with humor when he's uncomfortable. But underneath, I can still feel his anxiety through our bond.

"Hey." I squeeze his hand. "Just be yourself. That's all they want. The real Cash who makes terrible cowboy puns and can't go five minutes without touching me and who once spent three hours teaching the kittens to fetch."

"He still won't do it consistently."

"Not the point." I lean across the console, cupping his face. "You're amazing. And this interview is going to help save our home. We can do this."

He stares at me for a long moment, blue eyes soft. "What would I do without you?"

"Probably still be letting Brittany drape herself all over you."

"Hell, don't remind me." He shudders dramatically, then checks his watch. "Okay. Let's do this before I lose my nerve."

The station is exactly what you'd expect from rural Montana radio... Wood paneling that hasn't been updated since the seventies, signed photos of local celebrities, mostly rodeo riders and one country singer I've never heard of, and a receptionist desk that's currently unmanned but has a bell with a handwritten sign saying *Ring for Service!*

Cash dings it, his other hand finding mine immediately.

A man appears from a back hallway, late forties, beer belly straining against a KMTN polo shirt, face lighting up when he sees us.

"You must be Cash and Sophia! I'm Dave, afternoon drive time." He pumps our hands enthusiastically. "Been following your story online. It's got so many people invested. Big corporation against the farmer. Anyway, follow me so we can get started." He guides us down the narrow hallway, past walls covered in old concert posters and faded bumper stickers.

The studio is smaller than my closet back in Chicago was. Two microphones face each other across a scarred wooden table, an ancient soundboard taking up one wall. There's barely room for three people, and when we squeeze in, Cash's thigh presses against mine.

"Here, put these on." Dave hands us headphones that have seen better days. "When the red light goes on, we're live. Just talk normal, don't eat the mic, and try not to swear."

"No swearing?" Cash mutters with a grin. "You know who you're talking to?"

"That's why I said *try*." Dave smirks, settling at the soundboard. "Okay, we've got about thirty seconds. You both look great, by the way. Not that anyone can see you, but still."

Cash adjusts his black hat, the one he wears for special occasions, and I resist the urge to fix my hair even though, as Dave pointed out, no one can see us.

"Going live in five, four..." Dave holds up fingers for the last three counts, then points at us as the ON AIR sign lights up red.

"Good afternoon, Montana! You're listening to KMTN, your home for country classics and community news. I'm Dave Morrison, and, folks, do I have a treat for you today. Sitting across from me are two people you've probably been hearing about: Cash Winslow from Wild Hearts Ranch and Sophia Hollis, the Omega blogger who's captured hearts across the internet with her story. Welcome, you two!"

"Thanks for having us," I say, surprised by how steady my voice sounds in the headphones.

"Pleasure's ours," Cash adds, his drawl more pronounced than usual. Nerves, definitely.

"Now, for anyone who's been living under a rock," Dave continues, "tell us what's happening this weekend and why it matters."

I lean toward the mic, finding my rhythm. "This Saturday, Ridge Colter, three-time rodeo champion, is coming out of retirement for one last ride. We're calling it *Eight Seconds to Save Everything* because that's exactly what it is. We need to raise money to save Wild Hearts Ranch from foreclosure."

"And not just any foreclosure," Cash adds, warming up now. "This is about keeping local land in local hands, not letting developers turn it into another shopping complex."

"How much are you trying to raise?"

"Half a million," I answer, watching Dave's eyes widen. "We're at three hundred twenty thousand now, with four days to go."

"The response has been incredible," Cash adds, and I can hear the emotion in his voice. "People from all over, not just Montana, stepping up to help."

"And this is all documented on your blog, Sophia?" Dave asks me.

"Every crazy minute of it," I confirm. "From inheriting a ranch I'd never seen to falling in—" I catch myself, cheeks heating. "To finding my place here."

Cash's hand finds my knee under the table, squeezing gently.

"The phones are already lighting up," Dave says, grinning. "Let's take our first caller. You're on with Cash and Sophia."

"Oh my God!" The voice is young, female, and very excited. "Sophia! I've been following your blog since day one. We've been dying to hear your voice for real!"

"That's so sweet," I say, genuinely touched. "Thank you for reading. It means the world to me."

"And, Cash," the caller continues, "you sound just as good as she says you look."

Cash tips his hat even though she can't see him, a grin spreading across his face. "Ma'am, I reckon that's the nicest thing I've heard all day."

The caller does a small squeal, which I can only interpret as a swoon.

"And, Sophia, you are keeping all three cowboys as yours, right?"

Dave's eyebrows shoot up, clearly not expecting the

conversation to go in this direction. I'm chuckling, as my blog comments are filled with these kinds of questions.

"They're all mine," I confirm, chin up, daring anyone to judge. "And I'm theirs."

"That's the hottest thing I've ever heard." The caller sighs. "You're living every Omega's dream."

"*Dream* is one word for it," I tease. "Though Cash here has a habit of embarrassing me with details that don't need sharing."

Cash's mouth curves slowly, wickedly. "Like how you sing when you're alone in the barn or the kitchen?" He drawls it into the mic, and my whole body lights up.

"Cash!" I smack his arm, laughing even as my cheeks burn.

Dave is laughing. "I'll paint a picture of Sophia's face blushing pink and her whacking him in the arm. It's hilarious to watch."

"What?" Cash shrugs innocently. "World deserves to know their blog queen sings to the chickens."

"Oh, fine," I shoot back, leaning toward the mic. "Then the world deserves to know Cash practices his pickup lines on horses."

The caller gasps, then dissolves into laughter.

Dave nearly falls out of his chair, wheezing into his sleeve. "All right, folks." He chuckles. "Sounds like Honeyspur's got more going on than rodeos and ranch work. Let's take the next call."

"Hi!" Another female voice, bright with excitement. "Cash, this is embarrassing, but we've been begging Sophia for photos. Do we finally get to see what you look like?"

Cash groans low, dragging a hand down his face before shooting me a look that says *Traitor*. "See what you've done to me, sugar?"

"You're a hot commodity, cowboy." Dave laughs. "These ladies want the goods."

I can't resist. Mischief bubbles up in my chest. "There will be a cowboy calendar, which features my three Alphas, available at the event, and the best part is, they are each cuddling kittens," I tease into the mic, sweet as honey. "Part of the money goes to help our fundraiser."

"I need ten copies, please," the caller says mid-laughter. "I'm being serious."

"Next caller!" Dave jumps in hastily, clearly trying to keep things family friendly. "Line three, you're on."

"This is Bob from the local Livestock Supply shop." The voice is gruff, steady. Businesslike, but warm underneath. "I've been listening to you two, and I want to up our donation. We were in for five thousand, but make it ten."

I actually gasp. "That's... that's incredible. Thank you so much." My throat tightens, unexpected tears pricking my eyes.

"You are a good man, Bob," Cash adds. "Much appreciated."

"Of course. Besides, my wife would kill me if I didn't help after reading your blog. She cries every time."

The lump in my throat turns to a burn in my chest. I glance at Cash, and for once, he doesn't hide the emotion in his eyes. Pride, grief, and something sharper that makes me want to kiss him right there in front of the whole county.

"Tell her thank you," I manage, my voice wobbling with emotion even though I try to laugh it off. "Though maybe don't let her read the comment section, or she'll cry for a whole new set of reasons."

Bob chuckles. "She already does. But she swears you write like Rose would've. She misses her too."

I press my hand against my chest. That belonging swells until I'm afraid my voice will crack if I speak again.

Cash lays his hand over mine beneath the table, grounding me. Strong, steady. "We'll make her proud," he says, simple and sure, his words more vow than promise.

More calls come in, locals sharing memories of Rose, fans of my blog asking questions about ranch life, someone asking if Ridge is single. He's not, I confirm firmly. Through it all, Cash relaxes more and more, his natural charm coming out.

"Tell us about Ridge," Dave says during a break in calls. "How's he feeling about Saturday?"

Cash's expression shifts, all playfulness gone. "Ridge is the strongest man I know. What he's doing, coming back after three years, after the injury that ended his career... it's brave as hell."

"He's been training like a man possessed," I add, pride swelling in my chest. "Five hours a day, minimum. Mechanical bull, strength training, rewatching old footage until he can call the moves before they happen."

"Is he nervous?" Dave asks.

"We all are," Cash admits, his voice low, steady. "But Ridge has this focus, this determination. When he sets his mind to something, nothing stops him."

"Even a two-thousand-pound bull?"

Cash's mouth quirks, that flicker of dark humor back. "Especially a two-thousand-pound bull."

Dave glances at the studio clock. "We've got time for one more caller."

"Sophia?" The voice is older, female, hesitant. "This is Martha. I just wanted to say... my husband and I lost our farm two years ago to developers. Reading your story, watching you fight... it helps. Even if we couldn't save ours, knowing someone might save theirs... it matters."

Her words slam into me. I grip the mic tighter, swallowing hard. "Martha, I'm so sorry about your farm." My throat burns, but I push through it. "This fight isn't just about us. It's about everyone who believes land should mean more than money. About families, and roots, and—"

My voice cracks, and I have to laugh softly at myself, blinking fast. "Sorry, I'm a mess."

"That's why we're donating," Martha says, her tone steadier now. "It's not much, but every bit helps, right?"

"Every bit really does," I manage, though the tears slip free this time. My vision blurs, and I don't even care if half the county hears me sniffle live on air.

Cash's hand slides under the table again, warm and solid over mine. He doesn't say anything, but the weight of him there steadies me.

"And that's what this is all about, folks," Dave says. "Community. Supporting each other. If this is any sign of how the weekend will be, we're in for something unforgettable."

The ON AIR sign clicks off, and I rip off the headphones, swiping at my eyes with the back of my hand. *Professional radio personality right here. Somebody give me a medal.*

"You two were perfect," Dave explains, standing to shake our hands again. "Absolutely perfect. The phones are still ringing. And before you leave, can we get a quick photo of you two for our website?"

Cash takes off his hat, running a hand through his hair, and I catch the glint of sweat at his temples. He looks rugged and untouchable, and yet entirely mine.

"Thanks for having us," he says easily, that smooth charm sliding back into place like it never left. Then we head out of the studio and out of the building.

Cash leans in closer. "Don't worry, sugar. If you keep cryin' on air, folks'll just donate more. Nobody can resist a teary-eyed Omega fightin' for her land."

I elbow him gently in the ribs, laughing. "So you're saying I should ugly-cry my way through the whole fundraiser?"

He grins, wicked and soft all at once. "You do that, and we'll have enough money to buy the whole damn county."

Night Before

The ranch house is unusually quiet for eleven at night. No music from Cash's room, no sound of Walker's late-night cooking experiments. Even the cats have settled early, with Chonkarella curled on the bed with her kittens. But I can't sleep. Tomorrow Ridge rides, and my nerves are frayed.

I pad through the dark house in one of Walker's shirts and sleep shorts, checking rooms. Cash is passed out, fully clothed, on the couch, still wearing his boots. He'd been setting up at the arena until past ten. Walker crashed on our bed, already sleeping.

But Ridge is nowhere to be found.

I know where he'll be.

The night air is cooler than expected as I step onto the back porch, cicadas creating their symphony in the darkness. There's no moon tonight, just stars scattered across the sky like spilled sugar. I grab the blanket off the porch swing and head toward the old oak tree.

Ridge is there, of course. Sitting on the massive stump.

His silhouette is unmistakable with broad shoulders hunched forward, elbows on knees, hat tipped back. The bottle of whiskey beside him catches starlight.

I approach quietly, bare feet careful on the rough ground, but he knows I'm coming. Ridge always knows where I am, like there's an invisible thread between us.

"Couldn't sleep either?" he asks.

"Bed's too big without all of you in it," I say, settling beside him without asking permission.

He hands me the bottle of Maker's Mark, and I take a sip, immediately grimacing as it burns down my throat.

"Still can't handle whiskey, city girl?" There's a ghost of his usual teasing in his voice.

"Still can't understand why anyone drinks liquid fire voluntarily." I hand it back, watching him take a longer pull. "How long have you been out here?"

"Hour. Maybe two." He stares at the horizon where tomorrow the sun will rise on the day that changes everything. "Couldn't stop thinking."

"About?"

"Everything. Nothing." He rolls the bottle between his palms. "You ever play out every possible scenario of something until you've convinced yourself they're all disasters?"

"Only every night since we started this fundraiser."

"I keep seeing it," he admits quietly. "The moment I can't hold on. The moment I fall. The moment I fail all of you."

"Ridge—"

"We're so close, Sophia. Four hundred thousand as of tonight. I know the donation is what counts, but what if I fail again, fall off in front of everyone coming to support us?"

"They're not paying for a show," I interrupt, putting my hand over his. His skin is cold despite the warm night.

"They're paying to support us. To save the ranch. To stick it to developers and banks and assholes like Ronan."

"They're paying to see Ridge Colter ride again." His tone turns bitter. "The comeback kid. The fallen champion rising from the ashes."

"So?"

He looks at me then, really looks at me, and I can see the fear he's been hiding. "What if I'm not him anymore? What if that Ridge died in that arena three years ago?"

"Then the Ridge sitting next to me is enough," I say firmly. "The one who's spent every day for weeks training until he could barely walk. The one who comforted me through my heat and protected me from Ronan. The one who stays up fixing fences and managing horses and keeps this ranch running. *That* Ridge doesn't need eight seconds on a bull to prove his worth."

"The bank doesn't care about that Ridge."

"Fuck the bank." I take the bottle, managing a longer sip this time. "You know what I see when I look at you?"

"A washed-up cowboy drinking alone in the dark?" he says.

"A man who was willing to risk everything for his family. Who didn't hesitate when we needed a solution. Who literally put his body on the line for the people he loves." I turn to face him fully. "You already saved us, Ridge. Just by being willing to try."

His jaw works, that muscle ticking that means he's fighting emotion. "What if my hip gives out? It's been screaming for three days."

"Then it gives out."

"What if I freeze? What if I get up there and can't—"

I stop his words by kissing him. It's soft at first, just pressure and promise, but then he makes this broken sound and pulls me closer. He tastes like whiskey and fear, his hands tangling in my hair with desperate need.

"You won't freeze," I whisper against his lips. "You're Ridge fucking Colter. You're going to climb on that bull tomorrow, and for eight seconds, you're going to remind everyone why you're a champion. And then you're going to come home to us, whole and victorious."

"You sound very sure."

"I *am* sure. Because I know you. Because I've watched you fight through pain every single day. Because you're the strongest person I've ever met, and I don't mean physically."

He kisses me again, deeper this time, like he's trying to draw certainty from my mouth. When we break apart, we're both breathing hard.

"I fucking love you," he says quietly. "However tomorrow goes, I need you to know that. I love you more than I thought possible."

"I love you too. We all do."

As if on cue, we hear footsteps approaching. Two sets, one heavier than the other. Cash and Walker materialize from the darkness, both in sweats and T-shirts, looking rumpled from sleep.

"Thought we'd find you here," Walker says, settling on Ridge's other side.

"Can't have a pity party without us," Cash adds, dropping to sit on the ground, leaning back against my legs. "Pass the whiskey."

Ridge hands him the bottle. "Who says this is a pity party?"

"The brooding alone in the dark gave it away." Cash takes a swig. "Very dramatic. Very on-brand for you."

"Fuck that," Ridge teases.

"You're definitely brooding," Walker adds, accepting the bottle from Cash.

"You two are assholes," Ridge says, but there's warmth in his tone.

We sit in comfortable silence for a moment, passing the

bottle around. The cicadas continue their chorus, and somewhere in the distance, one of the horses nickers.

The bottle makes another round, and I notice it's getting low. We've been out here longer than I realized, the temperature dropping enough that I pull the blanket tighter around my shoulders.

The stars wheel overhead, and gradually, I feel the shift in energy. The fear is still there, but it's tempered now by determination. By love. By the understanding that win or lose, we're in this together.

"We should sleep," Ridge finally says when the bottle is empty and Cash is yawning every thirty seconds.

We stand, joints protesting from sitting on hard wood. "Whatever happens tomorrow—" Ridge starts.

"Is going to be great," I interrupt. "Because we're together. Because we fought for this. Because Rose would be proud."

Inside, we gravitate toward the master bedroom without discussion. The two king beds pushed together are ridiculous but perfect for us. I crawl into the middle, immediately surrounded by warm Alpha bodies.

Ridge curls around me from behind. Walker's hand finds mine in the darkness, squeezing once. Cash is in front of me, his back to me, and I embrace him, snuggling my face against his neck.

"We're going to be okay," Ridge whispers.

"We're going to be more than okay," I whisper back. "We're going to be legendary."

33

Thunder Creek Arena pulses with an energy that makes my skin prickle. Every single seat is filled, people are in the aisles getting food and drinks, kids are perched on shoulders, and the noise is this constant thrum that vibrates through my chest. I've never seen anything like it and certainly never imagined I'd be at the center of it.

"Your hands are shaking," Cash observes, his fingers interlaced with mine.

"That's because you're both cutting off my circulation," I point out. Walker is gripping my other hand just as tightly, like I might disappear if they let go.

"We're not that bad," Walker protests, but he loosens his grip slightly.

"The radio station posted those photos they took from our interview," Cash says, nodding toward a group of women wearing matching T-shirts with our faces on them. "And the calendars are already circulating."

"Apparently, Mr. July is very popular," Cash boasts, grinning and referring to one of his photos where he's shirtless on a horse.

"I still think they photoshopped your abs," Walker mutters.

"They didn't need to," I assure him, which makes him preen.

The truth is, seeing my cowboys' faces on calendars being sold for the fundraiser is surreal. Four weeks ago, we were just trying to figure out how to save the ranch. Now we're here, surrounded by thousands of people who care about our story.

"Sophia! Oh my God, Sophia!" a female voice calls out my name from somewhere in the distance behind us.

I turn toward a woman standing and waving frantically our way from four rows back, wearing a City Omega Blog T-shirt I set up and sold with quotes from my posts printed on it. This one says *I came for the ranch drama, stayed for the cowboy measurements* in bold pink letters.

"That's, like, the twentieth person," Walker observes quietly. "We're basically celebrities now. Still processing the fact that thousands of people know about the measuring tape incident."

"I've embraced it," Cash says cheerfully. "Someone asked me to autograph their tape measure in the parking lot."

"You didn't," I gasp.

"I absolutely did. Even wrote 'Size Matters' above my signature."

"Cash!"

"What? It's good marketing. We should sell branded measuring tapes as fundraising merch."

"We are not—"

"'Wild Hearts Ranch, Where Everything's Bigger,'" he continues, grinning. "It writes itself."

I'm laughing at Cash when I spot June leaning forward, sitting on his other side.

"Seriously, this is insane. I've lived here my whole life,

and I've never seen anything like this. They opened the standing room only section. That literally never happens."

Belle, two seats down from June, nods enthusiastically. "Kitty from the café said she sold out of food at her booth in thirty minutes. She brought enough for the whole day, and it's gone."

"Wow," I mutter, still surprised by how popular this event has turned out to be.

The sound system crackles to life, and a booming voice fills the arena. "Good evening, Thunder Creek! I'm Tom Garrison, owner of the arena and here to welcome you to the most important night in our arena's history!"

The crowd roars in response.

"Are you ready to save Wild Hearts Ranch?"

The noise gets louder.

"Are you ready to witness Ridge Colter make rodeo history?"

The crowd is on its feet now, screaming.

"Then let's get this started! Fifteen minutes to show-time, folks. Fifteen minutes until we make miracles happen!"

My stomach turns with anticipation. "I need to move," I announce. "To walk or something or I'm going to—"

"Sophia!"

That voice. That particular combination of Chicago accent and excitement that could only belong to one person.

I spin in my seat so fast my neck protests. There she is, Meredith, my best friend since college, pushing through the crowd with the determination of someone who's navigated Michigan Avenue during the Christmas shopping season. Her blonde hair with fresh pink tips catches the arena lights, and she's wearing her super skinny jeans, paired with a Western shirt that definitely came from some boutique's *urban cowgirl* collection.

"Meredith!" I scramble over Walker's lap, definitely

kneeing him in the thigh accidentally in my haste, practically falling into the aisle.

"Girl, look at you," she says, catching me in a hug that smells like expensive perfume and airplane. "You're glowing. Is that what good dick does? Because I need to move to Montana immediately."

"Could you not?" I chuckle, though my face burns while several people nearby clearly eavesdrop with interest.

She pulls back, mascara already smudging from tears. "I've been reading every post. Every. Single. One. The heat one? Girl, I had to take a cold shower, and I was at work."

"Why didn't you tell me you were coming?" I ask, still halfway between shock and joy.

"Because surprising you is half the fun. The other half is meeting these cowboys you've been hiding." She grins and peers over my shoulder. "Please tell me those are them, because if Montana has more where those came from, I'm never leaving."

I roll my eyes as she waves flirtatiously at the guys.

"Oh," she adds, tugging her bag up higher on her shoulder, "and before you ask, I brought a small bag. Just a few of your clothes, toiletries, the essentials. But in hindsight... I probably should've arranged to have my entire closet shipped here. Tragic oversight." She laughs, completely unbothered.

I take her hand in mine and turn to my guys.

"Meredith, this is Cash and Walker," I say as she practically prowls toward them, all confidence and sharp heels. "Cash is the one with the quick smile, impossible charm, and zero chill when it comes to competition."

Cash tips his hat, grinning. "What can I say? I like to win."

Meredith laughs, eyes sparkling as she sizes him up. "He's a keeper."

"Don't encourage him," I mutter, then gesture to

Walker. "And this is Walker. He's the one with a heart of gold and the ability to make actual edible meals. Basically a unicorn."

Walker shifts a little, offering her a polite, almost shy smile as he reaches for her hand. "Hi, nice to meet you."

"Marry me. I'm serious. A man who can cook? In this economy?"

I bark out a laugh, and Walker is grinning, lifting his chin with pride. "I'm taken, sweetheart."

"All the good ones are." She sighs dramatically, then flashes him a wink. "No offense, Cash."

"None taken," Cash says. "But if I *were* available, I'd be too expensive anyway."

"Oh, I don't doubt it," Meredith shoots back, clearly loving every second.

I turn toward June, who's already leaning forward with a welcoming smile. "And this is June, my local ride-or-die. She's got emergency chocolate in her purse, a radar for drama, knows the best places to have fun, and gives the kind of hugs that reset your whole day."

June laughs and immediately pulls Meredith into a hug like they were best friends in another lifetime.

"Any friend of Sophia's is a friend of mine," Meredith says.

"I knew I'd like you," June says, squeezing her back. "You have warm-hug energy."

"And that," I continue, pointing down the row, "is Belle, who somehow made posing with livestock look glamorous in every single calendar photo."

Belle waves. "Great to meet you."

"We need to sit," Cash says, already shifting to make room as everyone shuffles like a chaotic, half-choreographed dance, eventually squeezing Meredith in between June and Cash.

Meredith settles in, glancing around. "Third cowboy

down there, I assume?" She points to the chutes where the bulls and riders come together.

"Yep, this is Ridge's moment, and he is going to do amazing." I'm smiling, so damn proud of him.

Meredith grabs my hand with both of hers, drawing me over Cash's lap, her expression suddenly softening beneath the sass. "Seriously, though, Sophia. I'm so proud of you. Look what you've built."

My throat tightens just a little.

"Don't make me cry at a rodeo," I say, nudging her shoulder. "I'm wearing mascara."

"It'd better be waterproof mascara," she says with a grin, and I'm nodding, smirking, while Cash has his hand on my back, Walker's touch on my thigh.

Before I can respond, the lights shift, and Tom walks back to the center of the arena.

The crowd roars before he says a word, and someone behind us blows an air horn that makes my ears ring.

"Easy," Walker murmurs, his arm sliding around my shoulders, warm and solid.

"As you all know," Tom begins, his voice echoing through the speakers, "we're here tonight to save Wild Hearts Ranch from foreclosure. But this is about more than just one ranch. This is about community. This is about standing up to those who think they can buy our way of life, our heritage, our homes."

The crowd cheers louder, and I see signs everywhere with *Save Wild Hearts Ranch*, *Ranches Not Developments*, *Rose's Legacy Lives*.

"Now, I've got some updates that might interest you," Tom announces, pausing for effect. "First, this event is being livestreamed to viewers worldwide. And not just that, it's also being streamed live on the *Confessions of a City Omega* blog by one of our own and newcomer to Honeyspur Meadow. Sophia!"

The crowd erupts, a wave of whoops, claps, and hollering that rolls through the arena like thunder.

I gasp, my cheeks going instantly, traitorously red.

Cash squeezes my shoulder, steady and warm. "You did that, sugar. Every single one of them is here because you shared your story."

"Second," Tom continues. "The current fundraising total, as of five minutes ago, stands at four hundred and fifty-five thousand dollars!"

The arena explodes. People are on their feet, screaming, crying, hugging strangers. We're so close I can taste it, feel it humming in my bones. I exchange glances with Walker and Cash, who are holding me tighter against them.

"And third," Tom raises his hand for quiet, though it takes a moment for the crowd to settle. "To put us over the top, I'm personally pledging forty-five thousand dollars."

The crowd starts cheering and whistling, but he holds up his hand again.

"But only if Ridge Colter makes his full eight seconds."

The sound is deafening. I'm crying, not pretty tears but full-on sobbing, as Cash and Walker pull me against them from either side.

"No pressure, though," Meredith says dryly. "Just the entire ranch depending on eight seconds of bull riding. Totally casual."

Through my tears, I spot Ridge by the chutes. He's stretching against the fence, already in his chaps and protective vest, the black helmet I kissed for luck this morning locked in place. Even from here, I spot the tension in his shoulders, the pressure.

I blow him a kiss, exaggerated and dramatic, not caring who sees. He looks up at exactly the right moment, catches it, and presses his fist to his chest, right over his heart. The gesture makes my throat tight.

"The sexual tension could be cut with a knife," Meredith observes. "How do you function on a daily basis?"

"Usually with less clothing," Cash says, which makes Meredith cackle and me turn crimson.

The first exhibition riders enter to warm up the crowd. These are professionals who donated their time and money to our cause. Tom introduces Sean Washington from Austin.

"That's Black Lightning he's riding," Walker explains, leaning forward to see better. "Mean son of a bitch. Ninety percent buck-off rate."

The gate opens, and a big brindle bull with horns that look like they could punch through steel explodes out. Sean makes it look easy on exit, flowing with the bull's movements like they're dancing, but he barely holds on for two seconds, and he's sliding off the bull, trying to free himself before he gets trampled. My heart is in my throat.

"Fuck," Meredith states, reality twisting her expression into one of fear. "Why would anyone climb onto one of those beasts?"

"That's what she said," Cash mocks and winks my way, which has me chuckling despite the tension.

Walker leans forward slightly, his gaze still locked on the arena. "It's about more than adrenaline. For some of these guys, it's legacy. It's proving something to their families, to themselves. Eight seconds on a bull can feel like control, purpose... even healing."

Meredith blinks at him. "Damn. Okay, cowboy philosopher."

The second rider, Bobby Garrison, Tom's nephew, is next. His bull, a coal-black monster named Midnight Terror, is in a mood. The moment the gate opens, Midnight Terror goes vertical, all four hooves leaving the ground. Bobby lasts exactly three seconds before being launched into orbit.

He lands hard, wrong, his leg bending in a way that makes me gasp. The bull wheels around, spotting him on the ground, and charges. Bobby rolls desperately as hooves the size of dinner plates slam into the dirt inches from his head. The safety riders sweep in, but Midnight Terror dodges them with surprising agility for something that size.

"Get up, get up, get up," I chant, gripping both my men's hands.

Finally, someone gets a rope on the bull, directing him away while medics rush to Bobby. He manages to stand, limping badly but waving to show he's okay. The crowd applauds, but my heart is trying to escape through my throat.

"Ridge can't get hurt," I whisper. "We just got everything figured out. We're finally together, finally home, finally—"

"He'll be fine," June says firmly, but I can see the worry in her eyes too.

That's when I glance around and spot Ronan, stumbling down the aisle like he's navigating a ship in a storm. His face is red and sweaty, shirt half untucked, and he's gesturing wildly at nothing.

My stomach hardens, fear pinching down my spine.

"Incoming," Walker mutters, already standing. The tension in his body is immediate, predatory.

Cash rises too, and I notice several other ranch hands throughout the crowd turning toward the disturbance. We're not alone here; we have an army.

Ronan is close enough now that I catch his slurred shouting. "Thieves! Fucking thieves! That's my inheritance! My grandmother's ranch!"

Cash and Walker move fast. One second, Ronan is storming toward us, red-faced and shouting, and the next, both of them have him.

Cash grabs one arm, Walker the other, lifting him clean off his feet like it's nothing.

"This is my ranch!" Ronan screams, spit flying, eyes wild. "You stole it! You fuckers!"

"The only thing stolen here is the oxygen you're wasting," Cash snaps, his voice low and razor-sharp, loud enough to cut through the crowd. His jaw is clenched, eyes blazing. "We warned you once about coming anywhere near Sophia and us."

Walker steps in closer, his grip like steel. "And now you're gonna find out what happens when you don't listen."

"You're gonna be sorry you ever set foot on this dirt," Cash growls. "Real sorry."

The crowd starts booing, voices rising with a mix of outrage and glee. "Get him outta here!" someone shouts. Popcorn sails through the air and bursts across Ronan's head like snow.

A chill dances down my spine, not from fear but from how fast my cowboys moved, how fiercely they stepped between me and danger like it was instinct. Like protecting me wasn't a question, just a fact. My heart is pounding, not because of Ronan's threats, but because of the way they carry him out despite his shouting and thrashing.

The arena *erupts* in cheers.

This isn't just loyalty. It's something deeper. Fiercer. Territorial.

And terrifyingly beautiful.

"This is better than reality TV," Meredith says, casually filming on her phone. "Your followers are going to love this."

"It's also stressful. Don't forget that," I say, trying to calm my breathing. June is reaching over to take my hand. "We're all in this together."

"I love Montana," Meredith declares with a grin. "In Chicago, someone would already be calling their lawyer. Here you have freaking cowboys taking out the trash."

They're gone for what feels like forever. Another rider enters, Jake something from Wyoming, and this time I watch the bull as much as the rider. It's a spotted beast, white and brown like a deadly dairy cow, spinning in the chute before the gate even opens. When it does, the bull corkscrews out, and Jake lasts maybe less than three seconds before eating dirt. Then three more riders, and I'm starting to worry about my men.

Finally, Cash and Walker return, sliding back into their seats, both of them still buzzing with the kind of quiet rage that simmers even after the fire is out.

I lean in, my voice low. "All okay?"

"Lucky for us," Cash says, brushing dust from his jeans, "the cops were already out front. They arrested him for public intoxication and being a potential threat to others."

Walker nods, gaze still tracking the edge of the arena. "We made sure they knew about what happened at the house too. The bathroom incident—with you."

My stomach twists.

"They said we might need to give a statement later," Cash adds, voice softening as his eyes meet mine. "But he's not going to bother us."

Relief flares over me, leaving my limbs just a little shaky.

"Ladies and gentlemen, the moment we've all been waiting for," Tom's voice booms through the arena, pulling every head toward the gate.

The crowd goes silent. Completely, eerily silent. Thousands of people holding their breath at once.

"Returning to the arena after three years, riding to save his family's ranch and prove that legends never truly die— Ridge Colter!"

The silence shatters into thunder. People are on their feet, signs waving, and someone starts a chant that spreads like wildfire: "Ridge! Ridge! Ridge!"

I can see him at the chute, climbing onto the bull with the grace that clearly made him famous. But I also see what others might miss, the slight hesitation as he swings his right leg over, the way his jaw tightens.

"The bull tonight is Apocalypse Now," Tom continues, and my blood turns to ice water. "Twenty-one hundred pounds of pure aggression. This red devil is ferocious. Only two riders have ever made eight seconds on this beast."

The bull is huge, a deep rust red with a white face and horns that curve wickedly forward. Even in the chute, he's throwing his head, slamming against the metal rails with impacts I can hear from here.

"Apocalypse Now?" I squeak. "That's what he drew?"

"Random draw," Cash murmurs, but I sense the tension in his body where it presses against mine. Walker's hand tightens on my thigh.

Ridge settles onto the bull, and I watch him wrap his hand in the rope. Around and through, around and through, then pounding his fist to set the grip. He looks up once, finding us in the crowd. Even from this distance, our eyes lock.

"I love you," I mouth, exaggerated so he can read it.

He touches his chest, right over his heart, and nods to the gate operator.

My heart stops.

Those around him are double-checking things.

Then the gate swings open.

Apocalypse Now doesn't just exit; he detonates. All four hooves leave the ground as he launches from the chute, his chunky body twisting in midair like he's trying to turn himself inside out. Ridge moves with him, but barely, his free hand high and already fighting for balance.

One Mississippi.

The bull lands and immediately spins left, hard and violent, his body nearly horizontal with the force. Ridge's entire body whips to the side, his legs losing their grip for a terrifying moment before he clamps back down.

Two Mississippi.

A damn monster of a buck, the kind that sends most riders flying. Apocalypse Now's back hooves kick higher than his head, and Ridge's body compresses and extends like he's being worked by invisible hands. His face is pure concentration, and I can see the pain there, the strain on his hip.

"Hold on, baby," I whisper, not even realizing I'm standing, everyone around me standing too.

Three Mississippi.

The bull changes tactics, crow-hopping in tight, vicious jumps that rattle Ridge like he's in a paint mixer. For a second, I see his eyes, wide, determined, maybe a little terrified.

"Come on!" Cash shouts beside me.

Four Mississippi.

Apocalypse Now does something that shouldn't be possible for an animal that size, but he drops his left shoulder while spinning right, a move designed to catch riders off guard. Ridge lists dangerously to the left, his entire body weight shifted wrong, sliding down the bull's side. The crowd gasps as one entity.

"No!" The word tears from my throat.

But Ridge does something I've only seen in his old videos where he throws his weight in the opposite direction without touching anything for balance, using pure core strength and momentum to right himself. The crowd explodes with relief and amazement.

Five Mississippi.

The bull is furious now, his bucks becoming more violent, more unpredictable. I can see Ridge's hand slipping on the rope, the wrap loosening with each jarring impact. Sweat flies from both man and beast, catching the arena lights like diamonds.

Walker chants beside me. "Come on, Ridge."

Six Mississippi.

Apocalypse Now tries to scrape Ridge off against the fence, getting close enough that Ridge has to pull his right leg up high, tucking it against his body. For a terrifying moment, he's riding completely sideways, all his weight on his left leg and wrapped hand, defying physics and logic.

"I can't watch," Meredith says, but she's peeking through her fingers, all of us unable to look away.

Seven Mississippi.

The bull gives everything he has, a combination of spinning, bucking, and twisting that looks like special effects. Ridge's body is held on only by his wrapped hand and sheer determination. His legs come completely off the bull, his body flag-poling out to the side, and I know, *I know*, he's going to fall.

Eight Mississippi.

He made it, held on for eight seconds. I'm so tightly wound that tears are pricking my eyes.

Ridge releases immediately and gets launched like he's been shot from a gun. But even in flight, I can see him tucking, preparing. He hits the dirt on his right side, rolling even as Apocalypse Now's hooves slam down where he was a heartbeat ago. The safety riders move fast, roping the bull and leading him out of the arena.

The crowd detonates with cheers and screams that ring in my ears.

Ridge springs to his feet, and he stumbles slightly, throwing both arms up in victory. His face is a mix of disbelief, pain, and pure joy. Dirt covers him from head to toe, sweat has soaked through his shirt, and there's a cut on his cheek from something, the rope, maybe, or flying dirt.

He looks absolutely beautiful.

Cash lets out a whistle beside me. "Well, I guess Apocalypse Cow didn't bring the end of days after all."

I nudge him, chuckling.

Meredith snorts into her drink. "You've been sitting on that one, haven't you?"

"I have more ready if he tries to rematch," Cash says proudly. "Heifer Reckoning, Udder Destruction."

We're all laughing, still half teary, adrenaline and relief tangling in my lungs as Ridge grins up at the stands like he just conquered the world.

Because honestly?

He did.

The crowd is on its feet, the noise powerful. People are hugging strangers, crying, screaming Ridge's name. Someone starts setting off fireworks even though the sun has barely set.

Ridge is climbing the fence, coming toward us. I'm moving before my brain catches up, pushing past Walker, climbing over some railing, I don't know, scrambling closer to him.

He vaults over a barrier just as I reach him, and he winces at the impact, his hip definitely screaming, but then I'm in his arms and nothing else matters. My legs wrap around his waist, my hands in his hair, and I'm kissing him while thousands of people lose their minds around us.

"I knew you could do it," I sob against his mouth, tasting dirt and sweat and victory and him. "I knew it, I knew it, I fucking knew it."

"Couldn't disappoint my Omega," he says against my lips. "Couldn't let us lose our home."

His eyes are bright with unshed tears, and there's a vulnerability there I've never seen before—like he can't quite believe it's real.

Cash and Walker reach us, and suddenly we're a tangle of limbs and tears and joy. Group hugs are complicated with four people, but we make it work, all of us crying and laughing and holding each other like we might fly apart if we let go.

"Five hundred thousand," Walker says, his tone cracking completely. "We did it. We actually fucking did it."

Cash whoops, lifting me off my feet and spinning me. "We're free! The ranch is ours!"

"Ladies and gentlemen, with my donation, the final total is five hundred and three thousand dollars! Wild Hearts Ranch is officially saved!" Tom states.

The crowd somehow gets louder. More fireworks go off. Someone starts playing music over the speakers—some country song about home and family that makes me cry harder. Meredith appears with June, and suddenly we're all hugging and crying and probably looking like complete disasters.

"That was the hottest thing I've ever seen," Meredith tells Ridge. "And I once saw Henry Cavill in person. Oh, and I'm Sophia's bestie from Chicago. Hi."

"Thanks?" Ridge says, holding me like he's never letting go. And I'm chuckling, hugging her and June.

The crowd roars approval, and someone starts chanting, "Kiss! Kiss! Kiss!"

Walker steals me back, and suddenly I'm between all three of them, right there in front of Montana and thousands of livestream viewers. Let them see. Let them know.

This is my family. My pack. My home.

And we just saved all of it.

Eight seconds that felt like eight years.

Eight seconds that changed everything.

Eight seconds to save everything.

And Ridge Colter, my beautiful, broken, brave Alpha, he delivered.

Cash and Walker were right there too, my protectors, my constants. I don't know what I did to deserve all three of them, but today, they reminded me exactly what love looks like when it fights back.

EPILOGUE

SOPHIA

"How do you own this many books? Do you have a hoarding problem?" June teases, dragging another box through the front door. "You could build a furniture set out of these."

"This is not hoarding, trust me—"

June arches an eyebrow. "Six boxes, all labeled *BOOKS* like they're endangered species. It's giving romance-librarian-with-light-hoarding-tendency vibes."

"Well," I say, grabbing a box from her, "the guys hired a delivery service to bring everything Meredith packed up for me back when I thought I'd only be here for three months. And now... I'm moving in. Funny how the universe works, huh?"

"Yeah, yeah," Meredith says, entering behind her, already brushing her hands off. "I packed the boxes, but somehow only now seeing them *here* am I realizing how absurdly skewed your kitchen logic is."

"What do you mean?" I ask.

June pushes a box aside so she can reach the couch.

"I *knew* something was off," Meredith says. "Sophia, you

own seventeen coffee mugs, three corkscrews, and *two* plates. Were you hosting brunch for ghosts?"

"Coffee is essential. Food is... optional."

June flops onto the couch, grinning. "I see your priorities —caffeine first, basic survival later."

I toss a cushion at her.

She ducks, chuckling as it flies right over her head.

"I gave up my entire garage corner for this, by the way," Meredith says. "Packed and labeled and everything. I had to put my kayak in storage to make room for your emotional baggage in paperback form."

"I love you for it."

"I know."

"Okay, Meredith, if you ever decide to stay in Montana, I already have a list of places with bottomless mimosas and one sketchy karaoke bar that will absolutely ruin your life in the best way," June adds.

"Oh, we'd get arrested together so fast," Meredith says brightly.

"Bailed out before midnight," June replies without missing a beat.

I laugh, sinking into the armchair with a happy sigh, watching them bounce off each other like they've known each other for years, not just a few days. It's all warmth and rapid-fire sarcasm, the kind of effortless connection that feels familiar.

And I love it.

I love having them both here. Watching them bond this easily feels like the universe giving me permission to want more.

So now I'm doing what any reasonable woman would do: secretly figuring out how to convince Meredith to move here too.

"Oh my God." June pulls out a candle from a box. "Why

do you have one that smells like Cash? Is this supposed to be cologne-scented?"

"It does?" I go over and sniff it, and instantly my body burns up. My face goes hot. "Wow, it does smell like him."

Both girls are grinning wickedly now, sniffing the candle. "This is hilarious," Meredith says. "You bought a candle that smells like your boyfriend before you even met him!"

"The universe was telling me years ago about my scent match," I add, chuckling.

Meredith laughs. "I've missed this. You, I mean. Our chats and banter."

"You're staying the whole week, right?" I ask, suddenly worried she'll leave early.

"Already requested the time off. Told them I was visiting my sister who joined a commune."

June laughs loudly.

"Well, you're living with three men on a ranch in Montana. That's basically a commune with horses."

"Doubt that," I answer.

"You share everything, work the land together, and probably have group meetings about feelings."

"We don't have—" I pause. "Okay, we had one about feelings, but that was Ridge's idea, and it was awkward for everyone."

June cackles. "Please tell me there were talking sticks involved."

"Walker made a presentation," I admit, and both of them lose it, laughing so hard that Meredith falls off the couch.

"I'm dead. I'm actually dead. Your boyfriend made a presentation about emotions."

"Why do I tell you things?" I tease, gripping my hips.

"Because you love me."

The front door suddenly opens, and all three of my

cowboys walk in, looking dusty and pleased with themselves.

"Ladies," Cash greets, tipping his hat. "How's the unpacking?"

"Slow," Meredith says. "Your girlfriend owns every book ever written."

I shake my head, blowing kisses to my men.

Ridge picks up one of the boxes, checking the label. "This one just says 'More Books.'"

"I ran out of creative labels!" Meredith pipes up.

"How many boxes are there?" Walker asks, surveying the chaos.

"Twenty-three," she announces. "I counted. Twenty-three boxes for someone who claimed she didn't own much."

"That's not that many," I say weakly.

"I moved here with one backpack," Cash points out.

"You moved here with the clothes on your back and a bad attitude," Ridge corrects.

"And look how that turned out." Cash grins, pulling me against him for a kiss that's entirely too heated for company.

"Get a room." Meredith throws a sock at us—where did she even find a sock?

"This is our room," Cash points out. "Whole house is our room."

"Gross. Also, Meredith and I are going to the book club with Sophia this week," June says.

"We are?" Meredith asks.

"We are," June confirms. "You need to meet these small-town ladies who've introduced us to so many interesting books."

June and I exchange looks and giggle, leaving Meredith slightly perplexed.

"Actually," Walker says, his expression shifting to something more serious. "We just got some interesting news about our friend Ronan."

"Is he dead?" Meredith asks hopefully.

"Meredith!" I say.

"What? He's terrible."

"Not dead," Walker continues, fighting a smile. "But possibly wishing he was. Remember how he claimed to have no assets to avoid the bank?"

"Yeah?" I ask.

"Well, he had a girlfriend, the one whose name he put everything in a few months before he took the loan out, so he could then get it all back once he got the ranch? Turns out, she's disappeared. Took everything and ditched him. The house, the trucks, the investment properties, all of it."

"Holy shit!" I gasp.

"That's the beautiful part," Ridge states, and I've never heard him sound so satisfied. "He can't report her for stealing because he legally transferred everything to her. If he admits it was to avoid the bank, he's admitting to fraud."

"So he's screwed either way," Cash adds proudly.

"Still, the bank has already filed charges for fraudulent transfer of assets," Walker continues. "He's looking at serious legal trouble."

"Karma really said, *Hold my beer and watch this*," Meredith says appreciatively, and we're all laughing.

"What about the money we paid the bank?" I finally ask. "The donations everyone gave?"

It still feels surreal, even now. A week after the rodeo, we paid the bank the money and were given official documents that said, in black and white, that the ranch was mine. No debt. No threats. No more countdown. Just... *mine*.

I still haven't figured out how to hold that kind of relief in my chest.

"Money stays with the bank. The debt against the ranch

is satisfied unless they can somehow get money out of him, but I doubt it."

"So he loses everything and hopefully goes to jail?" June asks.

"Potentially," Walker confirms. "Couldn't happen to a nicer guy."

"This calls for celebration drinks," Meredith declares. "Please tell me you have wine."

"We have beer, juice, and milk," Ridge offers.

"Beer works," Meredith agrees. "June, Sophia, you in?"

"Always," we answer at the same time and break into giggles.

We all head into the kitchen, and Meredith's shoulder nudges me. "Girl, you are so lucky. You've found the perfect family here for yourself."

I gush, smiling. "I know. My cowboys mean the world to me."

"Speaking of family," Walker says with that dangerous grin. "We should probably start working on expanding it."

"Not this again," I groan.

"What again?" Meredith perks up.

"We want babies," Cash says gleefully, like he's announcing that we won a raffle.

I nearly choke on my drink.

"Babies, plural?" June says. "Ambitious."

I laugh *too* quickly and take the beer she hands me, mostly so I have something to hold. Something to do.

They talk about babies like it's already decided. Like it's not this *massive*, irreversible thing that reshapes everything.

I've been trying to slow the guys down. To breathe. To catch up.

They've already built the future in their heads, fenced it in, named the horses, hung curtains in the nursery.

And me?

I'm still learning how not to flinch when someone calls this "home."

So, yeah... *babies?*

It's too fast.

Too big.

"We have the space," Ridge points out, totally unfazed.

"And the help," Cash adds with a grin. "Whole ranch to raise them. Plus you two," he says, nodding toward June and Meredith like he's just offered them a favor.

June snorts. "You just volunteered us as ranch nannies?"

Meredith raises an eyebrow. "Do I look like I have maternal energy? I own shoes I haven't even committed to."

Cash only shrugs, smug. "You've got strong auntie vibes."

"Oh, I'll be the fun aunt," June says, cracking a beer. "The one who teaches them to swear in five languages and lets them have cookies for breakfast."

Meredith leans back dramatically. "And I'll teach them how to emotionally repress things until they become funny. You're welcome."

"But it *would* be perfect for kids," Walker adds, softer, but with that spark in his eyes. "Teaching them to ride, to work the land... giving them space to grow up grounded."

I look at *my* cowboys all talking so openly, so casually, about this wild, beautiful future like it's just a few fence posts away.

And my brain?

Fully short-circuiting.

Because somewhere between the guys' ridiculous baby-planning and their heartfelt vision of little boots in the dirt, something inside me starts melting. Not in a scary way, but in a *dangerously tempting* one.

Do I want this?

God help me, I *might*. But I'm also leaving it to see if it happens naturally.

"You're all insane," I tell them, but I'm smiling. Because the truth is, I can see it. Little kids running through these rooms, learning to ride, growing up surrounded by love and chosen family, and yes, probably learning to avoid Brutus.

"Good thing you love us anyway," Ridge says, pulling me in for a kiss.

"Come on, let's sit outside on the porch," Walker offers, already heading that way with a beer in hand.

We follow, one by one, settling onto one of the two wooden bench swings and the weathered chairs scattered across the porch. The drinks are cold, the air is warm, and the sun spills gold across the fields like a blessing. The land stretches wide and quiet before us, the mountains standing watch in the distance.

It's beautiful. All of it.

And as we sit there, Meredith and June plotting how to terrify the local book club into choosing even spicier reads, and my three Alphas pretending they're not already scheming up a schedule for baby-making, I feel it.

That slow, breathtaking ache of *rightness*.

This is it.

My happily-ever-after.

Messy, ridiculous, and perfect.

We're mid-laugh when something shifts in the corner of my eye.

Across the yard, just beyond the guesthouse, there's movement. Big. Heavy. Dark.

"Oh, hell no," Meredith says, already half standing. "Tell me that's not—"

"Brutus," Cash groans, eyes widening. "Why is Brutus out?"

Before anyone can answer, Meredith screams, and that's all it takes.

The enormous black bull turns sharply toward the noise. Locks eyes. And starts *charging*.

There's no time to think.

We *explode* off the porch, cushions tumbling. Laughter and swearing and thudding boots as we scramble for the front door like a stampede in reverse.

June yells, "Why is he so fast?"

Ridge slams the door behind us.

We pause in the entryway, and I'm panting and laughing so hard my ribs ache, reminded so much of my first day arriving on this ranch.

I look around at them, my wild best friends, my insane soulmates, the accidentally terrifying livestock, and grin.

"My God," I say, breathless. "I *really* live here."

Confessions of a City Omega
The Final Chapter (Just Kidding, You're Stuck with Me Forever)

Dearest Diary,

So. Just over three months ago, I inherited a ranch from my ex's grandmother and thought the universe was playing a cruel joke.

Plot twist: It was actually the universe's way of saying, "Girl, hold on to your panties. Shit's about to get WILD."

And wild it got.

Things That Happened:

- Inherited a ranch I'd never seen
- Met three Alpha cowboys who turned my world upside down
- Discovered the term *scent match* can come in different forms that aren't just about smell
- Learned to feed goats (badly)
- Went viral on the internet (accidentally)
- Saved said ranch with the help of 50,000 of you beautiful humans

- Found my home, my pack, my everything

Things I Learned:

- Cowboys are even better than the romance novels promised.
- Brutus the bull is an agent of chaos, and we respect that.
- Small towns will rally around you faster than you can say *fundraiser.*
- Three Alphas are exactly two more than you think you can handle (but somehow perfect).
- Sometimes the worst thing that happens to you leads to the best thing.

Never let anyone tell you what you can or can't do. They said:

- City Omegas can't run ranches (watch me).
- You can't crowdfund half a million dollars (already did, thanks).
- You can't turn your disastrous life into a love story (*gestures at everything*).

We did all of that. With style. And only minor property damage.

Current Ranch Status:

My best friend is here for a week, and she's already trying to steal one of my cowboys (not happening). The cats have claimed every soft surface in the house. The guys have started a subtle campaign called "Operation Breed Sophia," which is both alarming and oddly sweet.

About that last one... They've gone from hints to leaving parenting magazines around the house. Cash bookmarked a baby names website on my laptop. Walker has been pricing cribs just to see. Ridge mentioned something about good breeding stock, which earned him a night on the couch (for about an hour before I caved).

My heat is returning soon. We'll see what happens. * *

The Real Talk:

This blog started as a way to process my grief and confusion. It became a lifeline, connecting me to all of you who've laughed, cried, and rage-quit reading when I was trying to feel like I fit somewhere as an Omega.

You proved that community isn't about proximity; it's about connection. That love isn't about perfection, it's about choosing each other through the chaos. That home isn't a place, it's the people who refuse to let you face your battles alone.

Thank you for being part of this absolutely unhinged journey. For caring about our story. For donating, sharing, and shouting at your screens when I was being an idiot about my feelings.

This isn't goodbye. You're stuck with me and my ranch adventures forever. But this is the end of "How did we get here?" and the beginning of "What happens next?"

Coming Soon to the Blog:

- Meredith vs. Book Club Ladies
- Why We Can't Have Nice Things (it's Brutus)
- Garden Adventures: Everything I Plant Dies but I'm Still Trying
- Small-Town Dating: A Guide for Visiting City Girls
- Baby Watch (they're wearing me down)

Tonight's Omega Wisdom:

Sometimes you have to lose everything to find what really matters. Sometimes the scariest path leads to the best destination. And sometimes three cowboys, a bunch of cats, and a demonic bull are exactly what you need to build a family.

Life is weird. Embrace it.

City Omega out. (Still claimed. Still loved. Still can't believe this is real.)

PS: If anyone knows how to build a Brutus-proof fence, I'm begging you to share. He learned how to open gates. LEARNED. TO. OPEN. GATES.

PPS: The *good breeding stock* comment was romantic in context, I swear. Stop judging.

BONUS SCENE
SOPHIA

Weeks Later

The swimming hole at Wild Hearts Ranch is one of those secrets that the ranch hands guard jealously, which is why I only recently found out about it. Hidden by a circle of blossoming trees and willows, the pond stretches maybe fifty yards across, fed by an underground spring that keeps the water crystal clear and cool even in the heat. Today it's ours alone, the afternoon sun filtering through leaves to dapple the surface gold and green.

"I still think I should be the one teaching her," Ridge calls out from his spot on a large flat rock, arms draped over his bent knees. He's wearing dark blue swim shorts and nothing else. And damn, he's captivating with all that sun-warmed skin, strong lines, and effortless ease. Like he belongs to this place. To the water. To the heat. My chest tightens, and I swear, for half a second, I forget the lake exists at all.

Walker, already waist-deep in the water, lifts his gaze in

Ridge's direction. "Yeah, well... I drew the longest straw. So I'm teaching her."

I laugh, because of course they actually drew straws.

Three grown Alphas. Dead serious about who got to give me a swimming lesson.

God help me, I love them.

I'm standing ankle-deep, trying not to be too obvious about staring at all three of them. The water is cool against my skin, clear enough to see my painted toenails through the ripples.

"You planning to swim in that sundress?" Cash asks from where he's stretched out on a fallen log near the water's edge, red swim shorts riding low on his hips. "Because that's gonna be hell to swim in. All that fabric? You'll sink."

I chuckle at his attempt to get me to remove my dress.

Ridge snorts from his rock. "Subtle. Real smooth."

I pull it up and over my head in one motion, tossing it onto a nearby rock where it won't get wet. The afternoon air kisses my skin, and I hear the exact moment all three of them register the black bikini.

Cash lets out a low whistle that echoes across the water. "Sweet Jesus, Mary, and all the saints."

"It's just a bikini," I say, but my skin flushes under their attention. The way they're looking at me, like I'm water in the desert, has me heating up.

Walker is suddenly diving into the water from where he stands, disappearing under the surface with barely a splash.

I track his shadow moving beneath the clear water, powerful strokes carrying him toward me. When he surfaces, water streams down his chest in rivulets that catch the sunlight. He shakes his head, sending droplets flying like diamonds, and every muscle in his torso flexes with the movement.

My mouth goes completely dry. The water runs down the grooves of his abs, following that V that disappears into his black shorts, and I'm definitely staring but can't seem to stop.

"Come on," he says, extending his hand toward me. "Water's perfect. Not too cold."

I wade deeper, the water climbing up my thighs, sending goose bumps across my skin. His hand is warm when I take it, calloused from ranch work, and he guides me farther from the bank until I'm waist-deep.

"Okay, I can't watch her eye-fuck you like that," Cash announces, pushing off from his log. "That's just fucking cruel to the rest of us. We have feelings too, you know."

"You could have won the draw," Walker points out, keeping hold of my hand, his thumb tracing circles on my palm.

Ridge chuckles from his rock, stretching like a large cat.

Cash dives in, surfacing right next to us with a spray that soaks us both. "I'm here for supervision. Making sure Walker doesn't abuse his position of authority."

"What authority?" Walker asks. "She's not going to be graded."

"There could be grades," I suggest. "Like a report card. 'Sophia shows improvement in not drowning.'"

"An A minus for effort," Ridge calls out.

"Why not an A plus?"

"Lost points for wearing a bikini."

Ridge stretches on his rock one more time, then stands in one fluid motion that makes his abs flex. "You know what? This rock is getting boring. And hot. And I'm feeling left out."

He rushes into the water, diving in and swimming toward us. When he surfaces, his auburn hair is slicked back, water droplets on his eyelashes.

"Thought you were judging from the sidelines," I tease, unconsciously moving closer to Walker as all three of them surround me.

"Changed my mind. Your bikini convinced me that hands-on learning is essential. For safety."

I laugh out loud. "Sure it is."

"Absolutely. What if you need multiple rescuers?"

"This section is only five feet of water."

"That's where accidents happen."

They're all around me now in the chest-deep water, and the sight of them has me gasping, my heart racing. The mountains frame the horizon like a painting, our ranch visible in the distance with its red barn and white fences, and I'm struck by how perfect this moment is.

"Actual teaching now," Walker says, moving behind me. "Breaststroke first. Easiest to learn, most practical for distance."

He demonstrates, and I absolutely watch the way his shoulders move, the stretch of his arms, the powerful kick that propels him forward. Then he's on his feet by my side again.

"Your turn. I'll support you."

His hands slide to my waist, warm against my cool skin. "Lean forward, let the water hold you. Trust me to keep you up."

I lean, and suddenly I'm horizontal, his hands steady under my stomach and at my hip. The position puts us impossibly close, his breath warm against my neck.

"Arms out front, then sweep them back in a circle while you kick. Like you're pushing the water away."

I try the motion, hyperaware of everywhere his skin touches mine, of Cash and Ridge watching with expressions that are half amused, half hungry.

"Good. Again. Think about making yourself longer in the water."

"Longer?"

"Stretched out. Like you're reaching for something."

We practice like this for what feels like both forever and no time at all, him patiently adjusting my form, murmuring encouragement. My kicks are too shallow, then too wide. My arms don't quite coordinate with my legs. But his hands never waver, never let me sink.

"You're thinking too hard," he observes after my tenth attempt. "Swimming is about rhythm, not perfection."

"Easy for you to say." Then I try another stroke cycle, and this time something clicks. The rhythm Walker mentioned starts to make sense—reach, pull, breathe, kick. It's like dancing, except horizontal and in water.

"Better," Walker says. "Feel that?"

"I think so?"

"Trust the water. It wants to hold you up."

"Water doesn't want anything. It's water."

"Everything wants something," Cash philosophizes. "Water wants to flow. Fire wants to burn. Ridge wants to brood."

Ridge chuckles.

When Walker finally releases me to try on my own, I immediately forget everything and sink, coming up sputtering and laughing at the same time.

"Forgot the kicking part!"

"And the arm part," Cash adds helpfully.

"And the breathing part," Ridge contributes.

"So, basically, I forgot the swimming part of swimming."

"Practice," Walker says, pulling me back into position. "Again."

It takes so many attempts that I lose count. Twenty? Thirty? My arms ache and my legs feel like jelly, but each time, I get a little farther. The breakthrough comes when I stop thinking about every individual movement and just let my body find the rhythm.

Three strokes. Then five. Then seven before I have to stand.

"I did it!" I shriek, jumping up and down in the chest-deep water. "Did you see? I actually swam! Like, real swimming on my own."

"Beautiful," Walker says, catching me as I launch myself at him in celebration. "Few more weeks and you'll be racing us across the pond."

"Let's not get crazy. I managed seven strokes."

"Okay, game time," Cash announces. "Swim between us without touching the bottom, and you get a prize."

"What kind of prize?" I eye him suspiciously.

His grin promises the best kind of trouble. "The kind that'll motivate you."

They spread out in a triangle formation, maybe ten feet apart. It might as well be the Pacific Ocean.

"Ridge first," Walker suggests, turning me in the right direction. "Remember, rhythm, not speed."

I push off, managing two strokes before my form completely falls apart and my feet instinctively find the bottom. But Ridge catches me anyway, pulling me against his warm chest.

"Partial credit," he murmurs, then his hands slide down to grip my ass, squeezing just hard enough to make me gasp. "For effort."

"That's my consolation prize?"

"Would you prefer a handshake?"

"The ass grab works," I admit, which makes him chuckle low in his chest.

"Try for Cash," he suggests, spinning me around. "And actually swim this time."

This attempt is better because I make it halfway before standing. My body feels lighter in the water now, like I'm starting to understand the physics Cash mentioned. The water isn't something to fight against but something to work with.

"Better," Cash approves when I reach him, standing to catch me. "Much better."

He pulls me in for a kiss that's mind-blowing, his tongue sliding against mine while his hands span my waist. When he nips at my bottom lip, I moan into his mouth.

"Swim to Walker now," he challenges, eyes dark with promise.

The distance feels achievable now. My breathing is getting better. When I make it without standing, colliding with his chest in victory, I'm so proud I could cry.

"Perfect," he says, then his mouth claims mine in a kiss that's different from Cash's but equally devastating. His hands slide up my ribs, thumbs tracing the edge of my bikini top, finding sensitive skin that leaves me shivering.

"Back to me," Cash calls. "No standing. Show us what you've learned."

I push off, determined now. The water feels friendly instead of foreign, and when I reach Cash, he catches me with a sound of approval that vibrates through his chest.

"Knew you could do it." He draws me flush against him, and I feel exactly how much he's enjoying this lesson through the thin fabric of his shorts. "Want to celebrate?"

"We're still celebrating the last success."

"Then we're multi-celebrating," he decides aloud, rolling the thickness in his shorts against me, and fire spreads through me instantly.

I laugh and push away from him playfully, attempting to swim toward the shallows and away from them. But three splashes behind me signal pursuit, and I shriek with delight, trying to swim faster.

"No escaping!" Cash calls out.

Strong arms catch me from below, standing me up in

waist-deep water. Ridge surfaces behind me, caging me against his chest. The other two on either side of me.

"Where you going, little fish?" he asks, his voice rumbling through me.

"I was trying to escape!"

"No escape clause in swimming lessons," Walker informs me.

"That seems like an oversight in the contract."

"We'll review the terms later," Cash suggests. "Right now, we're implementing the capture protocol."

"That sounds vaguely threatening."

Walker's hand finds my waist, then guides me gently through the water, his hand steady on me. "Keep your head up. You've got this."

I nod, focused, until water splashes across my face.

I blink, sputter, and catch Ridge backing away, smug and unapologetic. "What?" he says. "You looked too serious."

I reach for him, but he's already gone underwater.

A second later, Cash slides in from my other side without warning. "Didn't hear you call for backup," he says, his mouth brushing my neck, not quite a kiss. My legs forget what they're supposed to be doing.

I twist away, only to be caught by Ridge. His teeth skim the slope of my shoulder. "Didn't know you were ticklish," he murmurs, fingers sliding over my ribs.

"Stop," I say, breath hitching, laughing and squirming at the same time.

Walker leans in, his mouth close to my ear, drawing my earlobe into his mouth with his tongue.

Heat flares low and hard, catching me completely off guard. My pulse spikes. It's too much and not enough all at once. I want to pull away, but I also want to sink into all of them—into this feeling of being wanted, surrounded, claimed. My skin hums under their attention.

I break away, finally, breath catching for entirely different reasons now. I drift to the shallows, arms out, letting the water hold me. The sky above is wide and blinding. My skin feels electric. They surround me at a lazy distance, like they've all agreed to let me breathe—but not go far.

"Synchronized swimming is next," Cash says, slicking his hair back with both hands.

I roll my eyes. "And that's useful how?"

He shrugs. "Could be anything. Group emergencies. Bachelor parties. End-of-the-world situations."

Somehow, miraculously, I'm floating. Actually floating.

They circle me like smug sharks, half treading, half leaning in.

But I need air. A second to steady myself.

So I ease out of the circle, expecting one of them to pull me back.

No one does.

They let me go.

I blink up at them, startled, until I realize they're still close, watching me float away but not chasing.

That's what surprises me most.

They stay in the water, watching me drift toward the shore without a word. No pressure. No chase.

When my feet touch the lake bed, I rise slowly, water streaming off my skin as I move through the shallows. The air is warm on my face, cooler on the parts of me they touched. Every nerve is awake. My legs are shaky.

"Where're you going?" Cash calls out.

"To dry off! I'm getting pruny." I turn and hold up my wrinkled fingers as evidence.

"Pruny is beautiful," he insists. "Very fashionable."

"That's not a thing."

"Could be. Come back and we'll show you."

I settle on Ridge's abandoned rock, which is warm from

the sun, and watch them in the water. They look like they belong here, three gorgeous men in their element, water droplets glinting on their skin.

"I need five minutes to not be wet," I tell them.

"But wet is our favorite look on you," Walker says with a grin that burns me up.

"That's a terrible line," I reply.

"But accurate," Ridge points out.

That's when Ridge does handstands that admittedly display his abs beautifully but also make him look like a show-off. Walker merely floats there looking gorgeous and knowing it, which is somehow the most effective technique. And Cash just stares at me like a wolf.

"I'm right here. You can see me," I say.

"But we can't touch you," Cash points out. "That's basically torture."

"It's been two minutes. You're all acting like I abandoned you."

"Already too long," Walker declares.

"Fine!" I laugh, sliding back into the water. "But only because you look at me like that."

"Absolutely," Cash agrees, pulling me against him immediately like he's been starved for contact.

"Completely lost," Walker confirms, pressing against my back.

"Utterly hopeless," Ridge adds.

The sun stays high, baking the surface of the pond and glinting off the water like scattered gold. I make it all the way across the water again, slow and clumsy, but upright and breathing. When my feet touch the muddy bottom, I turn around, beaming.

"That's it!" Ridge shouts. "You're officially a swimmer."

Cash throws both arms in the air. "Where's your medal? Someone get this woman a podium."

Walker smiles, treading water near the center. "Your technique is questionable, but your stubbornness is elite."

I can't help it—I laugh, water dripping from my hair and face. "You're all lucky I didn't drown just to prove you wrong."

Then I see Cash's grin. Ridge's quick glance to Walker. The look of pure mischief passing between them like a spark.

"Oh, no," I say, already backing up.

Suddenly, a wall of water hits me, then another straight across my face. I gasp and stumble, sputtering, wiping my eyes.

"You jerks," I say, blinking through the spray.

"Hydration," Cash says, completely unapologetic.

Ridge sends another wave my way. "You looked too dry."

Walker stays just out of range, watching with a calm smile like he's waiting to see how I retaliate.

I charge into the middle of them, splashing like it's my only mission in life. The pond erupts around us, a mess of arms and water and laughter. Ridge catches my wrist, but I slip out of his grip. Cash tries to grab me from behind, and I twist away, sending a splash straight into his face. Walker finally gets involved, dunking Cash with one hand while using the other to flick water at Ridge.

Eventually, we all tire out, panting, dripping, floating in loose orbit around each other.

Ridge lies back in the water, eyes closed, his chest rising and falling slowly. Walker is near my side, his fingers brushing mine now and then under the surface. Cash reaches out and grabs my foot.

I raise an eyebrow at him. "Seriously?"

He just shrugs. "Still counts as holding hands."

I roll my eyes but don't pull away.

None of us talk for a while. The water settles around us, warm and quiet. I float on my back, eyes to the sky, arms spread wide. My body feels weightless, held. My heart, steady.

This is it.

Not perfection. Not some dream. Just this.

Their laughter. Their touch. This place. This peace.

This is what love feels like.

And when the water pulls us to the deeper part, I know they'll be right there with me.

They always are.

ABOUT HARLEY KNIGHT

Hi, I'm Harley Knight! I'm a romance author who's absolutely obsessed with books, writing, and happily-ever-afters. I love creating stories filled with emotion, passion, and unforgettable characters that stick with you long after the last page. When I'm not writing, you'll find me lost in a good book or dreaming up my next big adventure. For me, there's nothing better than crafting love stories that remind us all why love is worth fighting for.

Contact: knightharleyus@gmail.com